FIRE & ICE

Patty Jansen

Icefire Trilogy book 1

Print Edition

Cover design by Patty Jansen

Sign up to be notified of new works by this author: http://pattyjansen.com

CHAPTER 1

SOMEWHERE NOT FAR from the edge of the plateau, where the goat-track snaked up the rock-strewn slope, the rain had turned to snow.

Cocooned in his cloak, his view restricted to the swaying back of the camel, Tandor had failed to notice until a gust of wind pelted icicles into his face.

He whipped off the hood and shook out his hair. The breeze, crackling with frost, smelled of his homeland. Oh, for a bath, to wash off the clinging dust and the stink of the prairie lands, of steam trains or the bane of his existence: this grumpy camel.

To his left, the escarpment descended into the land of Chevakia, its low hills and valleys bathed in murky twilight. To his right, the dying daylight touched the forbidding cliff face that formed the edge of the southern plateau, accessible only to those who knew the way.

Something flashed where the ragged rocks met the leaden sky. A tingle went up Tandor's golden claw, pinching the skin where the metal rods met the stump of his arm. Icefire.

Ruko?

He peered up, shielding his eyes against the snow. Golden threads of icefire betrayed the boy's presence, flooding Tandor with feelings of relief, of urgency, of panic.

Wait, wait, Ruko, not so fast. Tell me what's going on.

There was no answer, of course. Ruko conversed only in images, and Tandor needed to be close to the boy to catch those.

But Ruko's emotions had spoken clearly enough. By the skylights, something had happened while he was away. He flicked the reins to jolt the camel into a faster pace. The animal grumbled and tossed its head, but did as it was told.

Ruko waited at a rocky outcrop to the left of the path, seated cross-legged in the snow. An ethereal form, his skin blue-marbled, his brooding eyes black as a lowsun night. His chest shimmered where his heart should be. A lock of hair hung, dark and lanky, over his forehead; he shook it away in an impatient gesture.

Tandor slid off the camel's back.

He held out his two hands, one of flesh, the other a golden claw. *Come.*

Ruko rose, towering at least a head over Tandor.

By the skylights, did that boy ever stop growing? While Tandor had been away, he had discarded his soft childish look for planes and angles.

Ruko put his hand in Tandor's. The intense cold of it made Tandor gasp, but he steeled himself and sent a jolt of icefire into Ruko's arm.

The image of the two hands, the live one and the blue one, faded for a scene of chaos. Huge birds with tan-coloured wings, white heads and yellow beaks swooped down on the village, carrying Eagle Knights in their traditional red tunics and short-hair cloaks, the swords on their belts clearly visible. They landed their birds in front of the guesthouse, jumped in the snow and ran to the houses, banged on doors, dragged out occupants. Adults, children.

"What, Ruko? What happened?" All those children Tandor had saved. He thought Bordertown was a safe haven, no longer frequented by merchants, no longer of interest to the Eagle Knights.

Images flowed through Tandor's mind. Snow under his feet as Ruko ran from the village, screams from women, shouts from men. Trees flashing past. Crossbow bolts thunking into wood. And later, the main square, empty, except for deep tracks in the snow and a single child's mitten.

Ruko's shoulders slumped. There was a brief glimpse of the red-cheeked face of a girl, smiling. Shame. And grief.

Tandor pushed Ruko's chin up. "No, Ruko, it's not your fault."

If anything, it was Tandor's. He had left the boy alone; he couldn't have done otherwise. He had needed to travel to Chevakia, and Ruko couldn't leave the southern land. Across the border, where there was no icefire, Ruko would simply cease to exist.

"I'm sorry."

Ruko batted Tandor's hand away.

"Being angry with me doesn't help. What can I do about it?"

Ruko's fury burned inside him. His screams for his girl dragged away by a Knight. His pounding on the Knight's back with insubstantial fists. Without the presence of the master, a servitor was little more than a ghost.

Ruko reached for Tandor's belt for the dagger and the Chevakian powder gun.

"No—you're not to kill anyone. Stay here. I'm going into town to see how many children they took." There had better be some left, or his plan was in tatters.

Tandor swung himself back in the saddle. "Behave yourself." In case the order wasn't enough, he let icefire crackle from his clawed hand. Golden strands snaked around Ruko's legs and then into the snow.

Ruko glowered at him.

"Behave, and you will get your revenge, I promise."

He flicked the reins and the camel turned towards the town.

The southern plain spread before him, white, flat, the horizon bleeding into the grey sky. A gathering of low buildings lay in the snow like scattered fire-bricks.

Smoke curled from the chimneys. Light radiated from the windows, golden rectangles that were the only spots of colour in the grey dusk, occasionally interrupted by the silhouette of a head: someone checking out this late visitor.

There was no sound except the squeak of the saddle and the croaking of the camel's footsteps in the freshly-fallen snow. The soft blanket had long since erased the signs of the events Ruko had witnessed in the town streets. How long ago had that been? A few days, he guessed, no more.

If only I'd come back earlier. Stupid Chevakian trains, stupid Chevakian bureaucrats not allowing the camel on the train.

At a house with a deep front yard which held a shed, Tandor tapped the camel's shoulder. The beast sank stiffly to its knees, uttering a protesting howl.

Tandor slid from the saddle and led the beast through a creaky gate, through the yard to the shed which stood slightly apart from the house. He pushed aside the bar across the doors, dislodging clumps of snow which rained over his glove and golden claw, and went inside.

The plainsman had kept his part of the bargain. The box in the corner contained straw and a bale of hay, albeit a very dusty one.

He tied up the camel and left it to attack the hay, and ploughed through knee-deep snow to the house, a sturdy construction of rough stone. The top floor was dark, but warm light peeped around the frayed edges of a curtain in a ground floor window.

He knocked. Locks rattled; the door creaked open. It was the plainsman Ontane himself who stood there, unshaven, dressed in a loose woollen robe. For a moment, he squinted into the dusk, but then he shrank back into the hall, pushing the door half-shut. "No, no. She isn't here."

Tandor stopped him slamming the door with his golden arm, the points of his pincer-claw cutting gouges in the wood. "Where is your daughter?"

"Inside, but you can't see—"

"I can't see her? Is that what you're saying? Fifteen years ago, I saved your daughter's life, but I can't see her?"

"The man said—"

"The man? Most likely, he came from the City of Glass, didn't he? Most likely, he rode an eagle, didn't he? And most likely he told you to give up all your citizens with . . . defects." With each sentence, he thrust his golden claw closer to Ontane's chest. "Imperfects. Like me. Huh? Is that what he said?"

Ontane licked his lips and straightened his back. "He said we be punished if the Knights found people like them. They got us all to come out of our houses and ransacked the place if they thought we's hiding something. Then they lined up the children and took them all away."

"To the City of Glass?" *Please, let this not be true.*

Ontane shrugged. "How do I know?"

"All of them?" Tandor clenched his good hand into a fist.

"Yes, except . . ."

"Except what?" Tandor almost screamed.

Ontane tried to retreat further, but already stood with his back against the wall. "No, no. I can't tell you."

"Except the one who was born since the others left, is that what you were going to say? Except your daughter and her child?" All those children he had saved over the last fifteen years. All gone?

"Not born. Not yet. They said they wasn't going to take my daughter in the condition she's in."

"Let me see her."

"No!" Ontane planted his hands at his sides.

"Why not? Would I pay for your daughter's food if I wanted to harm her child?"

"You'll do to the child what you did to that poor boy." Ruko.

"*That poor boy* lived with an abusive family from which I saved him. *That poor boy* is only poor because you turned your backs on him."

Ontane muttered, "Not a surprise, that is. He crackles with icefire, and the cold of him would freeze the kindest heart. Stupid as we be in your eyes, the villagers are not letting such in their houses as they do not understand. You know you can see through him? Here?" He put his hand on the position of his heart.

Of course you could. Ruko was a servitor. He had given his heart in exchange for his missing foot, and in exchange for never having to eat or never to be cold again. Tandor took a deep breath to calm himself.

"Have you spoken to him since?"

Ontane gave Tandor a what-do-you-take-me-for look.

"I have told you many times: he won't harm you."

"So you say, so you say. But many of us can't even see him, and to the rest of us he looks like a spirit."

Unbelievable. The Imperfect children had lived here for as long as fifteen years; the villagers should be used to them. "I'll be taking Ruko. There is no point in leaving him here any longer. I want my sled to be ready tomorrow morning with a bear and supplies."

A look of business came to Ontane's eyes. "Usual fee?"

Tandor nodded. "The usual fee." He let a silence lapse and added, "Can I see your daughter?"

Ontane opened his mouth, but Tandor said, "No look, no business."

A silence, shifty eye movements, before Ontane said, "Jus' a look then." Still eyeing Tandor suspiciously, he moved into the house. Tandor followed him through the hall, where a flapping candle cast long shadows over unpainted walls and a threadbare carpet.

They entered a dimly-lit room with a blazing fire in the hearth.

In the chair against the far wall sat a girl, barely fifteen, propped up on pillows. Her face was pale and delicate, her hair dark but fine and straight. Her cheeks were red from the cold. A plain woollen dress stretched tightly over her extended belly.

Tandor breathed in deeply. The tingling of icefire snaked out from the child inside its mother's womb: golden strands only he could see. Wild, untamed power. It called out to him, sang to him, like the voices of the mythical sirens said to be luring sailors on the iced sea.

He was sure: the child would be Imperfect. His life's work had finally brought success.

The girl's eyes widened. "Da, what's he doing here? Take him away!"

Her father pulled at Tandor's cloak. "Now leave, you sorcerer. You've seen her."

With regret, Tandor let go of that tingling and retreated into the hall. He forced his breath to calm. "See? I mean her no harm."

Ontane said nothing; the suspicious look didn't vanish from his face.

Tandor forced a smile. "I'll let the child grow up with her, don't worry." After all, it was only in adulthood that the child would be of use to him.

Ontane snorted. "Well, let's just say I believe that when I see it."

He accompanied Tandor through the hall back to the door. When he opened it, an icy breeze blew in a flurry of snowflakes. Tandor stepped into the cold.

With his good hand, he dug in his pocket and flicked Ontane a silvergull. The coin caught the light as it span through the air, before Ontane closed his fist around it.

The language of money convinces you easily enough. "My sled, with a strong bear. Provisions for six days."

Ontane nodded once and shut the door.

In total silence, Tandor strode through the village, trying to ignore heads vanishing behind curtains.

All you shallow greedyguts. Took my money while it was

available, but cared nothing for the lives of the children who lived with you?

In all these fifteen years, nothing had changed. In fact, nothing had changed since his mother had fled the City of Glass. Well, things were going to have to change now.

The front desk of the inn was unmanned, but Tandor's ring of the bell brought the matron hustling from a back room.

"Oh." She hesitated in the doorway, her eyes wide. For a moment, it looked like she was going to comment on Tandor's long absence, but she didn't. Clever woman, had a nose for business. "Usual room?"

Tandor nodded.

He followed her up the stairs where she opened the door to a musty room and bustled in the fireplace to light the fire.

He asked her to fill the bath with hot water.

"My maids have gone home, but I will do it myself. I always be glad to give the best to our best customer." She winked at Tandor.

Once, he might have responded, but the villagers' shallow bids to please him made him feel sick. The woman was about his age. Her face no longer held curves of beauty, but the lines of long, hard work. She cared nothing for him, or for the children. She only wanted his money.

"You be going after the children?" she asked when he failed to react.

"I'll do my best."

"Oh, it's such a disaster. My poor daughter lost her little boy as well. He was only four, like a child he were to her. Every day poor Poony has been asking about her brother. Tell me, what do you think they will have done with the children?" Her eyes glittered by the lamplight.

Tandor shrugged. He truly had no idea. Most Knights were from the Pirosian clan who couldn't even see icefire. They had been on a fifty-year mission to eradicate all remnants of the Thillei clan, but they wouldn't have bundled the children onto sleds if they wanted to kill them.

"And then that mean bastard Ontane gets to keep his Myra. Y'know what I think? I think he's paid the Knights so he could keep her. He's willing enough to bargain with money. I think he—"

Tandor held up his hand.

"Yes, yes. The bath. I know. I'm going."

Soaking in the tub not much later, Tandor transformed himself. First, he rubbed dirt from his skin. He washed dust from his hair until it was once again golden. Then he ran his golden claw through his locks until the colour leaked from it like honey, leaving his hair deep, glossy black.

Standing in front of the mirror, he blinked his eyes, let icefire crackle from his fingertips onto his face, and blinked a few more times. With each blink his eyes faded from brown, to grey, to green to a brilliant dark blue. The colour of his birth.

Then the hardest part. He called up a ball of icefire and shaped it into two symmetrical curls floating in the air. The curls descended towards Tandor's cheeks, one on each side. He closed his eyes and braced himself. Searing pain. The smell of burned flesh. His mouth opened in a scream of pain, of punishment, of lust or satisfaction.

Panting, he opened his eyes, staring at his sweaty face in the mirror, where symmetrical curls of golden paint marked his cheeks, like the tattoos noble men in the City of Glass received when they became adults.

The Knights might have dealt him a blow, but he wasn't defeated. The children were in custody, but they were most likely in the palace, exactly where he wanted them.

He needed to know if he had enough Imperfects to freeze the guards for long enough to get into the palace.

By the light of the fire in the hearth, he dug in his luggage and brought a heavy book on his knees. Let's see, the guard level on the palace gates would be at a minimum because of the Newlight festival. He guessed there would be ten Knights. That meant he needed . . .

His pen scratched over the paper as he added up the numbers as he had learned from his grandfather's diary. Body weight by strength. Himself, Ruko, the boy in the city . . . that was not enough. He did have one other Imperfect: Ontane's daughter Myra. He crossed out the numbers and re-calculated. Yes, that would give him enough power to take out ten guards, and once he was in the palace, he could draw on the fifty Imperfect children.

Yes, he could do it.

CHAPTER 2

ONTANE CROSSED his arms over his chest. He leaned back against the shed door, which he had just closed after dragging the sled out into the yard. "I told you, she's not for sale. Here in Bordertown we don't do the women's things like they do in the City of Glass."

"How much do you want then?" Tandor asked, while casually dumping his travel chest on the luggage rack of the sled. The white bear in the harness gave an annoyed snort. Ruko leaned forward over the driver's seat and patted the animal's furry rump while giving Tandor an impatient glance. Yes, Ruko wanted to get going. He had been waiting outside the inn at daybreak. That in itself was worrying enough. Ruko should not have been able to break those bonds Tandor had put on him yesterday.

"You don' give up, do you?" Ontane growled.

"No. A hundred silvergulls?"

"My daughter is not for sale!"

"I don't want to buy her. I want her to come with me to the City of Glass. I'll take her there, and I'll bring her back. Two hundred silvergulls?"

Ontane shrugged. He cast a shifty-eyed look at the shed doors, as if wondering if his wife or daughter were listening. "The Knights thought it be too risky to take her a few days ago, why should you take her now? She'll be needing another mother to be with her when she . . ." He spread his hands.

"My lady friend is one of the best midwives in the City of Glass. She has delivered hundreds of children and birthed nine of her own. Do you want a more experienced woman?" *Or do you want me to take your wife off your hands as well?* "Two hundred and fifty silvergulls?"

Ontane tightened his arms over his chest. "It's not up to me to agree on something like this. Dara's gonna kill me if I do anything to the girl."

Tandor had only met the girl's mother once, a dumpy, unattractive woman with a permanent scowl on her face.

"Your wife will be glad you have the money to buy her a new carpet."

"There be nothing wrong with my carpet!" A blush rose to Ontane's cheeks. He snorted and looked down. "Although it's not exactly new . . ."

"Precisely. Women notice these things, take it from me."

"Hmph. What do you know about women?"

"Enough to know that I'm right."

Ontane sniffed and raked hair away from his face. "I don' like it. Why do you want her to come anyway? I thought you were hiding her with us here."

"I was, but your stupidity of bringing the Knights down on Bordertown has changed everything—"

"How many times do I need to tell you: it weren't *my* fault."

"Whoever's fault it was, I need to go into the City of Glass to get the children back. Including, I presume, your grandson's father. Don't tell me none of the other families in Bordertown question why you got to keep your daughter."

Ontane's face went red. "I told you: the Knights din' want to take her like this."

"I've not known the Knights to show such compassion. Maybe there was a bribe involved?"

"Hmph." Ontane scuffed his feet in the snow. "I want three hundred silvergulls."

"That's robbery!" But Tandor knew that now Ontane started negotiating, he'd won.

"It may be, but I'm the one that's happy with my daughter being where she is."

"And with an old carpet on your floor. Two hundred and sixty."

"What do you think I am? I want two-ninety."

"A man with a nose for business. I could just walk away from this deal and you'd get nothing. In fact, I'm in a hurry, so I best get going." Tandor picked up another of his packs and set it on top of the chest, then went about lashing both items to the luggage rack.

Ruko was jiggling his leg and fiddling with the reins.

"No, no. It's not as easy as that, mister. Two-eighty."

"Da, what's going on?" The shed door had opened and the girl poked her head out.

"Go back inside, Myra," Ontane said.

"You're talking about me."

"We weren't."

"You can't fool me, Da. I heard you. What's it about?"

"The sorcerer wants you to come with him."

The girl squeaked. "Go with him? Like this?"

She spread her arms. She was a thin, mousey thing with a fine-featured face, narrow shoulders and slender arms. One of her sleeves flapped empty below the wrist. While there might have been an element of beauty to her, Tandor's gaze was drawn to her swollen belly. It was hard to believe a female belly could stretch that much and still be part of her.

Tandor repressed feelings of discomfort. "My lady friend in the City of Glass is a very good midwife. She will look after you. Certainly a country girl like yourself would like to see the marvels of the City of Glass? You would like to buy some nice dresses from the city's best merchants, and go to the Newlight celebrations?"

The girl's eyes widened. "The Newlight celebrations? In the City of Glass? See the games? People competing from all over the land?"

"That's what I think I said, yes."

"Oh Da, it doesn't sound so bad. Can I go?"

Ontane snorted, and then shrugged. "I suppose your mother . . ." He shrugged again and met Tandor's eyes. "This, uhm, lady friend of yours . . ."

"Mistress Loriane, one of the city's midwives."

"And what if she . . . if it happens on the way? I'm guessing *he* doesn't have any experience." Ontane nodded at Ruko.

Tandor repressed a shudder. "Look at it this way: the Knights will be back. If they find her here, you will never see her again. If she comes with us, there will be a good chance that you'll see your grandchild. Anyway, my lady friend tells me that such . . . women's things have a habit of happening safely by themselves." He was groping for words. By the skylights, every word spoken delayed him further, with the chance that this dreaded thing would indeed happen before he got to Loriane's house. He'd heard a woman's birth screams once, while he stood, powerless, hidden between stuffy clothing in a dressing room. *Oh my love, if I knew I'd do that to you.*

"It's all about your daughter's safety," he said, pushing away those memories.

"Hmph safety. I want your guarantee that you'll bring her back here alive and healthy, not blue and cold like that ghost over there." Ontane raised a warning finger, the nail chipped and blackened from work.

Tandor met his piercing eyes. Ontane wasn't stupid. He knew that Tandor would have to turn Myra into a servitor if she was to be useful to him.

"She will be back here as you know her." Once he had control of the City of Glass, all the power of its Heart would be his, and he could return her in the original state. "Are we agreed then?"

Ontane fixed his gaze on his daughter, who smiled at him. "Please, Da?"

"Right then," Ontane muttered.

"Oh, thank you." She gave him an awkward hug.

Over his daughter's shoulder, Ontane mouthed, *two-seventy.*

Two-sixty, Tandor mouthed back.

Ontane's face twisted into a snarl, but he didn't protest. "You'll be the ruin of me." He hawked and spat in the snow to seal the deal. "Go get your things then, girl."

Tandor put his attention to securing his luggage to the sled.

Promises, promises. His life hung together with promises. Once he had established himself in the City of Glass, there would be no more promises. He raised his eyes to the sky. *Not even to you, Mother.*

CHAPTER 3

CARRO PICKED UP the cup from the merchant's table, feigning interest. A mother and a daughter had come to the stall and the mother had asked if the merchant had any good sets of tableware for sale, and she had unwittingly saved Carro from doing what he dreaded.

While her mother spoke to the merchant, the daughter studied the items on the table, a dusty collection of bric-a-brac, the sort of things that remained after grandmother had died and all her relatives had scavenged her possessions.

The girl was nervously winding a thin strip of leather with a gull's tail feather attached around her fingers. One of the newly blooded virgins.

She let her eyes roam over Carro's shorthair Knight's cloak and the straps of his riding harness, which dangled from underneath. Her expression was one of fear or interest; he couldn't decide which. He knew her vaguely, like he knew most people here, or they knew him. His stomach churned. He did *not* want to do this, not in the safe haven of his childhood.

He glanced over his shoulder, between the crowded stalls, the garlands of yellow paper hung from their canopies, and the steady stream of patrons that tottered out of the meltery, faces red from bloodwine. All the signs that the Newlight festival was in full swing.

The Junior Knight Captain leaned against the wall, the map in his hands. He was looking straight at Carro.

"Can I assist the dear sir?"

Carro started. The mother and daughter had left.

"Uhm . . ." He put down the cup he was still holding.

The merchant was a middle-aged man, his short-cropped hair and beard more grey than black. Age had lined his face, but his eyes were clear and blue. He wore black. Everyone in the Outer City knew what that meant.

"Oh, it's you." The man smiled. "I had been wondering how you were getting on with the Knights."

"Very well, thank you."

"You know that all of us in the Outer City are proud of you?"

Carro stands at the stall; the table has suddenly become a lot taller. The cover of the book feels rough under his fingers. He opens it, marvelling at the beautiful print on pages of glossy paper. The book's scent floats on the breeze, releasing the smell of fifty years of hiding in a musty cupboard.

I want this one, he says.

The merchant reaches across the table. He wears a short beard, black, the same colour as his clothes. It's the colour of the Brotherhood of the Light.

The merchant says, *I don't think your couple of foxes of pocket money would pay for that.* He eases the book out of Carro's hands. *Besides, I don't think you want to be seen with this. Your father would whip you if he knew you had it.*

Carro shivers. His father would, too. His father doesn't like the Brothers. It's illegal to possess anything that belonged to families who supported the old king. But he promised his friend Isandor. And the book is so *beautiful*.

Carro puts his hand in his pocket and closes his fingers on the gold eagle, the metal warm and heavy against his leg. It's not his money, well, some of it is, but most of it is his friend's. He takes it out and puts it on the table.

He says, *I want the book.*

"You'll be flying in the race today?"

Carro gasped. The words of the past were still on his lips. *I want the book*. He blinked at the merchant, who was waiting for a reply.

"Oh—uhm—the race. Yes, I will." His heart thudded. He hated how he had these spells where he drifted off into his memories.

"So you're here to visit your parents?"

Carro glanced over his shoulder again, where the Junior Knight Captain was still looking at him, drumming his fingers on the side of the sled. No way to get out of this. He closed his eyes and sighed.

"No. I'm afraid I'm on patrol. Do you have any illegal items?"

The merchant took in a sharp breath. His eyes widened. No, he hadn't expected that either, after Carro's history.

Carro ploughed on, speaking rehearsed words with a tongue that felt like tanned hide. "You can give illegal items to me now, and there will be no fuss. If I have to call my Captain . . ." He shivered. The merchant might tell the Captain that he had sold Carro some of those illegal items.

"No, no, you needn't do that." The man rummaged in the space under the bench and retrieved a box with a dusty assortment of bric-a-brac. There were some forks, silver, richly stamped with the crests of the old families, the Thilleian house. There were metal stands for lights—the silver globes gone of course—a couple of sheets in neat print. Carro ran his finger over the paper, feeling the raised profile of the ink. Familiar. His books were like that. The old people used to have machines that melted ink onto the paper. The books that were still under his bed in his father's house, the books Carro hoped no one would find.

Carro took the box, meeting the merchant's eyes. He cringed with the anger in the man's expression. "I'm sorry, but I'm asking every merchant."

"Sure," the man said, his voice stiff. "You know this sort of stuff turns up every now and then."

"You should hand in any illegal material as soon as you get it." Carro hated his own words.

"I hadn't gotten around to doing that."

All lies. Carro wanted to hear no more, lest the merchant dig up uncomfortable truths from Carro's past. This was enough warning, for both of them.

Seated on a mound of snow, with his peg leg sticking out awkwardly into the narrow alley, Isandor opens the book on his knees. His skinny fingers trace the writing. He whispers, *Wow*. A lock of glossy hair falls over his shoulders.

A real diary from the time of the old king, Carro boasts. *The best he had. You should have seen his face when I showed him the money.*

You're a real hero, Carro.

Carro smiles. No one else calls him a hero.

Who wrote this? Isandor has a dreamy look on his face.

The king's court historian. Carro bends forward and flicks the pages, trying to ignore his numb and cold fingers. Heroes are not cold.

Wait. Isandor stops Carro's hand. There is a drawing on the page with many lines leading from one box to another. *Look at this. It's a map of the city with this thing they call the Heart.*

The Heart? There is no such thing. Carro feels uncomfortable. His father has spoken of this thing once and he'd seen it when he flicked through the book.

It is the Heart, Isandor says. *It says so in the book. It's a machine under the palace. They say it's the source of icefire.* Isandor raises his head. His eyes are distant. *You know this book sings?*

Sings? Carro shivers.

Yes, can't you hear it?

Carro shakes his head. *What song?*

There isn't a song. It's like the band in the meltery. The music just plays on and on, but no one takes any notice of it until it stops. That's what it's like.

Carro shrugs. It's strange. Then again, Isandor has Thilleian blood, Carro is sure about that.

The old king only needed to reach into the air and icefire would spark from his fingers. He would kill people with it. Old people still tell the stories.

Carro carried the box across the marketplace to the sled, repressing memories unlocked by the musty smell. Other merchants, all people he knew, followed his every move. Stone-hard looks on stone-hard faces. He wanted to scream that it wasn't his choice to do this job, that he'd been told to do it, that the Knights with him were all older and hated him, that . . .

He dumped the box on the luggage tray of the sled. The Knight Captain strolled to the sled and rummaged through the contents in a bored fashion.

"Another load of old junk," he drawled. "You know, we've collected so many light stands over the past few days, one wonders where the lights are."

Carro didn't meet his gaze. The silver light globes were always gone by the time these items came to the market. Even if the lights had been complete when the merchant obtained the items, he would know better than take the globes to market. They were worth a fortune, those bulbs that needed only icefire to glow.

The merchant hadn't given up everything he had, Carro was sure of that. He had just hoped that by going to the Brother's stand first, he would have spared the man a more thorough inspection.

No such luck.

The Captain flicked his fingers and pushed himself off the sled.

The other two Knights of the patrol moved towards the stall. One spoke, but they were too far away for Carro to hear. The merchant shook his head. Then the second Knight grabbed the edge of the table and turned it upside down. Pots and plates flew everywhere, shattering on the frozen ground.

As Carro had suspected, there were more boxes underneath, ones that held far more damning material than the few stands and leaflets he had collected. He could see the spines of books and items of clothing in black and silver: the colours of the Thilleian house.

"You said you inspected that one?" The Knight Captain raised his eyebrows at Carro. "Are you Apprentice puppies capable of anything?"

Carro clenched his fists. The Brotherhood merchant was looking straight at him.

"I thought you would actually be of some use to us here," the Captain continued. "That's why I asked your Tutor if you could come. You *did* weasel your way into the knighthood from this slum, didn't you?"

Carro shrugged.

"Answer me when I ask you a question." The Captain slapped Carro in the face. "And look at me when I'm talking to you."

"Yes, Captain." Carro met the man's eyes.

"Then go and carry all that rubbish onto the sled."

"Yes, Captain."

Carro set off to the ravaged stand, past the yellow garlands that seemed to mock him. His cheek stung, but he resisted the urge to wipe it. Every merchant and many of the market's customers were looking at him. Carro, the pride boy of the Outer City. Carro, the son of a lowly merchant who had made it into the Eagle Knights. Carro, who had come back to betray his own people.

"I want that merchant watched," the Knight Captain said behind him to another member of the patrol. "See who visits him and what they bring, or buy."

CHAPTER 4

THE SLED swished to a halt at a spot where a mound of snow broke the monotony of the plain. Tandor peered into the low sun, which trailed long shadows over the snow. Little diamond-like specks twinkled in the powdery surface untouched by man or beast. At the horizon, the sky faded from pink to the most delicate of blue. The tall buildings of the City of Glass were mere specks in the distance, glittering needles that reflected the sunlight in their glass facades. What tranquility, what incredible beauty. This was home, this was what his heart had been denied all those years his mother had forced him to live in the dust and noise of Chevakia.

"What are we doing here?" a whining girl's voice said. The bundle of furs that hid Myra from view stirred. Her head poked out.

"Enjoying the view," Tandor said. He'd grown wary of her complaints. Her back hurt, her head hurt, she was cold, she needed to piss. "You asked for us to stop somewhere you could piss behind a tree. Well, there aren't any trees on this plain as you might have noticed, so it will have to be a stack of ice instead. Here you go."

He jumped down from the sled, his footsteps creaking in the snow. The cool air that charged his lungs made steaming puffs of mist when he exhaled.

He unlashed a net from the back of the sled and took an ice pick and a shovel.

"What are you doing with those?" Myra asked.

"Some big business."

She wrinkled her face, but pushed herself up awkwardly. With a bit of luck, she would go for a walk to the other side of the mound.

"You're welcome to watch."

"You're not just creepy, you're disgusting."

"At your service, lady."

She sniffed, let herself down from sled with a wince and waddled off. Good.

Tandor positioned himself so that the peak of the snow mound and the glittering buildings of the City of Glass aligned. His gaze tracked the barely perceptible line that marked the shore of the Frozen Sea, the flat plain of the iced-over bay to his left, soft undulating snow-covered hills on his right.

Yes, he was at the place the diary had described.

He glanced around, checking if Myra had gone. Ruko stood at the sled, glaring into the light. The bear fidgeted, shaking its shoulders and jiggling the harness. Steam blew from its nostrils. Ruko patted its back, to which it responded with an angry snort.

Tandor glanced at Ruko. *You deal with it.*

Ruko gave Tandor his usual fuck-you look and flicked his hair out of his eyes. Tandor had tried to cut it, but the boy wouldn't let him near. With every step they came closer to the City of Glass, Ruko grew stronger. He had heaved huge blocks of ice out of the sled's path with his bare hands. He had run after the bear when it got it into its mind to chase after a group of gulls and he had dragged the bear back by the scruff of its neck. Tandor had needed a lot of icefire to make Ruko let go of the bear.

Tandor swung his ice-pick up above his shoulder and drove it hard into the mound. Ice chips flew in arcs of glittering diamonds. Two more hits and the point of the pick hit a hard object under the snow with a "ping".

Good. He was definitely at the right place. The secret had not been disturbed. There was hope yet.

A few scrapes with the shovel later, he had unearthed a door handle, a few more and the rest of the door had become visible, a plain metal surface, pitted and weathered over time. Tandor stuck the pick and shovel in the snow and yanked at the handle. It wouldn't turn.

He gathered strands of icefire from the air—much stronger this close to the city—and directed them at the door. Steam hissed. The metal vibrated and glowed. He yanked at the door again and this time it opened. Cold and stale air spilled out of the dark maw.

The bear gave a low growl, lifting one corner of its dark lips.

Tandor let his hand stray to the Chevakian powder gun he carried in his belt. Icefire oozed from the door, against which the gun was of course perfectly useless.

He felt a stab of anger at having shown such a basic Chevakian reaction. All his life he'd lived in the blasted foreign country. It had corrupted him.

He had even known that there was *supposed* to be a field of icefire here.

This was not the time to hesitate or make silly mistakes. He'd best hurry up before the nosy girl came back. If the past day was anything to go by, she'd be asking plenty of questions already.

He stepped inside and tripped over something. By the skylights, it was dark in here. According to the maps in the diary, there should be a light somewhere on the wall.

He stumbled to the side, hands outstretched, until his palms met slime-covered stone. A waft of cold air drifted in from outside.

Ah, there was the lever, the metal ice cold under his fingers. He pushed it up. A light flicked on, cold and white and incredibly bright. It came from a round globe unlike the oil lamps used by the common folk in the city or the gas lamps in Chevakia.

The beauty, the wonder of it. How could the Pirosian Eagle Knights have denied the people of the City of Glass this technology? How could they have condemned the citizens to living in poverty as primitives while these wonders existed?

The room was dank and moist. Against the far wall, a staircase wound down into the earth, much like the dungeons in the palace, with which he had made unfortunate acquaintance, and just as slippery. Unlike the one in the palace, this staircase was covered in slime from disuse, accumulated over all those years that water had seeped through the stone.

Tandor made his way down, groping along the wall for additional lights. A fear grew in him as to what he would find at the bottom of the stairs. What would remain of his plan if the machine was ruined by meltwater?

The stairs ended in a round chamber. A table stood in the middle, and on it, an array of jars and tubes, a large metal box with levels and buttons. He ran his finger along a glass tube. A tingle of icefire crept up his hand. What purposes had this strange equipment served? There might be some records of it scattered in the antique shops of Chevakia and Arania, where refugees from the palace had taken their goods, but it was likely that no one would ever know. *That* was the crime the Eagle Knights had committed. All that knowledge lost. They had plunged the City of Glass into the worst period of backwardness history had ever seen, condemned anyone who was not of Pirosian noble blood to poverty. Simply because they were afraid of icefire, and jealous of those who could see and use it.

At the far end of the room a bank of tables lined the wall, their surface a maze of controls and dials, many of which were rusty and probably no longer worked. In the old days, this machine distributed the power for the city's heat and lights and for trains that flew along rails, much like Chevakia's steam trains, but without the smoke, the stink and the noise of the engine.

In those days, the machine they called the Heart of the City beat strongly in the catacombs of the palace. The more power was channelled away, the more the Heart produced. Now, ignored and isolated, cocooned in its underground prison, its beat had faded to a feeble throb. Even after they'd seized power, the Knights hadn't been able to turn it off. Its fuel was contained within the machine, which dated from much further back.

Tandor sank in the chair that faced the panels, and slowly extracted the key which he had spent months travelling to find from under his clothes. Discovering it, after a lifetime of searching, in a box of curiosities on a market in northern Chevakia, had been the culmination of his work. If he could turn the distribution network back on, the Heart would again be powerful, and increased icefire would be available to all who could use it around the city. Then those people, the Thilleians, would make the southern land great again. Of course it wasn't quite so simple, even though his mother would like to think so, but it was a start.

The key was a strange thing, a thin strip of metal as long as his thumb, with two ridges on either side. He slipped the chain that held it in place from around his neck, feeling the stern eyes of his dead ancestors prick in the back of his head. They knew what he risked, and they knew of the glory of days past, and of the disasters. They also knew that he had no army to control the icefire the machine would produce.

They're in the City of Glass already; they will help me because they are destined to do so.

But he had to obtain their hearts for them to be unconditionally obedient to him. They had to be servitors, like Ruko. At the thought of Ruko, an unpleasant thought surfaced.

If I wait any longer, I won't be able to control him anymore. If I wait any longer, the Knights will kill the children, and then all my work will have been for nothing.

He stared at the controls. Dust coated engravings in the metal surface. Levers stuck out of slots, their handles made from Chevakian wood inlaid with river pearl. There were little silica windows with silver embossing, now dark and lifeless. The work oozed beauty and craftsmanship.

I owe it to the souls of all the Imperfects who have been killed since the Knights took power.

There would not be a second chance. This was the best time of the year to find the Eagle Knights distracted with the Newlight celebrations. Half of them would take part in the competitions and the other half would be drunk or in some woman's bed.

He didn't have another fifteen years to scout out another army. It was make do with these children, or not at all. He *did* have enough power to get into the palace.

I am no quitter, Mother, no matter how much you think I am.

He breathed in deeply and slotted the key into the panel. Strands of icefire bent to his hand. He pressed a button. A tiny light lit up, under a cover yellowed with age. Silver engraving reflected the glow. Underneath the ice on the plain between here and the City of Glass, in a pipe that contained threads that Chevakians called *wire*, a signal would travel to the underground power network to come to life. And under the palace, the Heart would respond.

Tandor went through the motions he had memorised from the diary. The network needed water to cool down. The underground passages needed to be opened up to let the heat escape. He slid up levers and turned dials. More lights blinked into life.

Everything seemed to be working the way it should. He had five days before the machine would come into its full power. This would be one sizzler of a Newlight celebration.

Cramped, shivering, Tandor rose from the seat.

He charged back up the stairs, across the slippery bunker and out into the brightness of the snow-covered ice. He heaved the door back into its place and used his pick to push snow over it.

Ruko waited in the driver's seat, the reins in his hands, an impatient scowl on his face.

Myra sat in the sled, rummaging through her luggage.

Tandor jumped onto the seat. "Ready to go? From here straight to the City of Glass. We'll be there today."

He expected a keen response from her. The prospects of visiting markets and shops had kept her happy for the past two days, but she wasn't looking at the horizon at all. Her underwear was bunched around her knees. His heart jumped. *Please, no.*

"Anything wrong?"

"I'm bleeding." She sniffed, wiping a tear from her cheek.

"What does that mean?" His heart thudded.

"I don't know!"

"Does it hurt?"

She shook her head. "It's only a tiny bit." But her voice sounded unsteady. Her face was very pale. He glanced at her underwear, spotting streaks of blood-tinged slime. Was that normal?

"Do you have any . . . pains?"

She shook her head again.

"You think you can hang on for a bit longer? We're almost there." *By the skylights, please.* He heard a woman's screams in his mind. Then the feeble cry of a baby. The horrified voice of the midwife, *This one's deformed.*

"I think so," Myra whispered.

Tandor took a deep breath to calm his thudding heart. "Let's go then."

CHAPTER 5

THE EYRIE of the eagle knights perched atop the second highest tower in the City of Glass. A place where windows had been removed and eagles and their riders could fly in and out freely.

Yellow feet outstretched, Carro's eagle glided into this dark maw that was its home. Air disturbed by its flapping wings propelled straw in little eddies to the corners of the landing area. From their tethering spots further into the building, other eagles squawked and ruffled feathers.

Carro unclipped his harness and slid off the back of his eagle. He swayed with the effects of too much bloodwine, but he forced his feet to move. Never mind the Newlight festival, there'd be trouble if he was caught drunk in the Eyrie.

Six birds stood tethered to the central bar. One of them was ripping at a mass of blood and fur that might once have been a Legless Lion cub. Two other birds were preening themselves, and one regarded Carro with a roving orange eye.

Carro tied the reins to the far end of the bar and threw the bird a hunk of meat. As if it knew that he was supposed to rub it down before leaving, the animal cocked its head and gave him a disdainful glare before it pierced the meat with its claw to claim it. Yet it didn't bend down to tear strips off the meat. It arched its neck. A series of spasms rippled through the animal's body. It opened its beak wide and spat a fur ball onto the floor.

A stable boy skittered past and shovelled it, still steaming, into a bucket. His eyes were wide. "Did you see that, how fast I got it?"

If he expected coin, Carro had spent his last money on drink. He shrugged, and continued to the door, bloodwine churning uncomfortably in his stomach.

That was not an honourable thing to do. But he had no coin left.

After the market raids, the men had gone to the meltery. The older Knights had been drinking hard and had challenged him to keep up. Which he had, just, including two trips to the alley at the back of the meltery to spew, standing over the pink-stained snow, hating himself for the waste of money. His father might be a merchant, but he was an Outer City merchant with nowhere near as much wealth as the city nobles whose sons usually went into the Knighthood.

He avoided the young stable boy's questioning gaze.

Later. He'd give double the going rate later. The thought only added to the misery he already felt.

The merchant's shocked face. *I trusted you*. All those others watching him. He'd *betrayed* his own people. What would they do when he came back, when he and Isandor flew in the race? Would they still cheer? What would the Knights do if they knew the full truth about him? There was no way, *no way*, he'd go back to his father.

He left the eyrie for the darkness of the corridor. Against the wall stood an eagle statue carved from opaque glass, with orange gems for eyes.

The Knight served his eagle; the eagle served the Knight.

It was said that the first eagles had been bred in the palace from the much smaller birds that lived in the mountains. Rumours went that icefire had gone into their blood and that this was the reason they were big enough to carry a fully grown man in leather armour.

The Tutor said that this was nonsense spread by "certain elements", by which he meant the Brotherhood. But the Brothers said they spoke the truth about the eagles being giant forms of wild eagles, and many Knights believed it. This statue symbolised the first of those birds.

The Tutors and upper command didn't like it, but most Knights placed small offerings at the glass eagle's feet. For luck. The Tutors didn't like that either.

Carro stopped and stroked the cold glass neck, smoothened by the passage of many hands. He leaned his forehead against the glass, hoping it would clear his drunken head. *If you have any power at all, help me.*

Then again, why should it help him? He had never been brave enough to give an offering.

Carro's mother sits across the table, yelling at him.

If I hear one more word about that nonsense . . .

It's not nonsense. Just because his mother fails to understand why the Brotherhood does things such as calculating the power of sunlight doesn't mean that it is *untrue.*

It is true; he and Isandor did the experiment as it said in the book. They went out into the alley and let the light shine through the looking-glass they bought at the markets. The intense spot of light caused the paper to burst into flames. The book told them why this happened: because of the shape of the glass and the direction of the sunlight. It also explained that you could do a similar thing with icefire.

They were laughing at their success when his mother found them.

Carro hangs his head. No use arguing.

Go and help your father in the warehouse. She flaps her hand at the door, already bored.

Yes. mother.

Carro froze, his heart thudding, his cheek still against the glass beak of the eagle.

Voices echoed from lower levels of the eyrie, the meaning inaudible. Carro heard his name in every shout, mockery in every bout of laugher. Even the winds whistling through the howling staircase shrieked his name. Carro, the betrayer. Carro, the gutless. Carro, who had to follow his cripple friend to the Knighthood.

"There you are, Apprentice Carro."

Carro gasped.

The Tutor Rider stood behind him, hands on his hips. A man with a beak-like nose, much like an eagle.

Carro scrambled away from the statue, kicking a few coins across the stone floor. Blood rose in his cheeks. Had the Tutor seen how he'd embraced the glass eagle?

"Where were you? I expected you at training."

"With the Knight patrol. You gave me permission—"

"I did?"

"Yes, the patrol Captain—"

The Tutor slapped Carro's face, hard. "The Eagle Order has five pillars: Obedience, Honour, Honesty, Humility and Silence. You disregard all of them. May I remind you that your status is of no import amongst the Knights?"

Status? He had no status. His father was a lowly merchant. Oh, his status as the only Outer City Apprentice? His status as the Apprentices' pissing post?

His gaze on the toes of his boots—scuffed, unpolished—he said, "The Patrol Captain asked if I could come with them to the markets. You gave me permission to go." He'd done nothing wrong—except getting drunk.

The Tutor pushed Carro's head up and spat in his face.

"You disrespect me. And you're drunk. Go to your dormitory and sleep it off. Report for cleaning duty tomorrow."

The Tutor turned and made for the door. "And be glad I'm not giving you worse punishment."

Carro looked up defiantly, wiping saliva off his face with the sleeve of his tunic.

"And wash yourself. You're disgusting!" the Tutor yelled in the confined space of the corridor. The sound of his footsteps faded.

Carro went down the staircase which took him down to the Apprentices' dormitory, a long room with rows of mats against both walls. Blankets lay neatly rolled-up at the head-end of each.

A few older Learners huddled together on one mat, casting furtive glances at the door as Carro came in.

"And then," one boy was saying, "Then I could see her, right through her dress, you know, and man, does she have puppies."

The boys guffawed. One or two glanced at Carro.

"Heh, you look like you fell off your bird again," snorted one called Jono.

They always had to remind him of *that* moment, in the second lesson, when his eagle had taken off so quickly that he hadn't secured himself in the harness.

Clamping his jaws, Carro crossed the room to the shelves at the far end, and took a clean uniform from the shelf labelled with his name.

"Listen to me then," another Apprentice said. "I seen her the day before yesterday. She were going into the baths. There were guards outside, and some went inside with her."

"Do you think they . . ."

More guffaws.

"Nah. She'll pick the real pretty ones. Like that one."

All boys turned to Carro. A grin spread across Jono's face.

"Hey, pretty boy."

One elbowed the speaker in the side. "Hush. He be selected, I think. I heard some Tutors talking about him."

"And they let him stay with us? Do they want him undamaged?"

Jono laughed aloud. For some reason, he'd been picking on Carro since the first day of their training. It started with comments on Carro's clothing, and his parents. Then there had been taunts about the Outer City, and about his clumsiness and his girl-like curls—which Carro had cut off at the earliest opportunity.

Carro kept his gaze to the floor. *Do not talk back, do not talk back*. With everything at the eyrie, that only made things.

"Hey, boy? You be a virgin?"

Carro stares across the room. The girl has hair like bronze. It dances over her shoulders when she moves her head. She's come with the seamstress who is going to make some new dresses for his sister to wear to dinner parties to show off the material his father has imported from Arania. Then rich women will come from the city to buy the fabric.

Business. Fabric on the table and patterns spread out over the couch.

The pretty girl should be wearing the dresses, not his dumpy sister. The girl would look like a goddess. She should be outside, celebrating Newlight, but instead she's here with her boss on his mother's whim.

She smiles. Around her neck she wears a strip of leather with a gull's tail feather tied to it. She's freshly blooded and free to consort with whomever she wants. And she's watching him.

Carro's cheeks burn with heat. Distant thumps of festival music roar in his ears.

Carro, I told you to get the account books. Why haven't you done it yet?

Carro gasps. That's his father. He'll be in for another punishment when the seamstress leaves.

He jumps up, but still looks at the girl, and doesn't see the table. He hits the corner with his knee. Cups go flying with loud clanks and clatters. Tea seeps into the tablecloth.

You clumsy boy! his mother yells.

The girl giggles.

Carro flees, blood throbbing in all sorts of uncomfortable places.

Carro snuck into the bathroom as quietly as he could, trying not to catch the boys' attention.

Here, his footsteps echoed in an icy silence of tiles and stone. Puffs of mist lingered in the air from his breath. The fire from the drying room barely brought any warmth. A fat icicle trailed from the tiny window in the top of the opposite wall almost to the ground. The city buildings were so different from those in the Outer City. These buildings were open, square and cold. The houses in the Outer City were round, without windows, and with a central stove that kept the house warm all day.

Being a Knight wasn't meant to be comfortable.

He undressed himself, and rinsed the smell of bloodwine out of his clothes, shuddering at the memories of the Learner Knight from the patrol who had kept buying him drinks, while his stomach was already protesting. To get him punished no doubt. He poured several pitchers of ice-cold water over his head and then got to work on the bathroom floor. Cleaning duty, he'd done his fair share. He collected the broom and scrubbed the tiles.

When he went to hang his clothes to dry, the Apprentices who had been in the dormitory blocked the door of the drying room. Jono was in the middle of the group. He said lazily, "It think it's time the pet got a lesson, don't you?" He scratched the crotch of his trousers.

The girl's name is Kaila. She holds his arm and talks and giggles. Carro listens to her cheerful babble and wonders how he can guide her into the furniture-maker's warehouse. It's big and empty, and young people go there to lose their innocence during the Newlight celebrations. And now he's managed to sneak her out of the house, he can think of nothing else. His whole body aches for it.

A couple of older boys block the street. Carro recognises some of them as his sister's friends. The pleasant pulsing of blood fades for an icy cold.

The leader of the group, a lanky boy whose name he doesn't know, pulls Carro's cloak off.

Hey, Carro yells. His voice sounds high and boyish. Not the way he wants the girl to hear it. He wants to be manly; he wants her to think he knows all about having girls.

The boy holds the cloak out of his reach.

You don't need that. You have enough blubber to keep you warm.

Give that back to him, Kaila says. She lets go of Carro's arm—leaving a warm spot—and yanks the cloak out of the boy's hands.

Hey, what have we here? The boy grabs her arm. He reaches out and pulls the feather from under her cloak with a broad grin on his face. His mates are cheering.

You keep your hands off her! Carro shouts.

Ah, she's yours, is she?

Another boy laughs. *Do you guys reckon he knows where to*

put it?

A volley of laughter cascades through the street.

You know what, the leader says. *We will let you go.*

Carro breathes out heavily, but doesn't understand. Let him go? They never let him go without humiliation.

Then the boy says, *And we'll come. We're going to watch.*

One of the boys pushed Carro face first into the wall. Others laughed. Hands yanked away the towel, which slipped past his thighs into a puddle on the floor. An icy breeze made his skin break out in goosebumps.

No. He would not think of what happened that day in the furniture-maker's warehouse, about the girl and her pale flesh and his own unwilling body, the laughter at his flaccid member, shrunken and shrivelled in the cold. The girl was crying; the boys were cheering, pushing him, jostling him. He could *not* do it.

And he would *not* go and relive it. He needed to toughen up; his father said often enough, and as much as he hated his father, the man was probably right. He was *not* a pretty boy with too much fat and no muscle. He was *not* an artist with certain parts of his anatomy removed. He was *not* a boy lover.

Carro stands in his father's room. His father sits in his chair by the hearth, smiling.

Carro doesn't like the smile. When his father is angry, things are bad. When he smiles, things are worse.

But his father doesn't speak. He sits, saying nothing.

Carro grasps his hands behind his back and stands there, determined not to say anything.

But the silence lasts on.

Eventually he can't stand it anymore.

He asks, *You wanted to see me, Father?*

His father doesn't answer.

Uhm—Father? I'd like to continue with my study.

His father says nothing. Doesn't even look at him.

What sort of silly game is this? Carro balls his fists, but knows getting angry will not do much good. Whatever he does, his father always wins.

So he stands there, and stares into the fire.

But his father still doesn't speak.

He gathers all his courage. *Father. I really need to study. Please tell me why I needed to come.*

Another silence.

Well, if you won't . . .

A raised eyebrow, and then his father goes back to staring into the fire.

Father, I'm not going to stand here if you won't tell me what this is about. I have a lot of study to do. I won't let you keep me here and then punish me for not doing my work.

Carro turns on his heel and leaves the room.

In the hall he stops, panting, listening to his thudding heart, stilling his trembling limbs. He can't believe what he's just done.

Carro mustered his strength and pushed himself back, slamming his elbow hard into the nose of Jono, who was fumbling with his trousers.

Jono swore hard.

There were shouts, cursing, a jostle and few more boys pushed Carro back against the wall. The mixed taste of plaster and blood was too familiar. Two boys on each side held Carro's arms.

"What did you think you were doing?" Jono stroked Carro's

naked shoulders and let his hand slide down his back, between his buttocks. A cold hand closed around his balls.

"You thought you could beat me, pup?"

Carro dared not breathe. He whispered, "No."

The hand let go, and slid over the skin. Carro broke out in goosebumps.

"You like that, huh?"

"Yes." No other reply was possible, not without making this worse than it already was.

Both hands now grabbed the sides of his thighs.

"I didn't hear that. Can you say it again?"

"Yes!"

"Beg me."

Carro pushed his eyes shut.

Jono hit him hard on the back of the head. "Beg, I said."

"Please!"

Jono came up from behind and rammed hard into Carro's arse. Carro couldn't restrain a moan. His whole backside was on fire.

"You like that, huh?" Jono's breath tickled in the back of his neck. Warm fluid trickled over his shoulder. Blood, from Jono's nose.

"Do I have a choice?" Carro snarled, with one cheek pressed against the wall.

Jono grunted and pushed deeper.

Goosebumps broke out on Carro's skin. The pain had subsided and now he was starting to go hard. It always happened. They'd fuck him, use him, and leave him, sore and aching for release. He hated how his body betrayed him. He hated everything.

Carro clamped his jaws. He would *not* scream or cry. Next time, he would hit harder and in a more delicate spot.

CHAPTER 6

"THE CITY OF GLASS," Tandor said, gesturing at the horizon.

Since stopping at the cave early that morning, the sled had skirted the frozen bay, cutting across points and peninsulas. Now at last, the sled had crested the last hill on their path and they had an uninterrupted view of the snow-swept white bay where it joined the southern ocean. To the right, fluffy clouds hung over higher hills that would eventually become the mountains that formed the border with Arania.

Straight ahead, where stacks of ice floes met the bay, the jagged peaks of the City of Glass reached towards the heavens, tall structures that reflected the light of the low sun. The palace tower protruded from the cluster like a broken stick. That was where Queen Jevaithi looked down upon them all from her rooms with the soft carpets, the ruffled curtains, the stuffed armchairs and the huge bed. Oh yes, the bed.

To Tandor's eyes, the City lay at the centre of a golden web that spread out over the plain, always moving and shimmering. By the skylights, he had never seen it as strong as this. In days to come, it would get stronger, and that was all his doing. Power returning to the Thilleian clan.

Myra sat straight, wincing. She had stopped complaining but kept casting Tandor angry looks. It alternately annoyed Tandor or he ignored it. At the moment, ignoring it was the better option. He had made it here without mishaps. Loriane would probably scold him for taking Myra, but now the women could worry about the women's things.

"You'll soon be warm in mistress Loriane's house."

"It's not the cold why I'm shivering. There's something creepy about this place."

She let her eyes wander to the jagged out lines of the city. Tandor wondered how much icefire she saw.

Ruko was pulling a hooded cloak from the luggage. Good boy.

Tandor nodded his appreciation; Ruko glared back and sent Tandor images of an infirmary ward. People wore the cloak for fear of contamination.

No one will bother you, Tandor said by way of excuse.

Covering up avoided risky situations. If people saw a driverless sled moving by itself, there would be panic, or worse, arrests and questions.

A rush of images flashed through Tandor's head: the same infirmary ward, but the patients bloody and injured in their beds. Red sheets. Some people decapitated, some with their bellies slit open and their intestines spilling out. A madman looking like Ruko, with a knife—

Tandor clamped down on the visions. He gathered icefire in his hand, and threw a loop of it around Ruko's legs.

The images faded, except for one: that of the girl Tandor had seen in Ruko's mind before.

Ruko's inaudible angry howl rang through Tandor's mind.

You love her? Tandor asked.

The girl's image smiled, and reached out.

If you do what I say, we will free her from the palace. If you disobey me . . . Tandor cast a glance at the chest strapped to the luggage rack. Ruko's heart was in there. Returning it to his body would not only turn Ruko back to a weakened, mortal state, it would make him Imperfect, and persecuted in the city.

Ruko pulled on the hooded cloak with jerky movements that oozed anger. While he stepped back up onto the driver's seat, his eyes met Tandor's. They both knew that Tandor's threat was useless. He needed Ruko to be a servitor for his plan to succeed.

Ruko flicked the reins. Even that simple gesture made Tandor's skin creep. With every step the bear took towards the city, the boy's power grew.

The bear started moving again.

The Outer City lay on a hillock to the right, a jumble of snow-covered humps which were houses built by those who had been exiled from the city after the Knights had taken over power. Initially, it had been nothing more than a camp, frequently razed by Knights to weed out the last remains of Thillei blood. These days, the settlement was a decent town in its own right, a gathering of buildings that had been thrown together without plans or foresight, home of commerce, and crime.

The traditional festival grounds were a temporary town made of colourful tents on the plain separating the Outer City from the City of Glass proper. It was busy; the breeze brought shards of music and clapping, and grumbles of bears from the sled parking area. There were fences, a course for racing Tusked Lions. They even had igloos for the animals. Tandor spotted the flapping wings of an eagle, and the grey and red uniform of a Knight. Yes, they would be out here in force, too.

Newlight meant free unlimited girls, most of whom were throwing themselves at the Knights, so most of them wouldn't look so closely at what went on in the Outer City.

Ruko steered the sled along a track that had many marks from passing traffic, no doubt made by Lion-catchers returning to the city with the first of the to-be-slaughtered animals.

Soon, they had reached the ramshackle collection of houses,

with Ruko negotiating the twisty streets. Getting lost was easy in the Outer City. No street was straight and the houses, structures locals called limpets, all looked the same from the outside: large conical shapes of ice. The ones that had just been resurfaced were pristine white, while the older ones had gone dirty and grey. Usually, the only other thing that distinguished individual houses was the colour of the doors, but during the Newlight festival, most doors were yellow.

There were people everywhere: talking on street corners, watching artistes in colourful clothing juggling balls while standing on each other's shoulders.

The sled progressed at walking pace. The people would see a noble and a girl heavy with child—a man from the city proper with his breeder woman, nothing out of the ordinary. Nobles came to the Outer City for shady business, and as such they were best ignored when they were there.

A juggler performed an act with a set of black coals and a huge butcher's knife. At his feet lay a stuffed pillow made from bear fur, symbolising the animal that would be ritually killed at the height of the celebrations. Newlight celebrated the end of the long, dark winter, when the sun rose above the horizon and hunting trips were again possible. It was the start of a time of plenty, of new life, and of fertility.

The sled had gone past the juggler before the man got to the part of his act that involved stabbing the stuffed bear and ripping it apart. Usually, there was something inside for the children. Chevakian sweets, or bits of saltmeat. Tandor could taste it on his tongue.

By the skylights, the memories. His mother used to take him here for visits almost every year.

Myra looked wide-eyed at the scenery sliding past. For a short time at least, she seemed to have forgotten to complain.

They crossed the markets, with busy stalls and roaring fires, where people were eating hot food and warming themselves. Tandor felt the pull of icefire from the merchant who usually had his stall in the very corner. To the common people in the street, he sold crockery and bits and pieces he scavenged from old estates, but under his benches, he held forbidden items from the past. Little portraits of the King, a piece of cutlery with the Thillei emblem, scavenged from the palace storerooms. Today there was no opportunity for Tandor to see the man, but he'd come back later. First he must deposit this complaining child in mistress Loriane's hands.

Ruko halted the sled in front of a newly-covered limpet with a blue door. So familiar, down to the white snowflake patterns on the blue paint—Tandor had painted them—and the mark on the door which he had made trying to manoeuvre a chair inside. So many times had Tandor stepped through that door into Loriane's soft arms. He could taste her lips against his, he could feel the softness of her breasts under his hands. He could—

"Is this it?" Myra asked, frowning.

Tandor shook himself out of his memories. "Yes."

He jumped off the sled. A young couple came past and stared at him as he lifted the knocker and let it fall on the door. Why *would* a noble come to mistress Loriane's house? Good question.

Tandor ignored the gazes. He imagined the big round stove that was the centre of the limpet, where Loriane would make her heavenly soup. He could almost see her determined face, the cheeks red with cold, the slightly crooked mouth and the way one of her eyes always seemed to squint. No, Loriane wasn't pretty either. Her beauty was on the inside.

Why had no one opened the door yet?

"Well, your woman obviously isn't at home." Myra's voice sounded peevish.

Tandor wanted to snap at her. Yes, he was sore and tired, too—and how was he to know that Loriane would be out?—but he bit on his irritation.

"She might be at the festival," he said.

The remaining Imperfect boy would be fifteen. He might take part in some of the competitions. Loriane's brother was a butcher. He would have an important role in the festivities. Yes, that was it.

He climbed back into the sled.

Ruko's questioning mind touched his.

Tandor forced his thoughts back on the snow-covered field where the crowds and the tents had been. *And the eagles.* The place crawled with Knights, since a lot of them would be competing. Well, that was not to be helped.

Ruko steered the sled away from the house, and they went back through the same busy streets, drawing annoyed glances from pedestrians.

When they reached the festival grounds, the sled could go no further. The designated parking area was already full and the igloos occupied with bears. But never mind; they wouldn't stay long.

Tandor jumped out, after which Myra pulled up her legs and settled sideways on the bench. "You go and look for her. I'll stay here."

"No, you won't." He couldn't risk losing her now.

"I'm tired."

"No, you come. I promised your father I'd look after you." *And I didn't take you to play stubborn adolescent either.*

Her face scrunched up briefly, but then she pressed her lips together and rose. "I don't know why you wanted me to come. So far, you've only been disgusting and nasty to me."

"You'll find out." He held out an arm. She took it, clambering awkwardly from the sled. A man walking past shot him a look that might have been disdain. Noble men of the City of Glass paid their breeder women to have their children but did not, ever, fall in love with them. He wanted to scream at those curious people *the child isn't mine.*

A man walked past pulling a sled full of barrels. Bloodwine. That load was worth a lot of sore heads tomorrow morning.

To his right, at the bottom of the slope, stood several bright-coloured tents. Clouds of steam rose into the air from food stalls.

A bit further away over the plains, a group of eagles were coming in. The tail end of the long-distance race for Apprentice Knights, Tandor picked up from a shard of conversation.

A couple of youngsters were walking in the snow in bare feet, with bare legs protruding from blankets. Ah, the swimming. Didn't they make that race harder every year? Jump in the water, swim to the ice floe, climb on, get the token, jump back in and return to the start? By that time, most of the competitors were so cold they needed rescuing, to loud jeers of the audience. Oh, the memories were coming back.

Soon, they were amongst the thick of the activity. Tandor wanted to run from tent to tent. Now he was so close, he hungered for Loriane's touch, the twinkle in her eyes and the caress of her hands.

Loriane had once said she manned the drinks booth, so they looked at the food stalls. It was so busy that Tandor had to hold Myra close for fear of becoming separated in the throng. She shuddered under his touch.

The crowds at the swimming were so thick that even he, tall as he was, could only hear the splashes and the shouts. Further past the tents, nurses' sleds marked with green were doing a brisk trade shipping contestants off to the various Outer City healers.

Ah. As midwife, Loriane was a healer of sorts. Maybe she was on duty in the medical post.

A huge queue lined up there. Tandor pushed past the line. People glared, but said nothing at the sight of the golden curls on his cheeks. The advantages of being a noble.

In one tent, a couple of frazzled nurses were treating a young man with cuts all over his upper body. Tandor guessed he had fallen on the ice.

In another tent, a group of young men continued to brawl while Tandor tried to make himself heard. Where was Loriane? The young nurse thought maybe in the main post. Where was that? Her reply was interrupted by a loud burp. The next thing one of the brawling youths projecto-vomited bloodwine all over his mates and collapsed face first onto the floor. Then everyone started yelling.

Tandor retreated. The smell of vomit made him feel sick.

"Have you seen anything that might look like a main medical post?" he asked Myra.

She didn't reply. Her face was pale; she seemed not to have heard anything.

A stab of irritation shot through him. "What's wrong with you?"

"What's wrong? Well, you're so good at being crude. In case you haven't noticed, having a child inside you puts a lot of pressure on your rear end. In case you don't understand that: my butt hurts and I feel like pissing myself with every step. I want to use the outroom." Her voice spilled over.

"But you did only just before we came here."

"Didn't you listen to what I said? I feel like that. All. The. Fucking. Time."

People were stepping back, leaving a small circle around them, keen expressions on their faces. At Newslight, fights were entertainment, no matter who was fighting.

He grabbed her arm. "Come. You're making a spectacle of yourself."

"No, I'm not coming anywhere. I've had enough."

She yanked her arm out of his grip and ran, shouldering people aside. Oh, by the skylights!

Tandor pushed between curious onlookers, but she had vanished. Great. That was just what he needed.

He stood there, gnashing his teeth when a shiver crawled over his arm. Icefire. A brief golden thread snaked through the air. That had to be from Myra, but the thread had not come from the direction of the sled. Where was she going? Was she lost already?

Women.

He pushed through the crowd. The sensation grew stronger. Golden threads shivered and dissolved into sparks. At that point he realised that this icefire didn't come from Myra: the boy was here.

Stupid. He should have realised that. Myra had Thillei blood, but it wasn't half as strong as the boy's. Isandor had turned fifteen and would be out here looking for girls, maybe drinking if he had money, or taking part in a competition or two.

All Tandor needed to do was follow the tug of icefire and collect another of his children. Except the strand led him . . . to the eagles' pens.

Tandor spotted Myra before he found Isandor. She was at the fence, staring into the pen where at least thirty eagles were tied up on bars. She was even leaning her Imperfect arm on the fence. *By the skylights, get away before anyone sees you.* The place was crawling with Knights. There were at least ten of them in their distinctive red tunics with grey cloaks.

"Myra, come," he hissed at her. "I promise we'll go back to the sled now."

She didn't move, but stared ahead.

Tandor followed her gaze. In a group of a few young Knights stood a distinctive young man, lean and quite tall. His skin was milk-pale and his hair black as lowsun night. Since Tandor had seen him last, his face had become more mature. He even sported a dark fuzz of hair on his chin. But his eyes were the clearest, darkest blue, that colour people called royal blue. It was Loriane's boy Isandor, and he was wearing an Eagle Knight uniform.

CHAPTER 7

ICE FLOES, belly slithers, what would they think of next?

Loriane pulled the thread and knotted it close to the young man's skin. She cut the needle free and covered the wound with a dab of paste to stop it going bad.

"That will become a nasty scar, I'm afraid," she said. On his forehead, too. Stupidity forever engraved on his face.

The man blinked, looking up at the canvas ceiling of the treatment tent. Light from the central fire flickered in his eyes. He was too drunk to respond, too drunk to feel pain. He also had been too drunk to swim probably, otherwise he would not be sitting here.

"I've finished with him," she said to his friends who waited by the fire, hands outstretched to warm themselves. "Take him home and make sure he rests for a tennight."

They mumbled agreement.

Loriane heaved herself to her feet and tossed her instruments—scalpel and needles—into the cooking pot that hung over the fire.

"Help me put his clothes back on."

One of the young men came forward and pulled his mate up from the chair while Loriane wrestled unwilling limbs back into armholes, sliding cloth over wounds she had bandaged earlier. The stench of bloodwine around the men made her gag.

The man's cloak, blood-splattered and dirty, went over his clothes. The two shuffled out with the patient.

Loriane sighed and sank down in the chair that still held the young man's lingering warmth. *Rest.* Like that would ever happen. More likely, she'd see him back here tomorrow with . . . Let's see . . . alcohol poisoning, cuts from the ice, bruises from his fellow's fists or deep ugly scratches from trying to mount an eagle. Seriously, had she ever been that stupid at that age?

She so much preferred her usual patients: pregnant women who came to her for advice and who asked her to come to the palace birthing rooms to help deliver their children.

She should pack up and go home before someone brought the next victim. During the Newlight festival, there was always a next victim. She had been on her feet since this morning. They hurt. Her belly hurt.

As she picked up her cloak, the tent's outer flap whispered like it did when someone entered. A girl stood there, barely out of adolescence. Loriane knew her; she lived a few streets away, the daughter of a merchant.

"Mistress Loriane! Am I too late?"

Loriane sighed. "I was about to go home. Be quick."

"I'd like to get my ichina." The girl's eyes shone. "I got my first bleeding, just in time for Newlight."

All girls went through this trial, the ritual deflowering of their innocence. When they bled, they were allowed to consort with whomever they liked whenever they liked during the Newlight celebrations.

Loriane went to her medicine chests. She rummaged through her medicines for the jar of ichina, and measured out a small quantity of the red powder on her scales.

"You must take it on the first day you stop bleeding. You should mix it in a drink. It's most effective if you use it in the morning."

The girl nodded solemnly, but her eyes shone.

"Are you sure you want it now? Because you would have more chance next year. A girl's bleeding usually takes some time to settle before you can conceive." If that happened at all. Far too many women went barren.

"No, I want it now." The girl blushed.

All right—she fancied someone.

"Anyone important? If it is, you have to make sure you get a contract negotiated if you fall pregnant. Don't ask too much. They might use you again if they're happy with you."

The tent flap rustled again, letting in Aera, one of the Outer City's regular healers, an older woman with a severe bun on top of her head. She advanced silently into the tent, put down a bucket and peeled off her cloak. Underneath, she wore a study dress. She rolled up the sleeves and started transferring chunks of ice from her bucket into a large pot of water that hung over the fire.

Loriane rattled off the other things in a business-like manner. The girl left, happy and red-cheeked, clutching the treasure in her pocket.

"You go home," Aera said into the silence. "I'll take over. You look tired."

Loriane nodded. She *was* tired. Somehow, this child exhausted her more than the previous nine had.

"How long until you drop that child?"

"A tennight, no more." Or tonight, she wished with all her mind, but so far none of the concoctions she gave her girls had worked.

"Urgh. Rather you than me. Whose is this one?"

"Yanko."

"Good catch. Hope he'll pay well for the suffering."

Loriane nodded non-committally. The world of breeders was

far removed from this woman's life. Most of the bright-eyed girls who came to ask Loriane for ichina never came back again. Like so many of the city's women, they were barren. If they were lucky, they would snare a decent husband who would pay a breeder to have his children. If they found no husband, well, there was always the street, the pleasure parlours and the merchants were always looking for workers in poorly-heated warehouses.

Loriane donned her cloak, bid the healer good luck and left the tent.

She had feared there would be more people waiting outside for treatment, but the queues had gone and a sense of quiet had descended over the festival grounds in preparation for the night, when revellers moved to the Outer City's melteries.

Soon enough, the stream of patients would recommence, bringing unconscious drunks choking in their own vomit and men with gashes from fights.

With a shiver, she wondered what Isandor was doing. He'd been a boy this time last year, talking about the races with wide-eyed wonder. Now he was with the Knights, there was brooding handsomeness to him that made her sure that by the end of Newlight, he would no longer be a virgin. If a girl came to her door claiming to carry his child, would he have the money to deal with it? Could she cope with raising another one of those strange children that made her skin crawl? He was fifteen, not ready for any of this.

I was thirteen when I let myself be taken by the young noble Knight with the curly hair, and fourteen when I pushed out his son. After a day of pain, a beautiful baby with big bright eyes. She had fed the child and had never wanted to part with him. But the palace midwives had taken him away. The boy would be sixteen and living a world away in the towers of the City of Glass.

Oh, she had done well enough. With the Knight's money, she had been able to leave her embittered father. But no amount of money could take away the pain.

She wanted a different future for Isandor. She wanted to tell him not to touch any girls, but knew he wouldn't listen anyway.

"Loriane," a male voice called.

"I'm on my way home. Go to the help post at the festival." Then she realised she sounded snippy and added, "Unless it's an emergency."

"For you, there is always an emergency."

The next moment warm arms enclosed her from behind. The man's clothes smelled of exotic spices and oil.

"Tandor!" Could it be true? She leaned away from his male warmth.

Tandor indeed. By the skylights, where had he been? His blue eyes smiled at her. The street lamps glinted in golden curls on his cheeks. He was wearing his noblemen's disguise again. He looked so good; he was here for her.

"What are you doing here?"

"Shh." He put a finger to her lips and pulled it away when his lips came closer. His kiss was hungry, and for a moment, she lost herself in desire.

His hands strayed to the taut skin of her belly. "Another one, eh?"

"It pays my food."

"Oh, Loriane, how many times do I have to tell you that you don't have to do this."

"And I'll tell you just as many times that I have no other option. I'm a fertile woman, and there'd be talk if I wasn't carrying."

By the skylights, she was angry all of a sudden. Why hadn't he let her know he was coming?

"So, what *are* you doing here?"

"It's a long story. We need a safe place to stay, and I thought—"

"Isandor's bed is empty so you can stay with me." By the skylights, he was so transparent. "Tandor, you don't need to find silly excuses to stay with me, even though you always manage to think of some." Wait—he had said *we*?

She glanced over his shoulder. His familiar sled waited in the street, with the equally familiar cloaked and hooded driver. She had never seen the man's face, and had never heard him speak. Tandor had told her the young man had an accident and couldn't speak. His face had become terribly disfigured, he said. Would he have to sleep in her house, too? He never came inside.

Fur stirred on the back seat of the sled; a head lifted from what had looked like Tandor's luggage a moment ago.

"Can we go now?" asked a female voice.

Loriane stiffened. "Who's that?"

She pushed himself out of his embrace. Her heart thudded like crazy.

"This is Myra, from Bordertown."

His eyes met hers, intense, and she had no idea what that look meant.

Her lips felt stiff when she spoke her next words. "It'll cost to stay with me. This is the time of Newlight. There are no beds for hire anywhere in the city. If you stay in my house, I'll have to cancel a paying visitor I'd agreed to take."

"Loriane, Loriane, you know you're the worst liar in the world?"

Damn him. She shrugged and let a silence lapse. Then she let go of his arm, severing the last bit of physical contact between them. "Let's go."

He guided her to the sled, where he sat between her and the girl. She was a wisp of a thing, barely older than Isandor. It looked like she had travelled with him for quite some distance, with the amount of furs that covered her and her wind-blown rough cheeks.

Tandor never said a word to the cloaked driver, but the man flicked the reins and the bear loped into action. Once they were out of the street, the going was slow. Groups of drunken youths came out of side streets, laughing and pushing each other, and generally not looking out for other people, let alone sleds.

"Busy," Tandor said into the uneasy silence. He kept his gloved hands ostensibly on his lap, as if uncomfortable with showing either her or his young lover affection.

Loriane turned her head away, seeing shops and groups of revellers pass through a blur of tears.

She thought he travelled to collect knowledge and to conduct his Chevakian stepfather's merchanting business. She thought he *belonged* to her; she thought that was why he visited the Outer City. She thought . . .

What did it matter?

The sled stopped in front of her limpet. Loriane stepped from the sled fighting her pricking eyes. She opened the door and stumbled into the short hallway. The air was cold and still in the space between the outer layer of ice blocks and the inner wall of the limpet structure. She had tossed a few bricks in the stove this morning, but they had burnt a long time ago. Not even Isandor waited for her these days, not since he had moved to the eyrie in the City of Glass.

Loriane charged into the central room, not waiting to see if Tandor and his mistress followed. She opened the door in the side of the huge stove and flung in a few fire bricks—rubbishy ones. No point wasting her good bricks on someone who cheated her. With a wick of fire, she then went around the circular room and lit the lanterns. Greasy curls of blubber oil rose past the sleeping shelves towards the ceiling. She indicated to what had been Isandor's shelf, above her head.

"The bed up there will be yours, once I've—"

She turned. Tandor and the girl had come in after her. In the flapping light of the oil lamps, she saw how pale and tired the girl looked, and how young she was. And how incredibly pregnant.

Loriane froze, looking from Tandor to the girl.

Impossible. If Tandor had the necessary equipment, all her ten children would have been his. Or had he perhaps found a way . . . Why this girl? She'd been available for him all these years.

The girl gave her a desperate look. "Mistress Loriane, can I please, please use your outroom?"

Loriane played with the notion to refuse, but tucked it away just as quickly. She was a midwife first, always. "Sure, it's at the back over there."

The girl stumbled past the stove to the door Loriane had indicated, clutching her belly, leaving Tandor and Loriane facing each other in an uneasy silence. The fire bricks sputtered and hissed in the stove.

"Don't tell me that you took her all the way from Bordertown in that condition," Loriane said.

"She's in danger."

"From dropping the child on your lap, yes. What do you know about delivering a child, Tandor?"

His face hardened. Right, one didn't go there with him. "Must've been some pretty big danger to do something as stupid as that." She flung a pan onto the cookplate and re-opened the door on the stove.

"Loriane—"

She grabbed the poker from its spot against the chimney and stabbed the dying coals underneath the bricks more vigorously than necessary. A volley of sparks flew into the chimney.

"—I will explain. There's a real danger to her—"

"No, just leave it. When you talk like this, everything that's real to you isn't to me." She hated how her voice sounded unsteady. Tandor was the only bit of colour in her dull life. She waited for his visits. She dreamed of travelling with him. *Why, Tandor, why?*

A small noise indicated that the girl had finished her business in the outroom, and remained standing by the door. Loriane couldn't help feeling sorry for her. Had she asked to carry his child, did he pay her, or—she cast Tandor a glance—had he played some sort of trick on her? How had he done it?

Loriane, jealousy is an ugly emotion.

"Come on, shut the door, come here and sit down. Let me have a look at you."

The girl sat down on Loriane's old couch and folded her hands in her lap. No, wait, one of her sleeves hung empty; she had only one hand. The other ended in a stump just above the wrist. Oh. That explained a lot. Tandor had said something about other

Imperfects during his last visit. It was so long ago, she struggled to remember what it was.

Loriane kneeled on the carpet and pushed her hands under the girl's dress. The skin on her belly tensed into a hard ball. The girl took in a sharp breath.

"Does that hurt?"

"A bit."

Loriane prodded the skin, feeling bumps of the child's elbows and feet. "How long do you have to go?"

The girl shrugged.

"Do you know when you slept with a man?" She tried to see how Tandor responded to this question, but he had gone to the other side of the stove and studied the contents of her pantry, where she couldn't see his face.

"Many times," the girl whispered. "My father didn't like it, so we climbed into the hay loft. My father was furious when my belly started growing." Her face crumpled. "I wasn't the only one either, just the first one. Tandor says the Knights took the others to the City of Glass. Do you know where they are?"

Others? A chill went over Loriane's back.

Just what had Tandor been doing?

"The Knights discovered the sanctuary I set up for Imperfect children in Bordertown," Tandor said, still speaking at the wall.

Loriane could tell from the tenseness in his posture that this was important to him. So he had found himself a bunch of teenage lovers and was breeding an army of Imperfects?

He continued, "That's why I took her with me. The Knights didn't take her because of her condition, but they will be back."

"So you brought her to the one place in the land that's crawling with Knights. Some days you make so much sense to me, Tandor."

She pulled down the girl's dress, a coarsely-knitted thing which barely fit over her stomach. Tears trickled down the girl's freckled cheeks.

Loriane hated herself for being so jealous, for admitting how much she had longed for him to come back. It had all been a waste of time.

She rose. "Come." And charged across the room.

When he was a small boy, Isandor, with his peg leg, had fallen down the ladder to his sleeping shelf a few times, so her brother had built him proper stairs. The girl followed Loriane up these steps to where Isandor's bed stood, untouched and musty. It was dark up here, and the air thick with rancid smoke from the lanterns. The light that reached from downstairs was feeble and orange.

"Take off your clothes and get in the bed."

Loriane snipped another lantern into life as the girl obeyed. First she took off her cloak, her jacket and her dress. In the pale light, she looked like a misshapen troll. Too skinny.

The girl hesitated. "Bottoms, too?"

She wore a coarsely woven pair of shorts, tied with a ribbon under her belly. Her bellybutton stood out like a weak spot on a waterskin.

"I'll give you some clean bottoms."

Myra undid the ribbon and let the garment fall to the floor, not looking at Loriane. She wore a piece of cloth between her legs, covered with blood-streaked slime.

By the skylights. "How long have you been bleeding?"

"Started yesterday." Her voice trembled. "I didn't know what else to do. I couldn't tell Tandor . . . Does it mean . . . the child is harmed?"

Loriane picked up the cloth. The discharge was slimy, and brownish. "You've been having pains?"

She shook her head. "Is that bad?" New tears threatened in her eyes.

"I don't think so. It just your body getting ready for the birth. It means that you will be having a child very, very soon."

"It hurts a lot, doesn't it?" Her voice was barely more than a whisper.

"If you panic and fight it. You should let the pains come over you and it will hurt a lot less." *But as skinny as you are, it will be a very hard job.*

The girl nodded but her face was pale. Oh, she was so young, and obviously no one had taught her anything about becoming or being a mother.

Shivering, Myra slipped between the covers of Isandor's bed. Loriane draped the blankets and Isandor's bear skin spreads over her. Poor girl.

"I'll be back to bring you some soup. Eat it all. You will soon need your strength."

The girl nodded, but was already drifting off to sleep. Loriane guessed soup—and sleep for herself—would have to wait.

Before going downstairs, she pulled the string to open an air vent at the limpet's very top. For Myra's health, air laced with smoke and smells would never do. Too many people died from stale air inside their limpets.

Tandor paced around the stove.

The orange light made his golden tattoos glitter. His hair was smooth and glossy, tied back in a loose ponytail from his face bronzed by the Chevakian sun. He was so handsome, so mysterious it made her heart ache.

Tandor looked up to where she had stopped on the stairs, white-knuckled hands gripping the railing. There was a look of concern on his face, a look that said you-shouldn't-be-doing-this-in-your-state. Loriane raised her chin, daring him to say it, but he didn't.

"I'm angry with you," she said instead, still shivering. "You let that poor girl suffer. She's scared and in pain. She needs a mother to show her what to do and I have no time—"

"No, Loriane. I'm angry with *you*."

"Angry with me?" she whispered. "*You* are angry with *me*?"

"About Isandor. I saw him this afternoon. He's wearing a *Knight's* uniform. What's this, Loriane? How could you allow that?"

"Allow it?" She gave a hollow laugh while trying to keep her voice down so Myra wouldn't overhear. "You try and raise an adolescent boy alone and tell me how you can or cannot *allow* him to do anything. It was either the butcher's or the Eagle Knights. It was his idea to sign up. I'm happy for him. The uniform looks *good* on him."

Next thing she knew, Tandor had crossed the room and was looming over her. His mouth trembled.

"Looks good on him? By the skylights, *looks good on him?* Have you forgotten?" Spit flew into her face. "Have you forgotten who made me what I am, who killed my family and made me an outcast in my own country? Have you forgotten who is killing all people of my clan?"

He had to take a panting breath.

"No, I have not forgotten, but that's your life, not his."

"It's his life as much as it's mine. I saved him. I asked you to keep him safe, and where is he? With the *Knighthood* by the skylights. He's Imperfect, and the Knights will kill him. I don't understand why they haven't done so already."

"Times have changed, Tandor."

"They haven't. What do you know about it? How could you let him join?"

"Well, I never received instructions that he couldn't. And I couldn't have stopped him if I wanted anyway. He's a pretty wilful young man." *And much stronger than me, besides.* Frankly, Isandor was starting to scare her, with the wild look in his eyes. Those times, she wondered who his parents were, and wondered why Tandor had brought him, red and screaming, to her door with the end of the umbilical cord still attached.

"Just leave it, Tandor. It's his life. What is it to you anyway? I've looked after the boy and you've never shown any interest in him. And now you have your little family . . ."

Tandor's mouth fell open. Then he threw his head back and laughed, not a pleasant laugh. Loriane motioned for him to be quiet, gesturing upstairs to the sleeping shelf.

He snorted. "So that is what you think? You think the damage the Knights did to me can be restored like that? Yes, Loriane, this is about family, but much wider than your narrow understanding of it."

"I don't care about my *narrow* understanding of family! You intrude into my life, impose yourself on me, let me think you feel something for me, and then you think you can get away with this and I won't mind?" She turned away before she would burst into tears and left the living room for the outroom, slamming the door behind her.

She stood there, panting in the dark. *Forget about him, forget him.*

She lit the wick and let its end sink into the oil reservoir of the light that hung next to the door. It was cold here in the washroom, and her breath steamed in the air. Tears were streaming down her face. She had been such a fool.

"Loriane."

She gasped. "Will you stop sneaking up on me like that? In my own outroom?"

"You're not using it." He glanced pointedly at the seat with the hole against the outer wall of the limpet's double layer. Natural sculptures of glistening icicles dripped down the inner cladding.

"I have used it." Loriane raised her chin and stalked past him back into the warmth of the central room.

Tandor spoke in a low voice. "Is that really what you think? That I have hidden all these young girls for my own fun and they're carrying my children?"

Loriane looked away. The accusation sounded silly when he spoke it aloud. She knew what the Knights had done to him, and if he'd been able to restore himself with icefire, he *would* have done so.

Tandor pulled out a stool from under the bench and sat down.

For a while no one said anything. The yelling and laughing of partygoers drifted in from outside.

Then Tandor said, "The father of Myra's child is a young man called Beido. He's fifteen, like her, and one of my oldest charges.

When the Knights came to Bordertown, he was taken with the others to the palace dungeons. Myra is very upset about it."

Loriane saw nothing except the flapping light.

Oh, she had been such a fool. Such an incredible stupid, jealous fool. She turned away from him, straining to hold back tears. They came anyway.

His arms closed around her.

"Sorry, Tandor, I'm so sorry. I'm just a big emotional fool."

She leaned against his chest, listening to the heavenly sound of his heart beating. He stroked her hair. Everything was all right now. Things would be as they were before.

"Loriane, did you think I had abandoned you?"

"I shouldn't have, but I did. You were away so long."

"I know, but I'm here now. I'm not leaving you anymore."

She turned and faced him, meeting his royal blue eyes.

"I love you," she said.

"I know."

His lips tasted salty with her tears.

CHAPTER 8

AT THIS TIME of the year, the land of the south knew no night. Day bled into dusk and slightly deeper dusk and then, slowly, the sun rose again.

Sick of watching Loriane sleep, Tandor had gone outside at the first hint of sunlight.

The drunken festival crowds had gone home, surrendering the streets to the humdrum of business: melteries replenishing their stocks of ice and distillates, cooks from the Outer City's eating houses haggling over the last vats of saltmeat, because certainly, it would be the worst of shame to ask one's customers to eat only tubers and beans, with the only sniff of meat that of the lard used to cook the pancakes.

No. Must not think of food. His stomach had felt queasy for two days in a row.

He yearned for freshly baked bread, and fruity muffins. *Chevakian* things. The food of his youth. He had become soft, corrupted.

In the chaos of the markets no one paid attention to a noble roaming the stalls. Tandor pretended interest in the wares offered for sale, but he listened for anything that might be of use. From merchants, he learned that there were no games on today that Knights were likely to enter. It looked like they were right, because the eagle pens remained empty.

Yet, he had to find a way to talk to Isandor, because without Isandor, he would need one extra Imperfect for his plan to get into the palace. There was no way he could get his hands on the *other* girl.

He lingered at a stall where two men were warming their hands in front of a grill sizzling with battered pieces of saltmeat while discussing swimming races which would be held today. One man said that girls would win because they suffered less in the freezing water, to which the other man argued—

"Excuse me, do either of you know what's on tomorrow?" Tandor asked.

Both men turned to him, eyebrows raised.

"You're not from here?"

Tandor cringed. His accent always gave him away. *I'm a blasted Chevakian*. "I've been away."

"Good time to return," one man said.

"Tomorrow's going to be a big day," the other man added. "There's the long distance race for the Apprentice Knights, and the choosing of the Queen's Champion."

So— Isandor was likely to be back here tomorrow. He must find some way to talk to the boy and offer him something he could not refuse. But he had to be careful. He was not as young and strong as he used to be. As soon as he asked Ruko to help, Isandor would be suspicious. He was a trained Knight, and knew how to defend himself. On top of that, Isandor would be able to see Ruko very well, and with his interest in old books, Isandor might even know what Ruko was. Few books said good things about servitors, and fewer still fully understood the concept. That was one thing he would have to change, once he had his victory.

Meanwhile, securing Isandor's cooperation was going to be hard enough. Damn Loriane for allowing the boy to join the Knights. No, Tandor hadn't forbidden it, because the thought that Isandor would want to join the Knights had never even entered his mind. Why would a Thilleian do such a thing? Did he have so little regard for his heritage?

By the skylights, all his children were in prison, weakened, like Myra, or corrupted, like Isandor, and even Ruko.

What a mess.

Tandor arrived at the second-hand bric-a-brac stall that was run by a man who was an ordained member of the Brotherhood of the Light. Last time he visited the stall, probably a few years ago, the man had sold him some interesting material from the old royal family, which had probably come out of the palace. He still remembered showing his mother the purchases. She had gone all misty-eyed over a small bronze statue. *I can still see it standing in his study*. That statue now stood on her desk in Tiverius.

"Can I help the dear sir?" a man asked.

Tandor started and looked up into the bearded face. The stall owner had gone grey in those years, but this was indeed the Brother.

"I bought something interesting from you a while ago," Tandor said. "A bronze statue that belonged to the royal family."

The man obviously hadn't recognised him before, but he so did now. His lips formed the letter *O*, but his eyes showed an emotion not quite so indifferent. Surprise? Fear? It was hard to tell.

"Do you have anything new for me to look at?" Tandor kept his voice low.

"No, no. I don't have anything like that. It's illegal. The Knights took all I had. I should have handed it in before—"

"What sort of things?"

"All sorts. The usual knick-knackery, plates, cups, some napkins with the royal crest. All gone."

"Books?" Those were the most precious. Those books should *not* fall into the hands of Pirosians.

"Yes, there were books, but they're all gone."

"You have nothing left?"

"Nothing, nothing, nothing. It's a disgrace. I'm an honest businessman. What harm can a few cups and some forks do anyway? I mean—without the old royal family's stuff, what would we have to sell? Nothing good's been made since the Knights came to power. Nothing that people want to buy."

"Shhh." Tandor waved his hand. "I agree with you, but saying it aloud is dangerous."

"Not here at the markets it isn't. In most of the Outer City, it isn't. Many people are fed up. We'll no longer live in poverty while the Knights and nobles get everything. We'll no longer have any children taken away from their mothers' arms."

Tandor was surprised by the anger in the man's voice. He didn't know the resistance against the Knights had grown so much and was delighted with this turn of events. Maybe he didn't need to go as far as snatching Isandor away from the Eagle Knights' eyrie. There might be other Imperfects in hiding.

He clasped his live hand in his claw behind his back, feigning a relaxed pose.

"So," he said and licked his lips. "If I were to tell you that *someone* who's sympathetic to your cause might be looking for a person with a certain . . . imperfection, is there a chance I'd find such a person in the Outer City?"

A shrewd expression crossed the merchant's face. "There might be."

"Could you tell me?"

The merchant glanced aside.

"The Knights have been rather keen to investigate us. I was searched recently, and things were taken. We fear . . . a raid, maybe. We might be . . . interested if someone were to offer this person shelter . . . If there is a certain . . . remuneration."

"An Imperfect?"

Another glance aside. "There's a boy. He's eleven years old. I've been expecting the Knights to get word of him soon. Rumour goes that you saved . . . others."

"This boy of yours, he's in the Outer City?"

"Yes."

"In your compound?"

The merchant gave a single nod.

Tandor considered his next response. At eleven, the boy was too young to be of much use, but it might be all he could get. He attempted some provisional calculations, but he couldn't concentrate under the merchant's hawkish gaze.

By the skylights, it had been so long since he had found an Imperfect, and for one to spring up just when he needed one so desperately could be a trap.

Tandor let the silence linger for a little longer before he put his hand in his pocket and drew out a golden eagle, which he deposited carelessly on the table amongst the second-hand jumble of cookware. Then he picked it back up. The merchant watched every move. Oh, he was keen to have the money all right.

"I'd be willing to pay, but I'm not sure if this boy is worth my money."

The man gave an indignant sniff. "I have not deceived you, have I?"

"No, you haven't, but there is a first for everything." He grabbed some strands of icefire, which came so readily, and found and held the man's gaze until the merchant looked away.

"Don't stare at me like that. It gives me a headache. If you're going to stare me into revealing lies, you can stare all you want, because I don't have no lies. I won't lie about the money either. I'm broke."

Yes, Tandor was sure of it now: the man had felt icefire and had Thilleian blood. He took the coin out of his pocket again and put it on the market stall. "Tell me who this boy is and where to find him."

"You must promise you'll do him no harm."

Where did these people get the idea that he was out to kill everyone? "Would I harm one of my own kind?"

"Then come to the compound. But be careful, Brother, I can sense the Light in you. The Knights will sense it, too."

"Don't worry about me."

"May the Light guide you."

Tandor found it hard not to walk too fast from the markets, since it would only draw attention, but there was energy in his step that he hadn't possessed before. He pushed his way through the crowd waiting outside the door of the meltery. The shouting and bawdy music was audible even around the corner where Tandor stopped.

A cloaked and hooded figure came to his side, oozing out of the shadows between the limpets. Tandor tugged off his glove and parted the sides of his cloak. His hand of flesh and bone met Ruko's, blue and ice-cold.

Ruko, go and find me that boy.

There was no reaction, but he knew Ruko had understood. Moreover, Ruko was glad to have something to do. Without meeting Tandor's eyes, he pulled his hood further over his face and strode down the street.

Total obedience, that was how a servitor worked. It seemed Ruko's errant behaviour had been brought under control for now.

Chapter 9

JEVAITHI PICKED at her dinner, shoving bits of meat around the plate with a golden fork. They were perfectly cooked to her personal taste, but today even those morsels tasted bland. A feeling of pressure, an underlying thrum, coursed through her, a singing excitement she didn't understand. She couldn't say when it had started, only that she had first noticed it yesterday. All too easily, when she flexed her fingers on her left hand, did sparks leap off them. Those sparks her mother said no one must ever see.

Eyes unfocused, she stared out the window, where the glare of the light on the horizon silhouetted the buildings of the city. Directly before her, but lower down, was the Eagle Knight's eyrie. If she squinted, she thought she could see the great birds moving within. In the past few years, there had been days she had watched the Knights fly out and wished she could be one of them, but these days the sight of them just filled her with bitterness because she knew she never would.

She pushed her plate away.

"Not hungry, Your Highness?"

She glanced up at the dry sound of the male voice. Supreme Rider Cornatan stood a few paces from her, in the middle of her tower room. He was grey-haired, stiff and reedy, his short-haired Knight's cloak held together with golden clasps in a never-ending display of status. Why did *he* always have to be here? Chaperoning her, watching over her as if she were his possession.

He was the *regent*, not her father.

"I have enough of children's meat." She put her fork down with a clunk to illustrate her point, then counted the heartbeats before he would say something about her childishness.

One . . . two . . . three . . . four—

"You are still a child as I am sure I do not need to remind you."

Five. That was a poor score. He must be distracted. He deserved to work a bit harder for his presence here.

"It's almost my birthday."

"That's true, but until that day, you are a child and you will not eat any organ meat. We must consider your health. You know that, Your Highness, and you need not bring it up. Your birthday will come soon enough."

A chill crept over her back at his sideways glance and the change in the tone of his voice: from harsh to something she couldn't fathom. One thing she knew: after her birthday, nothing would be the same.

For one thing, she didn't think Rider Cornatan was going to give up his power as regent so easily, the power he had since she was ten and her mother died. Rider Cornatan devoured power and twisted it. He sat at the table of the Knights' Council, his chair before the empty throne, and rebuked anyone who challenged him. He thought he ruled the world. Jevaithi wasn't even allowed to attend the meetings. Too young, he said.

Just look at the smug expression on his face. He thought she was dumb; he never made a secret of that. He thought she would let him continue as before.

"Rider Cornatan, I would like to discuss my attendance of the Newlight celebrations."

"Your attendance of the—No, Your Highness. I don't think it's appropriate for a girl of your age." Through clenched jaws. Good.

Now she put on her most innocent voice. "It is not appropriate that I want to show myself to the good people of the city who celebrate in my name?"

"Your Highness, there are far too many inappropriate things going on at the Newlight celebrations."

"All I ask is to take part in the traditions of my own people."

"Traditions?" His Adam's apple bobbed in his throat.

Jevaithi straightened her back; he knew perfectly well what she meant.

She was no longer a girl; she was a virgin, blooded three moons ago. He knew that. He had stood, straight-faced, as she came out of the bath chamber screaming, with blood on her hands. He had stood by the door as his own elderly mother explained to her what it was all about.

"You weren't seriously thinking . . ." His voice was indignant. "Your Highness . . . the men in the Outer City . . ."

"The men of the city who are celebrating are deemed unsuitable to take my blessed innocence as they do with every other newly-blooded girl at the festival?"

"If you want to put it that way . . . Your Highness." His cheeks had gone red. "But I'd rather that you didn't—"

"Then, Supreme Rider Cornatan, tell me what the Knights have in mind for me, because surely the matter of my fertility—or not—must have come before the regent, and it is a matter that must be attended to as soon as possible. There must be an heir to the throne."

He nodded. "Yes, there must be." Dry-voiced and stiff-faced.

"If a young Learner Knight or an Apprentice isn't suitable for me, not even if he comes from the best family, then tell me, do I get a choice in this matter? Maybe we should discuss it?"

"Maybe." He sounded like he wanted anything but.

"Or maybe I should take it to the Knights' Council."

A shudder went over him. Oh, this was delicious. They *had* discussed it, she was sure. She was also sure that none of the Eagle Knights wanted to repeat the mess that surrounded her mother's succession. A virgin until twenty-nine, the Eagle Knights had squabbled over who from their midst would have the right to father her children, until they found that an unknown stranger had already done the job. But by that time Maraithe had been visibly pregnant, and in the face of the cheering citizens, all the Knights could do was smile with their teeth clenched.

"I don't think the Knight's Council should bother itself with such things," he said.

He turned to her, his expression now more soft. "But maybe we could organise an excursion for you to the festival."

Oh glory, he was giving in already. The threat of the Knight's Council must give him panic attacks. She must remember that.

"However, I insist that you would need to need to be suitably attired."

"Is anything wrong with the way I look?" She held up her arms, letting air breeze through her dress.

"No, not at all. It's just that your dress . . ."

"Is a little revealing?"

He said nothing.

"Then I will order proper garments." She hated these flimsy garments the courtiers made her wear anyway. Layers of gauze so thin the wind breezed through them even when she walked around the room. They were designed to keep her indoors.

"You could do that." Rider Cornatan stopped pacing and stared out the window, hands clasped behind his back. A couple of gulls sat on the outside windowsill.

"I want a dress such as the maidens of the city wear. One that's warm enough for outside. I want to go into a real meltery and meet real men."

He stiffened. "Out of the question."

"Why? I will speak the words you tell me to speak. I will dance only with men you have chosen. Hire the meltery if you wish. Tell the owner to put guards at his door and let in only Knights. They don't have too much trouble drooling over my puppies when I'm merely walking past."

"Your Highness, where did you learn to speak so? If you were my daughter—"

"Which I am not. I am your Queen, and this is how my men speak about me. I listen to their voices, Rider Cornatan."

He let another silence lapse. She knew he would offer a compromise of some sort. A trip in the royal sled—she didn't care as long as she could leave this room. She didn't really fancy getting a close-up view of Knights drooling over her anyway. The junior Knights maybe, but the Senior Knights scared her.

"We could organise for you to witness a race and a walk over the festival grounds. Every year one of the Apprentice Knights is chosen to be the Queen's Champion. You could choose the winner yourself."

Yes, she could, but it was just another boring official function, not something she wanted to do. "Could I see the Legless Lions?"

His lips twitched into a smile. Was he glad she no longer mentioned men?

Hoping for a kiss and awkward fumbling in the dark with a young man of her age was futile anyway. The man who took her would be older, experienced, and in her bed for only one reason: to get his blood on the throne. She was probably facing that very man right now.

She had known it all her life.

There is no point fighting, Jevaithi, her mother used to say. The Knights do as the Knights want to do. She could still see her mother over there in the bed, pale and sickly. Devoid of a will to live.

"We can certainly arrange for you to see the Legless Lions, and the bears. Perhaps you would like to see the ritual killing?"

She shuddered at the thought of guts and blood on some

beefy butcher's hands, but nodded. The longer she was out there, the more time she had to do *real* things and pretend she was a real girl. And real girls wouldn't mind to see an animal killed. For them, it meant work and food.

"Yes, I would like that."

Rider Cornatan bowed. "I will organise that for tomorrow, with your permission."

"You have my permission."

He bowed again and left.

Drained and still hungry, Jevaithi sank down on the bed. Her plate remained on the table, the sauce congealed into a jelly-like blob. A servant scurried to take it.

"You haven't eaten, Your Highness."

"No. Next time, I want you to bring me real food."

The man's eyes widened. "But Ruder Cornatan says—"

"Never mind what he says. Bring me adult food. If he tries to mistreat you, come to me."

The man nodded and retreated.

She gazed out the window, where the people of the city moved about like little black specks.

She would try to charge into a meltery once she was out there. When they were surrounded by the people, Rider Cornatan wouldn't dare to lay a hand on her. The people loved *her*, not him.

Mother, maybe you gave up the fight, but I will be free.

Chapter 10

ISANDOR TOSSED a couple of coins onto the bar and wriggled sideways between sweating bodies to pick up the tray of drinks the barman had put there. A maid burst out the kitchen door, yelling at two younger girls who were collecting tottering piles of dirty glasses. In the din of the meltery room, Isandor couldn't hear what she said, but the gist of it was written on her face. Hurry up, work faster. The girls were rosy-cheeked, their hands red from alternately washing up in ice chips and tending the roaring fire, or stirring the giant vats of meltwater and mixing in spirits and berry distillate to make bloodwine.

Isandor lifted the tray with drinks carefully over the heads of a couple of fishermen and backed into marginally less-crowded territory. Here, patrons sat at tables, every chair occupied. Some talked, some were gambling, and here and there, a few couples were engaged in other activities. A layer of smoke hovered over the patrons. It wafted from the fire every time the door was opened, which happened a lot.

A heaving crowd on the dance floor made so much noise that

it was hard hearing the musicians.

Carro and his cousin Daman sat alone at a table. Carro leaned his head in his hands and stared into the crowd, while Daman fiddled with the hem of his tunic.

"Hey, smile," Isandor said as he set the tray down. He regained his seat and distributed the drinks.

"That's easy for you to say," Carro muttered into his glass. His pale blue eyes had a haunted look to them.

Isandor laughed. "Yeah, we'll have this race in the bag, and then you'll just have the swimming and running races to win."

Carro clamped his large hands over his glass as if to retain the warmth of the wine. "The running and swimming are unfair competitions. I'm the only Knight Apprentice who can compete as Outer City citizen. It'd be embarrassing if I *didn't* win those races."

"Carro, have you noticed I'm from the Outer City, too and I didn't even enter."

"It's different for you." He let the reference to Isandor's peg leg hang in the air. "Besides, the flying race tomorrow is important. Knights *live* for flying."

"And so we won our selection heat. Smile, Carro. We won. We're in the final."

"I almost fell off," Carro said. "Look, why don't you find another partner. You're so much better than me, you deserve someone who can actually control their bird."

"Carro, please . . ."

Why did he go into sulky moods like this? Isandor had thought it would get better when Carro was away from that horrible father of his, but if anything, being in the Knighhood had made it worse.

Carro shook his head and drank deeply from his bloodwine, staring ahead. Daman still fiddled with his tunic. His eyes were following one particular girl swept in the tide of dancers. Tall, with curved hips and tresses of honey-coloured hair, and completely out of his league.

"Hey, good evening boys!" A girl dropped into the empty chair. Her cheeks were red from dancing and bloodwine and her perfume mingled with a faint scent of sweat. Around her pale-skinned neck, she wore a simple strip of leather with on it, a gull's tail feather.

"Uhm, good evening, Korinne," Isandor said. "Still here? I thought you said your father wanted you to come home."

Stupid. That's sounds too hopeful. Bloodwine had addled his thoughts. He had to clamp his jaws to stop himself laughing, because laughing at the daughter of Rider Cornatan's closest advisor would never do.

"What's so funny?" she asked.

"Carro was just telling a joke," Isandor said.

"What?" Carro woke up from his moody thoughts.

Isandor gestured, *You deal with her*. All day, Carro had been staring at this girl like a hungry pup whenever she came near.

Carro began, "Oh yeah, I can tell you a good joke. Did you hear about the two Chevakians who went fishing . . ."

Isandor stifled a groan.

The girl continued to look at him, batting long eyelashes over her clear grey eyes. She fiddled with her feather. Yes, he knew she was available. He'd hardly had a chance to forget it.

"I guess you already heard the joke," Carro said, his voice flat.

"I just wanted to congratulate you on winning your race. It was amazing. I saw you come back so far ahead of everyone else. You flew really well." Then she glanced at Carro. "Both of you, of course."

Carro rose from his seat. He'd already finished half his glass and stood unsteady. "Can I invite you to dance, Korinne?"

"Knights can always ask me to dance." She giggled, and as Carro led her away, she gave Isandor an intense stare and added, "Whether I agree depends on who's asking." She winked.

By the skylights, that stupid girl just didn't give up. She had been following him around all night.

Isandor drank deeply from his cup, letting the bloodwine

sting its way into his stomach.

"For someone who's had their first taste of booze only yesterday, you sure know how to put it away," Carro's cousin remarked.

Isandor had almost forgotten about him. "So," he said to Daman. "Do you know what happened when the two Chevakians went fishing?"

"I think we shouldn't joke about Chevakia. One day they will invade us. You know my father says"

Isandor let his mind drift off. He didn't mind discussing politics, but not today and not with Carro's cousin.

Carro and Korinne came past on the dance floor. He was talking to her, his hand on her shoulder—too close to her neck—and his head bent towards her. He was too tall, and his steps too large. She held her body stiff, so she didn't touch him, and stared past him at Isandor.

Isandor averted his gaze. Between the dancers, his eyes met those of a much older man, a noble from the city proper, with golden swirls tattooed on his cheeks. He sat alone at a table. More than twice the age of most patrons, he didn't belong here.

Isandor shivered. This was the man he'd seen after the race today, the man whose presence he'd *felt*.

"Heh, d'you think that one fancies you?" Daman asked, looking at Korinne whirling past.

"Does she really?"

"It's not fair," Daman went on, oblivious to Isandor's sarcasm. "The best girls are always taken by you Eagle Knights."

Isandor took another gulp from his drink, stifling the comment that Daman could have her if he wanted, and that if it was so unfair, maybe he should sign up for the Knighthood himself instead of whinge about it.

Before he could say anything stupid, and he was feeling rather drunk by now, Carro and Korinne came back to the table, both red-faced. Carro picked up his glass took a large gulp from his drink.

"Oh, Isandor, you're not going to ask me?" Korinne said.

"Oh, come on, be a man to her," Daman said. "She's throwing herself at you."

Carro sunk into his chair, his face hard and not meeting Isandor's eyes.

All right, so they had a disagreement. Let's see. It would have been about Carro treading on her toes or grabbing her too tightly? Next thing she would go back to her friends and gossip about it.

Oh, by the skylights. Isandor wanted to stay with his friend. No, he wanted to leave this stuffy place and walk with Carro back to the birds, or find some place more quiet, and away from pushy females, to have a drink and a good talk, but he couldn't refuse such a blatant offer by the daughter of Rider Cornatan's advisor. So the took the girl's hand and led her onto the dance floor, where it was so busy that bodies pressed into him from all sides. The musicians struck up a rowdy tune.

Soon, they were swept up in the tide of dancers, and Korinne attached herself to him, like a suffocating parasite. He had to concentrate hard to keep his gait even, to make sure that his empty boot didn't get stuck or pulled off his peg leg. The crowd heaved and surged. And he was attached to this girl, red-cheeked and bright-eyed with bloodwine, holding him more closely than necessary.

"You dance well," she said.

He just nodded. Never mind that he didn't think so, not when dancing had become a matter of life and death.

"I could dance with you all night," she said into the hollow under his chin. Her breasts pressed against his chest. When he looked down he could see into the deep crevasse between them.

Sweat rolled down his back. His hands felt like slippery fish. The scent of her perfume made it hard to breathe so he concentrated on his steps. One, two, three, four, one, two . . .

"It's so hot in here," she said.

This was the part where he should say *We can always go*

outside. And then they'd go into the chill air, and he'd have to keep her warm with his kisses and no doubt she'd taken her ichina and was after a bit more than kisses, and that was all fine during Newlight, as long as the girl fell pregnant.

Part of him wanted to go, badly. No doubt she could feel that part in the space between his hips and hers. But he couldn't. It would mean taking his clothes off, and she would see his wooden leg. And although the Knights at the eyrie must have seen that he was Imperfect, no one seemed to have actually *noticed* it. He didn't understand why, and knew that someone would, one day. And while he was vulnerable, literally with his pants down about to ride a girl was not the time for that to happen. Especially while he was so drunk that he could barely see the opposite side of the room. He wasn't supposed to have lived. He knew no other Imperfects. According to the books, Imperfect babies were left to die on the ice floes, not to join the Knights, win races, or attempt to get any girls pregnant.

But it was so hot in here. He concentrated on his dancing. Korinne pouted. Isandor's heart was going like crazy. Would it hurt just to give her a kiss and see if he could do that? To see what it was like? But no, his body might betray him, like it did sometimes at night when he dreamed of this girl who came to the markets sometimes. She didn't know him, or how beautiful he thought she was. But for some reason in this dream she would come up to his sleeping shelf—he was always at home or some other place that was a weird combination of home and the eyrie, and he was always alone—and then she would take off her clothes, but as soon as she folded back the covers to get into his bed, he'd wake up and then he would be all wet. But he hadn't actually wet himself, since it didn't smell like piss, and it wasn't unpleasant at all, just embarrassing. Definitely too embarrassing to be thinking about now, since the thoughts only made his . . . problem worse. Korinne would be able to feel it now for sure.

Carro was sitting at the table with his cousin, who gabbled away, probably about some political thing, but Carro stared at

Isandor with uncomfortable intensity, as if he knew what Isandor was thinking. His eyes said, *Get your hands off my girl.*

Sweat made Isandor's shirt stick to his back. Everyone was staring at him. He could see the question in their eyes. What was he waiting for?

Then, thankfully, the music ended. His face and ears glowing, he led Korinne back to the table, raising his eyebrows at Carro and hoping that Carro would get the hint and take her off somewhere to a dark warehouse. It might cheer him up. As for him, he felt like getting disgracefully drunk.

"Oh, do we stop dancing already?" Korinne said.

"I'm tired. I have to think of tomorrow's race and feed the birds. I think Carro would like one more dance with you."

A painful look passed over her face.

Carro was already getting up from the table, ready to take her hand, but she stepped back. "I promised my father I wouldn't stay out too long."

A feeble excuse. No girl promised their fathers anything during Newlight except that they'd do their very best to fall pregnant.

She extracted herself from Isandor's grip and ran out, her lips pressed together.

Isandor cringed. He hadn't meant to hurt her, and didn't know how he was meant to have rejected her without hurting her. What a mess.

"What, Carro? M . . . my sister laughed in your face, din' she?" The voice was haughty but the speech was slurred.

Oh no, Jono. He stood at the table, his usual smirk on sharp-nosed face. He had taken off his Knights' cloak, displaying the distinctive red tunic.

"Shut your stupid mouth." Carro took a step towards him.

"You in . . . ssssulted my sister," Jono said.

"She came here begging for a dance."

"Heh," Jono sneered. "Why sh . . . should my sss..sister ever want *you*?"

"Shut up!" Carro grabbed Jono by his shoulder.

A circle formed as other dancers stepped aside, faces keen and eyes wide.

"Oh, Carro, come, don't be silly," Isandor said in his friend's ear. "This isn't worth a fight."

Worst of all, the Tutor had warned that any Apprentices caught brawling would not be allowed to go out tomorrow.

Carro didn't move.

"Yeah, that'shhh right," Jono said, his arms over his chest. "Get y . . . your friend to sss . . . sort it out for you."

"Shut up!" Carro said again, this time louder.

"What? You're jjjjealous be . . . becaushe your friend gets more girls than you?"

Carro lunged.

But he was drink-addled and Jono evaded him easily. Carro lost his balance and almost fell, but Jono grabbed him by his tunic. He drew Carro back to his feet. "So y . . . you want to fight? Let'sh fffight!"

"Carro, no," Isandor called.

"Don't, Jono!" Korinne said. "You'll be in so much trouble."

"Shut up, all of you!" Carro shouted.

He grabbed Jono's arms and tried to push him over. Jono stumbled backwards into the crowd, and fell. Carro was on top of him, and then Jono was on top of Carro, thumping his face.

Everyone was shouting and cheering.

Isandor grabbed the back of Jono's shirt, but he didn't have enough strength to lift Jono off. He was afraid his leg would slip away under him.

"Stop fighting, you two!" These stupid oafs would get them all into trouble. "Stop it, Carro, stop!" But they weren't listening, and any moment some older Knights would come and haul Carro off to the eyrie. He needed Carro in the race tomorrow. He—

Golden threads burst from his fingers. They crackled over Carro, as if he'd been caught in a living net of icefire. Carro and Jono froze. And then the threads snapped into diamond-specks of light which scattered through the air and vanished.

Jono stumbled back as if stung.

Isandor's heart thudded in his chest so loudly that he thought the people around him must hear it. Had anyone seen that?

"That's right," Carro said while scrambling to his feet.

Isandor knew his friend couldn't see the golden glow, but his eyes had gone hollow and distant again, as they did when Carro scared him most.

Carro wiped blood from his brow. "I'm wasting my time here. I have better things to do than concern myself with the lot of you."

He pushed into the circle of onlookers and was gone in a few heartbeats.

"Carro!" Isandor shouted, but he had lost sight of his friend.

Isandor wrestled against the stream of revellers coming in through the meltery's doors. Young men pushed aside to let him through and young girls glanced at him with drunken longing. The bolder ones clapped him one the shoulder and told him good luck. He was *their* Isandor, from the Outer City, riding in the Champion Race tomorrow. Except he wouldn't be if Carro got into trouble.

Outside in the street, people lined up to get in. Some had their own drinks and were sharing flasks of wine around. An older Knight was kissing a girl in the light of a street lamp, his hands fumbling under her cloak.

Isandor stopped, both revolted and fascinated. Knights were supposed to hold up respectability. Much leering and inappropriate behaviour of course went on in the eyrie. Family visit passes being traded for the sake of going to the whorehouse. Money being used to bribe superiors to turn a blind eye. But it always went on *inside* the eyrie walls, never openly in the street.

Isandor stifled thoughts of Korinne's hips against his. He *could* have had her, snuck away somewhere in a warehouse. That was what *normal* boys did. *Normal* boys didn't run after their friends if they behaved like stupid oafs. *Normal* boys fought.

"Carro," he called into the emptiness of the street.

There was no reply.

He walked away from the meltery, breathing the cold and fresh air. The streets became deserted. A single man leant against a wall, his eyes closed. Isandor stopped, intending to ask if he was all right and needed help, but realised that the man was so drunk that standing up was probably the most he could do. The front of his trousers was wet and had been frozen over. His mother would love injuries like that. She'd talk about it in gory detail for days. *You know frostbite leaves blisters on your . . .* He jammed his hands into the pockets of his cloak. Well, if this was Newlight, it wasn't much fun.

CHAPTER 11

ISANDOR WALKED ON in the grey-blue light of eternal dusk. Above the roofs of houses, the skylights danced and shimmered in pretty displays of orange, pink and green. Far away, the sound of partying continued, the crowd cheering the jugglers in the markets, and the drummers at the festival grounds.

He had no idea where Carro had gone, but he didn't feel like going back into the meltery.

He might as well go back to the eyrie.

And then . . . golden strands snaked from the sky. Very briefly, they touched roofs and chimneys; they shimmered over the sloping sides of the limpets and crackled along the ground. A thread touched his hand and burst into a spray of diamonds. The display lasted a heartbeat before it winked out.

Icefire.

He stopped to look over his shoulder, his heart thudding. Icefire had never been this strong. Sometimes, when he stood looking over the city from the eyrie tower, the golden threads crackled over the city. They would bend to his hands, but they had never touched him, like they just had in the meltery. Icefire never ventured indoors.

"You felt that, didn't you, young Knight?" a soft male voice said in the darkness. The man had a lilting accent.

Isandor gasped. He'd thought he was alone. "Uhm—good evening."

The man was tall and lanky, with piercing eyes and a sharp face lined with age. There were golden curls tattooed on his prominent cheekbones. A city noble? With a foreign accent? Talking about icefire?

"Who are you?"

But he knew who this was: that man who had been staring at him in the meltery.

In answer, the man pushed back his sleeve and pulled off a leather glove. The white-skinned arm underneath shimmered and dissolved. The skylight gleamed on two golden rods extending from the man's elbow. At the end, they joined in a "wrist" of black stone, where he had a pair of crab-like pinchers.

Isandor stammered, "You are . . ." He reached for his wooden leg in an automatic gesture. In all his life, he had never come across another Imperfect person. When he had been little, his mother liked to remind him that children born Imperfect were left on the ice floes for the wild beasts to eat. Not even the Knights' riding eagles would dine on such contaminated fare.

"My name is Tandor, and I'm a Traveller. Come." He held out his good hand. A tiny crackle of icefire played along the skin.

"Why?" Isandor stepped back. Everything about this man radiated danger.

"We need to talk."

Need to? "I *need to* look after my eagle."

A flicker of distaste went over the man's face.

"You felt the icefire," he said again. "When you reach for it, the light bends to your will." It was a statement, not a question. "Do you know what that means?"

Isandor kept his silence. During the time of the old king,

there were people who could *use* icefire, and who had done so to bring terror to the people of the City of Glass, by enslaving them as servitors.

"You're Imperfect," the man continued. "You helped your friend win the fight. I saw the icefire."

"There was nothing I could do about it!"

"No, there wasn't. I agree."

"Then why are you bothering me?"

"Others might have seen the threads, too. Maybe one day others will see the illusion you weave about your leg. Or they will notice how every person in the Knighthood you meet looks anywhere except at your leg. Or maybe—"

"Stop it! What are you trying to do? Who are you, trying to destroy me?"

"To the contrary. I'm trying to help you."

"Some help."

"If you are aware that icefire weaves an illusion around your leg, you can make sure it never falters. That way, no one will ever notice, not even if you take off your trousers."

That last bit he added with a sarcastic tone.

"Just go away, will you?"

"You don't want to learn how to hide your imperfections?"

Isandor wanted to shout that he had no interest, but that wasn't true. Being found out was his greatest worry. The Knights had never said anything about it, and every day, he feared that the subject would come up. "You can't hide it. You can make it look like there is a complete arm or leg, but they'll find out as soon as they touch it."

"Not if you learned how to control it."

"Control it? Isn't the same as using it? Turning people into ghosts? Isn't that why, after the king was killed, all his people were sentenced to death?"

Tandor shook his head, an expression of pity on his face. "I see you're upset and confused. We should sit down somewhere and talk."

Every fibre of Isandor's being protested. This man was danger.

"Come," Tandor said again. "I'm buying. What I have to say is important. It will change your life."

His eyes met Isandor's in the light of a street lamp.

Isandor followed the stranger through the twisted streets of a quiet part of the Outer City. It looked like most people had gone to bed already or were hiding from the crowds inside the warmth of their limpets.

In an alley, away from the main streets, was an eating house, recognisable only by a small sign on the door of a limpet larger and with less steep sides than the surrounding ones. Tandor went in first.

Inside the circular room, most tables surrounding the stove were occupied by a selection of the best middle class citizens from the Outer City. Men and women in middle age, dressed well and wearing jewellery, a far cry from the rowdy melteries. The cook was stirring a large pot and a kitchen hand was kneading dough.

Tandor went to one of the few empty tables. Isandor sat opposite him. Already, the warmth made him drowsy. It was even hotter than in the meltery. Couldn't they open a vent?

A waiter came to them.

"Bring some soup and bread for two," Tandor said.

"I'm not hungry," Isandor said. The bloodwine sat heavy in his stomach.

"I am," Tandor said. "And you should be, too. Adolescent boys are always hungry."

Isandor shrugged. *Not when they're drunk*. But he wasn't sure if he was still drunk.

The waiter left and they sat among the quiet murmur of the customers. Snatches of conversation drifted past, mostly about the Newlight festival and its various circus shows. Firelight gleamed in Tandor's tattoos. At this angle, he looked older than he had appeared at first. Isandor guessed him to be about fifty. His hair was glossy and black, his eyes . . . he couldn't look away from them.

They had that elusive hue citizens of the City of Glass called royal blue. He knew only one person with eyes like that; he looked at him from the mirror above the sink in the dormitory bathroom every morning.

"Are you my father?"

Tandor lunged across the table. The pincher-claw grabbed the collar of Isandor's shirt so tight that he could barely breathe. Isandor uttered a strangled, "Hey!"

Up close, the gold tattoos on Tandor's face looked frightening. Come to think of it, why did he have that sign of nobility? Certainly, nobles wouldn't pay for Imperfect children?

Tandor let a tense silence lapse, in which all Isandor heard was the roaring of blood in his ears. Diners on surrounding tables had stopped talking and stared at him.

"Let me go if you don't like the people to notice us," he whispered in a croaky voice.

Tandor blew out a breath. He relaxed and let go of Isandor's collar, his gaze still boring into Isandor's.

Isandor inhaled; the smoke-tinged air stroked his lungs. What, *just what*, was he getting himself involved in?

"All right, since you don't know me, I will tell you, once, and once only. Moreover, you will never speak of this."

Isandor nodded, nervously, tucking his tunic back into his waistband, too conscious of the glances at him. He was still in his uniform, by the skylights, and he should do something. This man could not attack a Knight without repercussion.

Tandor leaned on his elbows on the table. "My mother had the courage of a bear pup. When I was born Imperfect, rather than give me up, she ran away to the northern lands where she had heard people do not mind Imperfects. In time, she found a family, and married a travelling merchant and lived in comfort. The merchant collected old books, and as a boy, I became interested in them. I read that Imperfects are special people who have the power to shape icefire, and that they need to be in the vicinity of the City of Glass to use it. So I wanted to use that ability, didn't I? I was young, I was curious and I didn't get along with my stepfather, so I came to the white lands of the south."

He gave a hollow laugh. "Sounds simple, huh? What did I know about the southern laws and the Eagle Knights? I was a boy, just like you are now. I came to the City of Glass at the height of the tension over the raids on Chevakian border regions. I was both of southern stock and living in Chevakia and a prime suspect for being a spy. I was captured by the Queen's guards. They saw I was Imperfect, and judged me to be a king's supporter and too old to be abandoned on the ice floes—I might find my way back and come to haunt them—so the Queen ordered that I be changed so I could never father an Imperfect child."

It took Isandor a heartbeat to figure what Tandor meant, but then he realised. *Ouch.* He winced. "I'm sorry."

"If you don't want to attract my wrath, don't be. But no, I cannot be your father."

Isandor repressed the urge to shove his hand down his pants to check on his private parts, which felt larger-than-life and throbbing.

"And . . . are you? A king's supporter? A Thillei?" He had heard of such things whispered in the melteries, of people who said that the king should return. It was said that the Brotherhood of the Light organised meetings for these people.

A serving girl turned up with a tray containing two bowls of soup and a basket of fresh bread. Isandor found that Tandor had been right: he was enormously hungry.

He attacked the bread, dunking pieces in the bowl. The bread came away dripping with fat, which ran down his fingers as he stuffed the pieces in his mouth. Taste exploded on his tongue. Just like his mother used to make it.

Tandor put his spoon down and broke a piece off his bread. "There is one thing you need to understand. The Thillei are a clan much bigger than only the royal family. You cannot become one. You are one at birth. And you, boy . . . enough Thillei blood runs through your veins to make your eyes turn blue. There are few of us left. You, me and a handful of others. If it wasn't for me, there would have been none."

Isandor had suspected this, but hearing it spoken out loud made his skin crawl. He ripped a piece off a roll and mopped his bowl with it, disguising unease. Then another thought came to him.

"Then . . . when I was born . . . you paid for my mother to look after me?"

"Yes."

"Why, if you're not my father?"

Tandor gave him an intense look. "Don't you want to know who your real mother is?"

"Why should I? She wanted to kill me."

"How can you be so sure of that? Couldn't it be that someone else wanted to kill you, and she had no power to protect you, and gave you to me to bring to safety?"

Isandor scratched his head. He was beginning to feel sleepy from the bloodwine, and Tandor's stories were so confusing. Why should he care? Children in the City of Glass never grew up with the women who had given birth to them. They were breeders, like his mother.

"What do you want from me?"

Tandor shook his head, his expression sad.

"It is not about what I want or what anyone else wants. This is much bigger than the wants of individual people. It is about making the City of Glass great again, and about stopping the slaughter of children."

He hesitated. "I know this may not sound important to you, but I see in you myself when I was your age. I didn't know what to do with my gift. I was scared. I have found out how to deal with icefire the hard way. There is no need for you to do the same."

"You want me to be a sorcerer's apprentice?"

Tandor breathed out heavily through his nose. "Sorcery? I wouldn't use that despicable word, but that's obviously what the Knights have told you to think. Tell me this, though: do you think there is a good reason you should be punished if you were discovered?"

"I . . . can use icefire. I'm Imperfect. There are laws that forbid—"

"Is there anything that punishment could stop you doing, if you wanted?"

Isandor shrugged. "It's not as if I could *help* being Imperfect."

"Exactly. You can't help being what you are, but they will punish you anyway. Is that the way you want to live? I want to see you out of this slum. I want to see you soaring in the sky. You, and all other Imperfects. We need to save them, and I'm going to need your help for that. As . . . Knight, you would be perfectly placed to do that. Give me the word and I will teach you about icefire."

And then Isandor saw what Tandor wanted: to single-handedly change the Knights' view on Imperfects, to become a spy, or an agent. Did Tandor really think he was as stupid as all that? He respected the Knights, most of them at least. They were harsh but fair. He was determined not to let his wooden leg be a problem. No one needed to know. But on the other hand . . . if they found out, he would have to leave the Knights.

Damn this man. He was caught now. He couldn't refuse Tandor's offer or tell the Knights about him, or Tandor would tell the Knights.

He licked his lips. "What would you want me to do?"

A smile ghosted over Tandor's face. "A few days ago, the Knights discovered my safe sanctuary where I had hidden the Imperfects I rescued from the ice floes as babies. Children who are now young people your age. The Knights broke into the sanctuary, flushed out all the Imperfects and took them away. As far as I know, they were taken to the palace bunkers, and we need to free them, if they're still alive."

"And you want me to do that. By myself." Isandor chuckled. "Do you know how many Knights there are at the eyrie? Do you know how many guards there are on the entrance to the prisons, if that's where those children are? How do you even think I could get into the prisons? I'm only an Apprentice—"

"I could provide you with a good illusion that would make you look like someone who *could* get into the dungeons. All you have to do is maintain it. That should be easy after I've trained you."

"Deliberately *use* icefire? Under the Senior Knights' noses?" Isandor found it hard not to laugh. This was getting ever more ridiculous.

"Then what are you doing with your leg? What were you doing back there in the meltery?"

"That was—"

"Icefire, strong and clear. You used it to scare that bully."

"I didn't mean to—"

"No, I know. That is where the problem lies, I've been trying to make it clear to you. You've been doing it and you have no control over it. One day, you will be found out. Or someone will betray you, like that halfwit friend of yours."

"Carro? He will never betray me."

But a twinge of discomfort tugged at him Carro had said such strange things recently.

"In the end, it comes down to a simple thing: children are killed and harmed because they were born with strong Thillei blood. You have the chance to help me save some of them. Will you do it?"

"If I help you, I will be cast from the Knights."

"You don't belong there anyway."

"Who are you to say where I do and don't belong?"

"You don't get the opportunity I'm offering, don't you? If you help me, I will give you *real* power." That last bit was almost a whisper.

Real power, like the old king, who had murdered thousands of people.

That was enough. Isandor strained his muscles to get up.

"I'm going. I'm sorry, but I can't do what you want." He tried to sound angry, but he thought he sounded scared more than anything. "I'm an Eagle Knight and I will obey by their laws. The Knights serve the Queen with honour. They wouldn't do anything without her approval."

"Stop your naive daydreaming. Do you know how much power one fifteen-year old girl has over an ages-old institute of men?"

Isandor shivered uncomfortably, remembering the thin figure of a young girl standing alone before a coffin. So lonely, so small. Jevaithi.

"Do you see that I'm right?" Tandor said.

"I don't see anything except that you're telling me stories so I will come with you. I don't know what you want, but I don't like it. Find someone else to bother."

Isandor rose from the table, catching glances of fellow patrons.

"Good night, Tandor."

He turned and walked back to the door. He expected a shout, but none came. He opened the door and let himself into the cold night.

When he looked over his shoulder, Tandor was still sitting at the table.

CHAPTER 12

THE FOOTSTEPS of his hard-heeled riding boots echoing against stone walls, Carro strode through the corridor. His cloak flapped behind him. His riding harness creaked. Polished, clean, his hair slicked and bound by a leather thong. He'd done his best to clean himself and look good, as if any amount of cleaning chased away the ominous feeling that had become infinitely more ominous since his return to the eyrie.

When the Tutor had said the *high command wants to see you*, Carro had expected to deal with the Senior Knight who dealt with Apprentices.

Instead, the Knight at the entrance to the command centre had informed him that he was to see Supreme Rider Cornatan himself. Carro hadn't dared to ask why.

His face tingled with cold from the flight back to the eyrie and the air in the corridor did nothing to dispel it. Here, in the lower levels of the eyrie, warmth was as sparse as furniture.

Eagle Knights lived hard, simple lives. There was some aspect in that he liked. He had never felt comfortable with his father's opulence or his sister's obsession with clothes and hair ribbons.

Obedience, Honour, Honesty, Humility and Silence. He mumbled the Knights' mantra silently, as if to remind himself of the meaning of those words.

He had violated several of them in fighting with Jono. The Knights lived for punishing each other. There was a certain humility, obedience and silence in being fucked in the arse, but honour and honesty?

It hurt, that was all he knew, on more levels than one.

Yet, if he ever wanted to be someone in the eyrie, he'd have to endure it. This was what older Knights did to younger ones. Fit in, shut up and don't show your weaker side.

He failed in all three accounts.

Carro stands in his father's room. His father has the account books open on his desk. Long lines of figures stretch across two pages.

Do you think I've calculated this right, Carro?

Carro hesitates.

Well? You tell me. You are so learned. There is mockery in his father's voice.

I'd need to figure out the numbers. I need time.

You need time. Ha, that's right. You have so many books, and you still need time to work out a calculation.

He laughs. He doesn't need to say that he thinks the books are a waste of Carro's time. Carro has heard it all before.

The books tell him that in the days of the old king, people had machines that could work out sums, but telling his father would make him sound cocky. Some things are not worth the punishment.

Carro stopped, counting the doors he had passed since coming down the stairs.

Two, three four, five. That's what the guard said: the fifth door. This one had to be it. Just a solid door, no different from the previous one, or the next one.

He knocked, and waited, glancing left and right into the featureless corridor.

Strange, he'd have expected guards. The Tutor Rider responsible for Apprentice Knights had guards outside his quarters. So why didn't the Supreme Rider have any?

Before Carro could knock, the door clicked and opened. A dark room yawned beyond, polished stone bathed in emerald light.

No one met him in the door opening, and no one spoke, so Carro stepped inside, his footsteps echoing in the emptiness.

A stone chair stood in the middle of the room like a throne on a dais of black marble several steps high and with corners that looked sharp enough to slice skin. There was no other furniture.

A voice said, "Sit down."

Except there was nowhere to sit. The room was square, and entirely made out of black marble of the kind found in the mountains. The walls, too, were smooth, reflecting the soft green light.

The voice said again, "Sit down."

On the throne.

It seemed obvious. It was some kind of interrogation chair. Maybe the chair would get hot, like the chairs he heard they had in Chevakia. That would be his punishment. Pain and suffering. Rider Cornatan wouldn't even have to set eyes on him.

The tutor stands at the window, reduced to a silhouette against the low sun. The man's shadow falls over Carro's work book, obscuring the print. He squints against the page, trying to read.

What does it say? The tutor's voice is harsh.

It's a history of Tiverius.

The tutor drags a chair near the fire so that it stands on the middle of the carpet like a throne.

Sit here. Read it.

Carro sits and takes the book on his knees.

Sit up straight. The cane descends on the desk with a thwack.

Carro stares at the long Chevakian words.

If you make one mistake, I'll hit you. I'll tell your father.

Carro wants to shout that he hates his father. Why does he have to learn Chevakian? His father hates the Chevakians. No Chevakians ever come to the City of Glass.

They would die if they did. He wants to die.

Gingerly, Carro climbed the dais, and sat down in the regal chair. The cold stone bit through his trousers, but he sat up straight as if he was a king.

Just like Jevaithi.

There was a tiny noise which made Carro straighten his back even more. He would not be seen slumping in the seat. His heart thudded against his ribs. Punishment would not be far off.

But nothing happened, and his back became stiff and his buttocks very cold. What sort of punishment was this? The sort of unfathomable thing his father did.

Carro stands in the dining room. The dining table is so high that he can barely see what's on top of it.

His mother sits in the seat closest to the fire, his sister next to her. Neither says anything, but his mother looks at the floor.

Carro's boots leak melting snow onto the carpet, growing brown puddles seeping into the precious wool.

The door clangs behind him. His mother flaps her hand, and all of a sudden, Carro is lifted off the ground by the maid.

He kicks and screams while she carries him across the hall. The maid opens the front door and dumps Carro on the ground. Shuts the door. The lock clicks.

Carro bangs his fists on the door, but no one comes. Shivering, he sits down on the mat. It is wet and soaks freezing water into his pants. He draws his knees up to his chest, and waits. He doesn't have his coat. The wind cuts through his thin shirt. It is snowing.

A rumbling of stone on stone made Carro start. He turned, but the back of the chair blocked his view. There were footsteps, long and slow, hard heels on stone. Carro straightened, staring ahead, his hands on the armrests. *Don't show your fear*. There was a swish of a cloak, the creaking of leather, and jingling of metal rings. It was said that although Supreme Rider Cornatan was too old to ride eagles, he wore his riding harness every day.

"Boy," said a voice that chilled Carro with its reminiscence of his father. "I'm glad you could come."

"Yes, sir." How was that for a sarcastic answer? The Supreme Rider was *glad* to see him punished?

There was a soft laugh, not unfriendly. "You have quite a lot of courage, for an Apprentice."

"Sir?"

"Quite a few discipline issues, too, I hear."

"I am sorry. I was not in my right mind. I'd been drinking." He didn't like this brand of humility. Jono had needled him on purpose.

"I accept your apology."

There was strange tone in the voice that puzzled Carro. Amusement, affection almost. Since when did the Supreme Rider concern himself with individual Apprentices?

"But that is not why I want to talk to you."

The Supreme Rider came from around the back of the chair.

Carro met the sky-blue eyes and then dropped his gaze, the wrinkled but powerful face etched in his memory. He pushed himself up from the chair. How had he ever thought *he* was meant to be sitting here?

"I'm sorry, I—"

"Stay seated."

"I'm sorry I got in a fight. I'm sorry I hit Jono."

"Forget Jono."

"Sir?"

"If Jono works hard and holds up the Knights' ethic like his father, he might get somewhere. For now, he's insignificant. Did you really think that's why I wanted to talk to you?"

"But I did start a fight. I'm not always very nice."

Rider Cornatan chuckled. "None of us are. If we were nice all the time, we would never get anywhere." He stopped in front of the dais, meeting Carro's eyes with his light blue ones. "The old king, for example, was a dreadfully mean person, but he was so powerful that even his family didn't dare disobey him. At the very end, he locked himself in the palace and sent his son and his daughter-in-law away. He said it was for their safety, but it was to distract the guards, so they were killed while he himself stayed in the palace."

Carro remembered the story, but he had thought the king had sent his family away and stayed in the palace as ruse, so that they could flee safely and that the unborn heir to the throne would survive. But he didn't dare disagree with Rider Cornatan's version. In fact he hardly dared breathe. Why did the Supreme Rider mention this?

"You know the story?"

"I do."

"Because you read the books."

"Yes." Carro looked at his knees. He wasn't sure if it was a reprimand. No one read those books in the City of Glass.

There were steps on the floor, and a hand touched his arm, weathered and wrinkled.

"Don't be shy. I'm impressed with you."

"Sir?" This visit was starting to puzzle him more and more. No one had told Carro he was impressed. No one. Ever.

Rider Cornatan smiled, and he looked more like a favourite uncle than a feared leader.

"I've brought you here, because I need you for a special mission."

Special mission? "Sir?" Doubt hovered in his mind again. He was only an Apprentice. What did he know that would make him eligible for a special mission?

"You haven't noticed I've already sent you on some unusual tasks?"

"You mean—when you . . . I went with the Junior Knights to the markets?"

Had Rider Cornatan selected him for that task? Carro felt sick. By the skylights, what was this going to be about? Who was he going to betray now?

"That was just a small job, that you handled well, I heard."

"Wasn't that because I am from the Outer City? That's what I thought."

"It was, but it was also because you are a very special young man, although I don't think anyone has mentioned it to you yet."

"Special?"

Rider Cornatan nodded.

Special as in good-special or bad-special?

"Come, boy, I'll show you something."

Carro rose from the cold stone chair, his head still reeling. Something very odd was going on here. There had to be a catch somewhere, there had to be.

CHAPTER 13

RIDER CORNATAN led carro through a corridor made of dark stone into another room, also illuminated with the same eerie green light. The polished black marble on the floor contained the shapes of leaves and many-legged creatures such as Carro had never seen. The room was bare except for a table in the middle.

On a table lay a variety of things Carro surmised must be weapons. Long sticks of metal, glinting in the emerald light that radiated from the walls. On the end of one of the sticks was a glass bulb with many carved facets.

Carro wanted to ask about it, but Rider Cornatan strode past the table and pressed a panel on the opposite wall. At his touch, an entire section of stone slid aside to reveal a hidden room.

There were four men in the room, two of them grey-haired Senior Knights in uniform. They stood near a stone chair similar to the one in the room where Carro had waited. On this chair sat a man in black, his hands and feet tied down by leather straps threaded through rings on the armrests and base of the chair.

The second-hand merchant who sold the books.

His eyes widened when they met Carro's, betraying an expression of utter panic. He was sweating, his face pale.

The man showed no signs of torture, but there was a strange apparatus on a table behind the chair. The last man wore a green protective suit with a helmet. The dark visor showed only his eyes. He was laying out snaking leads and sharp metal implements on the table with a heavily gloved hand.

Carro's knees felt weak. Oh, by the skylights. Was this all his fault because he'd betrayed the merchant? His dagger burned against his thigh. He felt like grabbing it and cutting the merchant free.

Rider Cornatan was talking to the Senior Knights.

One of them said, "Is that the boy?"

Rider Cornatan nodded, and his expression turned hard, as if he defied anyone to comment.

"You see, boy, what we're trying to do here is something very new. You will witness our first true application of knowledge we've acquired over the last few years. The Thillei have been saying it for a long time—"

"The Thillei? But I thought there weren't any left—"

"No visibly recognisable ones, no, but there are those who still practice the Thillei ways, and we might as well call them by their name."

Carro whispered, "The Brotherhood." He didn't dare look at the merchant.

"Very good." Rider Cornatan smiled first at Carro, then at his Senior Knights, as if he had proven a point. "Whatever can be said about the ways of the old king, the truth is that he had a vision for this land. When the Knights took over, they, naturally, abandoned his plans, but it has not been to the benefit of our land. Our people are poor. We no longer trade with our neighbouring nations. Instead, they laugh at us, and have erected barriers at their borders. They wish to ignore us and cut us out as if we were a festering sore."

He turned back to Carro, more intent than before. "It is said that because our land is frozen, we have nothing to offer, but that is a lie. We have much, and it has been right under our noses all the time. The power we call icefire can be used to drive machines that do incredible things: dig the ore out of the ground and make it into useful things, heat the caverns under the city and grow exquisite crops, then build fast trains to take produce to the borders. We have everything we need: we have water and we have unlimited energy. Why should we deny it exists?"

"But . . . but . . . that was what the old king did, and he became so powerful that he no longer needed his people, and he started turning them into mindless machines, the servitors."

Rider Cornatan chuckled. "Yes, that is the version commonly told at dinner tables, and it is also the very thing that has been holding us back. It's the belief that everything the king did was bad, the belief that we couldn't possibly use icefire differently and better. The power of icefire is ours. We have been blessed with it, and we should use it if we want to get ahead."

Carro realised why the sudden emphasis on confiscating illegal material: the Knights didn't want to burn it; they wanted to use it. That brought a whole new perspective to his own situation. He'd read about the old days—and *the Knights considered that a good thing.*

"Now of course re-starting fifty-year-old plans is not easy, but we've made some breakthroughs, one of which I'm about to show you. But I'm wondering, since you are doing so well, could you tell me what is the great weakness in our plan?"

All eyes were on Carro, as if this was some sort of test.

"Uhm . . ." He wanted to say *I don't know* but that would never do. "I . . . don't know much about icefire. I can't see it."

"Exactly!" Rider Cornatan smiled. "Most of us are unable to see or work with icefire. But there are those who can."

"Does that . . ." Carro swallowed. His gaze flicked to the merchant, who was sweating more than ever. "Does that mean you want the Thilleians back?"

"No. Their powers can be turned to true evil. Once infected

with the sense of power, they tend to become corrupted. But we can learn from them."

"But the powerful ones were all killed." And at the same time, his mind squealed *Isandor*.

"Exactly. And that is where this man comes in. Go ahead." He motioned to the suited man, who pulled some metal frame from the table. It went over the chair to cover the merchant's head in a lock, with plates fitted to both sides of his head so he couldn't move it. The pale green light showed the man's face sheened in sweat. Another suited man had come into the room while Rider Cornatan was speaking. He stuck a very thin needle into the skin of the man's forearm. It had a soft balloon of fluid attached, which he hung on a stand.

The merchant struggled at first, but quickly gave up, and a stupid look came over his face, his tongue lolling out. A dribble of spit tracked down his chin. Carro's stomach lurched.

The suited man then dragged the table with the strange machines so that it stood in front of the chair. With click of a handle, he brought a light to life. There were two beams, which he adjusted so each shone into the merchant's eyes. His eyes had gone wide, the pupils wide open.

He started speaking.

At first, his voice was a barely audible mumble, made harder to follow by drool dripping from his flaccid bottom lip, but gradually words formed.

". . . no money . . . no money. Have to pay the landlord . . . Sorry, dear, but the Knights came and took all my stock. Now I can't sell it to the collectors. I have no more money, dear. Yes, I remember that man. He came to me before. He bought some books . . ."

Carro clamped his hands behind his back. The merchant was going to mention him as purchaser for illegal items, and that was why he was here.

"I have . . . no more books, but the stranger has lots of money. I tell him . . . I will tell him about the boy, the one who's Imperfect.

He wants them, the Imperfects, you know. He pays lots. I can pay the landlord, dear. I'm sorry . . ."

The man blinked and then his eyes fell closed. The beams of light tracked over his cheeks, no longer focused on his eyes.

Carro's heart thudded against his ribcage. He was going to be punished for not letting the Knights know about Isandor, who had to be "the boy" the merchant referred to.

The suited man turned off the light and released the plates that pressed against the merchant's head. The merchant collapsed forward into the chair, gasping. He made a kind of *huuh-huuuh* sound while holding out a trembling hand as if trying to grab something he couldn't reach. The green-suited men were busy with their machine, and the Senior Knights spoke softly to each other, as if no one else was in the room.

But the man was still going *huuuh-huuuh-huuuh* and Carro wanted to do something about this whole awful business, but he didn't know what, and meanwhile the gasping and the *huuuh-huuuh* intensified, and the trembling hand looked like some sort of insect clawing at the chair's arm rest.

Carro couldn't stand it any longer. "Can you help him, please?" His voice sounded high and young.

"Take him away," one of the suited men said, muffled inside the suit.

Carro wasn't sure if he was the "him" referred to, or the merchant. The other suited man went to the chair and tried to untie the merchant's wrist straps, but he was leaning too hard into them, so he pushed the merchant back. As he did so, the man arched his back and with an explosive *huuuuh* projectile-vomited. It went all over the suited man's helmet and face mask. The suited man swore, and dragged the merchant out of the chair, out of the room, leaving a foul-smelling trail on the floor.

Carro felt sick.

"Come." Rider Cornatan's voice sounded far off. "We'll leave the staff to clean this up."

He sounded so matter-of-fact, as if seeing people in this sort of distress was *normal* to him. He led Carro out of the room, gingerly stepping over the vomit trail, while Carro still heard the *huuuh-huuuuh* in his mind. He was used to brawls, and fights, and fellow Apprentices drinking themselves stupid until they spent all night puking their guts out in the bathroom. He had never heard anything so desperate as this man.

It was all his fault.

Meanwhile, Rider Cornatan kept speaking.

"As you are probably aware, since you helped inspect this man's wares, we had this merchant watched. He wears the black of the Brotherhood of the Light, but no longer lives in the compound. It seems he has taken a wife, and he is desperate to get someone to pay for the privilege of using his son. The child was born Imperfect, and his wife rejected it. The boy has lived with the Brotherhood ever since. The merchant passed the knowledge of this boy to another man, a visitor to the Outer City. He paid two gold eagles for the information, and vanished. At the moment, the boy is still in the Brotherhood compound. We are going to get him first. And that is where you come in."

Carro stiffened, alert now.

"You are familiar with the Outer City. No one will find it odd to see you wandering around the streets."

"So . . ." Carro swallowed. "You want me to go to get this boy, while some sort of stranger is also after him?"

Rider Cornatan chuckled. "Of course I'm not going to let you go out without help. Let me show you something else." He walked to the table with the weapons in the other room.

Carro followed him, his head reeling.

It's cold in the lawkeeper's office. The room is bare with just a bench along the wall. There is a tiny window that lets in a meagre beam of bluish light.

Carro sinks down on the bench. Cold and shame bites through his trousers. This is where *criminals* sit.

Carro's tears run across his cheeks like icicles.

Isandor says, *Don't worry.*

It's easy for him to say. Isandor's mother comes to pick up her son. There is an officer with her.

The merchant has put in a complaint, he says. *He wants compensation for goods broken.*

Oh, why did they have to play with boomerangs so close to the market? Why did the boomerang have to hit the merchant's sled full of glasswork?

Isandor's mother puts an arm around her son's shoulder. Isandor looks up at her with his big blue eyes. *I'm sorry.*

She says, *Don't worry. I know things sometimes break when you play.* Her voice is warm. She smiles at the officer and the man smiles back. She radiant, glowing and pregnant, one of the city's best breeders. *I'm sure we can come to an arrangement with the merchant.*

They leave the room, their backs disappearing into the corridor.

Carro's parents won't be so kind.

No dinner, no oil for his lamp, and his books taken away from him, and that is if he escapes the whip.

He waits. It's cold in the room. The feeling inside him is even colder. No one is ever going to come for him. His parents are going to leave him here.

Rider Cornatan had turned around, giving Carro a concerned look. "Are you feeling ill?"

Carro's heart jumped a beat. "No, no, I'm fine." He tried to push away lingering nausea from the smell of vomit and the hazy remains of the memory, and the realisation: the recurring memories were getting worse.

How long before he had an accident while his mind was off somewhere else? How long before someone discovered and declared him unsuitable for service? Declared him *insane*?

Rider Cornatan's expression wasn't convincing. "You looked out of sorts for a bit. Not an advocate of medical procedures?" He glanced back at the room with the chair, where the wall panel was just sliding shut again, and two Junior Knights were mopping the floor.

"No, no. I'm fine." A drop of sweat trickled down Carro's back.

"Good, then have a look at this." Rider Cornatan gestured at the strange contraptions on the table.

They were definitely weapons of some description. Eagle Knights used crossbows and poisoned arrows, or in close combat, swords or daggers. Carro reached out for the staff with the shining stone, but withdrew his hand, casting a glance at Rider Cornatan. Touching it wouldn't be very humble. Stupid that he had even thought he *could* touch these weapons.

Rider Cornatan laughed, his eyes gleaming with pleasure. "You like that, boy?"

"Yes." Carro hated how his voice sounded too innocent. His father always said *boy* and never used his name.

"Take it."

Carro picked up the staff. The metal felt warm, almost alive, in his hands.

"Try some blows."

Try blows? Where? Rider Cornatan didn't expect to be sparring with him? He was an old man.

"Stand over there."

Apprehensively, Carro went to stand where Rider Cornatan indicated, in the middle of the room. To his dismay, the Supreme Rider threw off his cloak and grabbed another staff off the table. While he strode across the room, the eerie light made his white hair almost green. He took up position opposite Carro, his legs apart, as if he was about to start a sword fight.

Rider Cornatan ran his hand over the metal rod of the staff. There was a noise like lightning.

Icefire! Rider Cornatan did know he couldn't see it.

"Yes, boy. That surprises you, doesn't it? Thought we had forgotten that the curse that taints our land can be *used* in more ways than one?"

He thrust out with the staff. A line of dust lifted from the floor.

Carro cried out, turned and tried to run. What sort of defence did he have against icefire?

"Use the staff!" Rider Cornatan's voice grated like stone on stone.

Carro grabbed the staff in both hands, but had no idea what to do with it. Dust now crackled all around him, making his nose itch. He swung the staff into thin air, like a blind man swordfighting.

"That's right. A good, honest Knight doesn't run like a coward. A good Knight stands his ground and fights with whatever weapon he has."

"But it's not fair . . ." Carro panted.

"Warfare is rarely fair, boy. Yes, the enemy will use icefire. Then now, so do we. Come on, show me what you've learned." He swung the staff.

Sweat pouring down his stomach, Carro gripped the staff in both hands. He adopted a fighting stance, legs apart, swaying from side to side.

Rider Cornatan circled him. Slowly, watching with eagle-eyes. The heels of his boots clacked on the stone floor. Carro's skin pricked. He turned on the spot, as he'd been taught in sword fighting, always watching.

Rider Cornatan chuckled.

"I see you've been taught well."

And then he thrust up. Lightning crackled around Carro.

Carro swung his staff. Too late. He didn't know what he was doing. However was he supposed to fight icefire he couldn't see with nothing more than a stick? Rider Cornatan thrust again. The air was thick with the scent of singed clothing.

"Fight, fight," Rider Cornatan urged and punctuated each word with a thrust of the staff. He could still laugh. Or maybe he thought it was funny. Maybe this was Carro's punishment.

He thrust faster and faster. Dust swirled in the room. Carro whirled, swung his staff whichever way seemed right, but Rider Cornatan always went faster.

Eventually, Carro could no longer keep it up. "This is ridiculous. I can't see what I'm fighting!" He stopped, panting, embarrassed about his outburst. "I'm sorry. You win."

He hung his shoulders. Humility. Lost to an old man.

Rider Cornatan laughed. "No. You win. Give me this." He took the staff from Carro's sweat-slicked hand. "Notice how the metal is cold?"

It was. Ice-cold in fact.

"You noticed how none of the rays hit you?"

Carro blinked. He couldn't see the rays, but hadn't felt anything either, so he supposed it was true. The floor certainly bore plenty of marks.

"That is because when you hold this weapon, it acts as a sink for icefire. When you're holding this staff, instead of hitting the intended target, icefire is all absorbed in this staff."

Carro's spirits deflated. "So . . . Nothing would have happened to me even if I had not defended myself."

"Precisely." A smile curled the old lips. "You are special, because of what you are. Pure Pirosians are rare. Cherish it, keep it a secret and use it well."

Carro tried hard to feel misused or suspicious, but he only succeeded partially. He was *special* He was more than Carro, useless boy from the Outer City, who was only here because the Knights wanted to spy on the Outer City residents.

"Apprentice Carro, we have a dire need of your talent. How would you like to be promoted?"

"Promoted?" Carro swallowed. This was getting more and

more strange.

"The first Apprentice ever to skip straight to Learner? Your father would like that, wouldn't he?"

Carro flinched. What did Rider Cornatan know of his father? What did he know of what his father thought about him? Did his father have a hand in this? Was that the catch?

The carpet is dark red and has a pattern of squares within squares that Carro knows all too well. He stands just inside the door, his hands behind his back, his gaze on the ground.

His father gets up from the desk and walks across the office. Carro follows his father's movement from the corner of his eye. Don't go to the cupboard please, not the cupboard. He doesn't think he can stand any more work in the warehouse on the accounting books, but he will not cry, or the boys will tease him. All the boys who were already teasing him in the streets. It will just get worse.

His father opens the cupboard door. Takes a long time to select a big book. The stocktake records.

Carro closes his eyes and tries not to show his despair. He shivers with the intense cold in the warehouse.

He can feel the chill breeze as his father crosses to the rough table where he is sitting. The book lands on the table with a thud.

I want this done by tomorrow morning.

Carro just nods, his mind numb. He fights back tears of despair.

His fingers will be blue and sore by the time the night is over. Then his reading tutor will hit him for not paying attention. Then his father will order the stove to be tempered, because the luxurious warmth is obviously putting his errant son to sleep.

And then . . .

Carro wobbled. Oh, by the skylights, why was he seeing these things?

Fortunately, Rider Cornatan hadn't noticed the spell. He was putting the staff back on the table. When Carro moved to do the same, his hands trembling, Rider Cornatan put his hand on the metal. "Keep it. I'm allocating you two elite soldiers. Get the boy and come back here. The soldiers are waiting for you."

"What—now?"

"Yes. Everyone is asleep or too drunk to notice. You should be able to take the boy on your bird. He's only a child. Bring him back here as soon as you can. Report to me directly. Don't tell anyone else."

Rider Cornatan turned to Carro and lifted up his chin with a single finger.

"Go on, make your family proud."

"My family hates me, especially my father."

Rider Cornatan's eyes met his, blue, intense. "I don't know about the rest of your family, but I can assure you, Carro, your father loves you very much."

Chapter 14

THERE WERE many questions Carro should have asked, but his brain was so numb that he was out the door before he remembered any of them. It felt like it had all been a dream, except he had the staff in his hands and his Learner's badge on his collar, and a fuzzy feeling in his head that told him that, yes, this was real, and if he wanted to come out of this alive, he had better obey orders. Someone was testing him, or teasing him, or using him as expendable bait, and all he could do was run along and hope he wasn't going to get caught in something sticky.

The two elite Knights waited at the end of the corridor that led to Rider Cornatan's quarters, both sharp-faced, silent men at least ten years older than Carro. He had never seen them before. Their eyes were hard, their gazes neither approving nor disapproving, but Carro was all-too-aware of their muscled arms and lean physiques. Body-guards or child-minders?

Their faces remained impassive.

They started moving through the dark corridor in the direction Carro recognised as leading towards the howling staircase. At night, there was no wind to make the jagged edges howl, and they climbed its many steps in uncomfortable silence. The sky was dark blue, too light to show any but the brightest of stars. Pink and green skylights shimmered above.

"You know where to find this Brotherhood compound?"

Carro had grown so used to silence that the man's voice startled him.

"I do." Carro explained the location on the far side of the Outer City. The men only listened. Evidently, they had been briefed on their mission.

They reached the eyrie, where dark shapes of birds shuffled and fidgeted as they came in. One of the Knights flicked the light lever up. The bulb sprang into life with its too-bright glow. Heads lifted from under wings, baleful eyes blinked. Both men had their birds untied before Carro had even done up his harness. His fingers trembled. He was fumbling with the staff Rider Cornatan had given him, not sure how to carry it. He settled on lashing his belt around the glass head. The stick banged against his leg, a feeling that was clumsy and awkward.

Carro untied his eagle. It hissed at him and flapped its wings, which made a few other eagles hiss and squawk.

Clumsy, clumsy.

At the opening, the two Knights mounted with fluid grace. Their birds stood ready, their eyes alert.

How had Rider Cornatan ever thought he could match men like these? Normally, the Apprentices mounted their birds from a platform, but it had been taken away for the night. Carro put his foot in the harness trying to imitate the Knights. He heaved himself up and almost overbalanced. The eagle flapped with his sudden shift of weight. Carro salvaged the situation by grabbing the handholds at the top of the saddle with both hands. The reins slipped from his hands, but at least he didn't fall.

One of the Knights gave a quick flick with his eyebrows before he launched the eagle out. Carro clicked his tongue and the eagle followed the other bird out, hurtling into the air that cut his face with the sting of thousands of knives.

Carro was shivering, already struggling to hold onto the saddle.

Most of the buildings in the city were dark. Lights burned in the odd window here or there, but most decent nobles and proper folk of the City of Glass had gone to bed. Alternatively, they were partying in the Outer City, which was an island of light on the plain dark blue with eternal dusk.

Carro kneed his eagle into catching up with the others. The bird was unwilling and made no secret of its dislike at being woken up. The two Knights fell back and let him lead the way, over the festival grounds, mostly dark, over the market square, bathed in light and full of revellers, to the part of the Outer City furthest from the City of Glass. Here, Carro landed his eagle in a rough piece of land amongst warehouses. There used to be a warehouse at this plot of land, but it had burned down some years ago. He remembered the flames, which had been visible from his street. He had Isandor had climbed up the limpet roof to see the flames roaring into the sky. Now it was just an empty piece of land with mounds of snow and stone pillars which had once been the foundations of the building.

There was nowhere to tie up the eagles, and it would probably be unwise to leave them behind anyway, so he dismounted and led the bird by the reins into the street. Eagles were not fond of walking and the bird kept jerking its head up. Carro almost lost his grip on the reins twice before he noticed how the two Knights had the leather straps wrapped around their wrists. They also kept the reins very tight, so their birds didn't have the slack to get any force into the upward jerk. The Tutor didn't teach that. Interesting. It worked, too.

In silence, they progressed to the wall that was the back of the compound.

Carro hadn't expected guards at the gate, and indeed there were none. But now they couldn't take the eagles any further and there was still nowhere to tie them up. Instead, the two Knights tied their birds onto *each other*. Their reins were interesting as well. His tack was the standard length of leather, fastened onto the harness on one end with a metal ring and looped back onto the harness on the other end. Their reins were two separate pieces of leather, each lashed around the rider's wrist when in flight. They now tied one of these strips to each other, threading the knot through the reins of Carro's eagle.

Carro wanted to ask, *but what about if we need them?* He envisaged a tangle of feathers and wings as all three birds tried to take off at once and found they were attached to each other. But evidently, the Knights had considered this and had some sort of solution.

Carro felt so dumb. *I'm an Outer City pup, and they'll do their best to prove it with every step I take.*

The men took daggers from their belts. Carro untied the staff and unsheathed his dagger. He was unsure in which hand to hold which and his hands were too cold to do much with either weapon anyway.

They walked in through the open gates. On the other side was a small courtyard surrounded on three sides by a low building with a columned façade, very unlike the regular building style in the Outer City. Carro knew from earlier visits that the door was somewhere in the darkness between those columns, although he couldn't see it. This was the furthest he had ever gone into the compound, bringing a delivery from his father to the Brothers. Fabric for bed sheets, he seemed to remember.

Every time he'd come here, there had been children of his own age playing in the snow, those who had been rescued from abusive families, lived in the compound and received teaching from the Brothers. They had always seemed happy and harmonious. This was not a place of shouting and punishment; it was a place of learning.

Sometimes, in his darkest hours, Carro had considered seeking refuge here, but he had always thought it unfair to the children whose families actually *beat* them, the girls whose fathers came home drunk and raped them every night. Those children needed the Brothers, not him. Being ignored, ridiculed or scorned every moment he spent inside his parents' limpet didn't injure him or kill him.

He walked across the snow-covered yard and took the two steps up the porch. The two Knights followed him like silent shadows. From memory, the dining room was directly opposite the entrance, and the sleeping quarters were to the right. A glow lit up behind him. One of the Knights held a pebble no bigger than a fingernail, which gave off bright light. The first few windows they checked were store rooms with lots of boxes, or classrooms with benches and tables. There was a blackboard against the far wall, on which someone had drawn diagrams of squares and triangles. Carro was unsure what it meant, but he had seen similar pictures in the books he and Isandor used to read, ones that spoke of calculations of icefire.

The next window looked into a living room of some kind, but a thick layer of ice made it hard to see. The second Knight gestured to a window further ahead.

Inside was a dormitory-style room with two rows of beds against the walls. In each of those beds was a child. The Knight tried the window, but it wouldn't open.

The other Knight gestured that there was an entry on the side of the building. They headed back into the courtyard and the Knight led through a passage between the building and the compound wall. There was an outroom at the back, and facing it, a wooden door. It was locked, but it took the Knights no longer than a few heartbeats to prise it open.

The quiet efficiency of these men chilled Carro. They had spoken no more than a handful of words since he had met them, and now he wondered if these men *ever* spoke. They certainly didn't seem the type to attend Newlight celebrations and start rowdy brawls in melteries, nor to get distracted by the presence of female flesh.

These were *real* Knights in the way he was not. Real Knights didn't party, didn't fight in melteries, didn't try to get into a girl's bed. Real Knights didn't even show off their status to their families and old friends. Real Knights didn't *have* old friends. They only had their jobs, and their superiors.

Into the building. A straight corridor stretched into darkness.

The fur-soled riding boots made not the slightest sound on the floor. The Knight indicated, *in here*. He pushed the door open, again without sound. The air inside was impossibly warm and laced with the must-tinged smell of blankets.

The first Knight marched into the room, while the second shut the door, holding aloft the light. Meanwhile, the first Knight was yanking blankets off the beds, uncovering sleeping children who woke up to a hand pressed over their mouths. Carro clutched his staff and felt completely useless.

The Knight struck success with the fifth child. Carro felt a cold shiver in the staff before the Knight had pulled the blankets off the bed. He was going to say *that one* for the sake of being useful, but the boy already sat at the edge of his bed. The harsh light showed his missing toes. Imperfect. Two heartbeats later, the Knight had the boy wrapped in a blanket and was pushing him into the corridor. All silent.

The other Knight gestured, *Quick, let's get out of here.*

As Carro pulled the door to the dormitory shut behind him, the staff jerked in his hand, nearly causing him to drop it. He couldn't restrain a gasp.

Both Knights looked at him. One had slung the blanket with the boy over his shoulder.

"Someone's coming," Carro whispered. He wasn't sure if it was *someone*, but something was definitely happening. The metal of the staff was going alternately warm and cold in his hands.

The Knights had stopped. Neither spoke, but their sharp gazes roamed the corridor. Carro didn't even know their names.

They listened. All Carro could hear was the thudding of his own heart.

"Your imagination." The Knight closest to him gave him a

disdainful glance and turned towards the door.

Carro shrugged, trying to be careless. Fine; these men thought he was an idiot, everyone did. He could do nothing but follow, even though the coldness in the staff increased.

They walked back along the path between the wall and the building, into the courtyard. Carro looked over his shoulder again. Saw nothing.

The staff chilled in his hands.

"There's something . . ." He didn't know how to continue. Speak of icefire in the presence of older Knights? Did they know what Rider Cornatan knew?

But the Knights broke into a trot.

Carro didn't question their motivation.

Quick, back to the eagles. Hurry up. The staff was jerking now. He took the lead in the courtyard, the two Knights close behind. Almost at the gate. There was a noise, a soft sigh as if someone expelled a breath.

Carro glanced over his shoulder.

Something moved at the dormitory window, a smudge of distorted air.

Quick.

Puffs of snow blew up in the courtyard, coming towards them.

Carro ran.

A loud crack reverberated between the wings of the building, followed by a thump. Carro skidded to a stop. One of the Knights lay face-down in the snow. The second Knight, holding the boy over his shoulder, had his dagger in his hand, slashing uselessly in thin air.

Some artefact of icefire

Carro gripped the staff even though its surface almost froze onto his hands. Something was in the courtyard with them, *something* he couldn't see. But he could see footsteps forming in the snow as the apparition walked. He waved the staff. The second Knight glanced around, his eyes wide, his dagger ready. His comrade hadn't stirred.

The second Knight's head jerked back. His face froze in a surprised expression. There was a loud *crack* that echoed in the courtyard.

The man fell backwards as if in slow motion and landed on the icy ground with a dull thud, the blanket with the boy under him.

Carro wanted to run, but fear made his legs unwilling. He stared at the man's neck, bent at an impossible angle. The invisible thing *had broken the man's neck*.

Carro waved the staff like crazy. That *thing* was going to kill him next. "Begone, begone, whatever you are!"

A sudden gust of wind picked up, howling around the building. The air crackled. Snow sizzled, and blew into Carro's face. He stood stiff with fear. He wanted to scream, but could make no sound. It felt like his entire face was on fire.

And then quiet returned.

Carro stood there, holding the staff. His hands ached with cold. Snow had blown into heaps obliterating any footsteps the apparition might have left. Where was it now? All Carro could see were indistinct mounds of snow, two of whom contained the Knights' lifeless bodies.

"Please, help." The voice was soft and muffled.

The Imperfect boy was pushing himself up from under the dead Knight, shaking snow out of his hair.

"Come to me," Carro called, still staring at the snow, expecting to see footsteps coming towards him.

He waved the staff. The metal was so cold it steamed. His hands hurt from holding it, but he was too scared to worry about frostbite. A deep keening filled the courtyard. Wind tore through the gate, throwing up a cloud of snow.

The boy had pushed the Knight off him. The man's head flopped back like it was attached to this body only by skin.

"Come now!" Carro shouted into the howling wind.

The boy ran, clutching his blanket.

Carro grabbed hold of him with his free arm, while hanging

onto the staff with the other. The staff, and his hand, were rimed with frost. He ran, whistled for the eagle, and then remembered the business with the tied-up reins.

But the eagles came, all three of them, flying low through the street, with their wing tips almost touching the houses on either side. The reins dangled loose—snapped? The two Knights' eagles kept flying, but his bird landed.

Carro heaved the boy on the saddle and clambered on behind him. One stroke of powerful wings and they were off into the night. Carro wrestled to gain control of the reins. His leather loop had broken, too, no, it had been cut.

The boy was shivering.

"S-s-so glad you came," he said. His voice was young and hadn't broken yet. "I thought . . . that blue thing was going t' kill me like th'others."

Blue thing? "What did you see?"

Carro shifted his weight to free his arm so he could lash the dangling reins around his wrist. He now saw how the tying-up trick worked. The knot still dangled in the reins of the eagle flying to the left of him. At his whistle, the birds had simply bitten through the leather. The Knights would replace the straps once they became too short.

"Din' you see th' blue man?"

"I didn't see anything." His teeth chattered.

"He were all shimmery an' in places you could see right through 'im."

Just what was he talking about?

Carro had to concentrate on flying and the boy fell into silence. He didn't shiver so much anymore. Carro was too busy staying in the saddle to talk, and too busy worrying what Rider Cornatan would say about the death of two of his elite soldiers, men much more experienced than him.

Riding with the loose reins would have been tricky even during daytime, and the deadweight of the boy didn't help. The eagle laboured to stay in the air, but he made the eyrie.

Rider Cornatan was waiting at the back of the room, silhouetted by the light. Carro slid off his bird, the weight of the boy pressing him down.

It was only when he stood in the straw, and the boy slumped on the ground that he realised the boy had lost consciousness.

Rider Cornatan gave a sharp command. A Knight ran forward to lift the boy's prone body off the floor.

"Take him to the infirmary. Impress on the medicos that I want him to *live*."

Then the man was gone, and Carro faced Rider Cornatan. He couldn't bear looking up. He'd taken out two capable Knights and had come back alone. Rider Cornatan had given him the metal staff to protect the patrol, but he had run first.

"I can explain," he whispered, but the horror of that snap echoed in his mind. How strong was this invisible monstrosity that it could break a grown man's neck with such a loud crack?

There were footsteps on the floor, Rider Cornatan coming closer. Carro cringed. He would sure be beaten, punished for his failure.

Carro sits at the big table in the dining room. His sister is next to him, crying.

Why did you do that, Carro? his mother asks.

Because she is ugly.

That is such a horrid thing to say, I don't know how you these things come into your head.

But it's true.

His mother slaps him across the face. *You need to grow up. You want to be treated like a big boy, you act like one.*

But a warm hand touched his shoulder.

"Look at me, Carro."

Carro raised his head, blinking hard to repress threatening tears. He couldn't help it—he always did or said stupid things that got himself and, most importantly, other people, into trouble.

Rider Cornatan's eyes met his. It was impossible to guess what went on behind that gaze.

"I know what it means to face the horrors of the Thillei legacy," Rider Cornatan said in a low voice. "There are certain things we simple human beings cannot fight. That is the true reason I sent you: because you alone have a chance. Had you not been there, the boy would have been in the hands of the enemy. You did as well as you could."

"Who . . ." Carro swallowed. Did this mean that the death of two capable men would be written off as inevitable? While it was *his* fault? "Who is this enemy?"

"That is what we need to find out. We might have thought that all Thilleians were dead, but it seems they are not."

Isandor. And then Carro had another chilling thought: did his friend have anything to do with this invisible monstrosity? It was Isandor's idea to read the books, but what if he had kept the most important ones of them secret?

"Now, I want you to clean up and rest. Go downstairs to my quarters and use the bathroom there." He winked. "I know it's Newlight. Don't stay too long, though. I believe you're racing tomorrow."

He passed an arm over Carro's shoulders and squeezed them briefly.

Carro's head was full of questions. What did he mean—don't stay too long? How could Rider Cornatan be so indifferent about the death of two men? What was he going to do with that boy? Why, if he wanted Imperfects, had he not noticed the one right in front of his nose in the eyrie, and what would Carro do if asked to betray Isandor?

But he left the room and slouched down the howling staircase to the Senior Knight quarters. When he came to the bathroom in question, he understood at least the first part of Rider Cornatan's remarks, because he could heard the sound of relaxed talk and laughter before he opened the door. It sounded like there was a party going on.

The room beyond was huge and impossibly warm. Steam drifted from the surface of a huge bath. At least twenty people sat in the water, on a bench around the perimeter of the bath.

"Hey, there is the hero!" one young man called out.

The others cheered, holding up glasses.

The group included some of the noble sons who had always been indifferent to him, men who should know about the deaths of two of their fellows. And, by the skylights, there was Korinne, seated in the water.

Their eyes met, and Carro looked away, acutely aware of his filthy clothes. No way to face a girl.

In a corner filled with benches and wash basins, Carro slipped out of his clothes and washed blood off his hands. It was warm in the room, and the laughter and cheerful voices made his ears ring, where he still heard that snap, that awful snap, of the Knight's neck breaking.

Footsteps in the snow.

Crack.

A servant came with a tray of hot bloodwine. Carro accepted a glass and drained it in one gulp. The liquid burned a way to his stomach. There. That was better. He slipped into the huge bath, not meeting anyone's eyes. The water stung his cold-numbed hands.

Carro leaned back against the side of the bath, letting the talk in the room wash over him. His head was becoming comfortably dizzy with the heat and the effect of the bloodwine.

"Hi, Carro."

Korinne, on the underwater seat next to him. Her curls were flattened against her head and the bottom ends of her hair fanned out from her shoulders, partially covering her breasts.

"Uhm, hello," he said, and then he felt like he had to add something. "Have you been here long?"

Stupid question, really, seeing as what he'd been through.

"Not very long," she said. She took one of his hands and began rubbing it, examining blisters on his palms. "Flying out at night?" she asked.

He nodded, the simplest answer that didn't require him to lie.

"Didn't you wear gloves?"

Carro shrugged. He didn't want to talk about his mission. The flow of the water drew her hair away from her breasts, soft white orbs with dark nipples. He felt oddly detached.

"We were just getting ready for the party and were waiting for you." She ran her hands up his arm, meeting his eyes.

"For me?" Heat crept up his cheeks.

Was this the girl who had called him a clumsy idiot earlier that evening? By the skylights—was it only that evening? It seemed many days ago.

"Drink?" someone behind him asked.

Carro turned and took the bottle from the man next to him, a tall, dark-haired young man with olive skin. His shoulders were lean and corded with muscle.

The man met Carro's eyes; his were grey and uncomfortably intense. He had long eyelashes. His face was narrow, with a long, hook-like nose.

Foreign blood.

"Uhm . . ." Carro hated how he blushed. "I'm Carro."

The man chuckled. "We figured."

"And you are?"

"Farey."

His intense stare made Carro uneasy, but he felt he had to say something. He *wanted* to say something. Not to look like an idiot, for once.

"I haven't seen you at the eyrie before." It was an insanely stupid remark, he knew that as soon as it left his mouth. Apprentices only ever saw a very small part of what went on in the eyrie.

Again that chuckle, breathy and nervous and very strange at the same time. "You wouldn't have seen me. It's my job not to be seen when I don't want to." The grey gaze roamed Carro's naked shoulders, the pale skin of his belly.

Carro turned back to Korinne and made a show of unstoppering the bottle. His hands trembled. He drank a few swigs without tasting anything, and when he passed the bottle on, noticed how on the other side of the bath two noble sons faced each other. One was old enough to have the golden markings on his cheeks, the other was not much older than Carro. As he watched, the older Knight pulled the younger closer and kissed him full on the mouth. The light gilded the younger man's cheekbones, His eyes were closed; his hands slid down the older Knight's chest.

Blood roared in Carro's ears. He wanted to turn away, give his attention to Korinne, who was stroking his shoulders, but he couldn't. Men did these things to each other *by choice*?

Next to him, that strange Farey gave another one of his breathy chuckles. "You're not with kiddies anymore, boy." The tone of his voice made Carro shiver.

Carro didn't trust himself to meet the man's eyes. He forced his gaze back to Korinne, but saw sinewy, olive-skinned shoulders. "You . . ." He cleared his throat. "You have parties here often?"

"Not me." She laughed. "But Rider Cornatan invites his elite group here quite often, I hear. This is the first time I've been here. He asked me to come." Her eyes said *for you*.

She looped her arm around his neck. Her bare breasts pressed against his chest. Carro wondered what had made her change her mind about him. Nothing he had done, that was for sure.

But it was pleasant, and she was offering, and doing what she wanted, whatever the reason behind it, seemed easier than facing that strange Farey on his other side, and with all the uncomfortable feelings *that* brought.

He bent forward, pressing his lips on hers. She replied, eager and passionate.

The rest of the night passed in a drunken blur. When he

stood in the deeper part of the bath, Korinne could loop her legs around him. It was easy to lift her in the water at the height he wanted her. She swallowed him, and he didn't object. His body obeyed his mind. For those few crazy moments, he ruled the world. He was Carro. He'd show his father how "useless" he was. Let his father beg him on his knees for forgiveness. Let his mother learn what it was to live in hardship.

If we are nice all the time, we'd never get anywhere.

He didn't suffer any flashbacks all night.

Chapter 15

JEVAITHI PULLED ON her thick furs and looked at herself in the dressing room mirror. Lush, thick and pure white, the cloak had been made in all haste for this visit. It suited her, she had to admit, and brought out the lushness of her hair. She had the maid pin it up in a loose bun today.

Underneath the cloak she wore a thick dress, tall boots, woollen stockings and felt underwear over her usual silk finery. She twirled in front of the mirror, admiring her new clothes, feeling like a little girl again, like walking on her mother's hand. Exciting, as if the whole world was out there to be discovered.

She had even put some colour on her face. Lines of kohl and a fine coating of silver paint accentuated her eyes.

Not too much or Rider Cornatan would object. She could almost hear his voice *You are still a child.*

No, she wasn't. She pulled up the leather strap she had insisted her maid bring her, and let the feather dangle over her chest. It was a crude thing, but one such as the new maidens of the city wore. It made her feel grown-up. It made her feel like she was in control of part of her life, no matter how small that part was.

"Your escort is ready," a male voice said.

Jevaithi gasped and tucked the feather back under the white fur of her cloak, her heart still thudding.

Rider Cornatan strode into the room. The dressing room! She should really have to talk to him about that. She was no longer a girl and he would have to start treating her like an adult, and an adult of the opposite sex at that.

He stopped a few paces inside the door and stared. Oh yes, she did not mistake the look in his eyes. She saw it in the Knights who attended her.

"Your Highness, you look . . . magnificent," he said. His blue gaze roamed her body as if seeking something to criticise, something that was too daring or too revealing for the citizens of the City of Glass to see, and, having found nothing, came to rest on her right arm, which she held in her pocket. Nothing untoward there either.

She stared back defiantly. *No, nobody will know.*

"Are we ready to go, then?" she asked.

"We are, Your Highness, unless . . ."

"Unless what?"

"Unless you would decide it's not safe enough."

Not safe enough? She frowned at him. "Is there a reason why I should change my mind about this trip? A reason that wasn't present when you agreed to take me? Which was . . . yesterday?"

His eyes met hers. He opened his mouth. Hesitated. "No, Your Highness, there isn't."

"Then let's go."

He was lying, she could feel that. Something was happening right here in the palace. And she bet it was something to do with those golden rays that wormed their way up from the ground to her tower room. Icefire, stronger than ever before. Whatever it was, he was worried, but would rather endanger her than talk about it.

Interesting.

She left the dressing room straight-backed, without looking at him. The fur lining of the cloak swished around her ankles. It was an unfamiliar sensation that left her feeling wonderfully warm and covered. For once, she wouldn't have to look at the world from a great height. For once, people would look at her face rather than her dress, or what they could see through the fabric.

The door opened, the Knights stepped to the side and then . . . oh, freedom. She walked onto the landing in front of her quarters. A breeze of frost-tinged air wafted up from the depths of the atrium, an immense triangular hall filled with bluish light, glass and mirrors. It was said that the hall was formed through the collapse of one building against another. When seen from here, the very top of the triangle, the theory made sense, and as far as she knew, the floors did slope in most of the unused floors of the other side of the palace.

Down below, far down, the palace workers moved like crawling insects, past the fountain, a triangular basin of water in the middle of the hall. Although blue with salts, dripping water had frozen in grotesque stalagmites at the foot of the burbling fountain. Miniature ice floes bobbed on the pond's surface, carved in shapes of flowers and animals.

Lifts trundled up or down along rails set in the atrium's walls. There was the sound of ordinary people talking, laughing. It was intoxicating.

"Your Highness."

Rider Cornatan's voice broke her reverie.

A lift cubicle had come. Two guards stepped in, then Jevaithi and Rider Cornatan and then two more guards. The doors hissed closed. The cubicle jolted into action. Through the glass ceiling, Jevaithi spotted the jiggling chain that held the cubicle in place. The floors slid by. Sometimes they passed remnants of destruction that created the palace: twisted metal bent into elegant sculptures, haphazardly holding up sheets of grey stone. Molten glass carved into arches. Sometimes she wondered what weapon could twist stone and metal so.

Lights lit up above the doors to indicate that the lift had come to the ground floor. The doors opened and out came more Knights, forming a guard of honour across the polished tiles of the atrium floor.

Through the glass wall of the main entrance Jevaithi spotted a sled in the street, surrounded by yet more guards. Were all these Knights going to come with her? There wouldn't be anyone left to guard the palace. Never mind her desire for an unobtrusive visit. She was going out, that was the important thing. Once she was amongst the people, she would try to stay there as long as possible.

As they were about to leave the atrium, a stiff grey-haired man came up to Rider Cornatan.

"You're going out?" he said in a low voice and his eyes flashed hidden meaning. He was a Senior Knight, with golden stripes for years of service on his collar. There were more stripes than times Jevaithi had celebrated her birthday.

Rider Cornatan nodded curtly. "Newlight festival."

"When are you back?"

"Why? Anything wrong?"

"Well—about the young lad you brought in last night . . ." Then he must have realised Jevaithi could hear what he said and he lowered his voice. They stopped walking. Jevaithi stopped, too, a few paces off.

The two men exchanged a few comments in voices too low for her to hear. Rider Cornatan's eyes widened briefly then he turned to Jevaithi.

"Continue on to the sled, Your Highness, I will be there soon."

Jevaithi didn't move.

Rider Cornatan raised his eyebrows in a way he did when he was annoyed.

"I said I will be there soon."

"I am the Queen. I have a right to hear what is going on in my city, don't I? So I think I'd rather stay and hear about this problem."

"Your Highness, it's only a minor thing and not important enough even to discuss in the Knights' Council. It's certainly not important enough to delay our trip. You might miss the races." He turned to the Senior Knight. "We will discuss this later."

The man gave a stiff nod, but Jevaithi didn't miss the tightly-pressed lips. *He* obviously didn't think it was a minor concern. She wondered if it had anything to do with increase of the golden rays of icefire she had noticed. If so, it wasn't unimportant to her either. Or maybe it had something to do with the more than fifty criminals the Knights had caught in Bordertown. One of her guards had let slip that information, but Rider Cornatan hadn't wanted to tell her why those people had been caught and what they had done.

"I think I should like to attend when the Knights' Council sits next," she said.

Rider Cornatan turned to her, his expression stiff. "We should start to think in that direction, yes, but I'm not sure you need to be introduced to the politics of running the land just yet."

Politics? There were the Knights and the Knights. What was so hard about that?

"I want to."

"We shall see."

He kept his face neutral, since he could hardly berate her with all these people present, but he would probably like to do so if the twitch of a muscle in his neck was anything to go by.

Her people were her protection. Once she was back in her prison, she would suffer. She thought of the gull's tail feather on the leather strap around her neck. The token suddenly felt heavy as stone. Suppose *Rider Cornatan* was to take her up on her advertisement tonight . . .

Quite a crowd had gathered to watch in the street. Held back by a couple of Knights, the people were all nobles of the City of Glass, dressed in their fine furs and gaudy head-dresses. Women wore face paint and jewellery.

As soon as Jevaithi stepped out the door, a cheer went up.

She waved to the people as she had been taught. A Knight spread sand from a bucket so she didn't slip in the snow. Another held open the door to the carriage. She climbed up the steps and settled on the bench next to Rider Cornatan.

The sled was huge and white, drawn by four bears. Their white fur shone and was washed and groomed to perfection. They even had jewels even on their collars and harnesses, which were made from red leather. One of the palace guards sat in the driver's seat. Two Knights stood on the front runners, and two behind, all prominently displaying weapons. So she was to have four minders, and Rider Cornatan, and the driver, who would stay with the sled. She could handle that.

With a flick of the reins the bears loped into action and started moving down the street. Jevaithi saw herself in the sled reflected in the glass facades of the buildings that lined the street. Pompous entrances were guarded by sculptures carved of molten glass. Behind the windows, racks of the finest clothing by the city's finest leather workers, or brightly-lit benches with swathes of green plants. Customers stood in line for attendants to cut their fresh vegetables. No such things as mundane shops here. Through another window, customers sat drinking from bronze-coloured cups on dainty tables surrounding a giant glass sculpture of a dragon.

The going was slow in the streets. The Knights had to motion aside people, who then crowded along the street and in porches. They cheered. Jevaithi waved and smiled. A young man ran with the sled offering a tray of biscuits. They looked wonderful, but Rider Cornatan's sharp glance stopped her taking one. They could be poisoned after all. Silly. She didn't care. If she died today, she would die having fun. Fifteen years old, and she didn't care if she never saw the sun rise on another day. If she died, she would have denied the Knight's Council the pleasure of using her body to further their aims. If she died, it would be without having a Senior Knight's handprints all over her and his child in her belly. If she died, it would be because she wanted to, not because anyone said so. Although, of course, there were better things than dying, and possibly other ways to escape her fate.

Escape. The taste of the word on her tongue was like that of a rare exotic fruit. Being out here amongst the people almost felt as good as escape.

They passed the city gates and the bears moved at full speed. The white plains spread out before her. Sunlight poured gold over the snow, casting long shadows and millions of glittering gem-like crystals.

An icy breeze bit into Jevaithi's cheeks. Her maids would probably complain about what it did to her skin, but she didn't care; she felt alive. Out there waited young men who didn't yet know the newly blooded virgin who would throw herself at their feet. She'd take herself off into one of the melteries, she'd dance, she'd flirt, and when the young man took the bait, she'd make sure it was out in the open, when none of the Senior Knights could make a scene.

Escape.

The jumble of low buildings that was the Outer City grew on the horizon at the same speed with which the excitement bloomed in her heart.

The buildings had been designed by locals and the people called them limpets. She had never been inside one—another task to add to her list of things to do after she ascended the throne on her birthday.

Before long, she could make out the colourful tents that had been set up on the plain and the fences for the animals. No Legless Lions yet, but one of her maids told her this morning that the festivities included a Legless Lion race. She would *have* to see that. Legless Lions were fun to watch when they ran on their flippers.

A number of eagles rose from the festival grounds. Knights in the saddles rode with quiet confidence. Low and gliding, they escorted the sled towards the tents. More guards. She'd escape them all.

Children ran out onto the plain, cheering and shouting when they met the sled. They ran along, stumbling through the snow to keep up with the bears. Their faces were red; their eyes shone with wonder. Jevaithi smiled at them and waved. The kids laughed and waved back, excitement in their eyes. She could hear their young voices, *Mother, I saw the Queen today.* What would it be like to be one of these kids, to live anonymously, to ride sleds down the hill, to build snow castles, to just walk around here without anyone watching.

The sled passed a fence and then they were amongst the festivities. The driver slowed the bears to a walking pace. The audience grew quickly. People ran through the pens, poked their heads out of tents, came with their families. Faces bright with happiness. The driver stood up on his seat and shouted, "Make way for Queen Jevaithi of the City of Glass!"

More and more people gathered along the sides, cheering and shouting. Someone started a chant, *Jevaithi, Jevaithi,* and before long everyone was shouting her name. Jevaithi waved until her arm ached. These people were her safety shield.

The sled came to a halt.

Rider Cornatan jumped off first and bowed, holding out his hand. "Your Highness."

If he was still angry about her insistence to attend the Knights' Council, he didn't show it.

Jevaithi stepped from the sled onto hard frozen ground where again a Knight was spreading sand. *They sweep the ground I walk on.* Rider Cornatan held out his arm to support her, but she waved it away. Her new boots were soft and warm. She wanted to walk in the snow, away from all these eyes. She wanted to run, be alone and free. She wanted to slip and fall, tumble in the snow. It looked soft.

But more Knights were coming up to her, all older men with lots of gold on their collars.

"How wonderful of you to grace us with a visit," a Knight

said. She couldn't see his face because he bowed so deeply.

"Thank you for receiving me." She had to stay polite and formal, oh so boring.

"I have had the honour of being appointed as your guide, Your Highness. What would you like to see first?" He was still speaking to the snow at his feet.

"I should like to see the flying races," Jevaithi said.

"The eagle race pens are on the other side of the festival grounds," the Knight said.

"Then I shall walk there."

Rider Cornatan bent to her, whispering, "Your Highness, I don't think—"

"Walking is healthy."

He didn't dare protest.

"Lead the way, my good Knight," she said to the guide.

The guards cleared a path through the crowd. People crowded along the sides. Burly merchants, mothers with children, all chanting. *Jevaithi, Jevaithi.*

Jevaithi smiled and waved. She stopped to admire a young mother's baby, stroking the little head with hair soft as fur. A young man—the woman's older son?—stood, red-faced slaving over a vat of steaming oil. Whatever he sold, the smell made her mouth water.

"Rider Cornatan, I'd like to have some of what he's cooking."

"It's saltmeat," he hissed at her shoulder. "You can't eat that, Your Highness."

"Why not?" She breathed the delicious scent that rose from the pot. The young man blushed furiously. He was perhaps only a few years older than her. Did he see her feather?

"Yes, I will have some," Jevaithi said in a clear voice.

The man scrambled to ladle a spoonful of steaming meat into a bag. Jevaithi reached forward, but a Knight had already taken the bag.

"With the compliments of my family, Your Highness."

"No, I won't have that. I'm a decent person. Pay him, Rider

Cornatan."

He did. Unfortunately Jevaithi couldn't see the look on his face.

The Knight held the bag for her while she slipped the glove off her left hand to pick up a piece of meat.

"Do you want some?" she asked him.

His face radiated distaste. "Your Highness, you may want to be careful what you eat. This is the Outer City, and it's not as clean as—"

She put the meat in her mouth. It was very salty and crispy, but hot and spicy. The taste exploded on her tongue. The taste of freedom.

"I shall be just fine." Anything that was this salty couldn't possibly be contaminated anyway.

By the time the group had made their way across the chaos of the festival grounds, the bag was empty. She had eaten half of it, and offered the other half to children along the way. Those children now followed the parade, along with hundreds of other people. Some came up offering her presents. A young merchant boy ran up to her and gave her a shawl made of thin silk. It was a beautiful thing, and he insisted that she keep it and that he didn't want to be paid for it. If his mother, who wove the silk, heard that the queen was wearing her work, the light might return to her eyes.

Jevaithi found it hard to keep her composure. These people loved her more than she had loved them. These were her people, not the Knights.

They arrived at the eagle pens.

Hemmed in by a frame of temporary metal fencing stood at least fifty eagles, magnificent creatures with gleaming white feathered heads, bright yellow beaks and strong and tawny-coloured wings. The beasts fidgeted and flapped, no doubt sensing the tension and activity around them. Each eagle was being attended by its young Knight. Most of them were Apprentices, boys of between fourteen and seventeen years of age. As old as she was. What would it be like, to fly on the back of an eagle? Did girls ever do that? They should have female Knights. There were enough women in the city who were not fertile and lived as grumpy old maids. She should propose that, the first time she attended the Knight's Council. That would get those old men talking.

To the left of the pens was the official starting point, a square arena outlined by red paint in the snow.

Someone had made a viewing stand out of pieces of fencing. There were two benches, covered by bear skins and even a frame for a canopy, in case of snow.

This was where Rider Cornatan led her. Jevaithi felt embarrassed. Someone had made this just for her? She sat down, wrapping the furs around her legs. The Knights stood at attention. Rider Cornatan remained standing next to her.

A cheer went up around the pen. Eagles flapped and squawked, disturbed by the noise, which prompted their handlers to pull on reins while ducking out of the way of flapping wings.

"What are rules for the race?" she asked the Knight guide.

He bowed. "The contestants had a preliminary race the day before yesterday." She wished he would stand up straight and look at her. "The Knights you see here are the ones who came through that selection, the finest in the land. They fly in teams of two where they have to pass a message cylinder between them twelve times, and be the first team back here. If they drop the cylinder, they're out of the race. If they make an improper change, they're out as well. They're flying a distance of twenty miles. Part of it will be over ocean and dangerous terrain—"

A blast from a horn drowned out his words.

Something was happening in the pens. Each young Knight had untied his eagle and was leading his bird forward by the reins. Some birds walked stately, others found it necessary to snap and hiss at their neighbours. Silver coins glistened on the birds' harnesses. Bells tinkled on the reins. One Knight had painted gold spots on the bird's beak.

Jevaithi had been to the eyrie a few times, but she had never seen the birds so magnificently attired. Each Knight was dressed in a thick shorthair cloak and immaculate red tunic. They had keen eyes and proud faces, the sons of the city's nobles.

As they filed past, and lined up in the starting area, a young man amongst them drew Jevaithi's attention. He stood straight-backed and proud. His glossy black hair was tied in a plait. He wore no jewellery, unlike most other Apprentices, nothing that wasn't part of the uniform. His hands were red and rough from riding, his gaze was serious. He didn't wave at parents or wink at girls.

As she watched, a single strand of golden light snaked over his right leg.

She realised with a shock. *He's Imperfect.* How was that possible? All her life, she'd been told Imperfect children were killed after birth.

And there he was, looking at her, as if he knew . . . or felt . . . or saw what she hid, just like she saw what he was trying to hide.

The Knight next to her was still explaining the rules, but his words slid past her.

The Apprentice was about her age, teamed up with a boy taller and broader than him but much coarser in features, although this boy also stared at her, and at Rider Cornatan. Rider Cornatan even winked at him.

An older Knight blew a whistle. All the riders mounted their birds. Some put their foot in the stirrup and swung the other leg over. Some, like the Imperfect Apprentice, let their eagles crouch first. He definitely had only one leg, although it was cleverly concealed by a boot on the end of what she presumed was a wooden peg. Now that she was aware of it, she noticed the golden glow around his leg more clearly. Clever. Even his trouser leg stood up as if there was a proper lower limb inside. No one would notice. No one but her.

A second whistle sounded. Eagles poised, their wings spread. The crowd grew quiet. The Knights gripped their reins.

The Imperfect rider glanced at her. Jevaithi couldn't contain a smile. He met her eyes squarely. He had heavy eyebrows, high cheekbones and full lips. His skin was pale with a tinge of red excitement. One corner of his mouth curled up, leaving a dimple in his cheek.

Jevaithi slid her hand up to her throat, pulling the feather out from under her cloak, but at that moment, there was another blast of the horn and the Knights were off with a flurry of flapping wings.

"It will be a while before they return," Rider Cornatan said, while Jevaithi looked after the eagle silhouettes which were fast getting smaller. "We could meet some of the Senior Knights."

"Let them come here," she said. "I'll wait."

She'd wait however long was necessary to see that young man return.

Rider Cornatan raised his eyebrows.

"If I am to choose a Queen's Champion as you said, I better watch the riders."

Rider Cornatan seemed happy with that response. She guessed it made protecting her easier for him. He sat down next to her, and said in a low voice, "On the subject of the Queen's Champion, Your Highness, I shall point out to you which Apprentice has the highest points score."

"You already know that? Before the race has even finished? That's not how it should be done. I read the rules and it says the Queen or her representative can choose from all participants, as long as they completed the race and made all twelve changes. It is the tradition that the Champion is chosen from the first five, although my mother chose a different Apprentice on at least one occasion. The Queen's Champion is about fairness and skill."

He gave her a sharp glance, opened his mouth, but closed it again. "Yes, that it true, Your Highness. You read the books well."

"I thought I had better check the rules for what I'm supposed to be choosing." And it was not as if she had so much else to do.

She leaned back in her seat on mock-relaxed fashion. Her

heart was hammering in her chest. She'd been openly defying and needling him since she left her tower room. Would he punish her when they returned?

A wry smile played over Rider Cornatan's mouth, also not a pleasant expression. "Pardon me for taking liberties, Your Highness. I should have said I can give you some good suggestions."

Oh, indeed. "Go ahead, and give me the suggestions, then. I don't know any of these Apprentices by name."

So she listened to a string of middle-ranked Knights extolling the virtues of the young Apprentices who had just gone out to race. The name of the Imperfect boy was Isandor, and he was a native of the Outer City. Even the name made her shiver. She very much wanted to, but she didn't ask about him and the Knights volunteered little information. Her mother had always said, *If you want something that's not in your power to have, keep quiet about it until it is*. Several times, she found the question on her tongue, but one glance at Rider Cornatan stopped her.

She didn't want to bring the Apprentice in danger with her questioning, but she *had* to speak to him. No one, not even her mother, had mentioned that there were other Imperfects.

CHAPTER 16

ISANDOR HELD the reins tight and gazed at his destination over the bobbing head of the eagle. Even though he wore goggles and a face mask, his face was numb from the cold. There was no sun today, only a mass of dull white clouds. Darker clouds on the horizon promised more snow.

Isandor and Carro led a group of eagles which had detached from the main body of competitors about the halfway mark. One Apprentice had since dropped the cylinder in the frigid waters of the sea, disqualifying his team. Now they were on the home leg, the cylinder had passed from Isandor to Carro and back ten times. They still had two changes to make.

The other riders, led by Jono and Caman, were uncomfortably close. Carro wasn't flying well. He was using the reins too much to balance. He'd barely said anything since they got up this morning; he'd looked tired, but wouldn't answer questions about what he'd done last night.

Carro's eagle was fidgety and snappy, probably tired, too. What had Carro been doing? Yesterday was meant to have been a rest day.

They had to win, they just *had* to. The winners would be presented to the Queen, and her gaze still burned in Isandor's mind. *Those* eyes were true royal blue. Her smile was more beautiful than he had ever seen.

The second last exchange of the cylinder was due. A Knight on a lazily circling eagle patrolled the change point. Isandor steered his eagle into a circle and swung the cylinder. It flew through the air, catching the light. Carro caught it neatly. He grinned, although his face was hard with fatigue.

"Now, come on!" Isandor yelled and pulled the eagle out of the spin. "We've almost done it."

Jono and Caman were now circling the change point, only a few wingbeats behind, but Isandor could already see the festival grounds, and on the edge, the stands where the Queen was waiting.

Come on, come on, come on.

He saw her cheering—no not cheering, that was too undignified for a Queen—but clapping. He saw himself walking up to her to receive his medal. Queen's Champion.

No, he'd better keep his mind on the job. The Senior Knights always decided who would become Champion anyway, and they always chose a boy from the noble families.

Stop daydreaming. Do you know how much power one fifteen-year old girl has over an ages-old institute of men? Tandor's words came to haunt him.

The last change point. He brought his eagle into a tight spin so it circled Carro's.

Carro raised himself in the saddle. He was shivering, Isandor could see that even from his position. He lifted his arm and threw the cylinder. It flipped through the air, catching the light.

Short.

Isandor reached as far as he could, but his hand grasped thin air.

No.

For one horrible moment he stared at the twirling cylinder plummeting towards the gleaming ocean and the ice floes.

No.

Another moment and he had pulled the reins hard. The eagle screeched protest, but it pulled in its wings and dived. It went hurtling towards the ground. Isandor's stomach lurched. Freezing air cut into his face as the ground came up fast. His vision blurred from his watering eyes, but he focused on the tumbling cylinder.

Down, down, faster, faster.

He plummeted past the Knight who patrolled the change point. The man yelled out but Isandor couldn't make out the words.

He was not going to make it. *He was not going to make it.* The eagle couldn't dive fast enough.

Stop, stop, stop!

Golden light snaked out of the air. It wrapped around his hands, cocooned the eagle and caught the falling cylinder, freezing it in mid-air. Just a moment, and then Isandor had reached it and clasped his hand around the cold metal. A sharp pull of the reins brought the eagle soaring into the air again, its immense wings flapping. It gave a piercing cry.

Isandor stood in the saddle, balling his fist around the cylinder.

Yes, yes, yes!

"By the skylights, how did you do that, Isandor?" Carro shouted from his beast. His eyes were wide, pleading almost, scared. His lips were blue with cold and he shivered worse than ever. Isandor on the other hand, was hot and glowing from his victory.

Isandor smiled, but felt uneasy. Carro couldn't see icefire. But one day, Tandor said someone *would* see it.

"Never mind that, I've got it," he shouted at Carro, trying to sound careless. "Just don't fall off until we get there, all right?"

Carro returned a sharp look, and something flickered over

his face. Worry?

Isandor didn't like to think about it. He had to concentrate, or he would fall off himself, as shivers overtook him.

The eagle flew lower, spread its wings and stretched out its yellow feet. It landed in the snow with a thump. People were cheering, but he barely heard it. The truth hit him hard. He had just used icefire to win the race, not just bent it to hide his missing leg, but *used it* to his advantage. The old king used to do that, the old king, who had been the worst murderer the southern land had ever known.

In his mind, he heard Tandor's voice. *The Thillei blood is strong in you.*

No, he didn't want this. He wanted to be a good Knight.

The crowd had swelled since the start of the race. People were clapping and cheering. Isandor spotted his uncle in the crowd, waving wildly. He waved back, but felt sick. He had failed them all.

Isandor let himself slide from the saddle, clutching the cylinder against his chest. His heart was still going at a crazy rate. There was no escape. The bird handlers were hustling him and Carro out of the arena to the holding pens, where young boys threw steaming hunks of meat at the birds. He didn't dare look at his friend. Carro had all the rights to be angry. They'd lose all their points. Isandor didn't even want to contemplate what the Knights would do to him when he got back to the eyrie later today. Carro would never forgive him.

The crowd was yelling his name, and clapping and whistling and cheering. His eagle held its meat under a claw, but was hissing as the crowd, its wings spread. Isandor rubbed its head, burrowing his fingers in the feathers down to the hot skin. It was said that the animals were created through icefire and could feel its presence, and attached closely to those riders who could wield it. That's what he was: a dangerous freak.

"Apprentice Isandor?"

A Senior Knight was standing behind him.

"Sir." Isandor bowed, his heart thudding. This was it.

"Come with me," the man said.

Isandor followed him through the cheering crowd. He wished the people would shut up. There was nothing to cheer about. Hands were touching his arms, clapping his shoulder. Snatches of conversation drifted on the air.

". . . Did you see that?"

"What about the other one?"

". . . Queen is going to make him the Champion."

Oh yes, one of the boys would be the Queen's Champion, probably Jono, since he had the right family heritage. But first, his punishment, and the citizens of the Outer City loved that as much as they loved their bloodsports.

They stopped at the base of the stand. The guards moved aside, giving Isandor a view of the Queen's legs, wrapped in thick bear furs. He bowed, unable to face pity in her eyes. "Your Highness."

The furs moved aside. The feet in dainty boots descended the steps. Soft boots and a cloak of fur white as snow. He bowed more deeply.

"Do not be shy," the Queen said. "Look me in the eye, Champion."

Champion? His heart missed a beat. He blurted out, "That can't be right."

Her laugh sounded like the tinkling of crystal. "Oh, you Knights are priceless. Don't be so humble. You won fairly. I have the honour of choosing the Queen's Champion, and I have chosen."

Next to her, the reedy man Isandor recognised as Supreme Rider Cornatan sniffed, his lips pressed together in a thin line. Oh no, *he* didn't think Isandor deserved to be Queen's Champion.

"I don't deserve the honour." *I cheated.* He let his head droop again.

A soft glove entered his vision and pushed his chin up. A strand of golden light seeped over her arm and into his face. He exploded in warmth.

Isandor looked into those dark blue eyes, and found himself drowning in her gaze. Her face was pale, her lips full and marked with just a touch of red paint. Long eyelashes were dusted with silver. She blinked.

Isandor had to look away. His gaze slid down her soft, white-skinned neck to the elaborately-worked fastening of her cloak. She wore a crude strip of leather around her neck. The shaft of a gull's tail feather poked just above the neckline of the cloak.

Somewhere at the edge of his hearing, over the roaring of blood in his ears, she said, "You do deserve it, Isandor. *I* wish to declare you my champion. It is *my* title, and *I* choose whom I see fit."

The barbs in that remark weren't intended for him.

Again he heard Tandor's words. *How much power to you think a fifteen-year old girl has over an aged-old institute of men*?

At this very moment, she had all the power in the world over him.

A junior Knight approached him with a box that contained the medal and Isandor was forced to step back from the stand to make room for the man. The Queen's hand fell back from his cheek, severing the warmth between them. The Knight hung the medal around Isandor's neck, but Isandor had only eyes for the Queen, and how she kept her left hand in her pocket. He knew the signs. She didn't give him the medal herself, because she couldn't. She had only one hand.

Supreme Rider Cornatan came to stand next to her. "Your Highness, there are some jugglers who would be honoured if you could watch their act."

"Certainly," she said, still looking at Isandor.

She took Rider Cornatan's proffered arm and let him lead her away, but even while she disappeared amongst the Knight guards, she kept looking at Isandor. Her eyes were intense, and pleading.

Isandor stood there, numbed, barely aware that the Junior Knight was speaking to him. "As winner of the race you will also get the honour of making the first kill of the hunting season. That ceremony will be held this afternoon in this arena. Be here on time so we can instruct you."

Isandor swallowed away that embarrassing, glowing feeling and met the man's eyes, registering what he had said. "Don't worry. I used to work in a butchery. I know how to kill a Legless Lion."

"Be there on time," the Knight repeated.

He turned away, leaving Isandor was alone amongst the Senior Knights, some of whom congratulated him with stiff nods.

Someone said behind him, "Well I guess you don't need to have a drink with me anymore now you have all these new admirers."

It was Carro, with more bitterness on his face than Isandor had ever seen.

Should I warn him, should I not warn him, should I warn him?

Carro glared at Isandor who was receiving yet more congratulations from random patrons in the meltery. The man, someone Isandor must know from the butchery, clapped a meaty hand on his shoulder.

They had advanced barely a few steps into the main room. The door was still open, as more patrons followed, couldn't get it and then wondered what the hold-up was.

Carro jammed his hands in his pockets. He was tired.

Wan light slanted into the dimness, lighting up misty sections of heavy and smoke-tinged air.

The beefy man now left, towards the exit.

"Come on," Carro urged, pulling at Isandor's cloak. "You said we'd have a drink."

He dragged back a chair.

Seriously, if one more person was going to congratulate

Isandor, he was going to scream. What about him? Had he not won the race together with Isandor?

But if it had been up to me, we'd have been disqualified.

Carro slumped into the chair, clenching his jaws.

Isandor paid for two glasses of bloodwine from a passing waitress and sank down opposite him, plonking the glasses down. He leaned both his elbows on the table and sighed. His medal dangled from his chest, glittering in the smoky light.

"Oh, yeah, life as a champion is so hard," Carro said and knew he sounded petulant.

Isandor looked up, meeting his eyes squarely. It wasn't anger Carro saw in that blue gaze, but something else Carro couldn't place. It chilled him.

"Carro, I didn't ask for any of this. You can have this medal if it makes you feel any better."

A moment of regret passed between them. Carro knew he was acting like a jealous toddler, but he could not, he just could not . . .

"Carro, we are friends, right?" Isandor said.

"Yes."

Friends, as long as Carro didn't tell Rider Cornatan what Isandor was, as long as no one found out. Friends, as long as it was appropriate for a Learner Knight to associate with an Apprentice, and an Imperfect one at that. Yet, Carro had taken off his new badge, because he didn't want any talk in the dormitory about being favoured by the Senior Knights. He wanted to have *earned* his promotion.

"You are my friend. You can tell me what worries you," Isandor said.

"Nothing worries me."

Only that he had awoken late this morning, sweating and his bedding tangled around his legs, plagued by that nightmarish image: Korinne and her father, Rider Cornatan's advisor, at his father's doorstep.

We need to talk business with you.

As the maid let them in, Korinne gave him a sly look from under her curled eyelashes, and placed her hand on her swollen stomach.

Payment. They wanted payment for his few moments of stupidity, and he wasn't rich, and his father wasn't rich, neither of them *wanted* a child, and as soon as Korinne and her father were out the door, his father was going to kill him.

What were you thinking, stupid oaf of a son of mine!

Carro wiped sweat from his upper lip. What was he thinking indeed. It had been a setup from the beginning. She hadn't enjoyed it. He had, but he had known, even in his drunken stupor, that someone had ordered her to submit to him. Who was playing games with him?

And Isandor sat there looking at him with genuine worry in his eyes. Isandor, who had everything he wanted. His natural ability to fly well, his ability to make people listen, his innocence, and true innocent love. Oh no, Carro hadn't missed the look that passed between his friend and Jevaithi.

And that, he knew, was the root of it all.

You're jealous, Carro, simple as that.

Isandor slammed his glass down. He seemed to have taken to the drink just as badly as Carro had.

"You know," Carro said, swallowing discomfort. "You know I wish it was still last year?"

"Why?" Isandor asked, and then his face cleared. "Did she refuse you again?"

The truth was on Carro's tongue. *Get out before I can no longer hide you. It's the only way I can protect you.* He licked his lips.

The meltery door opened, letting in flash of wan light. People scrambled aside. Rider Cornatan had come in. The Supreme Rider looked around, spotted Carro and gestured.

Panic rising in him, Carro met his friend's eyes.

Rider Cornatan is after Imperfects. I don't know what he wants, but it scares me.

Someone is trying to buy me, and I don't know how long I can resist.

Treasure your virginity for as long as you can. Sex hurts and corrupts.

But he said none of those words. "Sorry, have to go."

"Me, too." Isandor rose from the table. His face looked drawn.

He faced Carro wordlessly, nodded stiffly as if greeting another Knight and left. By the skylights, was that what their friendship had become?

Carro drank the last of the hot liquid and set his empty cup on the table, clinging onto its lingering warmth. As he rose and crossed the meltery's room, his knees turned weak with fear. It occurred to him that instead of his father, he now bowed to Rider Cornatan, who treated him far better, on the surface at least. But why? What did Rider Cornatan expect in return?

Carro met his leader in the middle of the meltery room.

"Good, boy." Rider Cornatan put his hand on Carro's shoulder and squeezed it briefly.

Together, they walked to the far end of the meltery's room, where there were private alcoves against the perimeter wall.

As they settled in an alcove, Carro hardly dared meet the Supreme Rider's eyes.

People on the main floor of the meltery pretended to ignore them, but Carro didn't miss the furtive looks out of corners of eyes. Jono had been sitting at a table somewhere, raising his eyebrows as Carro walked past in the company of Rider Cornatan resplendent in his full uniform and riding harness.

"The young boy you brought yesterday woke up this morning," Rider Cornatan said.

"Oh?" Carro didn't know what else to say, but obviously there would be something of great meaning following this statement otherwise Rider Cornatan wouldn't have insisted on seeing him here in this very public meltery.

"He said that when you came out of the Brotherhood building a blue man attacked you and the other Knights."

"I can't tell. I didn't see anyone. I used the staff as you said

I should, but I saw nothing. I just grabbed the boy as soon as I could."

"Yes, you did well. But, according to you, the two Knights were killed by something that snapped their necks. Something you didn't—or couldn't—see."

The voice quivered with meaning. Intense blue eyes met his.

"You mean a servitor?" His voice was barely more than a whisper.

A chill crept over his back. He should have realised it earlier.

"That's what I mean, indeed," Rider Cornatan said. "The Brothers have confirmed that they have the Knights' bodies, but they're hesitant to cooperate with our investigation. I think they know more than they're willing to say."

"But how can servitors exist?" His books had spoken of the slave-servants of the old king. They had no will, and did everything their master wanted. They could not be killed except when their master died.

"There is only one way: there has to be a Thilleian in the Outer City. One who is strong and has the capability to make servitors."

Isandor. Carro's heart jumped.

Isandor runs through the street, holding out a box . *For you, Carro. It's your birthday.*

Carro stares. He doesn't have birthdays. His father made him work this morning. In the warehouse. No heating. No one said anything about a birthday at breakfast.

He takes the box. Opens it up and finds a book inside, a fat volume with a leather cover and thick, yellow pages. Doesn't know what to say. He's turning eleven today. *You shouldn't do that, Isandor.*

Why not? You're my friend.

Embarrassed, by someone who has so much less than he.

"But anyone . . ." Carro swallowed, hoping Rider Cornatan wouldn't notice his lapses in attention. ". . . any sorcerer who can make a servitor is very powerful." He didn't think Isandor could do that, but what did he know, maybe he could.

"We must find this person." Rider Cornatan's eyes fixed his with uncomfortable intensity.

Carro looked down at his empty cup, bloodwine churning in his stomach. Once it came out he had been friends with Isandor, what would that mean for him? Back to his father's warehouse? Death by accountancy?

Not that. Never that. He'd kill himself first.

"Did you enjoy last night?" Rider Cornatan's voice sounded far off.

Heat crept into Carro's cheeks. "Yes, I did."

"There were some elite young Knights invited, a special team of mine. Did you have a chance to have a word with Farey?"

The olive-skinned Knight who had been staring at him in a most embarrassing way.

"I did. We didn't say much—"

"Farey never says much. I've asked him to keep an eye on you. He leads a group of elite hunters. They scout out rogues that flee the city and spies to our lands. I was thinking that with your flying skills, you could possibly join them."

"*Hunters*?" They were special units of highly-trained men. Jobs that attracted whispers and rumours.

Rider Cornatan drank. He seemed to be enjoying himself. "I think you could make a valuable contribution to our search teams. I wouldn't rule out rapid promotions. You, boy, are destined to do well."

Carro didn't think so.

"No, don't look like that. I think it's time you showed leadership. It's one thing to tag along with a group of others, but you need to learn how to give commands."

He? Give commands?

"I notice you're not wearing your Learner's badge."

"I . . ." Carro stammered. "Some of the Apprentices will tease me. They're already saying that I have no right to be here."

"Ha—and you let them say that to your face?"

Carro shrugged. What else could he do? "Apprentices are not allowed to fight. I've already been punished too much for that. Fighting will just make the mocking worse."

Rider Cornatan put a hand under his chin and forced him to look up. "Boy, take it from me: men never mock those they fear. I am giving you the means to hold power over your peers. You are a Learner. You outrank them. They should fear you."

"But . . ."

"If they don't fear you, punish them for their insolence, and punish them hard. I can assure you: if you do it well, you only need to do so once."

"I'm not sure I—"

"Yes, you could do it. Tell me, you don't think you *deserve* being bullied by these cowardly boys?"

Bullied? How about raped? "No, but—"

"There you go. You don't deserve it. Those boys are insulting you. You are worth more than ten of them. You know that, Carro. Promise me you will do the worst you can imagine to anyone who defies your orders."

Carro nodded, his cheeks glowing.

The man was the opposite of his father, giving him compliments where he deserved none.

"You're very quiet today, boy."

"I'm . . . a bit tired."

Rider Cornatan laughed. "You would be. By the way, Korinne was most insistent in asking if you were available to come again tonight."

Korinne, asking for him. Offering herself to him without being asked. Did she like him after all?

He nodded again. “I will be there.”

“Very well, boy. That’s the sort of thing I like to hear. Lift your chin and make sure *none* of your peers tell you what to do. You obey your superiors, and no one else. You understand that?”

“Yes, Sir.”

Rider Cornatan hesitated, as if he wanted to say something else, but thought the better of it.

CHAPTER 17

TANDOR KNELT in the snow in the shade of the alley, tugged off his glove with his pincer claw and put his hand flat on the hard, icy ground. In the feeble blue light of not-quite dawn, the area around his fingers glowed with a few specks of gold before winking out.

Yes, Ruko had come this way. The trail was half a day old at least, but Ruko had been here.

There were footsteps behind him, and voices of women. Tandor rose quickly and pressed himself to the wall on one side of the alley. The women walked past, casting Tandor strange looks that said, *what is he doing here at this time of the day?*

Tandor waited until the women had disappeared from view and continued down the alley, kneeling and touching the snow. With each step he walked, and each time he looked up at the sky and saw it had lightened, his despair grew.

Ruko was in trouble somewhere, or he would have returned long ago. It meant that someone out here could see Ruko and had a means of injuring him.

To add to that, picking up Ruko's response became ever harder with the increasing strength of icefire.

Golden strands now frequently crackled through the air, escaped from the matrix that normally held its power.

The breeze carried the sounds of cheers, shouting and music. At the festival grounds, the common folk were watching the races. As yet, they were blissfully ignorant of the increased level of icefire, but that wouldn't remain so. The Heart was coming into its full power soon, and he had recruited not a single servitor to help him channel that raw energy. There were limits even to how much icefire the citizens of the City of Glass could stand without becoming ill.

Ruko!

A flutter of icefire responded, the tiniest of pulses.

Ruko?

The wind sighed through the alley, an exhaled breath of pain. The connection was weak. Ruko was injured and he was close.

The sound of children's voices drifted from the other side of a high wall at his back. Tandor couldn't make out the words, but the conversation held an edge of tense-ness, the voices curious, more than just children at play.

He crept along the wall until he came to a gate, which judging by the amount of snow piled up on the ground, was always open. It led into a walled courtyard surrounded on three sides by a building with a columned facade. Made of mountain marble, the building was ancient, because it was a long time since any marble had been brought from the border with Arania. It was also a long time since anyone had used the inscriptions which graced the building's facade. Tandor remembered learning the formulae off by heart. How to calculate the power of icefire at different points from its source. How to predict how many people could handle a certain amount of icefire, how to calculate how far the temperature would drop with increased power. How to convert icefire into heat and light. How had he hated those lessons with his mother.

A door opened in the rightmost wing of the building. A bearded man dressed in black came out, leading a group of children across the courtyard. Some were crying, some held the man's hand.

The Brotherhood of the Light. Named not after the sun, but after the power of the Heart.

On the far side of the courtyard, two men came into view, heaving a large object between them that looked suspiciously like a body covered with cloth. There was another one already on the ground.

A little boy came out of a door onto the veranda, but was ordered back inside with a sharp command. Both brothers in black stood silent, balling their hands against their chests. One of the men went inside, but the other hesitated and glanced at a heap of snow against the courtyard's wall. Icefire leapt from the air, a single strand which forked like lightning. It shattered into golden diamonds, which rained down onto the snow mound.

The young man didn't react to the light spectacle, but Tandor had no illusion that he could see it in some form. The Brothers of the Light had been the old king's spiritual order. Further back in history, the order had served as a handy depository for idle noble sons, including princes with minor claims on the throne. As such, many of its current members would have traces of Thillei blood. This Brother's Thilleian blood had located Ruko.

Bless the boy. Weak and injured as he obviously was, he'd gone and buried himself under the snow. Now all Tandor needed to do was wait until the courtyard was empty.

Loriane shut the door to the inner chamber of the limpet behind her. She crossed to the table and set down her tray.

Myra sat cross-legged on the mat in front of the stove. The fierce glow from the fire gilded the folds of the girl's thin night gown.

She didn't look up or open her eyes. Her hands on her knees, she sat there, counting and breathing slowly.

Loriane sat down and watched for a while. Maybe there was hope yet to prepare her for the birth. Her spot-bleeding had stopped overnight. Loriane might have a few days to teach the girl some relaxation routines.

She felt guilty about not being able to help at the festival anymore, but if she was honest with herself, Loriane didn't mind losing out on treating drunken louts.

Myra opened her eyes. "Was that better?"

"Much better," Loriane said. "Now if you can take that off, I can examine you, before Tandor comes back."

"Did he say where he was going?"

"No." If she sounded snippy, she meant it. "Does he think I have nothing to do but pamper him?"

"Tandor doesn't pamper—"

"What do you know?" Again, too angry. Loriane looked away, ashamed to have let herself go.

"I'm worried about him," she said to the room in general. "He comes here, he does whatever he wants. He makes promises. He disappears."

"Does he keep his promises?" A lot of anxiety hung in the girl's question. What had Tandor promised her?

"Usually." Loriane heaved a sigh. "Come, lie down here. After that we better make sure the washing is dry and we have all those oils poured in jars."

"I didn't think being a midwife was so much work," Myra said.

Myra slipped off her nightgown and lay down on the couch as Loriane indicated.

"Oh, preparing the medicines is just a small part of the job. You don't even know about the times I get called out in the middle of the night and have to stay all of the next day as well."

She grabbed her basket of supplies and kneeled awkwardly. Her own belly was getting in the way of this job. She rummaged through and then realised the bottle of disinfecting oil was empty. By the skylights. She had more, but she had left it in the tent at the festival grounds.

"All right, this will have to wait."

The girl stared at the basket, her eyes wide. "What were you going to do?"

Clearly, no one had ever examined her. By the skylights, had anyone looked after this girl? Did the people in Bordertown just let women have their children—and die giving birth—like beasts?

Instead, she probed the girl's belly. The womb tensed up under her touch, hard as rock.

Myra gasped. "It hurts, it hurts."

"Yes," Loriane said and withdrew. "You know what I think? I think your pains have already started."

"I've . . . I've been having cramps all day."

"That will be it."

"Is that all?" She sounded too relieved.

"No, it's not." Loriane rose. She really needed that disinfectant so she could examine Myra inside.

Myra pushed herself up. She was trembling when she reached for her gown and hesitated putting it on. "Or do you want me to leave it off?"

"We're not getting to that stage so soon. That will be a while yet. You better do some more of those exercises I gave you."

Myra nodded and wriggled back onto the mat, crossed her legs and went on with the breathing exercises.

Loriane studied the girl's shape. The weight in her belly restricted movement of her spine, which she held at an uncomfortable curve. Her shoulders and hips were narrow, with not a scrap of meat on them. Loriane hoped, for all she was worth, that the father of the child was not too broad or big-boned. Myra was heavy for her thin frame, and a gentle start to the process like this often meant a protracted and painful birth, especially in young girls.

"Loriane, how many children have you had?"

"This is my tenth."

"Ten?" A stunned silence. "I don't know any woman at Bordertown who has had that many."

And lived to tell the tale, Loriane added in her mind.

"When is your child going to be born?"

"Soon." *Should have been a few days ago.*

Another short silence.

"I've heard that women in the City of Glass . . . sell their children."

"Noblemen pay fertile women to have children for them if their wives aren't fertile. Many of them are barren."

"Why?"

"They say it's to do with icefire. It may not kill us as it does with the Chevakians, but many of us can't have children."

"Yes, icefire so strong here. I've never seen it like this before."

Loriane studied the girl's face. She had forgotten that one of the attributes of being Imperfect was the ability to see icefire. Even when Isandor was still at home, he had avoided this very subject. She couldn't see icefire, not a single scrap of it.

"Someone paid for your child?" Myra asked.

Loriane nodded. She thought again of Yanko, and how much she doubted the child was his, and how she had no idea whose it could be. She hadn't been with a man except Tandor a tennight earlier, but just last night she had seen again how he lacked the necessary equipment to do the job.

She glanced at Myra. Was there a way Tandor could have gotten both Myra and herself pregnant, even though he was no longer a man?

Yeah, that was wishful thinking. *Admit it, woman, this man has got you by the scruff of the neck.*

Loriane rose, rubbing her belly.

Now if Tandor would come back, she could send him out to get some disinfectant from the tent at the festival grounds.

Unless . . . She eyed his traveller's chest, which he had left open next to the bed. His thermals lay over the chest's contents. Whenever he visited, she usually gave him a few things from her practice, to use on his travels. He might still have some disinfectant.

She lifted the woollen underwear from the chest. There were clothes, neatly folded, and stacks of old books. A basket made of tough leaves unknown to the southern land contained an assortment of stoppered flasks, jars and boxes with foreign labels. She rummaged through the selection, recognising—she thought—ointment for cuts, syrup for upset stomachs and pills, but the latter were labelled in a language she didn't recognise. By the skylights, he even had face paint and perfumes. Did men use such things in the northern lands? There was a large jar with a wooden stopper that she had seen many times before, and the sight of it, with Myra watching, made her blush. Tandor brought this jar to her bed at night. It contained a gel which, when rubbed across certain sensitive parts, made those parts much more sensitive and made certain activities more pleasurable. She tucked that one away quickly. But: no disinfectant.

Tucked in the deep corner of the chest stood a jar made of clear glass with an elaborately-carved stopper. Clearly an item from an apothecary. The jar was heavy. The glass felt *warm* under her hands. There was pink fluid inside in which floated a fist-sized sac of soft flesh. A bundle of tube-like veins sprouted from the top, waving gently in the eerie bath.

The sac *pulsed* of its own accord.

Loriane stared at it, feeling sick. The pink sac was a human heart.

What had Tandor said again? That Ruko was restored in return for something he had traded? His heart? The old king used to do things like that.

Myra gave a soft gasp. "That *hurt*."

Her words broke Loriane from her transfixed state. With trembling hands, she put the jar with its hideous content down and dropped the woollen tunics back into the chest.

Myra had stopped her exercises. Her eyes were wide. "It hurts, Loriane."

"Yes, it probably does. Breathe as I've shown you. Nothing more I can do. It's all up to you."

Where was Tandor? What was he doing with that horrible thing in his luggage?

It took a long time before the courtyard emptied and Tandor dared enter it. When the last boys and the Brothers had finally gone, he ran across and fell to his knees at the snow mound. Faint golden strands of icefire showed the shape of a man underneath the snow. Tandor dug into the biting cold, scrabbling chunks of iced-up snow off Ruko's body. He lay curled up like an oversized sleeping child, and didn't move when Tandor uncovered him. He was no longer blue, but a sickly grey.

Ruko, Ruko!

The response was weak, a mere tugging at the edge of his senses. Tandor breathed deeply, stifling panic that crept up from his gut.

What, *just what*, had happened to him? Ruko was supposed to be invincible. A servitor. You couldn't kill them unless you killed the maker. And *not dead* was just about the only thing that could be said in favour of Ruko's condition.

Tandor pushed the snow off Ruko's legs and tried to drag him to his feet. The boy was too heavy for Tandor to lift, so he picked him up under the arms and dragged him across the courtyard.

Tandor stopped at the gate. Where to now? He could hardly walk back to Loriane's house like this, dragging a body that most people couldn't even see.

There was a narrow passageway between two houses opposite the gate. Tandor waited for the alley to empty of women returning from the markets before he dragged Ruko across. The recently-fallen snow had been trampled into a hard cover, on which industrious citizens had spread layers of sand. As Tandor dragged Ruko across, the heels of Ruko's boots scratched into the sand cover, leaving tracks of pristine white.

There was no time to grab sand from the bucket that stood next to the door of a nearby house—someone was coming.

Tandor cursed, sending a burst of icefire to spread the sand and cursed again when icefire lifted all the sand and blew it against the outer wall of the compound instead. Icefire was so strong already, and he was no closer to getting into the palace.

He dragged Ruko further into the alley, sending another burst of icefire to obscure the alley's entrance from curious eyes. Passersby would see something that repulsed them, and made them look away. A drunk man, a dead animal, a pile of rubbish, two lovers engaged in an indecent act.

Tandor proceeded further into the alley, past a side entrance to a house, past steps and a rubbish bin to where the passage ended. He tipped the snow off the bin's lid and fashioned it into a wall, grabbing icefire from the air to melt the snow enough so it would stick together. The structure didn't reach very high, but it hid Ruko from view in case someone could see past the illusion at the alley's entrance.

By the skylights, what now?

He eyed the wall at his back. It was ages since he'd sneaked around the streets of Tiverius as a young boy getting away from his mother, scaling walls and climbing onto roofs. It wasn't just that he'd become unaccustomed to moving around in such a way—he was a prince by the skylights—but the roofs of the City of Glass were too steep, ice-covered and utterly unfamiliar. *A man's survival instinct is honed and primed in his youthful scampering away from obnoxious adults* his weapons tutor used to say. And Tandor's experience was all in Tiverius. In Chevakia.

He was a blasted Chevakian.

He sat on the cold ground, his back against the wall, sheltering behind the rubbish bin. There was no way he could move until

Ruko recovered, but he didn't have the time. Someone was on the loose who not only knew he had a servitor, but who knew how to deal with servitors as well.

He loosened the clasp of Ruko's cloak and wriggled one of the boy's hands from underneath.

Tell me what you know.

Ruko's hand lay grey and pale in his live one. At first, Tandor didn't see anything, but when he grabbed strands of icefire and poured them into Ruko's prone form, images came to his mind.

The courtyard, the building of the Brotherhood shrouded in darkness. An unclear fuzz as Ruko walked through the wall. The boys' dormitory. There was someone walking around inside: three silhouettes escaping into the corridor. Beds against both walls, one of them empty but still warm. The three figures had taken the imperfect boy.

Blurry outlines as Ruko walked back through the wall, just as the three figures ran across the courtyard. One of them carried the Imperfect boy rolled in a blanket.

Two or three steps, and Ruko had grabbed the first Knight. Snapped his neck like an icicle, then the other one. But the third one, a slight man younger than the others, held a metal rod in his hands and waved it in the air indiscriminately. The rod pulled and tore at the very fabric of Ruko's being. Searing pain, blinding light. As the image faded, and Ruko slumped in the snow, the third Knight called out to the Imperfect boy, who scrambled from underneath the corpse of the Knight who had carried him.

Tandor ripped himself from Ruko's memories. The horrid image tore at him with the realisation of what the young man held. A *sink*. The third Knight, the inexperienced young man, was of pure Pirosian blood. No one could harm him, and while he held the sink, it attracted icefire. *Someone* had read the king's notes on the properties of icefire. And were using them against him.

What now. *What now?* The only servitor he had lay incapacitated at his feet. The Heart was beating and someone in the palace had started silly experiments with icefire.

He needed servitors. Isandor, the boy, Myra, or . . . did he dare hope that he could get the only other free Imperfect? Not without Ruko.

Ruko, I need you to recover.

He grabbed as many strands of icefire as he could and poured them into Ruko's prone form. The golden light resisted him. Making a servitor was easier than healing one. When the flesh was live and fresh, it would meld with icefire under the hands of a skilled worker. When he took Ruko's heart, it had fallen into his hands freely. As long as it beat, Ruko would live. But Ruko was his own entity, linked with the world through the heart in its jar in Tandor's travel chest. The flesh of his body had become old and scarred and resisted icefire from any other sources than itself.

Now that so much had been siphoned off by the sink, Ruko needed to absorb more icefire to recover. And his very skin was resisting it.

There was only one way.

Tandor felt at his belt for his dagger.

Ruko barely flinched when Tandor drew a sharp cut across the skin of his lower arm. He stuck the dagger into the flesh and lifted up a flap of skin. The dark blue muscle tissue underneath rimed with frost. A trickle of blood oozed out of the wound and froze on his fingers, a light blue coating of crystals. He dug the tips of the dagger amongst tissue, hitting bone. Bits of nerve and gristle slid under his fingers. All blue and lifeless. Was there any hope?

He made another cut, this time in Ruko's neck. After peeling away the skin, he found the jugular vein, pulsing faintly, a dirty brown-orange in colour where it should be gold and fat with icefire.

Tandor reached out with his claw hand. Icefire crackled through the air and sprang from his arm to Ruko's vein. It glowed bright yellow before the colour seeped into Ruko's body.

More, more. Icefire flowed down his arm. Ruko's battered body drank it in like a sponge. Tandor fed him as much as he could gather. Ruko stirred, a muscle twitched, but his eyes remained closed. Tandor let go of the icefire he was still holding. Its pull had become too strong for him.

Tandor breathed relief, tears pricking in the corners of his eyes. He couldn't restrain himself and bent over the boy in a hug. Intense cold crept through him. Frost rimed his cloak where Ruko touched it. Ruko's icefire still felt weak, but at least Tandor could feel it now.

So much of his plan hinged on Ruko.

Tandor sat with his back against the wall, holding Ruko's hand.

From his position in the alley, he could see a narrow strip of the street outside the Brotherhood compound.

A sled pulled by a bear came past. A Knight sat at the driver's bench, and a few more in the back, probably here to pick up the bodies.

Not much later three Knights walked back through the street. They were all young, with Apprentice badges on their collars. Tandor didn't move, counting on his disguises to keep him from sight. The fourth Knight was a Learner, and he looked straight down the alley in spite of the guards Tandor has put in place. Tandor didn't doubt for a moment: this Knight had seen him. This young man was a purest-blood Pirosian, who could not be fooled by icefire tricks. He would have been the one carrying the sink.

Tandor pressed himself hard against the wall, not daring to move. The young Knight was quite tall and broad for his age, with a determined face and a head full of soft black curls. He hesitated, but walked on.

Heart thudding, Tandor ran to the corner of the alley and looked into the street. The Apprentice Knights had stopped at the gate to the Brotherhood compound. The Learner was pointing into the yard. But Tandor didn't doubt that the young man would be back.

He needed to draw attention away from Ruko and the best way to do that was to give the Knights a more urgent problem to deal with.

Tandor opened the lid to the rubbish bin. Wrinkling his nose in disgust, he lifted up a slab of frozen fish bones and draped it half on top of Ruko. There. Now it looked like a snow fox had been at the bin.

The Knights still stood at the gates to the Brotherhood compound. One of the Brothers was with them, black amongst grey and red. They were in heavy discussion, gesturing and pointing.

Tandor turned into the street and walked away from the Knights. He disliked turning his back on them and it cost him all effort in the world not to run. But dignified citizens who had just come out of their house and were on the way to the markets did not run.

As he reached the corner, Tandor glanced over his shoulder.

The young Knight with the sink also looked up. Their eyes met. Tandor froze. A strand of icefire crackled from him to the shining staff on the Knight's belt, accompanied by a sharp jolt of pain in Tandor's chest.

Tandor gasped.

The man yelled, "There!"

Still clutching his chest, Tandor ran.

CHAPTER 18

CARRO STOPPED, panting, in the street. The Apprentices of his patrol came to a halt behind him.

"Where did he go?" Inran asked.

They had halted at the intersection of two streets. Patrons spilled out of the meltery on the corner, talking and laughing in groups. To the left the street led to the markets, but more people obscured a clear view. Ahead a troupe of jugglers was performing an act. To the right was another meltery which was so popular that people queued up to get in.

Some Junior Knights were in the queue, raising eyebrows at Carro, like they wanted to ask why he was working while everyone ought to be enjoying themselves, or why he seemed to be leading this group of Apprentices while he was only a Learner, and a very young one at that.

Well, some of us have to do the work. And he thought of the Knights he had met last night, the ones who had died on duty, and the ones who held their parties in Rider Cornatan's bathroom. None of them mingled with the drunken crowds.

"Have you seen a man running past?" he asked the Knight.

"Well, if you mean seen a man run after the girls, I've seen plenty." The Knight laughed.

His breath smelled of bloodwine, and he wasn't pronouncing his words properly. "Hey, boys, forget the work and join us."

Carro turned away, not trusting himself to shut up. He wanted to berate the Knight, but he was an Initiate, higher in rank than a Learner, and he didn't want to obtain the label arrogant upstart, because ultimately, the punishment that would earn him would not be worth it. That's what Rider Cornatan had said: punish the ones of lower rank, obey the ones of higher rank. Even, if they were drunk.

So he gave a half-hearted salute and led his group towards the markets, past the jugglers. Spectators blocked the way. Carro told Inran to clear the path. People glanced over their shoulders and frowned at them, at him, an Outer City boy so obviously obeying the other side. Yes, the Outer City loved the Knights, but only as long as they stayed out of Outer City affairs.

"We're not going to find him in this crowd," Jono complained at his side. "Why don't we go back to the festival grounds? The ritual killing must be about to start."

"Because that is not our job," Carro said. "We need to find this man." The staff at his side was only just warming up after that jolt of icefire that had gone into it, but he could still feel the cold burning through his trouser leg.

"He's gone," Caman said, not meeting Carro's eyes.

"Then we will start a search of all the streets surrounding the markets." Carro clenched his teeth.

Jono scowled.

Punish them, Rider Cornatan said, and Carro had threatened extra duties, but both boys still challenged him. Both Jono and Caman were taller than Carro. His former bullies. Rider Cornatan must have known that when he selected these Apprentices for the job. Maybe because Carro had mentioned Jono.

Punish them hard and you only need to punish them once. And clearly, Carro failed at the punishing department.

"Move now. Markets first. Quick, get on with it."

Carro waited until the other boys had gone first. When he walked past, Jono's eyes flashed a challenge.

Isandor hurried through the streets, every step putting more distance between himself and the Senior Knights at the festival grounds, and Rider Cornatan in the meltery.

Everything was wrong, even Carro seemed to sense that. Carro knew he'd used icefire to stop the cylinder falling, even though he hadn't seen it. His friend's voice still echoed in his mind. *How did you do that?*

He could still see the expression in Carro's eyes when the Queen had declared him Champion, a look that frightened him.

Carro frightened him.

A change had come over his friend since his inexplicable promotion. He was harsher, and to be frank Isandor didn't think the promotion was because of something Carro had done. Someone was advancing him for a reason. In his limited experience, those types of reasons were rarely good. Carro had been evasive at the meltery, as if he held some sort of secret, and what secret would that be other than that he knew Isandor had used icefire?

Maybe Carro was advanced under the condition that he spilled all he knew about the Outer City, and its inhabitants, about Isandor, about the Brotherhood and the old books they had.

There was only one option. Tandor was right: he had been born like this and couldn't undo abilities the Knights considered illegal. But rather than try to hide it better as Tandor suggested, he had to get out of here. Beyond the edges of the southern land there was a whole world he had never seen. Chevakia, Arania, a world without icefire, where no one would see what he could do, where no one even knew that using icefire was illegal, because there was no icefire.

He would run, before the senior Knights heard about his imperfection.

But he must bring food, and his own clothes. Beyond the border, a Knight's uniform would no longer be a disguise, or a reason for respect.

He opened the door to his mother's house, and stepped into the warmth of the hall between the outer and inner shell. The sound of voices floated through the door. His mother would be seeing some sort of customer, maybe that stupid Yanko, and he preferred to have as little to do with that business as possible. He was sick of defending his mother's reputation. No, she wasn't a whore, but while she carried Yanko's child, Yanko was entitled to see her as often as he liked. So she was a whore, of a kind. He didn't understand how she could easily give away children of her own blood. The whole business made him feel queasy.

The stand in the short entranceway held his cloak, but all this other clothing was next to his old bed on the sleeping shelf inside the main room. How to get up there without attracting too many questions? *Where are you going? What are you doing with that bag?* He could already hear his mother's voice.

There was a noise behind him.

A figure entered the limpet's front door and a burst of icefire hissed through the air.

Isandor didn't think. He dropped his cloak, raised his arm, sending a bolt to meet it. The strands clashed in mid-air, exploding into a rain of golden diamonds.

"So, you have *learned* something," a languid voice said.

Tandor.

"What are you doing here?" Isandor breathed quickly. Tandor had actually *attacked* him with icefire. "Are you crazy?"

"No," Tandor said. "But I'm getting impatient with your stupidity."

He stepped into the entrance hall, letting the door fall shut behind him. His complete hand moved to his waist and grasped the hilt of his dagger.

Isandor backed away, but there was nowhere to go. Tandor blocked the only way to the outside door. Worse, Isandor only wore the bare minimum of arms required for proper uniform rules. No crossbow, no sword.

"What do you want from me?"

"Same thing as before. Your help."

"And you'll get that from me when I'm dead?"

"Not dead. I wouldn't kill you. You know that. When you help me, I will give you unprecedented powers. You will not know pain, or death. You will never know hunger or cold. You will have two healthy legs."

The hand that held the dagger was covered in blue-tinged rime. Icefire crackled over the delicate crystals.

"I don't want any powers. Leave me alone."

"The Knights will find you out what you are, and you know what they will do to you." Tandor's voice was low and mocking. "There is nowhere to run for you except to me."

"You're crazy."

"Not crazy, I'm right. I'm finally righting all that has gone wrong for our land. No Imperfect should be murdered for his ability. No children should be left on the ice floes. I intend to put things right. I don't care what you think of me. I need you. You will come." Tandor's bloodshot eyes stared like a madman's. "I'm out of patience and out of time."

A net of icefire flowed from the metal of his pincer hand.

Isandor threw up an instinctive defence. Strands of icefire clashed in mid-air. Shatters exploded through the hall.

Isandor groped for the door handle behind his back. Tandor's net hovered closer. Isandor strained to hold it off, but his golden stream was weakening.

Tandor laughed. "Out of ideas, boy?"

The door to the central room opened. "Oh, I thought I heard

you, Tandor—"

Isandor stumbled back, into the heat of the room. The net of icefire melted away.

"Isandor?" she gasped. "When did you come in? Oh my boy, congratulations. The Queen's Champion."

Isandor hugged her, noticing over her shoulder how Tandor slipped the dagger back into his belt and smiled. Was he his mother's lover? By the skylights, no. She had to be more intelligent than that.

He was shocked how tired his mother looked, and how pregnant. He had never before realised she was quite so old and small and *fragile*.

"I . . . thought I'd come to see how you are." By the skylights, how could he get all his things and leave the city now?

She stroked his hair. "I'm sorry, but your bed is occupied."

"It doesn't matter. You know I can't stay. I have to get back to the Knights. I just needed to get . . ."

No, he couldn't say that, and he couldn't flee either. Tandor wasn't after him in particular, but was after Imperfects, and Isandor knew one other Imperfect. He must warn her. And he couldn't leave his mother to deal with this twisted madman alone either.

"I was . . . I was just going. I need to be at the hunt ritual." His courage sank. He had fully expected not to attend. He'd watched his uncle kill an animal often enough to know that he didn't want to do it.

"Oh yes, of course." She smiled. "I'm proud of you, my Champion."

Tandor still glared.

"Will I see you at the arena?" Isandor took another step towards the door, and then another one. Tandor watched him, but didn't move. *He didn't dare.* So Tandor cared about his mother.

"Maybe." His mother's gaze met Tandor's. "I was waiting for you to come back. You could give me a hand. I need to someone to go to the tent in the festival grounds to get . . ."

Isandor ran.

CHAPTER 19

THE DOOR CLANGED and Isandor was gone, leaving behind a tense silence.

"Champion?" Tandor asked.

"Yes, Isandor was made the Queen's Champion. Didn't you hear that?"

"The Queen's Champion." Wasn't that one of those silly titles?

Her grey eyes searched his face. "You could at least pretend to be proud for me. He flew very well."

"He shouldn't be with the Knights at all."

"Tandor, we've had that argument already. You can't change the boy's choices. I don't understand why you're always so nasty about him. I'm sure he would have liked knowing that you wanted him to survive."

Tandor bit his tongue. Giving her answers she wanted would only lose him valuable time.

"Loriane—"

"No, listen, I need your help."

"Loriane," Tandor protested. With all his being, he wanted to go after Isandor, but with all these people in the streets, there was no way he could do what he wanted. He searched Loriane's face for signs of what she had understood of their confrontation. As Pirosian, he knew she didn't see icefire, but she had to suspect something. She had seen him facing Isandor. By the skylights, since when had the boy become so strong? He had never received training.

And why had Ruko not turned up yet? He should have recovered by now.

"I need you to run up to the tent at the festival ground and get a few things. It really can't wait, Tandor. Myra's pains have started."

Tandor started to protest, "I can't go out there. The Knights—"

"Then can you look after her while I'm gone?"

"What—me?" By the skylights, no.

"I don't see anyone behind you."

"But Loriane—"

"Just sit here with her and give her water if she wants. Rub her back if you feel like being useful." She yanked her cloak from the hook on the wall.

"But what if the child—"

"It won't," Loriane said, her eyes intense. "Trust me. This is going to take a very long time. I'll be back soon."

Soon? Tandor took in a sharp breath. The dagger at his waist burned against his leg, a freezing burn from where Isandor's icefire had hit it.

"Please, Tandor. All I want for you is to sit with her so she's not alone."

Panic welled up in him. Did she know about his past experience? Loriane's eyes were pleading. "Please, Tandor, be my hero. I don't know who else to ask."

Oh, my Queen. He bent forward and brushed her lips with his.

"How long?"

"Not long. I'll be back before the hunting season ritual starts. I take it you want to watch it?"

"Uhm—yes."

Lies, lies, all such horrible lies. If only he told her he wanted to make her his queen after he had defeated the Knights, if only he showed her his grandfather's ring, the Thillei royal seal, if he told her why he needed Isandor and Myra, if he told her why he needed the crossbreed child she carried . . .

Loriane would hate him, he was sure of that. And that was why he loved her.

She tied up the cloak's fastenings over the bulge of her belly. "Well then the sooner I go, the sooner I'll be back."

A few steps and she was at the door, which Isandor had so recently slammed behind him.

Loriane, be safe.

If there were reasons out there for her not to be safe, he had created every single one of them.

She blew a kiss to him and was gone.

Tandor grabbed the door handle to the inner room door, gathering courage. He listened, but heard no noise. Heard in his mind the screams of a young woman. Fifteen years it had been, and he had never forgotten.

His hand strayed to the dagger at his side. Myra was Imperfect. What if he . . .

Another deep breath.

He could just wait here, outside the room, until Loriane came back.

No, he couldn't. Myra was young and frightened. Ontane would hear about it if he left her alone.

He pushed open the door. Stale warm air wafted out of the room.

Myra sat on a low stool next to the stove, leaning forward. She breathed heavily and didn't look up when he came in.

Tandor stood there, frozen, until her breathing slowed. She looked up.

"Don't just stand there. Shut the door." Her voice was husky.

Tandor did, although he would rather have bolted out. He took a few uncertain steps towards the couch. The dagger bumped against his leg.

As if he felt his thoughts, Myra's light blue eyes fixed on it.

He gathered courage. "Do you want me to—"

"Don't touch me." Her voice was sharp and full of distrust.

That nightgown wasn't very thick, and showed the tight curve of her belly. She was skinny, just like . . .

"I won't," he said, swallowing nausea.

He settled himself on the couch. Her sharp gaze followed him, even when her breathing became harsh.

Then she bent forward, uttering a low moan.

Tandor folded his arms over his chest, pulling them tight to stop his trembling. The metal rods of his arm bit into to bottom of his other arm.

Myra's moan became a cry.

Tandor cringed, clenching his teeth.

Stop it, be quiet.

In his mind, he went back to that dressing room, the smell of furs around him. The shrill sound of a woman screaming. *Keep your hands off me! Get out!* A blood curdling scream.

Footsteps, the clanging of a door, voices, male and female.

Someone else runs into the room.

A female voice yells, *push.*

Another bloodcurdling scream.

Tandor stands there, frozen, dizzy, while the woman screams and howls. There seems no end to it—

"Can I have drink?"

Myra's voice shook Tandor out of his nightmare.

"Yes, sure." He rose and almost fell from dizziness. He must forget what had happened and avenge what the Knights had done to her and his family. He must complete his life's struggle. His mother and other surviving Thilleians relied on him. She had not survived the massacre for her son to be such a coward.

Lies, lies, lies. He told everyone he was southern, but his mother had given birth in the merchant's house in Tiverius. He'd never even been to the City of Glass until his mother took him when he was about ten.

He was Chevakian, and a coward.

There was a carafe of water on the table. He took the glass out of Myra's sweaty and trembling hand and filled it up. His hand also trembled, and he spilled some water, which he mopped up with a towel.

By the time he had finished, she was moaning again, leaning forward with her elbows on her knees. The thin nightgown didn't do much to hide her pale skin. Her right arm ended in a withered stump just above the wrist

Tandor felt for the dagger at his side. If only he had the courage, he could solve all his problems now. He gripped the hilt, studied her back for where to cut. The dagger slid out of its sheath. He lifted it, gathering strands of icefire around his hand. And hesitated.

If he took her heart, what would it do to her? Would it freeze her in a permanent state of agony, making her useless for his purpose? What about the child? It could be killed. If he waited a bit longer, he could have two servitors.

He hesitated. Too long.

Myra pushed herself back up. Quickly, Tandor slipped the dagger back into its sheath.

"Can I have that water now?"

He handed the glass into her good hand. She gulped deeply and gave it back to him.

Yes, it would be better to wait.

The front door clanged.

Tandor flew up from his seat by the fire. Loriane came into the room, her cheeks red from the cold.

"And?" he asked. Behind him, Myra was still moaning.

She frowned at him. "And what?"

"Did you see where Isandor went?"

"No, I didn't ask. He went to the festival grounds, I imagine. He's got the hunting ritual to lead." Loriane looked past him, shrugging off her cloak. "Any progress?"

"I don't know. She told me to stay away from her."

"Tandor, I can't believe you." She dropped her basket and went to Myra, speaking soft words. The girl cried while Loriane rubbed her back. She gripped Loriane's hands.

"Don't go, please, don't go."

"No, I'm here now. Not going anywhere until you have that baby."

Loriane started unpacking items from her basket. Bottles, salves, bandages, all sorts of things. Tandor glared at her in the silence. Did she need all that? Couldn't she hurry things up a bit?

"There are a lot of Knights in the streets with a lot of gold on their collars," Loriane said without looking up. "I heard someone say that the Queen is there, and that it was her who declared Isandor champion."

"What—the queen? Jevaithi? In the Outer City?"

"I just told you."

Myra's gasps started again. Loriane was telling her to be quiet. Tandor waited for it to pass, scrunching up his hands behind his back.

When Myra had gone silent, Loriane wiped her face with something that smelled like mint.

"Thank you," Myra whispered. "You're doing so much for me. I'm sorry."

"Oh no, I wouldn't let another mother suffer."

Tandor clamped his teeth. Why didn't she hurry up with this dreadful business?

"What is the Queen doing here?"

"I don't know. Watch the races, I guess." Loriane dipped the cloth in water.

"I've heard rumours she wants to see the killing."

"Eeew. What's so great about that?" Myra said. Her voice was husky. "I never watch. The tavern's much more fun to be around after Newlight."

"Well, there is that, too," Loriane said. "But I think she'll be heading back before that time. The Knights were tense and didn't look very happy to let her come here. Poor girl."

No, poor Tandor. His whole plan was falling apart. The children gone, Isandor with the Knights and the last two Imperfect children either out of reach or unwilling to help. The street was crawling with Knights, and Ruko had not yet returned.

Meanwhile, the Heart was beating at a faster rate than before, feeding more and more icefire into the air. If the children were in the palace, they might absorb some of it, but if he couldn't get to them soon enough, who knew what would happen?

He heard his own voice echoing in his mother's palatial living room. *But it's lunacy! I can't do all that alone.*

The spirits of our family will guide you.

By the skylights, Mother, what good were spirits?

He was stuck here with two pregnant women. He could run out, but there would be nowhere for him to go, except to be discovered by the Knights, and have them follow him back to his last Imperfect children. Jevaithi was here, but he couldn't use her; there were too many Knights. He might be able to use icefire, but he was not invincible, not alone, and who said that Pirosian with his sink wouldn't be there?

He jumped when two hands grabbed his shoulders from behind.

"You are so tense, Tandor."

"Don't you have to look after . . ." He gestured at Myra.

"There's nothing much we can do except wait. She's not yet close to giving birth."

She massaged the muscles in his shoulders. Myra sat hunched over, breathing harshly through another pain.

Loriane continued in a low voice. "I'm worried about you, Tandor. It feels like there is something going on. You bring this girl here, I don't know why. Then what were you trying to do to Isandor? If I hadn't seen you come to my house with him as a baby, I might have thought you were trying to kill him back there. What has he done? I'd really like to know what this is about. Having you here is a risk for me, too. My clients are of the city nobility and I have taken enough of a gamble already looking after Isandor. You come here, barge into my house with a young girl about to give birth in the middle of the Newlight festival and I get no explanation. I'm busy, I'm pregnant, and I don't have time for your plans, even less so if you keep them secret."

"I told you life was too dangerous for Myra in Bordertown. I thought you understood that."

"Then why come here where there's even more Knights?" Myra asked

Tandor balled his fists behind his back. Why did sound carry so well in these damned limpets?

"She's right," Loriane said. "I believe she would have been much better off at home. She's only a young mother and it's not right to—"

"Don't talk to me about *not right*!" Tandor whirled.

A moan from Myra interrupted him. She clutched her belly, panting and crying.

"Calm down, calm down," Loriane said.

"It hurts, it hurts!" Myra screamed.

"Breathe like I told you."

Myra's screams faded into heavy panting.

Tandor turned away, looking at the door. All his hair stood on end. He could *not* stand this much longer.

When Myra's harsh breathing subsided, he continued. "I'll tell you what is *not right*. My family was murdered. My grandfather hacked to pieces as he tried to protect the wonders of the City of Glass and his throne. I was exiled. I have lived my *life* for this plan. I am not going to let it slip through my fingers."

"Tandor, what happened is a long time ago. It's not even something you personally remember." She let the shameful truth hang in the air, *You were born in Chevakia*. "Let it go."

"And let Imperfects suffer? Let Imperfect babies be killed?"

"I think Isandor is proof that things are changing."

"It is not. You know that. He would have been killed if it hadn't been for me, and he's only with the Knights because he shapes icefire around an illusion of the missing part of his leg, without ever having been taught how to do so, and because someone put it in his head that being with the Knights was a noble thing to do."

"Isandor is not stupid. He just doesn't care for your pointless quest for revenge."

Loriane's eyes blazed with anger.

Not pointless. Tandor saw his mother's proud figure, exiled matriarch of his family. Isandor *would* return to the Thilleians, no matter what. Tandor would send that message that would end his mother's pain: *it is safe to return home.*

"Loriane, they *killed* my family. They're continuing to kill any children born with my family's blood. The Knights took the fifty children from Bordertown. I *saved* those children, every single one of them." His voice spilled over. The Knights would have left those children on the ice floes.

"For what aim, Tandor? That's all I'm asking. Because you saved Isandor, and then hardly cared about him until now. You never told me who this boy is. You never gave me any guidance. And now it seems I have done everything wrong by letting him do what he wanted."

Tandor stared at her, raising his clawed hand. "Oh, I give up."

"Give up? You never even started. You try and bring up a child. It's not some . . . possession you can dictate what to do. If you wanted him to see your ways, why haven't you been around more, and explained to him what he is and what you meant for him to become?"

"I have—"

Myra let out a wailing moan. She was rocking backwards and forwards on her stool. Loriane turned away from Tandor and massaged the girl's back, speaking soft words.

Tandor heaved a sigh of frustration and strode up the stairs to the sleeping shelves. He was trapped here, *trapped*, with two crazy women, while outside the Knights were looking for him.

Icefire streamed in from all sides. The Heart was producing more than ever before, and he had lost Ruko and Isandor, and he couldn't reach his one remaining Imperfect.

He lay down on the bed, even though the room was stuffy enough to make him dizzy. Loriane should open a vent.

He closed his eyes and cast his feelings out for Ruko.

But even the pillow over his head did not stifle Myra's screams from below.

Come on, woman, shut up and get on with it.

Then a cold breeze drifted over him. Not just cold, but freezing. Was that . . . Tandor pulled the pillow off his head and looked up. The wall next to the bed shimmered. First the rough planks that formed the inner wall of the limpet dissolved. An amorphous blob of blue rose from the middle. The blue become clearer and took the shape of a young man. Ruko stood next to him, blue and shimmery.

Ruko, his saviour.

He wasted no time in grabbing Ruko's hands. The boy was strong again. His anger burned, not just for the Knights who had come to Bordertown, but the ones who had injured him. Ruko wanted his girl back, and he was angry enough to kill everyone in his path. And he was Tandor's to command. The time for trying to solve this nicely was over.

So he ordered Ruko, *I want Isandor brought here. Alive. I don't care how you do it. Make sure that the Queen doesn't leave the Outer City. I don't care how you do that either.*

Ruko said nothing, but Tandor knew he would obey. Ah, blissful obedience and none of the women's silly protests.

CHAPTER 20

ISANDOR RE-ARRANGED his cloak on his shoulders for what had to be the tenth time, ignoring the gazes of hundreds—no—thousands of people who were waiting for this ceremonial part of the festival to begin. The eagles in their pens at his back squawked and hissed, two of the Outer City's butchers were talking to each other accompanied with hand gestures to the animal pens and a young boy was sweeping the dull layer of sand off the snow-covered ground so it was again white.

Every time he put down his broom, golden sparks flew along the handle, but the boy gave no sign of having seen them.

To Isandor's eyes, the atmosphere in the arena thrummed with tension. Icefire sizzled and crackled through the air like he had never seen it before. Isandor couldn't believe he was the only one who noticed. Some in the audience would see it, too, but no one mentioned it, perhaps for fear of being labelled a sorcerer. Perhaps they hoped it would go away.

A large group of Knights gathered at the spectator stand to his left, where Jevaithi had come in moments earlier. Isandor had only spotted glimpses of her white fur cloak amongst the crowd of grey ones as she settled in the seating stand. The Knights carried daggers and swords, and Isandor even spotted a crossbow. The Knights might not be able to feel or see the icefire strands, but they knew something was going on, or they would not be as heavily armed.

He tried to catch Jevaithi's eye, but couldn't even see her head most of the time. He'd been silly to think that he would be allowed near her for the second time. And he'd even been so stupid to think that he should warn her.

The citizens of the Outer City crowded around the perimeter fence, bright-eyed, to cheer on one of their own. Young girls with ribbons in their hair, older girls with their hair pinned up, wearing pretty earrings, with their leather necklaces and feathers prominently displayed. Younger boys with dreams in their eyes of becoming an Eagle Knight themselves.

In one corner of the arena, a couple of men were dragging a large wriggling shape in a net. The bark of the Legless Lion cut through the chatter of the crowd. The men would have caught this animal on this morning's hunting trip. The first of the annual harvest.

The men moved the net into the middle of the arena and drove stakes into the ice to pin the corners down before retreating to the perimeter. They were all wearing butchers' aprons. A nearly bald man winked at Isandor and smiled. His uncle.

Oh yes, he would be happy. Isandor knew from past years that his uncle's back room would hold a number of other animals, waiting to be killed for the festivities, waiting for customers who would be flooding in after today to buy fresh meat.

From today for the next few moon cycles of highsun, the butchery would be a place of activity, of large vats with salted meat and oil, stacks of uncured skins and racks of drying meat. During highsun, the hunters harvested enough for the people to survive the dark lowsun days. Tonight, there would be a huge feast.

Jevaithi had settled on her bench, and the Knights stepped back to form a line around the stand.

"Are you ready, Apprentice Isandor?"

Isandor started, and nodded at the Knight who had come into the arena.

The three butchers came forward. One of them, Isandor's uncle, approached, handing Isandor a fearsome knife.

Isandor gripped his dagger's hilt, cold in his fingers and drew it out of its sheath. The blade, sharpened by his uncle, gleamed in the sun.

The two other butchers were at the net, one of them undoing the knot that kept it closed. He glanced at Isandor.

"Ready?"

Isandor nodded. He took up a fighting stance, his legs wide.

His uncle yelled and the man pulled away the rope that held the net. All three of the men retreated.

As they did so, a strand of icefire crackled through the air like lightning, and struck the ground at the other end of the arena.

Some people gasped, but most looked around confused; they hadn't seen the icefire.

The Legless Lion writhed on the ground, trying to free itself from the loose net, splashing its flippers in puddles.

Isandor stalked closer, holding the dagger in a white-knuckled hand.

The animal's mouth opened, showing yellow teeth, emitting its fearful bark and a waft of fishy breath. The eyes, liquid brown, roved the arena. Did animals see icefire or did it see the citizens who had come to witness this spectacle? Did it see Queen Jevaithi who had insisted watching her champion kill the beast?

Quickly.

Cut the heart, kill in one stroke, as it was done properly. Don't show his uncle his hesitation. He'd cut up carcases often enough in the butchery. There was nothing to it.

His uncle stood on the edge of the area, holding an axe at his waist. Ready for action.

The rope around the animal's flippers and neck dangled on the ground. Isandor grabbed it and with a sharp yank, he pulled the animal upside down, like he had helped his uncle do many times.

Before the animal could get up, he stabbed deep into the hairy chest. As the blade sank in, icefire crackled out of the ground. Strands exploded all around him. A golden glow burst, unbidden, from his fingers.

Oh, by the skylights!

The chest split open with a sickening snap, widening the cut he had made. The animal's heart jumped out. Isandor managed to catch it in his numb hands. Gold light poured from his fingers, filling the hole in the animal's chest. The lion barked and snapped at the rope around its neck, raising itself on clumsy flippers. Its fur had faded from mottled grey to an eerie blue, a faint glow. At the place where the heart should be, the chest shimmered.

Isandor stared from the throbbing heart in his hands to the animal. Severed arteries spilled no blood, but pure icefire. The golden threads snaked through the air, gathering to converge around the animal.

Around him, people in the stands stared. Some murmured in a tone of confusion. Someone said, the voice carrying across the pen, "Where is the Lion?"

A little boy pointed, but his mother clamped a hand over his eyes.

The Lion hobbled a few paces away from him, the net dragging through puddles, now half-frozen. It glanced at the end of the arena, where the plains beckoned.

"Oh no, you don't." Isandor lunged as fast as his wooden leg would allow, catching the Lion around the neck with one arm. Someone in the audience shouted. "Look, look!"

The animal's fur was rough and stank of fish, but Isandor cared not about the animal's snapping mouth.

But he was still holding the blood-covered heart, and the fur was greasy and slippery. The animal shrugged, and Isandor's arm lost its purchase.

He fell, painfully, on the ragged frozen ground. The heart rolled from his grip, still thudding, and came to rest against a block of ice. Sparks of icefire burst from it and leaked into the snow

On hands and knees in bloodstained-puddles, Isandor met the Legless Lion's deep blue eyes. Its fur rippled with tension. Whiskers twitched. The net lay free on the ground.

Isandor's ears roared, but through the sound, he heard the shouts from the crowd. *A servitor!* He scrabbled up, grabbed the netting, but before he could throw it over the animal's head, it waddled away, in the direction of the plain. A line of onlookers stood between the Legless Lion and freedom. People screamed and tried to run away from the animal, pushing into other people, some of whom looked confused, *because they couldn't see the Lion.*

The crowd cleared a small opening to the left, and the Lion took its chance.

Isandor shouted, "Hold it!" But it was no use.

A few heartbeats, and the animal was gone, a blue form fast disappearing amongst the tents. Isandor hobbled after it, but there was no way he could ever catch up.

Oh no, by the skylights!

People in the audience were screaming and pushing out of the arena. Others stood staring into the sky. Still others were talking to each other, confusion on their faces.

Isandor scrambled in the snow for the Lion's still-beating heart, scooped it up and slid it into his pocket, where it continued beating.

What now? Was there any chance of getting away unnoticed? Where to go in this confusion?

He looked up, straight into the Queen's eyes.

The Knights around her were shouting, but it was confusion, more than anger, that marked their words. Like Carro, most of them were Pirosians. They hadn't seen what had happened.

But Jevaithi just looked at him, unmoving, her eyes wide, her mouth open in an expression of shock. *She* had seen it.

In his mind, he was running past tents. People were screaming words he couldn't understand and running out of the way, tripping over their feet. He saw the shore where he belonged, where his females lazed on the ice floes. He couldn't get out of this maze; there was a fence in his way. A man ran after him, shouting unintelligible words.

No, no, he had to escape. He must get back to defend his females from the other bulls.

The image melded with the arena, the audience, Knights, his uncle staring with wide, bulging eyes.

All around him the Knights were stirring, and the first ones were already entering the arena.

He wanted to run, but his legs felt like they would buckle under him.

Carro stood with his patrol at the edge of the crowd at the arena. Being taller than many people had allowed him to see most of what had happened, but he didn't understand it. One moment, the Legless Lion was there in the net, the next moment, it was gone, and Isandor stood there, holding the animal's heart. And then Isandor ran, or tripped, and fell, and some people in the audience seemed to have seen something. Now, everyone was shouting and the whole festive atmosphere had turned into panic. Knights were forming a circle around the Queen.

"What happened?" he asked Inran next to him.

The young man was staring wide-eyed, at Isandor.

"I don't know what happened," another Knight answered. "One moment the Lion was there, and the next moment it was gone, become invisible."

A chill went over Carro's back. He had seen an invisible creature before: last night, when it snapped the necks of two

Knights. A servitor, Rider Cornatan had confirmed. And he had just seen who had made a servitor by taking the animal's heart, just like it was described in the old books. Isandor had been behind the servitors all along. Isandor had wanted to read about the old king's practices because he wanted to *use* them. Isandor had deceived everyone, including him.

His heart thudding, he searched the crowd for Rider Cornatan. He would be with the Queen no doubt.

The Apprentices in his patrol were just as confused as everyone else. Jono was looking over the roof of the tent on the opposite side of the arena. Caman was observing a group of Knights trying to get into the arena, while Inran kept glancing over his shoulder. None of them knew where the real danger was.

"You. Stay here," he ordered.

Jono gave him a sneering look but said nothing.

Carro pushed through the crowd, filled with the uncomfortable feeling that he would have to discipline his patrol when they came back to the eyrie. They should be afraid of him, and they were not. But he'd deal with that later. The praise for what he was going to tell Rider Cornatan now would give him the courage to do what needed to be done. Hopefully.

Knights were pressing each other to see into the central area.

Carro pushed them aside. "Let me through, let me through."

His voice had become deeper, louder. They actually listened, and, after glancing at his Learner badge, move aside.

Up to the viewing stand, where Rider Cornatan sat next to the Queen. All around, Knights were talking frantically, looking over their shoulders and left and right, frowns on faces.

Carro bowed before the viewing stand. Rider Cornatan acknowledged him, but the Queen just sat there, staring hollow-eyed at Isandor, her cheeks red, like she was deeply upset with his trickery.

Well, he should put an end to that.

The words burst from Carro's mouth. "The one you call a Champion shouldn't be here. He's a cripple. He turned the Lion into a servitor."

Rider Cornatan fixed him with his light blue eyes. "He's *what*?"

"A cripple. Ask him." There. That served him right. That horrid apparition last night had killed two good Knights.

"Imperfect?" Rider Cornatan lowered his voice and met Carro's eyes.

Carro nodded. The next question would surely be *Why haven't you told us before?* but he would have to handle that, too. *Because he has deceived us all.*

"Well, that would explain a lot." A smile crept over the wizened face.

Carro added, "There is another cripple in the Outer City, an older man. He was loitering around the area of the brotherhood compound. We followed him, but unfortunately lost track of him in the markets."

Rider Cornatan's face showed intense interest. He nodded, a satisfied smile on his face. "I see. You are proving your worth. Keep looking for this man. Let me know if you want more men." Then Rider Cornatan pushed himself up, his face set. "Now let's see about this young man. If what you say is true, you will have done the Queen a great service."

Rider Cornatan walked down the steps. A Senior Knight stepped in his way and held up a hand.

"The boy's dangerous," the man whispered.

"I know," Rider Cornatan said.

He pushed the man's hand away and continued into the arena.

Knights surrounded Isandor, but none had dared to touch him. In the confusion, no one seemed to have ordered them to do so. And yet Carro's friend wasn't arguing; he just stood there, with that gruesome heart in his pocket, still beating.

Carro could almost feel that someone was looking at him. He glanced over his shoulder into the Queen's eyes, which burned with pure hatred. She held her lips pursed and little white spots appeared at her upper lip and chin. Carro had to avert his gaze.

Isandor laughs. Gestures at the notice from the palace that Carro has brought. In curly letters, it says that Carro has been accepted into the Eagle Knights. Carro applied. His father was against it, but he applied anyway. Isandor encouraged him. He wants to be a Knight, too, and his mother doesn't mind. He has already been accepted.

Then we will join up together and we'll both be famous Knights.

Carro laughs.

Then Isandor's expression changes to one of wonder. *Do you think we'll get to stand guard for the Queen?*

Of course we will. All Knights do.

Isandor looks dreamy. There is something in those blue eyes Carro can't fathom. Something he doesn't want to fathom.

The Queen belongs to the Knights. She is *his*, with her honey-coloured hair and milk-white arms. Her eyes gaze into people's hearts. Carro has seen her twice, both from a distance. She is the most beautiful woman in the known world.

Yes, he will join the Knights, even though his father will hate him for it.

The Knights protect the Queen. He cannot trust a boy with a wooden leg to protect the Queen. The books say Imperfects are sorcerers. Carro is trying not to believe the books. They *are* only stories, after all.

"Apprentice Isandor?" Rider Cornatan's voice was hard and thin over the chatter of onlookers. He had pushed through the circle of Knights around Isandor and faced him directly.

Oh no, Rider Cornatan wasn't scared of sorcery. Real Knights weren't scared.

"Yes," Isandor said, his back straight and proud. His hair black and shiny, his eyes dark blue. Royal blue.

Carro's stomach squirmed. Oh, by the skylights, how did he hate Isandor. Even like this, he managed to look arrogant, like he owned the world, like he challenged Rider Cornatan to do something to him, even though he would know he could never escape.

And I am just a coward. Waited all this time to tell Rider Cornatan about Isandor. Can't even punish my own patrol.

Rider Cornatan looked Isandor up and down.

"Do you have any secrets, Apprentice Isandor?"

"Secrets, Sir?"

Rider Cornatan hit out, lightning fast and kicked Isandor's legs from under him. He stumbled and tipped backwards into the fast-retreating Knights, and then fell in the snow. A blast of wind went over the arena, whipping at clothes and hair. Isandor's trouser leg had moved up, clearly displaying the boot stuck to his wooden leg. Everyone in the audience stopped talking.

Someone whispered, "A cripple."

"How is that possible? I thought they were all . . ."

"Watch out, he's going to blast us."

In the alley and under the cover of gathering darkness, Isandor lifts up his trouser leg.

I do have a secret. I have a wooden leg, see? I can't run as fast as you can. People don't seem to like it. I don't know why.

Carro shrugs. *Why should people do that?* Isandor is just like him, someone people don't like him very much. He also doesn't understand why.

Isandor bends closer, and whispers in Carro's ear, like *real* friends do. *They say that anyone who is born like this has magic. You know, icefire*

Carros shivers. Stares. *Do you?*

Of course not. Do you see me making things disappear?

Uhm—no. But Carro doubts. His mother always told him icefire was real. She says she can see it. But his mother always lies.

There you go. It's all nonsense. But we won't tell anyone that, won't we?

Of course not. Certainly not his parents.

It's a secret.

A real secret, between friends?

Isandor nods.

Friends forever.

Onlookers fled. People pushed away. Knights retreated to the edge of the arena. In the holding pens, eagle attendants shuffled back, pulling their eagles away, wide-eyed. Isandor lay there alone in the snow.

"What is this?" Rider Cornatan kicked Isandor's wooden leg.

Isandor raised himself, stumbling to get the leg under him. He still managed to act dignified, but the look in his eyes frightened Carro more than anger would have. It was not anger, not hurt, but a withering look of determination.

"Who said cripples could join the Knights?" Rider Cornatan asked.

"No one said they couldn't." Isandor's voice was cold as the southern wind.

A cold gust of wind blew eddies of snow in the corners of the arena.

"You should well know cripples can't even live in this city. You are an abomination. I don't understand why no one has seen it before."

"I've not hidden anything." Again, that confident tone.

That was true. Isandor had come up to the registration as he was, with his slight limp. Why had no one seen it? Yes, why?

Everyone with half a brain could see that Isandor didn't walk normally. Yet no one had commented.

"How come you're even alive? Who hid you?"

"No one. I've lived with my mother in the Outer City all along."

Look at the cockiness of him. Look at him stand there.

"Well, whatever you did, you're finished now." Rider Cornatan stepped forward and tore the golden badge from Isandor's collar. "You will never darken the eyrie with your presence again. Thanks to my vigilant spies, I have saved the City of Glass from this evil. Take him away."

Knights closed in. Two grabbed Isandor under the armpits and yanked him up.

What were they going to do with him? Carro had flown over the jagged shapes of the ice floes earlier today. Anyone left there alone would be attacked by stray bears. Anyone put in the dungeons would die a slow death of hunger and disease. *Why did I say this? Isandor is my friend. He looked after me. He would never kill anyone. The fact that he made the Lion a servitor doesn't prove that he made the human one.*

Knights don't have Imperfect friends, the other voice in his mind said.

Isandor has been good to me. He's a good person.

But I've had enough of "good" people. I don't want pity. I want people to be honest. Right, they are honest, and don't like me. I want people to like me and be honest. No pity. I can't stand pity. I want to be accepted because of what I am, not because my father is a moderately successful merchant. I hate him anyway.

Oh, he was so confused.

CHAPTER 21

NO. ISANDOR!

Everyone was getting up, blocking Jevaithi's view of the arena. The citizens were filing out, most still uttering expressions of confusion and trading gossip. A whole group of Knights rushed into the arena and out again. Jevaithi presumed that they escorted the young Champion Knight away.

To the palace dungeons. She had to put a stop to it; she had to.

Rider Cornatan returned to her, his face red.

"With respect, Your Highness. We must take you to a safe place."

"What happened?" she asked, although she was sure she had seen it better than any of them. The animal had run off into the festival grounds in its blue state, leaving the Champion standing there holding the pulsing heart. The animal had become his servitor.

"It was inappropriate for your eyes. Rest assured, the Knight will be punished severely."

No. She saw an emaciated body, wounds from lashes, matted

hair. She remembered. She had only been young when she saw the man who had been blamed for poisoning her mother. He'd spent ten years in the dungeons. "I would like to set eyes on him, who dares to perform these deeds before the Queen." She was trembling, fighting to keep control over her speech. That day, last year, she had presided over the poor wretch's execution. She didn't believe the man had poisoned her mother any more than she wanted him dead. He'd been a palace servant. All the servants adored her mother. But the Knights had to have someone to punish.

"He'll be taken into custody." Rider Cornatan's voice sounded far off.

"Can I see him?" She ached to ask more, but anything she said could be dangerous. Rider Cornatan raised an eyebrow. He knew what she was, and probably had thoughts along the same lines as her fascination with the strange young Knight.

"I would think that inappropriate. Come, Your Highness, We must go now. It's getting late and this place is not safe at night."

Jevaithi stifled a sob. She must save that young Knight, the only other person of her kind. But how? The Knights controlled everything. They gave her the illusion of power as long as she did what she was told.

She took Rider Cornatan's arm and let him lead her away from the arena, which was completely abandoned now, save for a few remaining splatters of blood. To Jevaithi's eyes, they exuded a soft yellow glow.

People in the tents along the way cheered and waved at her, but she paid them no attention. In her mind, she saw those blue eyes, looking up at her with the boy's innocence. When she looked at him, declaring him her Champion, it was as if she had seen into his soul, as if their hearts beat in unison. If he was tortured, she would lie awake with the pain. If he was killed, part of her would die.

"We shall return to the palace as soon as possible," Rider Cornatan said.

For once, she couldn't find a reason to disagree with him. She longed for the warmth of her room, the comfort of her bed and the whisper of servants bringing her dinner.

She shuffled with her entourage, nervous Knights looking everywhere, Rider Cornatan holding her arm like an over-protective mother bear. They passed the food stalls, where it had become quiet. Stall holders were cleaning up for the night. Most of the revellers had gone into the Outer City to celebrate in the melteries. How stupid had she been to imagine she could ever dance with the local boys.

Stupid. Naïve.

Ahead, a woman screamed.

Rider Cornatan halted. The Knights at the front of the group had all stopped, a solid wall of cloaked backs. The woman's screams had turned into sobs. The Knights murmured. Hands went to swords, but most of the men just stood there.

"What's going on?" Rider Cornatan demanded.

"See for yourself, sir." The wall of Knights parted.

Jevaithi's royal sled stood abandoned on the plain. Splatters of blood marked the white paint and had seeped into the snow. The harness which had held the four magnificent bears lay empty on the ground. The bears themselves were bloodied humps of white fur in the snow.

Jevaithi took a gasp of stinging cold air and couldn't breathe out again. She clutched her throat, dizzy, blood pounding in her ears.

"No, no," she stuttered, fighting to repel blackness from the edge of her vision. Her beautiful bears, and the driver—where was he?

"Guard the Queen!" Rider Cornatan shouted, while he started running towards the sled with agility that belied his age.

Between the bodies of the Knights who closed in around her, Jevaithi saw how he jumped into the driver's seat and hauled up the body of the sled's driver. His head was bent back like a broken stick and his cloak dark with blood. His arms flopped by his side; his body hadn't been out here long enough to have frozen stiff.

"Don't look, Your Highness," one of the guards said.

"Who would do such a thing?" Jevaithi's voice sounded weak, even to her own ears. All of a sudden, she had trouble keeping her balance.

A soft warmth closed around her, the dense fur of a shorthair cloak, and a man's arms. It was one of the Senior Knights, a man normally calm and reserved. Jevaithi stifled her sobs in the man's shirt. She was shivering.

The Knights were shouting amongst themselves over her head.

"Who could have done this?"

"I'd say—*what* has done this? This wasn't done by a human."

"He's right. Look at the bears. No one can kill a bear that easily."

Jevaithi pressed herself deeper under the Knight's cloak, seeing images of a blue-tinged Legless Lion running from the arena. *No humans . . .*

"I want to go home," she said to no one in particular.

Why ever did she entertain such silly plans to go amongst the common people? There were *murdering* strangers out there. Poor, poor bears, poor driver. What had they done to deserve this?

"Shh, Your Highness. You are safe with us." The man's voice rumbled in his chest. He tightened an arm around her, while he continued to give orders to the guards.

Jevaithi felt warm, and protected. Was this the feeling kids had about their fathers?

She didn't know how long she had stood there when Rider Cornatan returned. She heard his voice before he came into view.

"Where is the Queen?"

"Safe," the Knight said.

Jevaithi extracted her face from the warmth of his cloak.

Rider Cornatan came to a stop. Stared at her and then at the

Senior Knight.

"I'll take care of her now," Rider Cornatan said.

A sharp look passed between the two men over Jevaithi's head. The Knight released her. Jevaithi reluctantly left the warmth of his cloak to take Rider Cornatan's arm. Even in times such as this, they jostled to be first in line to her bedroom.

The group started moving, away from the slaughter scene.

"What's happening now?" Jevaithi asked Rider Cornatan, doing her utmost best to sound composed.

"I've sent a messenger to the City. He'll bring back another sled. We'll wait for it to arrive."

"Couldn't I . . ." She licked her lips. "Couldn't I fly on an Eagle with a Knight? We would be back very quickly—"

The look he gave her stopped her talking. Obviously out-of-the-question.

They crossed the festival grounds through the maze of tents and fences. Legless Lions barked in the distance. There were now so many Knights around her that it was impossible for her to see the cheering people. The Knights walked quickly, ushering the crowd aside. Jevaithi wasn't in the mood to be cheered.

They left the festival grounds, and clambered up the slope that led into the Outer City. Through a wide street, where abandoned sleds stood in shop entrances, their terrified drivers holed up in alleyways by Knights. How many Knights *had* come from the city with her? How could someone still have killed the bears and the driver with all these Knights to guard her?

A person invisible to the Knights could do it.

They were now crossing the market place over trampled snow covered with sand. The Knights halted again in front of a cone-shaped building on the corner. The locals called these structures limpets. The writings had told her that there was a waterproof inner layer, made of ancient debris from the city before the Great War, a mantle of still air, and then an outer layer made from blocks of ice. This limpet was larger than most, and had three entrances. Someone had carved patterns in the icy outer cover.

A few of the Knights had gone inside. The glow of a fierce fire peeped through a crack between the doors.

There were shouts and bangs inside. The doors were flung open and lots of people streamed out, some speaking in angry voices.

Jevaithi shivered with the piercing breeze. She glanced over her shoulder to the Knight who had offered her the warmth of his cloak.

The Knights moved forward, through the door and a short hall with racks for cloaks—all empty—into a room where the air was impossibly warm and laced with a tang of liquor and smoke. The inner walls, made from sheets of metal and other unidentified material, sloped slowly to a high ceiling. A balcony surrounded the wall, with stairs leading up to it. There were tables and chairs up there. Empty.

A huge metal stove stood in the middle of the room, a blazing fire within. Surrounding the stove were many small tables and chairs. A couple of red-faced girls were hastily removing glasses from the tables, many still containing dark red fluid. A young man was righted chairs that had fallen over.

"Your Highness, what a surprise and honour to receive you in my humble establishment."

The man who bowed before her was rotund and almost bald. Although his words had been polite, his tone gave away his extreme annoyance.

Oh, she could see why. He'd had a room full of drinking, paying patrons and the next thing the Knights barged in and tossed everyone out on the street. The voices of those paying patrons now drifted in from outside, shouts and jeers. A crash, the tinkle of glass. Angry voices.

"I would be happy if you let your customers back inside," Jevaithi said, making her voice as clear and regal as she could.

"For once, Your Highness, be quiet and stop your childish demands," Rider Cornatan hissed. She had never heard his voice as tight as this.

The flicker of hope that dashed across the meltery owner's face died instantly.

"Sit here by the fire, Your Highness." He indicated a soft, high-backed chair that had worn fabric but looked very comfortable indeed.

There was another crash of glass outside. A man shouted and something thudded against the door.

"I'm sure," she said, as peevishly as she could, while sitting down in the chair, "I'm *absolutely* sure that a street brawl is just what you need to calm things down, especially if your men are out there attempting to catch a Legless Lion most of them can't even see."

In two steps, Rider Cornatan stood next to her. He grabbed a strand of her hair as he bent to her ear and pulled hard. His whisper sounded like a hiss of air. "I'm warning you . . . You're behaving like a brat. You want to be grown-up? I'll show you grown-up. When we come back to the palace, I will take you to your rooms and teach you a lesson you won't forget in a hurry." He let her go and stepped back as if he had merely conveyed a private message.

Jevaithi shivered and leaned back in the chair. Her eyes met the meltery owner's. His were wide, shocked.

Yes, the common people loved her and that love was her protection, but tonight, that would not be enough.

CHAPTER 22

ISANDOR TRIED to run, but he never had a chance.

The Knights had him blindfolded and tied his arms behind his back before he could do anything. They pushed him out of the arena and through the crowd. There were as many people cheering as shouting.

"Show them, show them!" a man yelled.

Show them what?

He struggled against the Knights' hands. "Stop pushing. I can walk. Where are you taking me?"

"To the only place sorcerers belong," the man holding him growled. "I hope you had a good look at the sky, because you won't see it again."

People around them were calling for the Queen, and then there were other voices from further away.

"Let the boy go, tyrants!"

"Down with the oppression!"

"Give us our houses back, and our businesses, and our money!"

"Death to Pirosian scum."

There were more scuffles and screams. People bumped into him. Knights shouted out. Out-of-control, hoarse voices. Daggers came out of sheaths. The sound of people running. Something heavy landed near his feet with a dull thud.

Isandor tried to free his arm to pull the rag from his eyes, but the Knights held him too tightly. He wanted to see these people. There were still supporters of the old king in the Outer City? The revelation confused him. The deeds the king had done, according to the books about the fall of the royal family, horrified him.

But what if those books had been written by Knights?

He did remember that last book Carro had bought, the one that described all the wonders of icefire, not just the bad things. Deadly, but very useful and powerful.

Why had he never known that people still supported the old king?

He was running through the street. Even though he was blindfolded, he could see. People were in his way, running, pushing each other. Their unintelligible screams filled the air. Their words were garbled bursts of sound that meant nothing.

Some had sticks and tried to push him. He kept slipping, his flippers finding no purchase on the trampled ice.

I am much faster in the water.

The water, where the fish were fresh and wet and where the females waited for him.

He needed to get back there.

Isandor stumbled and gasped, realising how he'd been holding his breath and how lack of air had made him dizzy. By the skylights, what was wrong with him?

The Knights were dragging him along at a fast walking pace, having left the shouting crowd behind. Judging by the echoing footsteps, they were somewhere in the alleys of the Outer City. The ground was uneven, and every now and then, the Knight holding his arm kicked his wooden leg, and then laughed when he stumbled.

"Hey," he shouted. "Where are we going? Where are you taking me?"

His angry shouts echoed in the street, and were taken up by other voices.

"Where you be taking him? He's done nothing," one man said in Outer City slang.

"You'll be taking him away like Merro," another man yelled.

"Where is Merro?" This voice was more educated.

The Knights sped up, tightening their grip on Isandor's arm. The sound of running footsteps followed them. Isandor was heartened by that. Certainly the Knights were less likely to harm him when there were witnesses. He had to face it. His time with the Knighthood was over. He might as well make the transition into evil complete.

He reached out for icefire. The strands sizzled and crackled. He could feel them on his hands bound behind his back. His body drank in the power he had denied for so long.

"You go, boy. Show them," the man with the educated voice growled.

They want me to do this? Isandor felt the rush of icefire swirl around him. A *satisfying* rush.

Next moment, the rag flew from his eyes with a gust of ice-cold wind. The rope that held his wrists fell to the ground.

Isandor stopped, panting, still holding the strands of icefire.

The Knights had taken him to one of the darker alleys behind the markets. There were many other people here, but strangely no one took any notice of him. The Knights were shouting and swearing, their weapons drawn, their backs to him.

Isandor couldn't restrain a chuckle. They hadn't realised that *he* made the icefire whip up the wind? Amusing. He grabbed another strand. It crackled and sizzled when he whipped it over their backs. The men shielded their faces with arms and hands.

Isandor ran as fast as he his wooden leg allowed.

Behind him, a man yelled, "The prisoner! Stop the prisoner!"

Isandor skidded into a side alley only to find many people

were already hiding there, all dressed in black.

A man at the front yelled, "Here he comes. Step aside, step aside everyone!"

People shuffled aside.

"This way!" a man shouted and opened a door for him at the back of the alley.

Isandor didn't think, didn't question; he ran through the open door, down a narrow passageway that zig-zagged between limpets, their side doors, their outroom collection buckets, composting trays and broken furniture.

He ran and ran, charged by the power of icefire. His leg worked better than it ever had before. He felt like he was flying, *running like a normal man.*

All the time, he saw the images of snow sliding under his belly, of partygoers in the streets running away and screaming their incomprehensible words. Where to go? Where was the ice plain with his females? Where was the ocean? This maze had trapped him. It was dizzying . . .

Breathe.

Isandor stopped, gasping.

He had to find that Legless Lion whose heart beat in his pocket. At times, he *became* the Lion, and Legless Lions could stay under water without breath for much longer than he could. If this went on, those images would kill him.

He made his way through the alleys, pulling his cloak tight around his neck so his red shirt wouldn't show. Shouts and cries rang in the night, sounds of fighting. The sky glowed orange ahead, and there were the telltale billowing clouds of a fire. Some of the limpets belonging to poorer families were made from light, foamy material that burned like fire bricks, and gave off thick smoke that made people who breathed it sick for days.

A group of youths tromped through the street, their faces hidden behind scarves, carrying sticks and shovels. He slipped in with the group, shaking his hair loose from the ponytail. No one protested the presence of one extra person.

"... yeah, and they took Indo, too," one boy was saying.

"What? He wouldn't harm a puppy."

"Everyone who was there, they said. Did you see what happened to the Queen's bears?"

"Didn't see, but heard. And they think *we* did it?" This boy sounded angry.

The other boy shrugged. "We're Outer City folk. Can't be trusted."

"Always the same. We got to stop the Knights, you know. Stop them right here. We can't be ruled like this."

A few others grumbled consent.

The street opened out into the market square. Two lines of Knights stood on both sides of the meltery doors. Isandor recognised their uniforms: these were Jevaithi's personal guards.

Jevaithi.

What was she still doing here?

The group of youths marched on, but Isandor stopped, barely aware of their receding footsteps. Jevaithi, the only other Imperfect he knew who lived in the city. Jevaithi, whose eyes pleaded him for help. And help he would.

Isandor stumbled across the square, deliberately unsteady, his eyes unfocused and his gaze directed at the ground.

"Hey, you!" one of the Knights said.

Isandor took the last few steps in a stumbling rush and leaned against the meltery's outer wall. His heart thudded in his throat. The Knights fell silent.

He swallowed a mouthful of air, and another one, and let it out in a mighty belch that made acid rise into the back of his throat.

"Hey, you. Move along," the Knight repeated.

"Be a moment," he said, slurring his words.

He dug under his cloak and undid the fastening of his trousers. He'd seen drunks often enough to know they always pissed everywhere. Cold bit into delicate skin, and all of a sudden, he *needed* to piss. A yellow hole melted into the ice of the meltery's outer wall. The Knights laughed and continued talking. He was no longer a danger to them, just another drunk.

Finished.

He re-fastened his trousers and leaned against the icy wall.

The door clanged and two Knights came out of the meltery. Their voices carried over the square.

". . . should have been here long ago."

". . . is so embarrassing . . . what do you think she . . ."

"And all this on the whim of a spoilt brat."

Then he ran through the streets, his flippers slapping on the hard ground. Someone threw a stick at him, but it missed. He barked at the man; he tore the cloak off his shoulders. *The fur of my fellows.*

A deep gasp of breath. His face pressed against the ice wall. By the skylights, he had almost passed out. The Legless Lion heart beat against his leg, in unison with his heart.

One of the Knights called out, "Thank the skylights, there he is."

Isandor glanced over his shoulder, still panting. Another Knight was crossing the square at a trot.

"Got the sled," he shouted to his comrades.

"Good. Let's get out of here." One of the Knights went back inside the meltery.

"Hey, move along, you drunkard!" This shout was directed at Isandor.

"Just . . . just a moment . . ." Isandor deliberately slurred his voice, stumbled a few steps, fell back against the meltery wall, swallowed air, and let out another burp.

"Disgusting," the Knight mumbled and went inside.

Isandor took as long as he dared to push himself off the wall, aware of the Knight guards' gazes on him. He moved away slowly, swaying on his feet. A faint breeze brought the sound of shouts and yells from elsewhere in the Outer City. The orange glow of fire had intensified. Once the surrounding ice had melted, those ancient building materials burned well. Isandor hoped the blaze was away from limpets of people he knew. He hoped someone was controlling the fire. He hoped his mother was all right.

The meltery doors opened, flooding the ice-covered ground with yellow light. A couple of Knights came out, long shadows over the empty square.

"We'll take you to the sled as quickly as we can, Your Highness."

Isandor couldn't believe his luck. She was going to walk right past him . . .

His vision faded. He ran on clumsy flippers. *I'm much faster in the water*. He shot out into the market square. Skidded to a halt. On the other side of the square was a building which glowed yellow light such as humans had. There were a bunch of people gathered around it. What they couldn't see was that a blue man hid around the corner.

Isandor gasped. He recognised the blue form of the man, taller than him, broader and with expressionless black eyes. He carried a dagger in his blue-marbled hand, blood dripping from the blade.

This was a true servitor. Tandor's.

CHAPTER 23

THE SKY had turned deep blue, and the meltery's owner had grown restless when the door opened, letting in a blast of cold air that made the fire in the stove flare up.

A group of Knights marched in and came to a halt before Rider Cornatan's chair. Saluted.

One stepped forward and bowed. "The sled has arrived."

"What took you so long?" Rider Cornatan's voice sounded annoyed. He broke his glare at Jevaithi, which he had managed to maintain for much of the time he'd sat opposite her. Undressing her with his eyes.

"There's a few houses on fire near the festival grounds, and the eagles had some trouble with the smoke, and when we got back, we had to come the long way. There are also too many people out to take the sled through the streets."

Rider Cornatan raised an annoyed eyebrow. "I hope you left an adequate guard with it."

"We did."

Rider Cornatan gave him a sharp look, but let the unspoken

truth hung between them. No normal person could have inflicted the injuries that had killed the driver of the other sled. No normal human could have slaughtered those bears, and so there was no guarantee that this not-normal apparition wouldn't attack the new sled with guards.

He rose from his seat. "Let's go then. Are you ready, Your Highness?"

Jevaithi scrambled for her cloak, which a Knight held up for her. She met the meltery's owner's eyes across the bar, where he was putting away glasses.

"Rider Cornatan, can you make sure he is compensated for the earnings he didn't take while we were in here?"

Rider Cornatan grumbled something to a younger Knight, who went to the bar. A few of the men gave her strange glances, but the owner took the money and bent his head to her.

"Your Highness, you are always welcome here."

"Thank you."

She met the man's eyes and held his gaze while walking to the door, in a daze. *Please help me, if you can*. The citizens were her saviours, if she could still be saved after tonight.

The man didn't give any sign that he had understood what was going on. As citizen of the Outer City, there was probably nothing he *could* do.

Jevaithi followed Rider Cornatan outside, every step bringing her closer to the palace, to her bedroom.

A thin mist hung over the marketplace, a damper over the voices of groups of revellers walking across. A powder-like drizzle of snow drifted from the sky. The air smelled of smoke.

The Knights started off across the marketplace, with at least six close to Jevaithi. They were all taller and broader than her, and she didn't see much beyond cloaks and hands on swords.

She shivered. Something pricked at her senses. Icefire was thicker in the air than ever. It buzzed and shimmered, lining roofs and gutters. It danced on top of a lamp post. It didn't touch the Knights; it bent around them.

Maybe—she was getting ideas—maybe she could use it to defend herself, later, when she and Rider Cornatan were alone in her room.

A voice rang out from beyond her circle of guards, "Watch out, Your Highness!"

She turned around, and saw nothing but Knights' backs.

"Keep moving, Your Highness," the Knight behind her said. "There's nothing—"

"By the skylights!" another yelled.

There was a sickening snap. All around her, Knights were yelling and pulling swords.

Jevaithi shouted, "What's happening?"

Someone shouted, "Move, move!"

A man at the back of the group screamed, his voice descending into a beastly wail, which was followed by a hard snap, and silence. There was the sound of a sword being drawn, and another. Footsteps scuffling in the snow. Knights closed in around Jevaithi.

Silence, except for the Knights' breaths, which made puffs of mist in the air.

"Where is he?" a Knight asked.

"Uhm—just what exactly are we looking for?" another whispered. "Did you see what killed him?"

In the silence, Jevaithi shivered. She couldn't see anything with all these men in her way, but she felt it well enough: icefire burst from something a couple of steps in front.

The thing that killed the driver and the bears.

Another scream, short, loud and sharp. It broke off abruptly.

"By the skylights," one of the Knights whispered. There was horror in his voice.

Bodies pressed closer to Jevaithi. The shorthair cloaks smelled of oil and beast. Slowly, the Knights shuffled back towards the meltery. They nodded signals to each other, and Jevaithi found herself being lifted off the ground by a couple of strong arms. The Knights went faster, first at a trot, then a full run.

Men screamed behind them. A few Knights stumbled. A waft of cold air descended on Jevaithi. Through the gap between two of the Knights, she saw what they were fleeing.

A blue shadow, like the Legless Lion had been. This one was a man, taller than any of the Knights. His face was hard and white with a blue tinge. His eyes were dark holes without expression.

The protecting group around her fell apart as Knights drew swords.

"Go away, you spawn of sorcery!" someone yelled.

Jevaithi stumbled back, and would have fallen if it hadn't been for Rider Cornatan behind her.

"Careful, Your Highness." He put her back on her feet, and peered into the semidarkness.

He couldn't see the blue giant, nor could any of the Knights, some of whom were fighting a band of brawling youths who had come out of a street behind them. The Knights weren't even looking in the right direction. The blue giant grabbed one man by the collar of his cloak and smashed him into a lamp post. He didn't even scream, but sank in a boneless heap into the snow.

Jevaithi cried, "There!" and pointed at the fallen man. The blue giant was now coming towards her.

The Knights, including Rider Cornatan, jumped in front of her, even though she was sure they still couldn't see what they were fighting.

"There, there!" She pointed.

"Stay out of the way, Your Highness," Rider Cornatan snapped. "Or, you'll get in the way of our—"

The first of her guards fell.

Another group of youths burst into the square. One was running so fast he crashed into a Knight. The young man screamed garbled words. Following him was the blue Legless Lion, snarling, jumping around. The youth, who could obviously see the creature, was backing away, flailing his arms and shouting.

The Knights, who could not see the creature, mistook the young man for an attacker. One belted the young man on the head. His fellows attacked the Knight. Within moments, everyone was fighting each other, while the blue giant tossed bodies aside and smashed his way through the chaos.

He was coming for *her*, and the Knights couldn't see him.

"Stand aside!" a clear voice shouted.

A shadow sprang forward, putting itself between the blue man and the crowd. Yellow threads sparked from the cloaked silhouette, fanning out over the street. People yelled and ran in different directions. Some of them also couldn't see the golden strands. Icefire whipped up cloaks and crackled over the street in sizzling bolts like lightning that encased the blue giant in a shimmering net of icefire.

The Legless Lion jumped and snapped at the blue giant who was trying to push himself free of the golden threads.

"Come." The mysterious newcomer took hold of Jevaithi's hand. His voice sounded like that of a young man and grip was warm. "Before he kills everyone. I don't know how long this will hold him back. I'll take you to safety."

Jevaithi didn't question the order. She ran. The young man dragged her along. He turned sharply into a narrow alley where they had to squeeze past overflowing rubbish bins, out into another alley, around a corner into a narrower alley, past another group of brawling revellers, into another alley. *He knows the way.* Her companion was tall and lanky. He wore a Knight's cloak, but if there was an insignia of rank on his collar, she didn't see it.

He stopped at the door to some sort of warehouse, in a dead-end passageway. Their panting breaths sounded loud in the sudden silence. Puffs of steam floated in the blue air. He fumbled with something in his pocket.

"Just need to find the key." He gestured at the door. "We'll be safe in here."

His voice sounded so familiar that she reached out and pushed the hood of his cloak back.

The soft light showed the face of her rescuer. It was the flying champion, Isandor.

A strand of icefire snaked through the darkness, over her head. Jevaithi whirled just in time to see the ice wall behind her shimmering. A section of it went blue. Hardened, grey ice formed into a booted foot, a knee, a leg . . . Jevaithi stood as frozen. A blue-hued hand emerged from the wall.

"It's him," she whispered to Isandor, gripping his arm. "It's that blue monster."

Isandor retreated, pushing Jevaithi behind him. They couldn't run any more.

The alley ended here, in the door to the warehouse that belonged to Carro's father, and the blue giant blocked the only way out. Isandor reached for icefire, but he found only weak strands. He looked frantically for a weapon and found a snow shovel propped up against the wall.

The servitor detached from the wall, his face a mask of blue marble, expressionless, with black holes for eyes. He lunged.

Isandor hit out at the man. The shovel struck his arm with a bone-juddering clang like he had hit stone. The giant's aching cold shuddered through his bones.

Isandor fell back, dazed. How could that man have walked through a wall?

His view faded and he was jumping and barking. He snapped his jaws together, got a hold of the blue man's buttocks, but the blue giant just shook the Legless Lion off. He rolled in the snow, into a pile of crates.

Remember to breathe.

Isandor gulped air.

The Lion scrambled to its flippers, never ceasing its barking and snapping at the servitor.

Isandor picked up a snow shovel and flung it in the man's face, but he just batted it away.

The giant was too strong. He blocked the only way out of the alley. They were trapped.

"I'll make a bargain with you," Isandor tried.

The giant said nothing. He simply grabbed both his and Jevaithi's arms. The cold of the blue-skinned hand went through Isandor's clothes into his very bones.

"Keep me, but let her go," Isandor tried again.

Again, there was no reaction, not even to Jevaithi, who pummelled her fist into the man's arm. Silly, servitors only listened to their makers. This blue giant only listened to Tandor.

Isandor held his breath and looked at the Legless Lion. *Bite him!*

The animal surged forward, snapping and snarling, but the blue man pushed it aside as if it were a small child. An icy cold hand grabbed hold of Isandor's collar. Jevaithi was similarly constrained, and she was bashing the giant's arms, but he took no notice of her.

He dragged Isandor and Jevaithi out of the alley.

Jevaithi's eyes were wide with fear.

"I'm sorry," Isandor whispered. If he hadn't intervened, she might have made it back to the palace.

Maybe, maybe not.

"What's happening now?" she whispered. Her voice spilled over.

Isandor shrugged, too much of a coward to say, *Tandor is going to turn us into slaves.*

The blue man dragged them through other alleys, staying away from main streets, until they came to another warehouse. The Legless Lion, which had hobbled after them, sniffed the air and barked. From inside the building, barks responded.

A butchery.

The giant pulled a door open, pushed Isandor and Jevaithi inside, and slammed the door shut.

They were in a butchery backroom, much like his uncle's. A single icefire light burned in a bracket against the opposite wall. It gave off an eerie white glow, much brighter than the oil lamps used by most in the Outer City. White tiles covered the floor and walls. There were cages under the benches which lined the perimeter of the room. Inside, dark shapes moved about, snorting and sniffing.

Jevaithi stared, white-faced.

"I'm sorry," Isandor said again, and he looked away. It was his fault that she was in danger.

"Sorry about what? You've already helped me. The Knights were going to—"

"The Knights know you're Imperfect?"

She stared at him, wide-eyed. "You can see that?" Like this, she sounded like an ordinary girl, a very scared ordinary girl.

"I can see it in you just as well as you see it in me."

"It's the icefire that gives it away." She licked her lips. Her breath steamed.

Isandor said, "We must get out of here as soon as possible. The servitor is going to get Tandor, his master. I don't know exactly what he wants, but I think he wants to turn us into servitors, too."

"*Us?*" Her eyes widened. "What for?"

"We will be strong enough to break a man's neck. We can use icefire as he directs us. We can't disobey him."

"But what does he want with that power?"

"Kill the Knights? Rule the City of Glass. I don't know. I know that I don't like it and I want to get out of here before he comes back."

He inspected the door. It was bolted. There was a small window in the door, but even if it had been big enough for a person to climb through, which it wasn't, it had metal bars. There was another door at the back of the room, but it led into a storage room without doors or windows. The shelves were stacked with piles of frozen meat and folded parcels of skin. Nothing to use as a battering ram. There was no way out except that tiny window with metal bars. If he could turn himself into a long and skinny animal, he could get through. Even a snow fox could, he thought. The books had mentioned rumours of people so powerful they could change the physical shape of their bodies. That would be handy right now.

He shivered.

In his mind, he saw the blue man walking through the wall... He saw the blue Legless Lion hobble out of the arena; he felt the Lion's heart thud against his leg.

"Wait—I have an idea. It's probably stupid, but..." He hobbled over to one of the cages, and fumbled with the latch.

"What are you doing?"

"Help me. I'm going to open this. I want you to slam the door shut after one animal has come out."

"Why?"

"I'm going make a servitor. I have an idea. I could be stupid, but we don't know until we try."

She gave a small squeak, but nodded, her lips pressed together in a thin line. She took up position on the other side of the door.

All of a sudden it struck him how ridiculous this was, asking the *Queen* to do these things. Isandor hesitated.

"You know... for a noble girl having grown up in the palace, you're not afraid of anything."

"I am afraid," she said, and her voice trembled. "I'm just a lot more afraid of what will happen if I don't get out, or if the Knights catch me."

"The Knights? You are afraid of the Knights? I thought they protected you?"

That was what he always believed the Knights were about. That's what he had been *told* the Knights were about. They were the eyes and hands of the Queen, noble, honest—

She nodded, once, her eyes blinking. "I live in a prison. I'm kept better than this animal here, but that is only while the Knights squabble over who out of their midst gets to rape me first. Tonight."

What?

"Don't look at me like that." Her voice spilled over. She covered her mouth with a white-gloved hand. Tears glittered in her eyes. "I don't want pity."

"Your Highness." Isandor reached out and touched her cheek.

She looked up, such a vulnerable girl, too young to deal with this. "Don't call me that. I don't want it anymore. I want to be free. I want to go to the markets. I want to walk into the meltery and dance with the boys. I like . . ." Her voice spilled over in a sob. A tear ran down her cheek. She wiped it. "I'm sorry."

Isandor repressed an insane urge to kiss her, but he feared it would lead to all sorts of other things, and they didn't have the time for that.

"And so you will be free." He took the stick that stood against the wall and pushed the rope that dangled off the end through the eyelet so that it made a noose. He'd seen his uncle do this many times. "Stand there. Open the door. Slam it after the first animal has come out. I'll show you what I've been thinking." He sounded more confident than he felt.

She pressed her lips together, wiped her eyes and grasped the metal bars.

"Ready?"

Jevaithi nodded.

He opened the door to the cage.

A small female Legless Lion came out. Jevaithi slammed the metal grille on the nose of its mate, a young male. He yelped.

Isandor only had eyes for the animal, which hobbled about agitated. It wanted to go back to its mate, but Jevaithi stood in front of the cage, clamping a hand over her mouth. Yes, the animal stank of fish.

The Lion hobbled away but came to the opposite wall. It ran until it reached the corner and couldn't go any further. Isandor aimed with the stick. After three misses, he managed to slip the noose over the animal's head, yanking backwards. The Lion lost its grip on the slippery floor and slid over its belly. Isandor pulled the rope tight and wound it around the stick.

"Hold this."

Jevaithi's face was white, but she flipped both sides of her pristine white cloak over her shoulders and took the stick.

He took the animal by the back flippers and turned it onto its back. Then he pulled the dagger from his belt, just like he had done this afternoon, and lunged, while calling icefire from the air. The blade sank into the animal's chest. The ribs split open with a crack. Icefire lit the inside of the warehouse, flowing into the animal's chest. Isandor lifted out the heart, still pulsing, and stepped back.

"Let the rope go," he said.

Jevaithi looked on, wide-eyed. She relaxed her grip on the rope.

The animal wriggled itself out of the noose and rolled into a running position. Its fur had gone pale blue. It stopped and looked at him, waiting for him to tell it what to do. That's what servitors did.

Go, he told it. *You're free.*

With a jump of joy, the animal ran for the door, straight through it, and then it was gone. Yes!

Isandor turned to Jevaithi. "That's how we can get out."

"You're not suggesting that I . . ."

"It's the only way. You cut me, and I cut you. Then I walk through the wall, you pass both the hearts through the window up there, and then you walk through as well, and then we put the hearts back."

"But I've never—"

"Try it. You can do it. There is so much icefire about that it almost happens by itself, if you do it, as Imperfect. Practise. There's plenty of animals."

She looked sick, but nodded. "I'll try."

Isandor went to open the cage to let the second animal out. As it hobbled onto the tiled floor, the servitor female burst back through the wall. Isandor lunged for its neck and pushed the pulsing heart back into its chest. Icefire crackled through the room. The fur lost its blue tinge. The animal was whole again and frolicked through the room with its mate as if nothing had happened.

"I can't do that," Jevaithi stammered.

"Yes, you can. Try it." Isandor held out the dagger.

She took it, looking doubtfully at the animal which was shuffling sideways, playing with its mate.

"Kill it?"

"It won't be dead. It will be . . ." *your servitor, and its experience will torment you.* "It's only for a while. It's how we can escape. Please."

She gripped the knife in her sole hand. Isandor caught the animal with the noose and held it down for her.

She tightened her stance. Hesitated. Isandor held his breath.

Don't say you can't do it, because I might just agree. Who was he anyway, to think that this noble girl could kill an animal? He had to be crazy.

She pressed her lips together and stabbed. Golden icefire flowed from her single hand, even from her stump. The knife sank into the fur. Icefire crackled. The cut in the animal's chest flowered open.

The heart jumped out. Isandor caught it for her, warm and pulsing. She gave him a triumphant smile, and letting out a relieved breath at the same time. The Lion raised its head and tried to wriggle free from the noose. Its fur had gone blue and eerie.

"See? You can do it."

Her eyes were wide. She swallowed. "I'm . . . seeing things."

"That's because you see the world through the animal's eyes. Wait." He returned the heart to the shimmering spot in the animal's ribcage. The golden glow of icefire vanished, and the fur returned to its normal mottled grey. The Legless Lion barked. Isandor let the noose go.

Then he faced her again, peeling back his shirt to bare his chest.

"Do it to me. We can get out."

"No."

"You have to."

"No, I'd kill you." She shook her head, her face white as if she would throw up any moment.

He pulled her closer, the fur warm against his shivering body. The tip of the dagger dug into his skin, staining it with blood.

"If you kill me, I will die happy and free." His hand touched hers, and he had to stop himself caressing her skin. "If Tandor or the Knights get here before we get out, we'll be dead anyway. Do it, and we'll escape. Together."

"Are you sure?" She stared at him.

He nodded. "Please. Do it. Now."

She hefted the dagger, her hand trembling.

Isandor closed his eyes. They should have practised on the Legless Lions more. They should have . . . No time, no time.

He held his breath. "Do it, please." *Before I change my mind and I get scared.*

Impossible. He *was* already scared. Terrified. About to piss himself.

He felt, rather than saw, how her arm descended. The blade bit into his chest. A brief shot of intense pain. His scream died in his throat as ice cold invaded him. Silent wind whooshed out the hole in his chest. His life, seeping away from him. Death awaited him; he was—

Floating in the wind—

Everywhere and nowhere at all—

You are mine now. The voice was soft, but insistent. *I think I'm going to like it.*

He opened his eyes. The world had turned inside out. Shadows were white. The light against the wall was dark. Everything the opposite of what it should be.

There was only Jevaithi, holding his life blood in her hands. Her hair gleamed silver against her skin which was deep golden brown. Her eyes were rich magenta. She was so beautiful it hurt inside. He wanted to speak but couldn't. *I'll do everything for you.*

Here, take this. She passed him the dagger, while unbuttoning her dress. He stared at the dark skin, wanting to touch it, caress it—

Take my heart.

He didn't question the order; he was hers. He hefted the dagger and stabbed. Her face turned white even before he had the heart in his hands. It pulsed strongly, but it now looked dark in his eyes.

There was no time to contemplate the reason for the changed colours.

Here, hold this. He handed her the other heart. She cradled both in her single hand against her chest, his heart and hers, together. Oh, how he wanted to kiss her. Her eyes were dark and full of longing. Her voice echoed in his mind. *We'll kiss later.*

Yes, later, when they were safe.

He walked to the door and pushed his hands against it. Material bent around them. He pushed his arms further in, then a foot . . . He drew back, staring down at his two healthy legs. Two feet! In his mind, he was running over the snow plain, he was jumping over cracks in the ice, he—

No, he couldn't get distracted.

He pushed further through the door. Blurred shapes moved around him, and chilled him.

His leg he came out into the clear air of the alley, followed by his hands. He pushed his head out. There was no one in the alley, so he pulled the rest of his body free of the door. Jevaithi moved in the darkness behind the little barred window.

Give me the hearts.

A white-blue hand passed through the window grille, holding an object that was too black for him to see. It fell heavy in his hands, ice-cold but pulsing. Safe. Then the other one.

The wall shimmered and Jevaithi walked through slowly, feeling her way with her hands. *Both* her hands. She stopped. Black eyes blinked at ten slender fingers, pale blue. The colour of her skin and eyes mattered nothing. She was so beautiful.

I'm free.

Her joy made him glow. He wasn't cold anymore. Tandor was right; he would never be cold anymore.

In two steps, he crossed the distance between them. He didn't stop to consider how he had never done what he intended to do; he bent and closed his mouth over hers. Her lips were soft and warm and willing. Her elation almost hurt.

I love you, I love you, I love you. Her inner voice sank deep into every fibre of his body.

He had to tear himself from her grip. *We must go.* They weren't safe yet.

Yes, I know that. Her gaze wandered to the hearts. *Will we put them back?*

He had intended to do that as soon as they got out, but he shook his head. Like this, they were strong. Like this, most Knights couldn't see them, and like this, Tandor couldn't make them his servitors. No, he had a much better idea, but that would have to wait until they were truly safe. He slid both hearts in his pocket.

Come.

They ran. The Legless Lion that was still outside hobbled along with them, even though the animal was now free. Or was it? Isandor felt in his pocket where he still had that animal's heart.

He ran, like a real person. His leg was whole and propelled him forward like as if flew. The joy, the elation, her warm hand in his. He was never going to let her go. He was going to rule the world, and put all the injustice right. He was—

Careful. Jevaithi's thought came like a shout.

She had stopped and yanked him back with tremendous strength. The Legless Lion couldn't stop quite so quickly and it slid into the street on its belly before finding grip with its flippers and hobbling back.

What is it?

Knights.

Isandor peeked around the corner and he could see them, too, a group of four.

They can't see us. He made to move into the street.

Wait.

What? He turned to her, to see worry crossing her face.

Don't you feel it?

Yes, he did. A pulling sensation that made him shiver.

Look. She pointed.

Black threads moved against the light blue sky, tendrils of mist streaming towards the Knights.

What is it? The pulling became stronger, as if threads were stuck to his skin and refused to let go.

Icefire.

Yes, in this state icefire looked black. *Leading to the Knights?*

The group of Knights had come closer. Their voices sounded far off, but the warmth in their bodies was close.

There were four Knights, and one, at the front of the group, held an object that attracted icefire, which wove over the Knights' heads.

Even through the tangle of black strands, Isandor recognised this Knight.

Carro. He was the one who held the object, a metal staff, poised as if it was a sword, with icefire streaming towards it.

"Which way?" one of the other Knights asked.

Carro waved the staff, his gloves covered in rime. "Something is very strong here." His voice sounded hollow.

He looked into the street where Isandor and Jevaithi stood, straight past them, and then moved the staff slowly so that it pointed at them.

No!

Jevaithi's shriek cut into Isandor's mind. She stood frozen like some grotesque ice statue. Dark strands of icefire flowed from her hands to the staff. The outlines of her right hand were already fading. Icefire flew from his body as well, dissolving skin into the air.

Oh, the pain. Like boiling water over his skin.

With all the force he could muster, Isandor shoved Jevaithi into a porch, out of the path of the black braid of icefire. Now it hit him at full force. Pain exploded in every part of his body. He wanted to, but couldn't, scream.

With immense effort, he picked up a lid from a composting bin and flung it at the Knights as hard as he could. It crashed into one of them, sending the young man toppling into the fellow next to him.

Carro yelled, "Watch out!"

The device had lost contact, and in that moment, Isandor covered the ground between them.

You betrayed me.

Carro couldn't hear him of course. He was wildly waving the staff, which made contact with Isandor again. White-hot pain flared.

He was dimly aware that a shadow leapt up between him and Carro. Something snarled. The next moment, the Legless Lion had thrown itself at the group. Carro stumbled and fell. The staff flew out of his hands, twirling and tumbling until it hit the ground.

Carro sat there, dazed, white-faced. His mates ran off down the street.

Isandor sat on hands and knees, panting.

The Legless Lion lay in the snow. It had jumped up to save him and had injured itself by touching the staff. Its body lay still, but when Isandor ran his hand through the rough fur, one flipper twitched.

Isandor flinched with the animal's pain. It lifted its head and blinked at him. He reached in his pocket and brought out the animal's heart.

Go, he told it as he slid it back into the hairy chest. *You have done enough*. The animal's fur shivered as it returned to its normal state.

The Lion let its head sink back onto the ground. *Sleep*.

Isandor rose. The animal would recover.

Jevaithi had come out of her hiding place and walked towards the staff which lay on the ground, absorbing lazy tendrils of icefire. Now that Carro wasn't holding it anymore, it had lost much of its power.

Don't touch it.

She bent over it, shuddering visibly.

Carro had retreated against the icy wall of a limpet, his eyes wide, trembling. He was looking at the Legless Lion, which had raised itself and slowly hobbled down the street.

Isandor grabbed the front of Carro's cloak, heaving him up until his feet came off the ground. His friend, taller than him, weighed no more than a sack of flour.

Carro's eyes bulged, still focused on a point behind Isandor. He gave a tiny squeak. "Where are you?"

Isandor hesitated. What would he do? He could easily slam Carro into the wall and kill him. He could break Carro's neck with a single snap. His hands ached to do just that. Carro had *betrayed* him. Carro had destroyed his life, his chance to be respected.

I would have been discovered anyway.

Isandor looked down into Carro's face. There were tears in his eyes. His lips were blue and shivered. One cheek was dirty from where the lid of the composting bin had hit him. A trail of blood ran over his face from a cut above his eyebrow.

He's just a coward. Carro did what people told him to do; he had always been like that.

Isandor got no pleasure out of killing cowards.

Prove yourself a real soldier, and we'll fight over this later.

He tightened his hold on Carro's cloak, swung his arm back and let Carro fly from his hands. His friend slid across the street like a rag doll, slammed into a heap of snow and remained there. For a moment, Isandor was afraid he'd used too much force, but then Carro raised his head.

Run, Jevaithi.

He took her hand, before he changed his mind, before he could no longer control his lust for blood. They ran through the streets, across the markets, where the merchants were guarding their stalls, eying a group of youths who stood outside the meltery. Isandor wondered if it was the same group he had joined briefly before rescuing Jevaithi.

The youths held sticks and shovels and stood together talking in low voices. Most of them had pulled their cloak collars over their faces. Acrid smoke billowed through the streets.

No one noticed Isandor and Jevaithi crossing the square. No one followed.

They went down the slope to the plain and the festival grounds, which still bathed in the blue glow of eternal dawn. Aisles between tents were deserted, the previous day's activity only hinted at by the trampled snow.

Two Knights guarded the eagle pens, standing in silent reflection, hidden in the warmth of their cloaks. Neither stirred when Isandor led the way through the pens.

The guards might not have seen anything, but Isandor's eagle certainly did. It lifted its head and gave a series of clicking sounds that signified alertness.

Shhh. Isandor lifted the saddle off the fence and slung it on the bird's back, checking several times over his shoulder if anyone noticed. The Knights were chatting to each other, facing the other way, where there were shouts and where flames rose above the roofs. He fastened the clasps and stepped into his riding harness, belting it up across his chest

Ready?

Jevaithi nodded.

Isandor hefted her onto the eagle. *Hold on.* She grabbed the handholds on top of the saddle. He untied the eagle's reins and jumped up behind her, whistling at the bird. It spread its wings and with a whoosh of wind and flapping of wings, launched into the air.

There was a shout below them. A couple of Knights ran on

the snow fields, waving their arms. Too late.

All they would see was a riderless eagle flying over the moonlit landscape.

But down there, just entering the festival grounds was Tandor, running and shouting. He could see what Isandor had done, but there was no way Tandor could stop them.

Isandor laughed. He had fooled them all. He clutched Jevaithi to his chest, guiding the bird with his knees. He didn't need to hold on. He didn't need to breathe. The cold wind didn't bother either of them. They ruled the world.

CHAPTER 24

LORIANE GASPED and stirred, lifting her head off something hard that hurt her ear. She sat, to her surprise, on the floor of Isandor's sleeping shelf, leaning on the chair by his bed. One leg had gone numb and her ankle hurt where it pressed into the floor.

The fire in the stove downstairs had died to a pitiful glow that barely lit the furniture.

She must have fallen asleep, although she couldn't remember sitting down. Myra slept in Isandor's bed, her mouth open, her arm twitching by her side.

Loriane heaved herself to her feet. She did remember giving Myra the sleeping draught which had stopped her pains. The girl was too tired to continue, not having slept for two days, and all the hard work was still ahead.

A soft noise drifted up from downstairs, the sound of scrabbling on wood. If she was not mistaken, there was someone at the door, and now she guessed that the knocking had woken her op.

As quietly as she could, Loriane went down the stairs, across the main room, into the icy hall. On the way, she glanced at her own bed, but it was empty. Where was Tandor? He hadn't said anything about where he was going.

She opened the outside door a tiny crack. Against the faint light of the midnight glow above the horizon, she could just make out a dark figure.

"Mistress Loriane?" A male voice, young. She didn't recognise it. The man was much taller than her and wore a cloak. A Knight? She didn't know any Knights except Isandor.

"Who is it?"

"Please, I need help."

Loriane hesitated, registered that he hadn't answered her question. Illegal business? Something to do with Tandor? She wanted to say *He isn't here*, but that might betray Tandor.

"Please," the man said again, and she heard a wobble in his voice. "I'm injured. I don't know where else to go. The post at the festival grounds is closed, and you are the only healer I know . . ."

No, Isandor wasn't the only Knight she knew. He had a friend who had gone to the Knights with him, a son of a fabric merchant, a pale and pasty boy. This might well be him.

Slowly, she undid the chain and opened the door.

He stepped into the hall, where the feeble light allowed her to see the young man better. She thought this was indeed Isandor's friend. He wore a shorthair Knight's cloak, wet and dirty. His face was covered in blood. It had plastered his hair against his forehead and had run into his eyes.

"Thank you. Sorry for . . . waking you up. 'S too much fighting . . . in the street t' go . . . somewhere else. Don't want to go home." He needed to breathe through his mouth because dried blood blocked his nose.

She ushered him into the main room, motioning for him to be quiet, and gestured for him to sit down next to the stove. "I have a patient asleep upstairs," she said in a low voice.

She grabbed a clean cloth, wet it with water from the jar that sat on the stove, and passed it to him.

"Here, wipe yourself with this. Wait here. I'll be back."

She rushed up the stairs to get her bag. What a bit of luck that she had taken her kit from the medical tent in the festival grounds this afternoon.

The sound of her footsteps woke Myra. She jerked up and coughed.

"Myra?"

It was hot and stuffy up here with the simmering fire, but Myra was shivering. Her eyes were wide and distant and her breath came in shallow gasps.

"You're having pains again?"

Myra nodded and the next moment vomited all over her stomach. It was mostly water, since she hadn't eaten anything all day, but her nightgown was drenched.

"Oh!" Myra cried. She wrestled herself free of the blankets, rolled out of the bed onto hands and knees and sat there, alternately coughing and gasping and retching.

"Myra, Myra, calm down."

But the girl wasn't listening. Loriane wrestled the sodden nightgown off and stumbled to Isandor's cupboard to find spare clothes.

Where was Tandor? He could have helped her with the young Knight downstairs.

She yanked a nightgown out of the cupboard. Myra was crying. She was drenched in sweat, and, Loriane realised with a shock, pushing. Was she ready yet?

"Come, Myra, let me examine you first." She managed to get Myra off her knees but before she was back on the bed her waters broke, with fluid exploding all down her legs. Myra screamed. "Let me go. Don't touch me!"

She grabbed hold of the back of the bed with white-knuckled hands and pushed until she was red in the face, gasped for air and pushed again. More fluid dribbled down her legs and puddled at her bare feet.

Loriane's heart thudded. She had given the girl a lot of sedative; she couldn't have gone from sleep to this stage so quickly.

"Myra, just calm down. Breathe deeply. I only want to check you."

"I know about this checking of yours. It hurts. You keep away from me."

Loriane put a hand on the girl's shoulder. It was slick with sweat. "Myra—"

"Keep away, I said." Myra lashed out and hit Loriane. Her nails bit into the skin of her arm.

"Ouch!" Loriane stepped back. Red scratches welled on her wrist.

The brat! She felt like hitting the girl in the face, but she knew that sometimes women in extreme pain reacted like that.

She schooled her voice to calmness. "Very well. I will leave you. I have another patient anyway." She started down the stairs.

"No! Don't go," Myra screamed. "I wasn't serious."

"But I was. I'll be downstairs."

And strode down, feeling raised welts on her face from where Myra had hit her. Oh, if Tandor came back . . . She balled her fists. Tandor, Tandor, all her trouble could be traced back to him. He came here, dumped this uneducated nutcase on her, and he spent all day gallivanting about town.

Oh, if he came back, she was going to tell him to pack up his girlfriend and leave her alone.

The young man still sat next to the stove, holding the towel to his face. His eyes met hers and a twinge stirred in her. Just briefly, the way the light played over his cheekbone, she was reminded of a young Knight in the meltery, many years ago. He was strong and handsome, and as they danced by the firelight, he'd enclosed her gull feather in his fist and yanked it hard and sharp, so the leather strap broke. His intense eyes said, *you're mine*, and she had been delighted. With this Knight, a Learner like the young man sitting next to her kitchen stove, there was no fumbling in freezing warehouses. He'd rented a room in one of the Outer

City's inns, a room with a large bed and a blazing fireplace. She had bled, just a bit, but he had been gentle, and he'd let her sleep next to him. In the morning, he'd given her a card with how to contact him, should that prove necessary. Which it did.

Never again had she carried a child for a Knight. Never again had she seen the young man, nor her baby boy with the face all squashed from birth. She very much doubted she would recognise either if she saw them again.

She set her things on the table next to the young Knight and proceeded to clean up his cheek, gentle around the edges of his cuts. She saw the handsome Knight's face, lit side-on by the fire. She felt his weight pressing on her, his warm skin against hers.

Once more, she was in the sled, with her father driving it through the snow storm. She sat in the back wrapped up in furs, and every bump in the ice had cut through her belly like a hot knife. She'd been petrified of giving birth out there, on the snow-covered plains between the Outer City and the palace, but the child had taken a whole agonising day of pains to arrive.

Wails from Myra drifted from upstairs.

"What's with her?" the Knight asked, concern on his face.

"Well, you know I'm normally a midwife . . ."

He raised his eyebrows, and then a look of understanding came over his face. "Oh. If I'm keeping you from your work . . ."

"Not at all." Loriane cringed and tried hard not to feel guilty for walking out on Myra. For once she was going to be tough like the midwives in the palace birthing rooms. Those women slapped misbehaving girls in the face, like that old hag had slapped her, not once, but three times. Myra would have to learn on the job what it meant to be a breeder. You only scream when it's bad.

She dabbed at the young man's face, dislodging clots of blood from his nose. Strangely enough, he didn't smell of bloodwine. "Well, someone certainly gave you a good beating."

A tiny shiver went through him. The shiver became a spasm. His muscles tensed up.

"Are you all right? Are you feeling sick—"

But he didn't react to her. His gaze was far off and his breath came in shallow gasps.

Loriane grabbed his wrist. His pulse raced like crazy.

Before she could do anything, he blinked and shook his head, meeting her eyes. Was there shame in them?

"What was that?" she asked.

He shrugged and looked away.

"Is there anything you're not telling me? Do you have a problem?"

His mouth twitched. He hesitated. "Well, I get these . . ." Then he stopped, shook his head again.

"These what?" she prompted.

But he would say no more and seemed reluctant to meet her eyes. She rinsed out the bloodied cloth, weighing up the risk of what she was about to say. She had seen little spells like this before, but he was a *Knight* after all, and Knights weren't *supposed* to be inflicted like this. But the condition could be quite dangerous.

"You know," she began. "Physical imperfection isn't the only type of defect caused by icefire. Some people have imperfect minds. They seem to find it hard to see the difference between a real experience and things that have happened in the past. They keep re-living memories, sometimes from long ago—"

"I'm *not* crazy." His voice was much too forceful.

"I'm not suggesting that at all."

"I'm fine."

"I'm sure you are."

A silence followed, broken only by Myra's moans. Loriane had washed all blood off his cuts, which were deep and nasty. What by the skylights had he done to himself? The cut had collected half a bag's worth of sand. It looked like he'd been dragged along the street. But his injury was not what concerned her. This young man had serious mental trouble, and he was in denial about it.

She took a deep breath, gathering courage to speak again.

"Just in case I want you to know ichina will help."

"Ichina?" He faced her now. "But that's for girls trying to . . ." His cheeks flushed.

"Ichina is a powerful medicine that will do much more than help girls conceive. It also helps a number of other conditions, although they're not common."

"So that's why we only hear about girls taking it?" He sounded relieved.

"Yes." She let a small silence lapse and then she asked him, "Do you want some?"

He hesitated. "If, say, a boy needed to take it for—uhm—other reasons, would that boy also have trouble getting a girl pregnant, you know, *before* he takes it?"

Loriane had to restrain a snort. Oh, these adolescents were so transparent sometimes. What had he been doing? Fooling around above his station, and now he was afraid his family would have to foot the bill?

"Quite likely." Although she didn't know this for sure. It wasn't important. The future would bring whatever it would bring.

He blew out a breath.

Loriane asked again. "Would you want some?"

He nodded, once.

At that moment the door clanged. Loriane turned.

"Tandor!"

His hair was wet, with frozen chunks of ice, and hung down the sides of his face in dirty strings. A dark stain marked his cloak and blood had dried up in a scratch across his cheekbone.

He wasn't looking at her, but staring at the young Knight.

"*What* are you doing here?" He spat the words out like broken teeth.

"Tandor," Loriane protested. "That's not how you treat—"

Tandor strode across the kitchen and grabbed young Knight by the collar of his cloak. "You let him escape!"

"I don't know what you're talking about, sorcerer!" The Knight's eyes bulged.

"Oh yes, you do, or you would not be sitting here with your face bloodied up. You let them out of that warehouse, didn't you? And then you found that your friend wasn't your friend anymore?"

"I have no idea what you're talking about!" the Knight shouted.

"Hey, no fighting in my kitchen!" Loriane yelled, but the men paid her no attention.

The Knight scrabbled for his belt. He pulled out a long metal stick and jammed the point in Tandor's chest.

Tandor froze, eyeing the glittering crystal that pushed into his shirt.

The thing wasn't sharp at all, but Tandor let the young man go, his eyes wide. "It was you with the sink?"

"It was me." He let the staff sink ever so slightly.

Tandor's eyes roamed the young man's face. "Oh, I see."

"I don't see, Tandor," Loriane said. "I don't see anything at all apart from the fact that you're bothering my patient—"

"Loriane, he is—"

"I don't care who he is. The Healer's Guild made me pledge that I would help every sick or injured person who comes to my door. Get out and make yourself useful. Go upstairs and see if you can talk some sense into that girl of yours."

A brief smirk went over the young Knight's face.

Tandor pulled the Knight's collar tight with his golden pincer hand. "Don't even dare say it."

Loriane rolled her eyes.

Oh, why did men get so hung up about their dicks or lack thereof?

Tandor looked down. The Knight had the staff once more directed at his stomach. What was that thing?

"You think you're so smart with that toy, don't you?" Tandor snorted.

The Knight pressed his lips together. Blood was again running from the wound on his forehead.

"I'll get you, sorcerer."

"You wouldn't dare."

Tandor grabbed the young Knight's wrist in his pincer hand. Pushed him back into the one of the posts that supported the sleeping shelves. He lazily withdrew a something from his pocket, a long metal barrel with a wooden handle. He pointed it at the Knight and poked the metal into the soft skin under his chin.

Loriane had only heard of the Chevakian powder guns, but she was sure this was such a thing.

The Knight's eyes widened.

"You should have known that you can't surprise me," Tandor said.

The boy swallowed hard. He clutched his staff.

Tandor laughed. "Ah, we *are* a coward, aren't we? Why don't you go and tell your Knights that the game is over? The game is over for everyone."

"Now stop this idiocy in my house!" Loriane yelled. "Tandor, leave him alone so I can treat him."

Tandor laughed, defying the Knight to make another comment. He didn't.

Loriane finished with the young man in silence, while Tandor leaned against the pillar. In a very demonstrative way, he took two bullets from his pocket, jackknifed open the barrel and slid the bullets into the magazine.

The young man gave him nervous glances. As soon as Loriane finished bandaging the wound, he jumped up.

Tandor clicked the barrel back into place and pointed the gun at the Knight's back while he ran to the door.

The door shut.

He had forgotten his ichina.

Tandor laughed. "If all else fails, a Chevakian powder gun will kill. Bang, bang."

Loriane whirled at him. "Tandor, are you crazy? What is this stupid behaviour about? That young man missed out on some important treatment because of you."

He smiled, but that only made her fury greater. The Knight was an angry young man, who might do silly things without treatment.

"He'll be fine."

"How do you know that? What do you know anyway? Why shouldn't he come back here with a bunch of Knights to question me? You haven't lived in the city for years. Things have been different ever since Maraithe died. She had the Knights in hand, but Jevaithi is much too young. They don't listen to her, and from what I've seen, they shelter her from the people. She hardly goes out, and the Knights just do whatever they want, so if they want to come back here and burn down my house, they will. I can tell you that. And it happens to people, I can tell you that, too. You know the merchant Merro—"

Tandor smiled. "Jevaithi is gone." Then he started laughing. "Jevaithi is gone with that boy of yours. I saw them fly off on his eagle. Towards the mountains. Bye, bye."

"Isandor?"

By the skylights, Tandor had gone mad.

"He was kicked out of the Knighthood for being Imperfect, to be imprisoned in the palace, but he escaped everyone, even me. He took Jevaithi from under their noses."

Tandor laughed, the sound a strange shriek.

Loriane had never heard him laugh, not like this. "Tandor, what's wrong with you?" He was telling lies, wasn't he? He was crazy; something had flipped in his mind.

"What's wrong, what's wrong?" Tears ran down his cheeks. "We're all going to die. That's what's wrong."

Loriane's heart thudded against her ribs, but she forced herself into calm.

"Of course we are going to die. Life is a terminal illness." *And you seem to suffer badly.*

"Loriane." He crossed the kitchen to her and scooped her in his arms. "Loriane, I love you." He bent forward and pushed his mouth on hers. His tongue met hers, hot and passionate. "There. I've said it. I love you, I love you."

Loriane pushed him away. "You're drunk." But she didn't smell any liquor on his breath.

"Now you're going to tell me what all this is about, or . . ."

"Or what?"

"It'll be morning soon enough and I'll have Knights on my doorstep, by which time you're long gone. I need something to tell them. What happened? What did you do? What am I going say?"

"Loriane, calm down."

"No, Tandor. I don't understand why you had to threaten him. I don't. You can't just come in here to create problems for me."

"Have I ever left you with a problem?"

"Are you kidding? My whole life is a problem of your making, starting with that baby you brought me. Who is Isandor, Tandor, why is he important to you and why have you never told me?"

"I mean a problem you can't handle?"

She snorted. "One day this whole game of yours is going to fall apart. Whatever game you're playing. And we're all going to suffer for it."

There was a scream from upstairs.

"By the skylights, Myra."

Loriane thudded up to the sleeping shelf. Tandor remained halfway up the stairs.

Myra was on her hands and knees on the floor, rocking from side to side. She glanced up between sweat-soaked strands of hair.

"I hate you." She spat out the words.

Loriane wasn't sure who she meant. Both of them, probably. Doubts about the father of the child re-surfaced. Tandor hung around Myra too much not to have involvement, and he still hadn't told her why he had taken the girl with him, rather than hidden her somewhere else. He'd lied to her. The child was his after all.

Why, Tandor, why? She looked at his handsome profile in the glare from the stove. She loved him, she hated him. It was time for her to break with him, stop waiting for him to make sense to her.

"Tandor, stop whatever silly games you're playing and give me a hand. Hold her."

His eyes widened. "Hold her?"

"He's not . . . holding . . . any part . . . of me," Myra panted. Her voice was hoarse.

"Then sit still. I'm going to examine you, and if you hit me again, I'm going to belt you so hard your head is going to hurt worse than the rest of you. Understand?"

Myra nodded, but a pain took over. She rocked, and moaned and cried. Loraine washed her hands, cringing as her own belly tensed up. Stupid girl, by the time it came to the hard work, she would have no energy left.

"Girl, shut up. You're not going to get that child out by screaming. Now sit still." She crouched on the floor, awkward because of her own belly. Myra was crying.

She slid her hand inside the girl's softness. The womb tensed up. Myra screamed.

"It hurts, it hurts."

"Shut up. It's not that bad."

But then she probed with her fingers and felt that it was bad. By the skylights, she should have checked earlier.

"Tandor, do you have that sled and driver handy?"

He raised his eyebrows.

"The child is facing the wrong way. I need to take her to the palace."

Tandor's eyes widened. "The palace?"

In one hit, his face had lost its madness.

CHAPTER 25

FIRE LIT UP the sky. Flapping flames reached over the rooftops, spreading foul smoke in the air. People ran through the street, mere silhouettes in the dusky Newsun night. Some carried sticks as weapons, others had their faces covered.

Carro walked through the dark streets alone, cold air biting through his cloak. His face hurt, his muscles hurt, his head hurt. He'd fled Mistress Loriane's house without the medicine, but he could hardly go back.

He was sure that the man in Mistress Loriane's kitchen was the same he'd hunted earlier that day. Who was he, and what was he doing there? He might be dressed up as a noble, but this was no noble of the City of Glass. The man spoke with a Chevakian accent.

Carro knew he should find Rider Cornatan urgently and tell him of this man, but on the other hand . . . Mistress Loriane had said that ichina would help stop the confusing memories. Surely there would be some ichina at the medical post in the festival grounds. The post was closed, but it was only a tent and he could easily get in. Taking medicine he needed wasn't stealing, was it?

He'd rather no one else found out about it. It was a medicine for *women* and he had seen his sister prepare it many times. It never worked for her. But his sister was only his half-sister, wasn't she? Born from a different breeder. And what was wrong with him didn't have *anything* to do with a girl's ability to conceive, did it? Or rather—by the skylights, Korinne. *She* had probably taken it and was now waiting until she and her father could come to his door to claim their prize. He didn't want the care of a child. His Knight's stipend would never pay for a house and a wife, and *servants*. A Knight couldn't very well live in the Outer City either.

And he just didn't, *didn't*, want that sort of thing. Knights, especially Senior Knights, often paid families to look after their children, since most didn't marry. However, they were from noble families and had money, and they had lineages and inheritances to look after. He was only Carro, and no one cared about any brats of his.

Then you should have thought about it before you acted. He could almost hear his father's voice. His father was right, but his father was a jerk, and Carro would rather *die* than accept any help from the man.

Was that how he himself had come about? His father had been careless during the Newlight festival, but didn't care, didn't want him, got him anyway, and now Carro was about to do the same to a child of his? Rejecting a little boy whose only wish was to be liked?

A strange thought occurred to him: what if Isandor got *Jevaithi* pregnant? Isandor had no money at all; he didn't even have a family. Oh, that would be priceless, with all the Knights drooling over her and all the speculation of who would father Jevaithi's children. And then the Knights found she would have the child of a dirt-poor boy from the Outer City, an Imperfect at that. Hilarious.

Carro chuckled, then he started laughing. He laughed and laughed and couldn't stop laughing.

A man stopped and asked if he was all right, but Carro couldn't see him. The street, the people, the limpets, the orange sky above all blurred into streaks of light and dark. Tears of freezing water bit into his cheeks.

"Yes, yes, I'm all right," he said and the man left.

But he wasn't all right, wasn't he? He was crazy, damaged, sick. A common Outer City healer could see that.

He moved through the streets with the flow of the crowd, under cover of darkness. The air resonated with angry voices. People looked at him from the corners of their eyes. Young men in black formed little groups and spoke to each other in low voices. In a street nearby people were shouting. In an alley between two limpets, he caught a glimpse of a blazing fire and lithe silhouettes running away from a patrol of Knights.

Carro jammed his hands in his pockets and bent his head, hoping not to attract any attention.

Who were these people coming out in support of the Imperfects? Why were there so many of them? Did this mean the entire Brotherhood of the Light and all their pupils supported Thilleians? That they *were* Thilleians?

He had read of the time before the uprising against the king, when the common people stirred against those who held all power. There had been hordes of looters in the streets, demanding for the king to come out of the palace. The people had *lynched* the king's guards, hacked them to death and cut them up into pieces.

Something like that could easily happen again.

Carro slumps on the table. Rows and rows of numbers dance before his eyes. He could put his head on the book and sleep. All night, he's been sitting here. His fingers are cramped, his toes frozen.

One mistake in his additions, and he can start over. The

figures never add up. Income and expenditure never balance. Records are missing or incomplete. One complaint to his father, and another book is added to the pile. No dinner until he's done.

He wishes that his father, like normal fathers, would hit him. Punishment by accountancy is cruel, slow, mind-numbing and in the unheated warehouse, incredibly cold. His hands hurt. His feet hurt and he is beyond shivering.

"Hey, watch out where you're going!" a man shouted.

Someone bumped into Carro, a hard knock of a shoulder against his upper arm. Carro just stood there, gulping breath.

Carro mumbled an apology, rubbing his arm. One way or another, he must get the ichina to stop those spells.

If he left it too long, he was going to be expelled from the Knighthood, and he would have no other option than to go back to his family.

He felt himself sliding into another vision and had to steady himself against a lamp post. It was getting so bad recently. He was mad, not fit for duty. He was—

"Hey. Carro, isn't it?"

Carro looked up, into the grey eyes of one of Rider Cornatan's private hunters, Farey. He was out of uniform, wearing a cloak as dark and sleek as his hair. He raised his eyebrows at the bandage on Carro's face.

"I . . . I was looking for my patrol," Carro stammered, his tongue feeling like an overcooked piece of meat. He was still struggling to hold onto the present.

The eyebrows rose further.

Carro squirmed. This man had the ability to make you feel uneasy without saying anything. He added, "They fled."

"Real brave hearts, huh?"

Carro nodded, and looked aside. He knew what Farey

would think of him: weak, unfit to command even a bunch of Apprentices. He had to *punish* the lot of them, and punish them hard.

"We . . . encountered some enemies . . . invisible ones." It seemed such a lame story, at least when facing this strange and very unnerving man.

"Ah."

It was too dark, but Carro thought a look of bemusement crossed Farey's face. His eyes glittered with mirth. Something in his smile made Carro shiver, not because he was cold, but because . . .

Both times when he had been to Rider Cornatan's bathroom, there had been more men than women, and both times, he felt the hunters considered Korinne a floozy who didn't belong there, and who was merely a plaything for a child.

Real Knights didn't play with girls, they played with other men.

Carro's heart thudded. What had Farey come to ask him?

"I'll . . . have to punish my patrol for running away."

"Yes."

"What about you?" He barely knew what he was saying. All he could see were Farey's grey eyes, intense and amused.

"My missions are always simple."

"Oh?"

"I was looking for you."

Carro's heart jumped. He saw Farey in Rider Cornatan's bathroom, his lean and muscled chest, his olive skin—

"I was asked to save your arse, and get you out of here before those riots blow up."

A nursemaid.

Farey had come as nursemaid. Rider Cornatan thought he needed a minder. He thought Carro was soft; Farey thought

Carro was soft.

Carro paced in the empty hall, up, down, past the pathetic members of his patrol, whom he had dragged out of the dormitory.

He was still shaking from his encounter with Farey and the flight back through the freezing night air. He was shaking with anger, at himself, at his stupidity, at everyone for playing games with him.

"You stupid idiots," he yelled. "You left your commanding officer like a bunch of screaming girls."

The boys stood there, white-faced, dirty, eyes downcast, not looking at one another, especially not looking at him.

"What the fuck did you think you were doing?" Carro yelled, replaying in his mind how the Tutors yelled at him, and trying to copy. "We were to stay together at all times. Isn't that one of the things we learn?"

"We can't fight when it comes to icefire," Inran said, his eyes on the floor. "It's not a fair fight."

"No fight is fair!" Carro grabbed Inran's collar. Just as well he'd learned so much from watching the Tutor. "I can't remember fights being fair when I was at the receiving end of them. Did I run? No! Look at you lot. You decide to run off—by yourself. *Deserting*. Do you know what the punishment is for desertion?"

"There were two blue ghosts." Inran's lip was trembling.

"There were—what?" Spit flew from Carro's mouth.

Inran cowered back. "There were two blue ghosts. I was scared. I thought you'd seen them, too."

"Thought? You *thought*? Apprentices never *think* anything. You are not here to do any thinking. Your stupidity nearly got me killed. Is that what you wanted? Do you know who appointed me in this position?" Carro had to stop yelling to catch his breath.

Inran shook his head, blinking. He was one of the boys who used to egg on Jono and Caman when they teased Carro in the dormitory, but he didn't look so brave now.

Isandor looks up at him with those strong, blue eyes.

All you need to do, Carro, is tell him you won't do it. You have been accepted into the Knights and you will have your own income. Your father can no longer demand that you do things for him if he's not paying for your upkeep.

It's easy for you to say. You don't have a father. That was a very nasty remark, Carro.

Isandor fell into a moment of silence.

Try it. Tell him you're busy. What can he do?

Give me a beating.

Isandor shakes his head, and Carro notices how fuzzy his friend's chin is becoming.

Carro, you're sixteen. Your father won't beat you. He's an old man and you are stronger than he. He's afraid of you.

They should be afraid of me.

Carro let Inran go and paced back to the middle of the room, then whirled to face the boys. Inran stared at him with wide eyes. Jono and Caman were quiet enough, but looked absent-minded. They hadn't even listened to what he had said.

"What are you staring at? Get your rotten arses out of here."

The boys saluted and made for the door. Jono and Caman glanced at each other, and Jono smiled, a smile that said, *We haven't been punished.* Rider Cornatan would think had he been too soft. Not fit to command a patrol. These Apprentices should be so scared of him they wet their pants.

"Apprentice." Carro made the utmost attempt to let his voice sound harsh. How did Rider Cornatan achieve that?

The boys stopped in the doorway, Caman furthest into the corridor.

Carro had not forgotten Jono's taunts. The boys hated him all right; they had hated him from the moment he'd joined. They'd never hated Isandor, because Isandor wasn't special in the same way he was. Isandor was never any competition in the eyes of those pampered noble boys. That's why they hated him, because his presence threatened them. *Then you must hate them back.* Rider Cornatan's words.

Carro joined the two at the door and paced around them, slowly and deliberately.

"Do you need to be taught a lesson?"

Meet violence with violence. Payback time.

"You." He pulled Jono's uniform by the neck. Why had he never noticed that he had grown taller than the bully?

"Hey! You can't do that!" Jono squealed.

"Yes, I can. I'm your superior, like it or not, and you will respect me and obey my orders."

"I was obeying—"

"You were not."

Jono gasped a few words, trying to prise his fingers between his neck and the collar that cut into the skin. His eyes went wide.

A hand comes into Carro's field of vision, a hand filled with snow. The next moment, the snow hits his face, and the hand rubs it into his stinging cheeks.

Carro screams.

Someone is sitting on his back, knees painfully pressing into his spine.

Stop it, stop it!

His mouth fills up with snow. Carro spits.

Someone pulls his hair.

Listen to me, you worthless runt, a boy hisses in his ear. *Any time we meet you again, we will repeat this. Understood?*

Carro nods. A cold lump of snow slides down his back between his clothes and his bare skin.

Understood? the boy says again, but louder.

Carro nods again.

The boy fumbles for the back of Carro's trousers, lifts the waistband and shoves in the handful of snow.

The other boys are laughing.

Carro hated them, he hated Isandor, he hated everyone. No one ever respected him. No one. Even Isandor, a *cripple*, treated him like a weakling, like someone who needed help. He didn't need help. He could punish these boys just as well as everyone else had always punished him.

He tightened his grip on Jono's hair and slammed him face-first into the wall. Jono whimpered. His arm trembled under Carro's touch. Yes, yes, this was how it was done. They had to fear him, or they would run circles around him. They would laugh at him behind his back.

He ordered the other two, "Hold him."

They did as told and each grabbed an arm. Very quiet and obedient all of a sudden. Oh, they knew what was going to happen. They knew, and they didn't want it to happen to *them*.

Slowly and deliberately, Carro undid Jono's's belt and let his pants whisper to the floor. His buttocks were scrawny and hairy, with a few angry red pimples. Goosebumps broke out all over his skin.

Carro squirmed and forced himself to think of Korinne—he repeated her name in his mind, saw her golden locks, her alluring eyes.

Come on boy, what are you waiting for?

She laughed, and her image faded. When he wanted the visions, he couldn't hold on to them. His cock was at best half-limp. Panic gripped cold fingers around his heart. Now he started this, he *had* to go through with it; this was how junior Knights were punished. He could of course use the belt to hit Jono, but that would be considered a backdown. His . . . ability would be questioned. Carro the dud, he could just hear it. He had to do it, he had to, he had to . . .

Inran and Caman watched him, their gazes hollow. They'd seen it before. They'd switched off in the same way they had when Carro was *receiving* this punishment.

They knew what was required.

Carro felt sick. Felt himself standing in the dormitory enduring the humiliation with clenched teeth. Oh, by the skylights! He had to do this properly. Rider Cornatan wanted it. *You must hate them back*. Hate, hate, hate . . .

Carro undid his own belt and clumsily pressed against Jono's backside. The skin was clammy with sweat. Carro remembered, felt the pain, his face pressed against the plaster of the wall. He ran his hands down Jono's sides in a mockery of a loving gesture, breathed hot on Jono's naked shoulder, and he grew hard. Jono squirmed away, but his fellows held him tight, white-knuckled fingers biting into purpling flesh, pushing him hard into the wall. Carro rammed in.

Jono screamed, his voice muffled into the wall.

"That hurts, doesn't it?" he whispered into Jono's neck. "You know what? It doesn't hurt for me. I never knew that."

He pushed harder. He was rock-hard now and should get this over with while it lasted, before he went limp and embarrassed himself.

"Ow! Stop. It hurts."

Carro grabbed Jono's hair from behind, arching his neck as far as it went. "Too right it fucking hurts. It's meant to hurt. You hurt me. Many times. The tables are turned."

Carro saw nothing, heard nothing. This was what he wanted to do to his father, his mother, to his sister, to the bullies in the streets. He was fighting, hitting them all back for pain they had caused him, slamming them into that wall. Carro won the fight, spilled himself with a triumphant roar. The feeling of ultimate power.

Carro withdrew, blood roaring in his ears. Jono was crying, and Carro tried to cut himself off from the sound. *By the skylights, be a man! Even I didn't behave like this when you did this to me.*

But there was blood in his crotch.

Carro ignored it, did up his belt and maintained a stiff and angry pose while the boys scampered from the room. When they were gone, he slumped against the wall.

The sound of Jono's cries would not leave him, and that feeling of power, and his unexpected lust. He kept seeing Korinne's face, and the image of Farey's eyes, the two Knights kissing in Rider Cornatan's bathroom . . .

His nails bit into the skin of his palms. Tears burned into his eyes. Who was he and what gave him the right to do things like this?

He didn't know how long he had been standing there when there were footsteps behind him. He whirled around to see Rider Cornatan coming into the room. The Supreme Rider said nothing, but approached Carro with quick steps.

"You're back." Carro heard a measure of relief in his voice.

Rider Cornatan's face looked relieved, too, more relieved than a leader should be over the fate of a single young man.

"I'm sorry," he said. He'd lost his quarry, then he'd found the invisible man, but had fled from him. And the other Imperfect, the older man, was still at large. He hadn't achieved anything, except that he'd punished his patrol as Rider Cornatan wanted.

Rider Cornatan shook his head. "This is bigger than you. Bigger than all of us, I'm afraid."

"Is that what's going on? What those riots are about?"

"The whole of the Outer City is in uproar over the young Champion's dismissal. They see him as *their* champion. There are a lot of troublemakers on the streets out for a fight. They seem to have support from locals."

The black pit in Carro's stomach grew. "Just like when the uprising against the king started," he whispered.

Rider Cornatan stared in the distance. He nodded, once.

"We must stop this," Carro said.

"I don't know that we can."

Rider Cornatan met his eyes. Carro could guess what would happen next. As only Knight from the Outer City, he would have to be involved in calming the people down. Except he could never do that. Didn't Rider Cornatan know that Carro wasn't exactly popular with many in the Outer City?

"I have an important mission for you."

See? There it was. Rider Cornatan was expecting far too much of him. And he was going to fail.

Carro sits at the desk in the warehouse. His father is pacing the floor.

You, boy, when you're here, you're nothing but the lowest-ranking of my workers. You do not chat to the customers, or to other workers.

Carro nods and looks down to the columns in the book. For the last two pages, his handwriting has been atrocious, but his fingers are too cold to write properly. He wasn't chatting to anyone; he was only accepting a warm drink from the girl in the office, who had felt sorry for him.

"Are you all right, boy?"

Carro shook the memory out of his head. By the skylights, he still hadn't been able to get the ichina.

"I'm fine."

Rider Cornatan frowned.

"Really, I'm fine." Even to his own ears, he sounded nervous. "Tell me what you want me to do." He might as well face the disaster head-on.

"I'm going to send you out of the city."

"Sir?" That was the last thing Carro expected to hear.

Rider Cornatan looked away, almost as if he couldn't bear to meet Carro's eyes. The black feeling increased.

"The trouble started in the Outer City because we took the champion in custody for having lied about his condition. He used his evil power and escaped. At the same time, in a different part of the city, someone killed the Queen's driver and her bears and destroyed her sled. When a new one arrived, Jevaithi and her escort were caught up in a riot. In amongst the fighting, we lost her. We've found no trace of the champion or the Queen. But someone freed the champion's eagle. It took off for the mountains. We suspect that he released it himself, and that he's with the Queen."

Isandor with Jevaithi? Yet Carro had seen that look passing between them and he knew it to be true.

"I'm sending you with the hunters to go and find her. Understand that it's a vital mission. If we can't produce the Queen, the people of the City of Glass are going to turn against us." He lowered his voice. "Unless we can find the Queen, the Knights will be slaughtered. The Brotherhood has become too strong, and understand icefire much better than we do. We *must* have the Queen, Carro."

A vital mission all right, but why would Rider Cornatan send him with vastly more experienced hunters?

"Maybe you ask why I entrust you with such an important mission."

"Yes, I'm not experienced enough—"

Rider Cornatan drew something from his pocket and he gave it to Carro: a bundle of velvet, heavy in his hand. "It is because I trust you like no other."

"Sir, what. . . ?"

"Open it."

Carro folded the material back.

Inside lay a golden medallion, with worked scalloped edges and patterns stamped into the flat surface. A finely-made gold chain hung from the eyelet at the top.

"Do you recognise this, boy?"

Carro ran his finger over the surface, depicting a Tusked Lion rearing on its hind flippers. He had seen this in his books. He swallowed. "Isn't this . . . the crest of the Pirosian House?"

A smile curled one corner of Rider Cornatan's mouth. "Very good. The crest of the Pirosian House indeed. You might have read, too, that there are only two of these medallions."

Rider Cornatan took the medallion from the velvet, unfastened the clip on the chain. He looped both sides around Carro's neck. He re-fastened the clip, and arranged the medallion on Carro's chest, a satisfied look on his face. Carro held his breath, but still smelled the waft of musk and harness oil that hung in the Supreme Rider's clothing.

"Only two. One of these medallions belongs to the male heir of Pirosians, the other, my son, belongs to his successor."

His heart thudding, Carro looked up, into the wrinkled face. "You're . . ." He hardly dare say it. "You're my father? My *real* father?"

The smile grew.

"But why . . ." All that hostility, all those sniping remarks, the cryptic questions, the nastiness. The man he'd known as his father had been *paid* to look after him. Just like he knew Senior Knights would deal with their successors.

"Why have you grow up in the Outer City, with a man hardly worth his spit and a woman who would have been better off a whore?"

Carro flinched, felt a brief urge to defend the man and woman he'd known as his parents, but then a feeling of rightness descended on him. He had never fitted in. His father had always hated him. His mother, too. He'd looked too different from his sister to believe they were related. He'd just assumed that his father had used different breeder for him and his sister, but now . . .

"I've not shared my rooms with a woman; that is not possible for me since Riders have sworn off such pleasures. But as Pirosian heir, I needed a successor. So I paid a young virgin of the purest Pirosian blood to give me one, for good money, and then hid you in a place I knew my enemies would not look and would not recognise you. The Thillei are more slippery than you think."

Yes, they were, Carro realised. The Thillei had tried to subvert him by letting Isandor befriend him. How could he have been so blind?

He clutched the medallion in a white-knuckled hand. He'd been stupid, stupid. "I won't let you down. I'll find our Queen."

Rider Cornatan's face hardened. "Listen, son. I'll tell you another secret. Jevaithi isn't *our* Queen. When the Thillei emperor was deposed, the people didn't want another dictator, so the Pirosian clan offered our female heir, since it was agreed that we should only have queens."

"Does that mean you are Jevaithi's father?" *I am royalty?*

"No, and that is where the problem lies. But we need to go further back than that. After the people had ousted the old king and instated the Pirosian queen, the Thilleians were desperate to recapture the throne. First, an agent infiltrated the palace and raped our queen. She fell pregnant, but the palace midwives managed to safely get rid of the child before it was born."

A visible shudder passed over him. "That was probably just as well. The child was . . . not normal."

"What do you mean?"

"Have you heard of the legend of the crossbreed? The children of the purest Pirosians and the purest Thilleians?"

Carro did remember from the books. Old prints showed demon-like figures with claws and wings. He nodded. "But I thought those were all stories."

"Some of it no doubt is untrue, but when we have the time, I will show you a sample preserved in a jar in the palace birthing room. It's not just any sample, but this very child, as big as your hand, but already showing its animal nature. Old measuring equipment showed that the creature—I won't use the term baby to describe it—attracted an inordinate amount of icefire. It even used the evil power to change its appearance into shapes too horrible to contemplate, before it had left its mother's body."

"The child was alive?"

Rider Cornatan nodded, once, pressing his lips together. "When the healers took it from the poor queen's womb, yes. It took five people to kill it."

Carro felt sick.

"Anyway, after that disaster, the Queen was shaken of course. We chose one of us to father the queen's child as soon as she recovered. It was done, and she gave birth to a healthy girl. However, we had never caught the Thilleian agent who was the father of the abomination. Soon after the birth of our princess, he, or someone else, came back and took the newborn baby, replacing her with another of the same age, who looked exactly like her, but grew up nothing like the Queen. You *do* know that Maraithe's mother killed herself?"

Carro nodded. Performers in the melteries still sang about the tragedy.

"That was because she couldn't live with the hatred she felt for her baby daughter, a baby that wasn't hers. You hear? *Maraithe* was a Thilleian impostor, but none of us realised. We thought we had eliminated all Thilleians."

But, Carro thought, that meant—

"Maraithe grew up normally, and never showed any sign of who she really was. We relaxed and, at that time, still suspected nothing. Things were good; the evil had been ousted. But then Maraithe reached maturity and we needed to find a father for her child. We thought to consider all possible candidates fairly. Some Senior Knights were engaged in battles of words and occasionally swords. Maraithe demanded a say in the matter as well."

Was that usual? Carro wondered, and then realized that there *was* no "usual". The system hadn't been in place long enough.

"Anyway, it was all a very lengthy process, and while we were debating a suitable father for Maraithe's children, time passed, and passed. Maraithe was twenty-nine, and all of a sudden, she was pregnant. She had said nothing, and one day she came into the Knights' Council and in a tight dress that was stretching around her belly." He shuddered with the memory. "We put on a brave face, since it was much too late to ask the midwives to abort the child. The people had noticed her pregnancy, and you know how popular the queens are. For all we knew back then, it didn't really matter who the father was. But it did. Maraithe gave birth not two moon cycles later. Early, the midwife said, but she was carrying twins."

"Twins?"

"Yes. Jevaithi and a boy."

"What happened to the boy?"

"He was left on the ice floes."

"He was . . . Imperfect?"

"Yes. So is Jevaithi. That is the dreadful secret we keep. Jevaithi hasn't a drop of Pirosian blood in her veins."

Carro's head reeled. Queen Jevaithi Imperfect and no one had ever noticed? No wonder why the queen hardly ever showed herself. Here was another betrayal. He'd sworn his allegiance. To protect her with his life. As many Knights did, he'd *dreamed* of her many a night, wanted her in his bed.

Rider Cornatan continued, "Now it appears that our enemies have taken Jevaithi back. I don't know what they plan to do with her, but with the potential of icefire, they could destroy everything and kill us. I don't think she'll have any hesitation in helping them. She hates us badly enough. That's why we must act now, before she has a chance to learn to use icefire. You must bring her back to calm the people. We must have her back here to control her. That's why I'm sending you. I trust no one else."

Carro wasn't trusting himself at that moment. *Jevaithi* was a Thilleian? A betrayer? A feeling of sickness welled up in his stomach.

"And the hunters?"

"My special team. You've met Farey."

"Yes." Carro fought to restrain a blush. Then he had another thought: every man in the Knighthood had known who he was all along? Now he understood the remarks the Tutor had made about his status.

"Find her and bring her back here, son, before it's too late and the evil spreads. Promise me."

Carro straightened his back. If he was highborn and Rider Cornatan said he was trustworthy, he must be. He'd sworn allegiance to the *throne* not to Jevaithi.

"I promise."

What about Isandor? Capture him too? His friend?

If that's what it took to get his father's approval . . . Isandor was not his friend anymore; he shouldn't be.

Rider Cornatan looked into his eyes. "Can you say the word to me, just once?"

"I promise, *Father*."

Rider Cornatan let go of his hands and closed his arms around Carro's shoulders.

"I love you, son. Never give up. The City of Glass belongs to the Pirosian House."

CHAPTER 26

THE EAGLE stretched out its feet, flapped huge brown and white wings and landed on the snow-covered hillside.

Isandor uncramped his stiff arms to release Jevaithi. She slid from the saddle into the snow, stretching her arms and stamping life into stiff legs. He unclipped his harness and followed her down, drinking in the silence after the roar of wind in his ears for so long.

The surrounding landscape bathed in soft pastel tones: pale blues of pristine snow, the golden light of the sun low above the horizon, and pink and orange hues of the sky.

Isandor squinted into the sunlight. The mountains rose at his back, and long shadows cast the valleys between the foothills in blue shadow. The City of Glass was well out of sight, almost a day's flying distance away, but he felt its constant pull inside him. The City of Glass was his home, it was Jevaithi's home. She was the queen and all the people should listen to her. They should go back and get rid of the Knights. They should . . .

A soft sound yanked him from the uninvited thoughts.

Jevaithi ploughed through knee-deep snow to a wooden hut half-hidden by a stand of gnarled trees. She pushed open the door—it creaked, and caused a big slab of snow to slide off the roof—and looked inside.

Anything? He was still feeling shaken, wanting to be rid of that need to return. He didn't *want* to return.

She shook her head. *There's cooking things, and a bed.*

We'll stay here tonight. Anything except to go back there.

Why would people build this hut here?

It's a camp for highsun herders. They brought their goats up here in the short period that the meadows weren't covered in snow. Isandor had seen the herders with their salted meats in the Outer City markets.

Jevaithi tracked back through the snow. Her blue-marbled form was not as substantial as it had been when they escaped. He could see *through* her. With the weakening icefire, their bodies would gradually disappear.

That was why the force of icefire pulled him back to the City of Glass. From here on, that feeling would become stronger, until it had grown into a physical pain in his ghostly body.

It was time to turn both of them back to normal.

He took the pouch from his pocket. To his eyes it was a solid black object that made him shiver. He closed his eyes and forced himself to put the bag into the palm of his hand. The hearts thudded, sucking in icefire with every beat. And with every beat, warmth in his hands grew.

Isandor had to fight the urge to fling the bag down the mountainside, to be rid of the thing and live without hunger and pain forever.

But he couldn't let this feeling win. Hands shaking, he gathered a fold of his cloak into a basket and upended the bag into it.

Both hearts beat strongly, pumping hard to keep the icefire going, to keep the illusion alive. Jevaithi stood with her hands over her mouth.

Both hands; she would lose a hand if he put the heart back.

She was perfect in her current state; she would never be any more perfect than this . . .

He would have to separate the hearts and they looked so perfect next to each other, beating in unison.

No.

Isandor closed a hand around his own heart, and lifted it to his chest, trying to absorb its warmth, but feeling repulsed by it. How could one be repulsed by life?

Here. He held it out to Jevaithi.

It lay, pulsing, in her hands. *Both* her hands.

Her eyes widened. *This is your heart.*

I know it's mine. I want you to have it. And he wanted it to be done quickly, before the urge to return to the city, or do something else stupid, became too strong.

You would forever be my servitor.

Isandor bent forward until the hand with which he still held Jevaithi's heart touched both their chests. He let his lips brush hers. She stiffened but did not withdraw. The tingle of frost made his blood stir. *And you would be mine. I want to be yours.*

I want you, too.

Her breath tickled over his skin. He sought her lips, teasing her with the most fleeting of kisses. She laughed and pulled him closer, pressing her mouth full on his.

A jolt of icefire bit through him.

Isandor withdrew. If he'd had a need to breathe, he would be panting. His need for her was so desperate, he would have ripped off her clothes and taken her in the snow, but that was not the sort of treatment she deserved.

He said, *If we take each other's hearts, we will be each other's servitors, but we will be whole at the same time. We can go beyond the influence of icefire, yet no one can ever make us servitors, because we already are.*

If I die, then you would die, too.

But you can't die unless I die. He smiled at her ethereal face. *Unless someone kills both of us at exactly the same time.*

A bright smile crossed her face. A glitter in her midnight-dark eyes, dimples in her cheeks. How he loved her.

She handed him back his heart. *Here. I want you to put it in.*

He took it and handed her heart back to her, his hands trembling. *You do it for me, too. Are you ready?*

To illustrate her readiness, she untied her cloak and unbuttoned the top of her dress, showing ethereal blue marbled skin, the fabric pulled back enough to show soft mounds of her breasts.

He pulled his tunic over his head. *Ready?*

She nodded, her mouth set. They both slid each other's hearts in their chests. Icefire blossomed in the sharp burst, snaking out over the snow-covered landscape. Strands turned from black to golden.

Isandor's vision blurred. Pain tore through him like he'd been dipped in boiling water. He opened his mouth and screamed. The sound echoed in the mountains. His voice had returned. Then he stood there, panting. Jevaithi had fainted in his arms, but she was already opening her eyes, blue once more, and put her left hand on his bare chest, whole and pink again, and her right hand missing again.

He kissed her, now warm and breathing. She gasped, clinging onto him, her breath warm over his cheek.

"Can you feel it?" She took his hand and placed it on her chest, between her breasts.

Their hearts beat in perfect unison. "I love you. I love you so much it hurts."

They stood motionless for a number of heartbeats. He let his hand slide under the cover of her dress. The skin on her breast was softer than he could imagine, but the nipple grew hard and erect under the touch of his fingers.

She giggled. "Your hands are freezing."

"Maybe we should go inside." He let a smile play around his lips.

She smiled back, nervously.

"Do you know how to make a fire?" he asked. "I need to look

after the eagle."

"I'll try. I've seen people make fires."

"Up in your tower room?"

"Yes." And then she smiled again. "Imagine. I'm free. I can do whatever I want. I'm free!" Her voice echoed against the mountain. A bird screeched a reply.

Isandor gave her a last kiss on the lips before she ploughed through the snow back to the hut. Even the sight of her back, and her messy hair over her shoulders, made him feel giddy.

Jevaithi. He mouthed her name, like sweets on his tongue. *Jevaithi, Jevaithi.* And then, *she's mine.* Unbelievable.

He tied up the eagle, rubbed it down and gave it a chunk of meat from the saddlebag. The meat was frozen solid and the bird gave him a baleful stare. It didn't bother him. His wooden leg didn't bother him. His blood sang, his mind flew, deep breaths of freezing air made him feel dizzy. He was free.

When he went inside, a fire roared in the hearth. Warmth fell on him like a blanket; it made his cold-stiffened fingers tingle. Jevaithi came to the door to help him out of his cloak, her eyes bright.

"This hut is well-organised. I found some saltmeat and flour and—"

He stopped her words with his mouth. Her one hand strayed up his chest, fumbled with his tunic, while he peeled the dress from her shoulders with trembling hands. Dizziness threatened to overwhelm him; he felt like he wasn't here, wasn't doing this, like he was on fire.

She broke the kiss. "Should we go . . . over there?" She glanced at the wooden bed in the corner.

He picked her up and carried her to the bed which had straw poking out and a bearskin cover that released a cloud of dust under the weight of her body. She laughed. Isandor slid the silk finery off her until she was entirely naked except for the leather strip and the gull's feather. Her gaze still meeting his, she reached behind her neck and undid the knot. The leather strips fell over her breasts. She passed the trophy to him, her eyes twinkling.

"Yours."

His. So beautiful. He sank down on the bed on his knees, awkwardly. He untied his wooden leg, put it on the floor, and then unbelted his trousers with trembling hands. The last of his clothing fell to the floor with a soft thud. She was watching him with wide eyes. Scared? Had she ever seen a naked man before?

"You're sure you want it?"

She nodded. A vein pulsed in her neck. Yes, she was scared.

He chuckled. "I don't know much either."

"What? You mean you've never . . ."

He shook his head.

"But I thought you Outer City boys all knew so much more than me." She laughed, but then her face grew serious. "Do *you* want it?" and when he laughed, she added, "What? It's a fair question."

He bent over her, supporting himself with a hand on each side of her shoulders and whispered in her neck, "By the skylights, I do."

"Well, that's settled then." She shifted her legs apart.

He could feel his heart going like crazy in her chest.

Isandor lowered himself, blood roaring in his ears. Naked skin whispered on naked skin. Oh boy, it was awkward. She had to wriggle her hand underneath to guide him to the right place. When he finally got the right position, she was so warm and so tight that the first time he pushed deep, he spilled himself in an uncontrollable shudder. Oh, by the skylights. He rested his head on her shoulder, still panting.

"I'm sorry. I didn't mean to do that."

"It doesn't matter." But in her voice he heard that it did. She was disappointed, had expected more.

"I'm sorry," he said again. "Did I hurt you?"

She shook her head, but he didn't miss the blood-streaked slime on the bedcover.

"It's all right," she said. "Girls bleed, the first time."

Isandor thought of his mother and the horrific stories she sometimes told about births gone wrong. "It's not fair. Girls get to take all the bad things."

He got up, filled the pot and set it to boil. In the future, he would have to do better than that. Look after her, love her better.

Jevaithi sat down on the bench while he stoked the fire. It was comfortably warm inside, and he was giddy with the feeling of love and independence. They could do this. He might be awkward, and she might not know much, but they would learn. They never needed to listen to anyone again.

He found some bowls and a pot and made hearty soup out of strips of saltmeat and herbs which he found on the shelf above the stove.

"Where are we going from here?" he asked. "Chevakia?"

"Chevakia! I don't care. We're free. No more Knights. No more Rider Cornatan to watch over me. Isn't it wonderful?"

He smiled, but deep inside suspected it wasn't quite so simple. That feeling of power he had as servitor still smouldered inside him. Jevaithi was the *queen*. People respected and adored her. He could wield that power to get rid of the Knights and give Jevaithi the throne that was rightfully hers. What would the people of the City of Glass do when they found out she was gone?

"Hey, dreamer." Jevaithi sat on his lap, pushing away the blanket slung over his shoulders. His naked body underneath responded pleasantly.

She gave him a sly look. "You want to try again?"

Sure, why not?

This time, things were much more satisfactory.

Afterwards, she fell asleep with her head on his shoulder. Isandor lay there, looking at her face by the glow of the fire, listening to the beating of both their hearts.

Yes, they would go back to the City of Glass one day, but not yet, not yet . . .

CHAPTER 27

RUKO WAITED by the sled outside Loriane's house. He had his back to the door, his arms crossed over his chest and was staring into the street, not meeting Tandor's eyes. Anger rolled off him in waves. Tandor saw a young boy and the same girl he'd seen a few times, in a darkened corridor with metal-barred doors on both sides.

Great.

Tandor strode to the sled, flinging furs onto the seat for Loriane and Myra to sit on. Earlier, when he went out before, he'd already taken his chest out here, in anticipation of his move into the City of Glass, when Ruko had told him he'd captured Isandor and Jevaithi. *You could have been on your way to your girl already. I told you to go after Isandor. Why didn't you stop the boy running away?* Ruko should have been more than strong enough to restrain two adolescents.

Images of Isandor struggling against Ruko's grip came into his mind. Jevaithi, too. The butcher's warehouse. The door shut, enclosing the two teenagers inside. Then Ruko on his way to get

Tandor.

All right, so Ruko *had* locked them up properly. That meant *someone* had to have unlocked that door. Tandor had seen the eagle fly over with Isandor and Jevaithi on its back, both in servitor forms and knew no one who could have turned them. Was there someone else who could make servitors? One of those pathetic Brothers?

Who saw you?

Ruko's arm muscles tightened.

All right, I didn't say it was your fault.

Tandor saw the rosy-cheeked face of a girl, one of the youngsters imprisoned in the palace.

Yes, I know it's taking a long time, but we can't go and rescue her until you help me to get enough Imperfects to get into the palace in the first place.

Ruko jumped up, blew a gust of frost-rimed air from his nostrils. He whirled at Tandor. Hesitated. Midnight-black eyes glared at Tandor from within the deep shadow of the hood of Ruko's cape.

No, you will not kill everyone. You will do as I say. I am the master.

Another snort of air, this one audible. Ruko whirled again and brought his fist down on the driver's seat with such force that the bench creaked. The bear let out a deep growl.

I am the master, Tandor repeated. He grasped for icefire and pulled it close around Ruko. The boy didn't move, yet Tandor could feel his anger strain against the icefire bonds. Did servitors ever break free of their masters? What happened if they did?

The door thudded shut behind him.

Draped in furs, Loriane and Myra shuffled into the street. Loriane had her arm around Myra's waist. The girl was crying, stopping every few paces.

Ruko settled into the driver's seat with a loud thump. He yanked the hood over his head and snatched up the reins so tightly that the bear grumbled.

Tandor pulled harder at the threads of icefire. *Careful.*

Loriane and Myra climbed onto the sled, very, very slowly. Tandor handed Loriane a few rugs, which she tucked around Myra. Tandor sat next to Loriane, on the far left of the bench, pressed against her because the sled only comfortably seated two people.

He released his hold on the icefire threads a fraction. Ruko snapped the reins. The bear loped into action, bouncing and kicking its hind legs in a way that was an indication that the animal was annoyed.

But now that they were underway, Ruko settled. He navigated the sled through the winding streets, avoiding busy thoroughfares. Through alleys and gaps between limpets, Tandor caught glimpses of fights, people running through streets with burning torches, buildings on fire, billowing smoke. The stench hung low over the Outer City.

Further, out over the plain, eagles circled, silvery shapes in the moonlight, Knights, no doubt looking for traces of the Queen. So many of them. Were there any Knights left to guard the city?

Tandor couldn't repress a smile.

While all the Knights were out looking for Jevaithi, he might not get a better chance to get into the palace, at least not any time soon. After a string of disasters things were finally looking up for him.

Ruko, to the City of Glass, as fast as you can.

Again, he saw the face of the girl.

Yes, we'll go and rescue her now.

Ruko flicked the reins. The bear increased its pace and soon, the sled left the twisted streets of the Outer City behind and came out into the open. Down the slope, past the festival grounds and onto the ice plain.

Myra was crying with every bump, and Loriane tried to comfort her. She cast Tandor poisonous looks. Did she have the faintest idea how pretty she was when she did that, her cheeks flushed, her lips slightly apart?

"Loriane, I love you." He gathered her in his arms and kissed her.

She pushed him away. "Spare your breath. You're up to something and I want to know what it is."

"I'll tell you." He kissed her again, tasting victory, in her, in the speed of the sled, in Ruko's anger. "After we come back."

"Now."

"No. After. Loriane, I love you. I wouldn't do anything to put you in danger."

"You swear you will tell me what this is about? I'm getting rather sick of your secrets."

"I swear it." *When I'm on the throne, you'll be the most powerful queen ever.*

"Deal." She gave him an intense glare that said *I'll believe that when I see it.* And she turned her attention back to Myra.

No one said much during the rest of the trip. Ruko urged the bear on as much as Tandor would allow it. Myra cried, but much less than before.

When the sled passed underneath a group of circling eagles, Tandor cast out a cocoon of icefire so they wouldn't see the sled. That was easy to do here, on the deserted plain, not so once he got into the city, where people with Thilleian blood might see it. The Knights didn't seem to be all that interested in who went into the city, though, because another sled ahead of them received no attention from the eagles either.

The tall buildings ahead grew and grew, dark and jagged silhouettes against a sky too dark for dawn and too light for midnight. Soon enough, the sled moved into the shadows of the buildings. Here, it was pitch dark and bitterly cold, with an icy wind gusting over the plain.

Ruko slowed down at the gates.

By the wan light of a single icefire globe, the three guards on duty were questioning a young noble man who was trying to leave the city, and waved Tandor and Loriane through, without much of a glance at Ruko's cloaked form. Myra was again crying and a noble man with a heavily pregnant woman in his sled could only be bound for the palace.

Once in the streets, the strong pull of icefire tugged at him. Golden strands of it snaked through the air, crawled up walls, slithered down windows, hugging all forms and structures that had once belonged to the ancient culture that had given rise to icefire. Tandor drank in the delicious feeling. By the sky lights, he could do it. The children were here—he could feel them. Together they could tame the Heart. Tonight, the throne would be his.

The sled arrived at the back entrance to the palace.

A twisted iron and glass structure hung as an arch over the entry to the courtyard in front of the passageway that led to the palace birthing rooms. A few snow-dusted sleds stood in the open space, and a single bear dozed in the corner of the yard. Two guards stood at their post, one leaning against the doorpost, his eyes half-closed. The other guard had his back to the courtyard. As the sled swished through the open gate, he turned slowly, and as he did so, his eyes widened.

Tandor's heart jumped.

Stop as far from the door as possible, Ruko.

Had the man seen anything? Since when did Thilleians stand guard at the palace?

The bear halted with a snort and a grumble. Tandor rose and pulled the hood of the cloak further over Ruko's head. Ruko batted his hand away, but Tandor grabbed the cloak's sleeve.

One of those men can see you.

Loriane helped Myra up, but when the girl stepped from the sled, she gave a cry and sank to her knees in the snow, clutching her belly.

Loriane glared over her shoulder. "This is ridiculous, Tandor, couldn't you have stopped a bit closer to the door?"

"No I couldn't." He glanced at Ruko.

Myra struggled back up. Loriane put her arm around the girl's waist. When they shuffled away from the sled, she said over her shoulder. "You do remember your promise, don't you?"

"I do." *I will do more than that. I will put you on the throne, my queen.*

By the skylights, he loved her.

Tandor waited while Loriane and Myra shuffled crossed the courtyard to the entrance before stepping off the sled. Ruko stirred and rose from the driver's seat.

Wait here.

Tandor's heart was thudding. The man's attention had gone to Loriane and Myra, who were at the entrance to the palace. Myra had stopped walking and was having another crying fit, but the guard still glanced at the sled even as he spoke to Loriane.

Ruko snorted audibly and jumped into the snow.

No, you can't come inside. He's seen you. Stay here.

Ruko took two huge steps until his chest almost touched Tandor's. Cold radiated from his blue-skinned hands that could snap a man's neck.

Ruko was half a head taller, but Tandor didn't back down.

What's this?

A blue hand lashed out and grabbed Tandor by the collar with such force that he could barely breathe. The image of the girl again. Ruko's young lover.

Set me down.

Ruko's eyes met his, black and deep as the ocean.

Set me down. More forceful this time.

He couldn't use icefire in front of these guards, or he would have lashed Ruko without mercy. What was it with the insolence? Who was the master?

If you don't behave, I'll turn you back into a cripple boy.

Slowly, Ruko let go of Tandor's collar.

Tandor drew a grateful and welcome breath, fresh air into his lungs.

Loriane and Myra had gone inside and Tandor was acutely aware of the guards' gazes in his direction.

Don't you dare do that again. Stay here.

Icefire flared in a web of strands coming from Ruko's hands. Images of the girl burst into Tandor's mind. He thrust up his golden claw, slashing through the net. Ruko held on, but wasn't strong enough. The network of strands shattered into diamonds. Tandor ducked to avoid the projectiles and grabbed a handful of Ruko's cloak. Icefire crackled the length of his claw.

What's this, Ruko? I am your master. I command. You obey. I tell you it's not safe to come inside—

In his mind, Ruko ran across the courtyard, grabbed the two guards and snapped their necks.

No, you can't do that. There are many more guards inside, and we can't fight them.

More images of violence. Blood in the snow.

No, Ruko.

Dark forms of guards and Knights slumped in heaps, their limbs bent at impossible angles. Dismembered shapes barely recognisable as human. Blue hands slashing through flesh and blood. Bones snapping.

Ruko trembled.

No, Ruko.

The cloak was yanked from Tandor's grip with so much force that he stumbled backwards. Ruko walked away from the sled.

There were images of the front entrance of the palace, the steps dripping with blood. Severed limbs, heads torn from bodies, eyes staring lifelessly at the sky, Knights' badges defaced, their swords bent and molten, crossbow bolts between their eyes. Noble ladies in the snow with their clothes ripped off bloodied torsos. Nail and teeth marks in alabaster skin.

Tandor grabbed as many strands of icefire as he could muster and, never mind the guards, lashed them around Ruko's form.

You obey me!

The strands met resistance. They stretched and snapped, and hit the glass and metal arch over the courtyard entrance. The structure glowed and gave out a shower of sparks, while Ruko ran underneath, out the gate.

Tandor stumbled back a few steps and stood there in the middle of the courtyard, panting, to regain his balance, the horrific images fading from his mind.

"Uhm—sir?" one of the guards asked. "Are you all right?"

Are you all right? That was not what they had asked last time Tandor had encountered palace guards. Maraithe had to officially pardon him. He'd had to kneel before the throne, pushed down by a Knight when getting to his knees with his recent wound was difficult. The pain, oh, the pain.

Maraithe sat on the throne, with two rapist Knights next to her, with her hands folded over knees. Her face looked drawn and pale. In his mind, he still heard her screams as she pushed out, unaided and denied medicine, the children he would never hold. It happened here, in the palace, a place stifled with haunting memories.

Tandor forced a smile. "I . . . tripped. I'm sorry. My son . . . he's at a difficult age . . ." A disaster. There was no way Tandor could get Ruko back under control alone. Servitors never disobeyed their masters. Never.

"Oh. I see." But the tone of the man's voice said that he didn't see at all, and worse, that he was expecting some kind of explanation, but there was no time for that now. Ruko was on the rampage and would kill anyone he encountered, and the only means of stopping him—Ruko's girl—was inside the palace dungeons.

He said, nodding at the door, "I'd like to wait inside, if I can. The lady . . ." He shrugged, feigning indifference, but his heart thudded. He *had* to get in, even if he was alone and helpless against the power of the Heart.

The guard eyed him. "Your breeder, sir?"

"Yes." Tandor kept his face impassive, no matter how much he hated these impersonal family arrangements.

The guard waved him through, but when Tandor looked over his shoulder, he noticed how both guards were leaning close to each other, and one was pointing into the courtyard.

The man had seen something: either Ruko or the icefire. Since when did the palace have Thilleian Knights?

And then he heard Loriane's voice, *That's your life, not mine. It happened fifty years ago, Tandor*. Could it really be that the citizens of the City of Glass were forgetting the clan feuds?

No, he decided. There were the Brothers, still teaching the Thilleian ways, and his mother, and all the people whose businesses had been destroyed by the Knights. They deserved revenge for what had been done to them.

Tandor would give them revenge, even if it was the last thing he did.

Chapter 28

TANDOR STOPPED in the darkness of a niche and pulled a cloak of icefire around him. He cast out his rays of power, and compared the picture that the rays brought back to him with the map he had memorised.

Getting into the palace was one thing, finding the entrance to the underground passages quite another. He'd been lucky so far that no one had come out of the birthing room to question him on his presence. Most of the Knights were at the Newlight festival; he'd planned it that way. But he could never plan for what he found in the catacombs. Right now, what he needed most was luck.

The trail of icefire led him into the darkness of the corridor. Here, the walls were ancient and bleak grey, spotted with age and rust. The icefire trail oozed from an ink-black hole at the end of the passage. Tandor plunged into darkness. It seemed his mental probe found the stairs to the underground chambers. His footsteps echoed in the staircase that seemed to have no end, zig-zagging down and down. A metal railing disintegrated under his touch, caking the steps with flakes of rust.

With each step he descended into the bowels of the building, the tang of cold increased. The vapour of his breath froze in his hair and on the collar of his cloak. Icefire called beneath his feet. Down, down, down. His lungs laboured to take in the stale, breathless air, laced with an unpleasant smell.

On every corner and every turn, he stopped, listened for footsteps, voices, slitherings or panting, jingling or clinking.

There were no sounds other than his own.

The stairs ended in a dungeon room where a single torch cast its flickering light over three walls of solid stone. The entrance to the stairs broke the fourth wall. There were no other doorways.

Tandor walked around the walls, inspecting the rough stone. From his time spent in the dungeons, he remembered the layout of the passages and cells.

Stupid, really, for Rider Cornatan to hold him prisoner in the dungeons all those years ago. Did the man know what icefire could do, of how he could scan and map the entire underground section of the palace, all its levels, its ramps and staircases, even down to the white lines painted on the floors by generations long past?

The flame on the torch flapped with a rancid breeze.

Tandor smiled. Of course.

That breath of air had to come from somewhere and had to be going somewhere. This was not a dead end at all. There was an illusion at work in this room.

For all he hated icefire, Rider Cornatan had no qualms using it, for the Knights of course would be unable to see the wall where Tandor saw it. With that knowledge, Tandor again walked the perimeter of the room, probing with icefire. This time, he found the passage, opposite the exit to the stairs. He pushed his clawed hand through the wall, then his other hand, his foot, and when it looked like his limbs were being eaten by stone, he walked through himself.

The familiar cold of icefire tingled his skin. A strong

construction, this one, and he recognised in it the mark of his family. This ward might have been in place since his grandfather had left the palace, and he was the first of his family to walk through it since that time.

The Thillei are coming home.

He could see himself walking up the steps of his mother's house . . . no, she would come to him, here in the City of Glass, where he sat on the throne his grandfather had been killed defending. His mother would fall to her knees for him.

Your Majesty. Yes, he could get used to that, especially when coming from his mother's mouth. It was time that she learned who was doing all the work and who had the right to get the top spot.

He had entered another passage which slanted away from the bottom of the stairs at a weak angle. An orange glow of fire or torches flickered at the very end. There were no wall niches, nowhere to hide.

He had not encountered anyone, but if the Eagle Knights still used his grandfather's wards, they would also use the listening bugs, or would maybe use his grandfather's famed live model of the palace, as his grandfather had described in the diary. If that was the case, they would know exactly where he was and where he was going.

There was no way of knowing how much the Knights had learned of using icefire, and what devices they were using. And this might all be a trap.

Yet, the children were here. He could feel them close by, perhaps in the chamber ahead.

Fires burned in the hearth at the opposite wall of that room. People moved back and forth, silhouetted against the glow. Some carried heavy things. The figures looked strangely out of proportion, with thick arms and legs, and with large heads. When he came closer, he saw that they were wearing baggy suits. Hoods covered their heads, sealed by a plate of glass in front, through which the occupant of the suit could look out.

The low light and the reflection in the glass made it impossible to see their faces. Chevakians needed to wear suits like that when they came to the City of Glass, not southerners . . . unless icefire was extraordinarily strong, like it would be around the Heart. *They're using it.* It was clear as it should have been before, when he encountered the sink. The Knights aimed to use this energy they couldn't see, or, for that matter, control. That's why they needed the children, as test subjects, as vessels and conduits for icefire. It was such lunacy. The children had no experience with using icefire, plus they weren't servitors. At crucial moments, they would never do as their masters wanted.

Oh by the skylights, did Rider Cornatan know what he was playing with?

He inched closer to the room, and the more he saw of its interior of tubes and machines, the more he knew he was right.

There was a commotion at the other end of the room. Two suited figures emerged from a doorway, dragging a third person between them. Thin, poorly dressed and not in a suit, the girl looked out of place, as if she'd been caught snooping. But the eyes drew Tandor's attention. Empty and hollow, they stared straight at him. She knew he was there. Icefire surged through him. He could barely clamp down on the crackling strand of golden light. Down here, he could no longer rely on the Pirosian inability to see icefire. Most of these workers would not be pure-bloods—Pirosians saved the best jobs for themselves; the part-Thilleian guard at the gate attested to that—and some would be able to see the strands, no matter how weakly.

Heart pounding, he leaned against the wall, listening to the girl's protesting screams. This was one of the Bordertown children. The others would be close by. If he could free just a few, he had the situation in hand. He could turn them into servitors and take possession of the Heart. Once he was there . . . He clutched his dagger to his thigh. The throne would be his. The Thillei would return. The south would again be a force to reckon with.

The two suited figures stopped. They put the girl on a table, and bound her hands to metal loops at the table's edge.

Another suited figure brought in a trolley on which lay an array of glittering instruments. The three gathered around the girl and covered her with a cloth.

The girl squirmed and bucked. The cloth slid off. The suited men yelled out. One pointed into the corridor.

Tandor released the icefire he had been holding. It crackled across the room in a jet of golden light. It hit the three suited men, knocking them to the ground, ricocheted off the wall, fractured and bounced back, until it formed a barrier across the room's entrances. Not much good against pure Pirosians, but he had to gamble that none of these people were pure-bloods. Tandor rushed into the room, drawing his knife from his belt. First, he yanked off the helmets of the suited men. If they had Pirosian blood, the bolt would merely have stunned them. He hit each of them hard on the head with the hilt of his dagger.

Then he went to the table.

The girl was thin, filthy, dressed only in a thin tunic. She looked at him, wide-eyed. "You are the man who came to Bordertown . . . The traveller . . ."

He put a finger to her lips and slashed the leather straps which held the girl bound to the table.

"Quiet," he whispered. "You thought I would leave you alone, did you?"

"They said you were dead." She met his eyes. Oh boy, could he feel the Thilleian blood stir in her.

He lifted the girl off the table.

She almost fell into his arms. Feeling her bony arms and the filth of her skin, a great anger surged through him. "Where are the others?"

Her eyes grew wide. "You can't get to them. You must get out. They'll capture you, too."

"I'll take that risk. Quick. Where are they? Show me. I'm here to free you all. There will be no second chances."

The girl hesitated, but pointed at an entrance, a dark maw of a passage leading further into the building.

"That way. There's a room . . ." She shuddered.

By the skylights, had they been treated that badly?

"Let's go then."

The girl stopped where the corridor ended in a t-intersection. Both ends of the new corridor vanished into darkness. Doors were set in the drab walls at regular intervals, all closed.

She pointed at one of the doors, unremarkable as the others. Tandor didn't need her directions; he could feel the presence of the children, enhanced by the strong glow of icefire beneath his feet. The Heart was close; and it was beating strongly.

"Stand back." He flung a burst of icefire at the door. It crackled over the smooth surface. The door vibrated and sprang open.

Tandor burst in through the opening before the display of icefire had died down. It was dark in the room, and the stink of human waste made him gag.

Oh by the skylights! He stumbled back out into the corridor staring into that dark maw from which the stench now rolled into the corridor.

There was a tiny pinprick of light against the back wall. He sensed, rather than saw, the children inside the room; he felt overwhelming pain and misery. They were stirring, mumbling, weak, confused.

Tandor trembled with anger, because the children were not in any state to help him, or to run. Anyone to be turned into a servitor needed to be healthy and willing for the best effect. Tandor was prepared to compromise on the "willing" part, but he couldn't skimp on the "healthy" as well.

"Any of you who can walk, get up and help the others." He would get the Eagle Knights for this, oh yes he would.

Sounds of movement—shuffling and scrabbling—came from inside the room. One by one, or in small groups, the children shuffled out. Rags, thin limbs, matted hair, many covered in their own filth. Many of them were wounded, sporting filthy bandages around arms and legs. They stood wide-eyed, blinking against the light. Tandor noticed a boy with a raw scar on his chest, and then another who had a filthy bandage in the same spot.

"What did they do with you?"

They didn't reply.

He examined the boy's scar. When he passed his hand over it, a chill went through him. "There's something underneath. What is it?"

The boy shook his head. He couldn't speak? Was he afraid to speak? He was not strongly Imperfect, just some of his toes were missing.

He turned to the girl who had brought him here. "What's been done to them?"

"The Knights put something under the skin. It makes you numb, like him. They were going to do it to me just now, when you came, but I'm one of the last."

"What is it?"

"I don't know. One boy opened the wound and took the thing out."

"What did he take out?" Tandor breathed fast.

The girl went back inside the room and came back with a filthy cloth. "We put it in here, so the men wouldn't see, but the boy died anyway."

Tandor folded back the filthy fabric. A clear diamond-shaped piece of glass slid out. As it rolled into his hand, strands of icefire bent and curled, stretching to its glittering surface, and simply disappeared there. The strands tugged at him, at the very power of his being. A low keening sound grew louder and louder.

Tandor snapped the fabric back over the stone. A sink.

All the icefire the children collected would be stored in that stone from where you could mine it but where it was useless to him, unless he could remove the sinks . . . He grabbed his dagger, but knew too well that his grandfather used to neuter Imperfects with sinks. Once the stone was inside the body, removing it always killed the subject. The Knights had outsmarted him.

While he stood there, wracking his brain for a solution, he realised that the children were shuffling in line, as if they knew where to go and were being told to go there.

The Heart.

It would come into full power today, and the sinks in their bodies made that they were attracted to it.

Tandor ran around the corner. The line already stretched into the darkness, slowly shuffling.

He grabbed one of the children by the shoulders. "Stop, stop!"

The girl, a skinny thing no more than twelve years old with empty eyes staring into the distance, pushed him aside as if he was an annoying pup. Already, icefire had made her strong.

Someone had made half-servitors out of them without being properly in control of their minds. Now no one could communicate with them. They would run rampant. Like Ruko.

There was only one thing he could do.

Tandor closed his hand around the Chevakian powder gun in his pocket and pulled it out. The girl next to him gave him no attention. He raised the gun and pointed it at her head. She turned, showing her sweet young face. She had the fine curly hair that was common to the inhabitants of the border regions. Her skin was soft and pale with a few freckles, looking at him like a fox cub.

Fifteen years he had lived as travelling merchant to provide for these children. Many he had saved personally by grabbing the newborn infants from before the hungry mouths of wild bears. While taking them to Bordertown, he had fed them, cradled them, kept them warm. In his mind, he had already assigned them positions in his royal guard, repaying their service, and that of their foster families, many times over.

He loved "his" children. He left the gun sink; the girl shuffled on.

By the skylights, he was too soft, he *cared* too much, for a job like this. For all his boasting, he was no killer and not even the direst need was going to change that.

Mother, if you wanted this done, why didn't you do it yourself?

There had to be another way to stop the children.

Find the Heart. Without protection, he would probably die from exposure, but he had to try, or there would be devastation on a grand scale.

Tandor ran.

Ahead in the corridor, the children were going through a doorway from where the smell of must and disuse mingled with strands of icefire.

Tandor followed into an eerie semi-darkness. In the dank room, the ceiling glowed with greenish light, casting harsh shadows on the walls. The floor sloped down in a spiral. Some time, a long time ago, someone had painted white stripes and arrows on the pale grey floor. There was a metal railing in the middle and flakes of coloured paint clung to some of the pillars that supported the roof. Others pillars had collapsed, or melted, causing the roof to collapse. In places, rust flakes piled up on the floor, mixed with bits of black that fell to dust when touched.

Tandor wondered what the old people would have used this construction for, and why this chamber had survived at all.

The call of icefire was stronger here than he had ever felt it in his life. His body sang with power.

He ran down the ramp. Two rounds of the spiral, three. Down, down, down. The light became ever brighter. All the children he passed glowed like beacons. His own skin also glowed, including the hand he never had, superimposed over the pincers of the golden claw. He resisted a look in his trousers to see if that part of him had been restored as well. Then again, he didn't need to check; he could feel it as he could feel his missing hand, move it and rake his non-existent fingers through his hair.

Around the last bend and his target came into sight.

About the height of two men, and much longer, the thing that was the Heart of the City glowed so intensely white that it was impossible to look at it. The Heart's shape was vaguely rectangular, and plates of metal lay scattered around it—presumably the protection the Knights had installed and then removed. Some of the casing still remained at the back, but all within was bright white. The air hummed so much that it vibrated in the light, creating an odd shimmering effect.

A single Knight guarded it, clad in a heavy suit, absurdly with a torch in his hand. What blindness that someone couldn't see this radiance!

Tandor let icefire rise to the tips of his fingers, but it wouldn't harm the man if he could stand here and had obviously strong Pirosian blood.

This would call for valuable bullets. He felt in the pocket of his cloak, shielding his eyes from the glow of the square in front of him.

At that moment, a shape of light stepped past him. Through the blinding rays, Tandor saw the face of an adolescent man, strong-jawed. Dark hair flowed over his shoulders. The young man hit the knight on the side of the head. The Knight slumped, without having given an indication that he had seen the young man coming. His torch rolled over the ground and went out.

Tandor was puzzled. Who was this young man? Ruko was outside and none of the other children had been older than thirteen.

He turned.

Behind him, all the children coming down the ramp glowed, no longer skinny and filthy, no longer cripple, no longer small. Some had tossed aside walking sticks. The girl he had rescued from the table had grown to adult size. Her skin was no longer scabbed and dirty, but milky white. Under his eyes, she pulled the tunic over her head and stood there, naked, inviting. She tossed her hair over her shoulder and gave him a mischievous look, very much like Loriane would do, a look that challenged him to do what he could never do. Except now he could.

Loriane appeared in the air before him, naked, alluring. Tandor trembled, tossed by emotions he could by rights no longer feel. Once again he was a complete man, not a pale shade of his former self, damaged by the man he hated most in the world of the living and the dead. He closed the distance between himself and the illusion that wasn't Loriane, ran his hands along her shoulders. She felt real enough. Goosebumps trailed over her skin.

Oh by the sky lights—what power!

Then he stepped back, forcing the image from his mind. This was an illusion, no matter that is was a very realistic one. Loriane was several floors above him in the birthing room. He was here in a desperate attempt to take control of this device, not to let it take control of him.

Several children sat on the ground, their bodies glowing, crying onto the shoulders of imaginary people they hugged.

Tandor understood. *This power shows us our deepest desires.* The young man who had just knocked out the Knight had been a boy whose wish it had been to become a strong soldier.

Wasn't it just disgusting that his deepest desire involved carnal pleasure. He should do better than that.

"Listen, everyone!" he called out. His voice barely rose above the humming of the device. None of the children paid him attention. He shook the shoulders of the nearest girl, who was so absorbed in her dream that she didn't react, not even when he slapped her in the face.

The young muscular man who wanted to be a soldier just stood there, staring at the brightness, eyes wide open.

They still have their hearts, Tandor reminded himself.

It was unlikely that he could still turn them into servitors, but he had to try. He fumbled for the dagger.

The girl had grown taller than him. Tandor grabbed her hand. She glowed and her touch burned even in the hand he was not supposed to have. With his real hand, he wielded the dagger and stabbed.

As soon as the knife made contact with her luminous skin, a surge of icefire went through him. It burned through his senses.

He held up his hands to catch the heart, but too late, realised the icefire was flowing *out* of him *into* the girl. The scar on her chest glowed white.

Tandor struggled, but couldn't let go.

A young man took hold of the girl's shoulders. Another jolt shuddered through Tandor's body. A third child joined. That figure, glowing too much in Tandor's pain-stricken eyes to determine gender, grabbed the next person. Tandor braced for the jolt, and still screamed when it came. He was still panting and sweating when there was another jolt, stronger still.

The rectangular shape of the Heart had lost some of its brightness. Still, the glowing figures were joining up, linking hands. Strands of icefire now flowed from the rectangular device into the children.

They were sinks. The device was voiding itself, its power flowing into the children's bodies.

The next jolt was so strong it turned Tandor's muscles to jelly. Shivering, crying, he fought to stand upright and found he couldn't. The two figures on either side of him had grown so much that his legs hung off the floor. His hand burned with intense cold. His trousers were wet from where he had lost control of his bladder. And still the rectangular shape became more visible, less strongly glowing, but more silver, like a giant metal box, with leads, pipes and other protuberances on the outside. Some ancient device the function of which he could only guess. A weapon.

Jolts of icefire made him scream, his voice raw. The pain made him sick, but his insides were empty.

Then the jolts stopped.

The circle of hands around the Heart was complete.

The children, or the grotesque, glowing shapes that had been the children, held its power now. The thing itself was no more than an ugly dented metal container.

No one moved.

The surface of the machine trembled, and shivered as if

someone had kicked it. Seams split apart. Shafts of light shone through, and expanded, etching into the ceiling. There was something *inside* it. The ground rumbled. The ceiling split open, hissing smoke. Debris rained from the stone and lit up where it intersected the beams. The children let Tandor drop to the ground.

Tandor sat there, dazed, while a firework of icefire raged over his head. The children, now constructs of light, breathed icefire. Their mouths spewed it when they spoke. Strands snaked away from their circle of hands, pulverising stone. Pipes burst, spewing forth water that glowed with icefire, ice-cold water too contaminated to freeze.

Tandor screamed. "Listen to me!"

But his voice didn't rise above the crackling and the rumbling. He gathered strands of icefire in his hands, tried to wind them around the legs of the grotesque figures. The strands fell away or snapped when the figures moved, as if they were simple threads.

No control, no control over this monstrous creation.

Too much exposure. The Knights shouldn't have removed the protective casing. They shouldn't have played with things they didn't understand and couldn't see.

He shouldn't have come here not knowing what the Knights had implanted in the children. He should have realised the danger. He should have shot the children.

It was too late. The power was out of control and he was no match for it.

Tandor ran.

Up the ramp, as fast as he could. His legs ached, his lungs burned, but he didn't stop. He ran and ran.

At the door that led out of the twisting ramp, he almost crashed into a group of Knights.

"Get out, get out!" His voice was hoarse.

They just stared at him, their faces already peeling from exposure.

Tandor ran through the experiment room, back to the stairs

that led up to the entrance of the birthing room.

Loriane! He had to get her out of here. He ran up the stairs.

Blood pumped in his veins. His face was burnt; he could feel the sting of cold air on raw skin. The numbness of the injury was wearing off.

Up, up. Black spots danced before his eyes. He missed a step and stumbled against the wall, bracing himself with his hand. By the skylights, the skin on his arm was peeling in big slabs, leaving raw and oozing flesh. The sight made him feel sick.

While he stared at it, the ground rumbled deep below his feet. Tandor listened, holding his breath. The floor vibrated with a low keening. The sound increased in pitch, and increased until the metal-and-stone construction of the building sang. Tandor ran. He almost blacked out, but he ran. Up, up, up, into the corridor. Into the room at the end.

"Loriane, *Loriane!*"

The room was empty, beds abandoned, a trolley of medicines upended in an aisle.

Tandor ran towards the exit.

"Loriane!"

The guard post was deserted. Shouts drifted in from outside.

"Loriane!"

The roar of an explosion overtook him.

CHAPTER 29

MYRA SAT stark naked, legs spread on the birthing chair. Sweat-soaked hair clung to her head.

The elderly palace midwife knelt on the cushion facing the girl, and placed a basket with soft towels under the chair. She nodded at Myra. "You're almost ready."

Myra's expression was distant. Her lips trembled, and then she muttered, "Help me, help me, help me." With each *help*, her voice became louder. Her breath sped up, her legs trembled, her one hand dug into the flesh of her thighs. She howled.

The midwife cursed. "Oh, come on, girl. It's not going to happen with screaming. If you want to be a breeder, you've got to do better than this. Push, by the skylights. Push, push."

Myra wailed and panted. Tears ran over her face. "I can't. Please help me, Mistress Loriane."

"She's right," Loriane said. "*You* have to do this. We can't help you any further if you don't want to be helped."

While Myra wasn't looking, the midwife reached between the girl's legs, trying to examine the baby's progress.

Myra screamed and kicked. "You're not touching me!"

"Right. That's *it*." The midwife wiped her hands on her apron and rose. "I've had enough. I'll be back when you decide to behave." She walked off between empty beds where women who shouldn't be walking had vacated their beds to get away from Myra's screaming.

Myra, her eyes wide, stared after the woman's broad back. "She can't just leave me!"

"Yes, she can," Loriane said. "You're behaving like an idiot."

"But I'm going to die."

"Yes."

Myra's eyes widened. She clearly hadn't expected that answer. Her lip trembled. "Mistress Loriane? You're kidding me?"

"No, I'm not. You *will* die if you don't do what we say."

"I don't want to die."

"Then for all you're worth *shut up*."

The girl was shivering with another building pain. "I'm scared. I'm so scared, Mistress Loriane, please help me, please . . ." She threw her head back.

Loriane covered the girl's mouth with her hand. "Shut up, shut up."

She kneeled at the pillow the midwife had just vacated, put her hands on the girl's sweaty and blood-slicked thighs, fixing her with a hard stare. "Or I'll tell Tandor that you behaved like an idiot."

Myra clamped her lips, her eyes blazing with anger. "I'm not an idiot."

"Good. Now shut your mouth and push."

Myra pushed. Her face went red until she gasped for breath. Then she pushed again. Loriane patted her knee, knowing that girls didn't like being touched at this stage.

She whispered, "Very good, keep going, keep going. You're almost there."

Myra pushed and pushed. Drops of fluid dribbled on the towel in the basket under her.

The silence was heavenly.

Two of the women who had left came back, peeking around the corner of the door. Their eyebrows rose. They had probably expected Myra to be dead.

Loriane glanced at the door. Tandor needed to come back quickly. If this was over, she could maybe ask the midwife for an examination, but after that, she could stay here no longer, neither could she go to the sled with a driver no one could see, or wait in the sled for a man who wasn't supposed to be in the palace.

Another contraction. Myra was really getting into it now. She pushed and panted, and pushed. The midwife came back and joined Loriane with set of instruments that included forceps and needles and gut thread. This was not going to be easy.

Loriane rose, sore and stiff from sitting in the uncomfortable position. The child inside her was kicking her in the ribs. It wouldn't be long before she had to come back here herself.

Myra pushed and howled and pushed. The midwife was easing out the baby's feet, and then the abdomen. Her calming words were wasted on Myra, who was hysterical. "It hurts, it hurts!"

"Keep going, keep going."

The head of the baby shot out, followed by a gush of fluid. Myra screamed. The child fell into the midwife's hands, wet and slippery and covered in blood-stained slime.

Loriane's stomach cramped. She turned away from the group, scanning the room for a bowl to throw up.

A healthy cry drowned all the women's talk

"That's a big boy," one of the women said.

But then someone gasped.

"By the skylights," the midwife said in the silence that followed. "He's Imperfect."

"I know, I know," Myra cried, her voice hoarse. "Give him to me."

"I can't. He . . ." The midwife licked her lips. She was still holding the squealing infant.

Loriane swallowed bile, and swallowed again, quelling her stomach.

In her haste to get Myra to help, she had forgotten the rule about Imperfect babies. She hadn't even considered it, since Imperfects were hardly ever born these days.

"Give her the child," she said, shouldering her way into the group.

The midwife gave her a strange look.

"The girl is from Bordertown, and will be going back there." She eased the squealing boy out of the midwife's hands and proceeded to cut the cord. She wrapped him in towels to still his cries. Everyone in the room had gone very silent.

Myra looked puzzled from one to the other. She was leaning back in the chair, still bleeding from a good tear, sheened with sweat, white-faced and totally spent. She had suffered for three days. It was probably a wonder she was alive at all. *If this had happened in Bordertown, she might not have been.*

"You had best fix her up," she said to the midwife.

Carefully, she lowered the child at Myra's swollen breast. The girl gasped when he latched onto the nipple and then started laughing, and crying.

Loraine's eyes misted up. How could she have forgotten her first time? That incredible relief after all the pain. The healthy baby at her breast. The boy would be sixteen now. Unlike her, Myra would keep her little boy.

"I'm still going to have to report this with the Knights," the midwife said. "They have been very strict on Imperfect births recently."

"The Knights are at the festival. The guard is really light. If I take her out tonight—"

"Back to your house? Like this? She needs to be under observation. We need to notify the father's family—"

"She is from Bordertown, there *is* no breeder's contract." Please, she really didn't want to argue about it now. Even the thought that Myra *might* lose her baby made her chest constrict. She still saw the nurse walk away with *her* beautiful boy.

"No contract? How can that be?"

"Because . . ." Loriane spread her hands. Tears pricked in her eyes. *Because she loves this boy.*

The midwife raised her eyebrows.

"Please, just let me take her home."

"I didn't think you would—"

The floor trembled.

"What by the skylights . . ." the midwife said.

The other women stopped chatting and glanced at each other. The door creaked open letting in a waft of freezing air, and a guard. He looked around the room, wordlessly and disappeared, leaving the door open. The frosty chill settled in Loriane's stomach. Tandor had gone down there. He was doing something stupid. He was always over-confident, that was how he'd become maimed in the first place.

She heaved herself to her feet and waddled towards the door. When she was halfway across the room, the floor rumbled again, more violently this time. Dust and plaster rained from the ceiling. A chunk of stone came down behind her, scattering bits over beds and couches. And something, *something* she couldn't see or describe made the air hum with tension.

Tandor, for sure. Tandor never came for just a social visit, and Tandor had *wanted* to get into the palace, that's why he was here.

Loriane turned, her heart thudding. "Myra, come, now."

All around, women scrambled for their bedding and warm clothes. Myra just sat there, clutching the child. She could probably not walk unassisted. Loriane ran back into the room and pulled Myra up. "Come on, Myra. We *have* to get out."

The girl's eyes were wide. "What's happening?"

"I don't know, but there are fifty floors above us, and I think I'd rather be in the street if this building is going to collapse."

The floor rumbled again.

A group of knights burst from the corridor into the courtyard, into the snow . . . which was melting into sludge. Steam rose from the ground. Bears bucked and pulled in their harnesses.

Loriane walked as fast as she could, dragging Myra with her. The girl's steps were insecure; she was probably close to fainting. The boy had started crying, muffled in the towel. Myra stumbled. Her face was deathly white. *Yes, yes, I know this is a cruel thing to do to you.* "Come, run, run."

Myra couldn't walk fast, let alone run, but Loriane pulled her along.

When they arrived in the courtyard, the floor heaved again.

Loriane pushed Myra into the sled and stumbled in herself. No Tandor. No driver.

"Go, go," she screamed at the bear and yanked the reins.

At that moment, there was a roar behind them. The ground trembled and bucked. Metal creaked. Glass crashed behind her.

The bear reared, pulling the front of the sled up with its harness. The animal sprang forward, and bounded out the gate.

Too fast, too dangerous.

The back entrance of the palace was in a narrow street, half-blocked with rubble. People were running out of every entrance; people lay in remains of collapsed facades. One woman hung on for her life on the crumbling construction that had been an apartment floor. A breeze stirred up her nightgown, giving Loriane a view of her pallid body. An instant, and then the sled whooshed past. People ran out of entrances on both sides of the street, screaming and pointing. The bear plunged into the fleeing crowd. Loriane yanked the reins, but couldn't stop the animal. In the mayhem, people fell, causing others to trip over them. People in flimsy clothes, people with bleeding wounds. Glass was everywhere.

The ground bucked and rumbled. Debris fell down from the towering buildings that lined the street. More glass. Pieces of stone. People screamed over the deafening noise. The bear was growling and snapping at bystanders.

Then there was a thundering rumble behind them, and a

huge whoosh. A cloud of smoke and dust filled the street. Every bit of glass that was still intact shattered. A rain of razor-sharp fragments pelted down. Loriane threw her and Myra's cloaks over both of them, and when the pelting stopped, she peeked out.

Silence, except for the creaking and groaning of metal.

The street behind her was blocked by a heap of rubble. In the dusty air all she could see was the structure of the palace gates, no longer attached to anything. The buildings were all gone.

The only people here were ones who no longer needed help, burnt and bloodied corpses, their skin blistered, limbs ripped.

Someone whistled; she recognised the sound.

"Tandor?" Her voice sounded like that of a lost child.

She shoved aimlessly at pieces of rubble. There was far too much of it, and she had no chance of finding him, certainly not without help.

The stupid idiot.

"Someone please help me."

No one replied. Everyone here was dead. The ground was freezing up in a hard layer of ice. Soon, the pieces of rubble would have frozen onto each other.

"Tandor, I love you," she screamed at the silence. She had never said those words aloud, but they were true, true as she stood here, carrying someone else's child, and wishing it was his, wishing for his arms around her, wishing for his voice to tell her everything would be fine.

On top of the rubble appeared a tall, bear-like figure, stepping from block to block without hesitation. At first, it seemed like the figure floated in the air. It looked like some kind of demon, with strange protuberances sprouting from its upper body. Then it came closer and Loriane saw that the figure carried someone, but still did not appear to have legs. The arms and head, too, seemed only half there. Tandor was real enough, but was he alive?

All his hair was gone, the skin on his face horribly burnt,

peeling in places, black with soot and blood. Parts of his shirt were missing and the skin underneath burnt. Blood dribbled from a deep gash in his good arm.

"Tandor!" She wanted to touch him, but the thing that carried him turned its head. It was human, of a fashion, but consisted merely of a thin skin of dust, transparent in many places, ethereal grey in others.

As it walked past towards the sled, Loriane realised that it was Ruko, the invisible sled driver, covered in dust.

He put Tandor down on the furs in the back seat. His skin glistened with weeping burns. His eyes were closed, his mouth slightly open. He breathed shallowly. Loriane took his arm and felt his pulse. It was regular but weak, although that could be because her hands trembled so much. Loriane and Myra wrapped him up and sat down on either side of him so he wouldn't fall over.

The driver flicked the reins and the bear started off through the street.

They passed many other injured, some beyond help. People with limbs blown off. People so badly burned that their faces were a mess. Some walked, but many did not, bleeding their life's blood onto the dirt-smeared snow. There were guards and Eagle Knights, all horribly burnt, trying help each other, or too busy simply with trying to stay alive as exposed skin grew blisters. The air hummed with tension.

You can't see icefire, Tandor had once said. *That doesn't mean it's not there and it can't harm you. It just harms you less quickly than it harms others.*

The buildings on both sides of the street were badly damaged. Glass blown out, floors collapsed, people's furniture sucked into the street.

The number of people increased as they went. Streets flowed with a sorry tide of humanity. Previously well-dressed nobles clutching jagged scraps of clothing, carrying their loved ones, some of whom beyond help. Old people fell and didn't get up.

Sometimes, someone would haul the fallen back to their feet, but no one stayed around to make sure they remained that way.

The ground still rumbled; buildings shuddered with some unseen force. People shielded their eyes to light Loriane didn't see. Exposed skin reddened with the blisters of icefire burns.

They reached the markets where a great number of people were crowded in the corner, with more people spilling into the square from the streets that led into it. Something Loriane couldn't see seemed to block the other side of the square.

Myra gasped.

"What is it?" Loriane asked.

Myra pointed. "Over there! Can't you see it? It's a huge . . . person. Like—made out of light. And there's another one, and . . . oohhh! Beido!"

Loriane stared where Myra pointed, and saw . . . nothing. No, that wasn't entirely true.

It had started snowing, and steam rose off the place where the girl pointed. Then Loriane saw them, too: huge shapes, at least thirty of them, maybe even more, outlines made of steam.

They formed a circle, towering over the city. The figure facing the people in the square held out its steam-wreathed hands.

"Beido! Beido!" Myra's voice barely rose over the screams of onlookers, but it seemed the figure heard her. A long tendril of steam curled towards the sled. Ruko tied the bears' reins to the sled.

"Look, this is your son." Myra uncovered the baby's head.

Ruko rose from the driver's seat, his hands planted at his sides, facing the steam figure.

Loriane said in a low voice, "Sit down, Myra."

"But that is Beido!"

"Myra, please—"

Loriane couldn't see the flash of icefire, but she could feel how it took her breath away. People around her fell . . . and died. Blistered faces froze in screams of agony. Eyes wide open stared at the sky.

Myra screamed, "Beido, no, don't, Beido!" Then she grabbed Loriane's arm. "He isn't listening. Make him listen!"

"I can't do anything. I can't even see him. Sit down." Loriane yanked Myra back into the seat.

But Myra continued to scream. "Beido, Beido! What are you doing? I'm here. Beido!"

A patch of steam grew in the sky directly overhead. Mist flowed out of the steam figures to join it and form a kind of dome, which was extending downwards.

Loriane reached for the driver's shoulder. The dust was ice-cold. "Please, get us out of here."

The sled remained where it was. People in the square were falling over, clutching burned faces, skin peeling from flesh, glassy eyes staring at the sky. The screams made Loriane shiver. This was hundred times worse than Myra's screaming.

"Come on, Ruko, if you want us to live."

Myra was crying. "I don't know what they're doing. It's like . . . evil. Something has bewitched them. Get us out of here, Mistress Loriane."

"I'm trying, but I think he only listens to Tandor—"

Ruko yanked the reins. The bear roared and raised itself on its hind legs, pulling the front of the sled off the ground. It charged forward, towards the steam figure, towards the crowd and the edge of the bowl-shaped steam shape that was growing fast in the direction of the ground.

Loriane shouted, "No, no not that way!"

Her shout was futile; neither of them could have stopped the animal.

The patch of steam in the sky had grown into a half-complete dome, blocking the view of the sky, but ahead, a path was still clear.

The bear growled. The sled jostled and bumped over the bodies, which flopped under the sled's runners like rag dolls. *They're all dead*. Loriane closed her eyes. It was so awful and they were not going to make it. The rim of mist was sliding towards the ground . . . *They were not going to make it.* They were . . .

The sled cut into the mist. Myra screamed. There was a gush of intense cold that took Loriane's breath away. She clutched the seat, squeezing her eyes tightly shut.

They were going to die, they were going to die, they were . . .

And then there was only the sled, the padding of the bear's feet and the swishing of the runners in the snow.

Myra cried, "Oh Beido. What happened to him? Do you think he let us go because of our son?"

Loriane looked over her shoulder to see the ring of steam shapes close the dome of icefire. For the life of her, she couldn't recognise a face in the steam shapes. Her heart was still thudding like crazy.

"Maybe," she said, but she had no idea what had happened. She stared, too numb to cry, at the destruction around them, at the people still running, many covered in blisters.

Ruko was urging the bear into a run. Much of the dust had blown off him, making him once again almost invisible.

No one spoke for a long time. Myra cried softly. The whole city was covered in the hideous mist, which was expanding outward, eating up shapes of buildings. The sound of shattering glass drifted on the wind. Loriane could barely breathe for the acrid smoke.

When the bear charged out the city gates, the Outer City came into view—a mass of fire, billowing smoke and flames.

Loriane felt sick. She muttered, "My house."

Eagles swooped low over the festival grounds, and a crowd of people were throwing projectiles at them. But even some of them had become aware of the destruction in the city itself, and the outward expanding deathly cloud.

"My house," Loriane said again. Her practice, her friends, her patients. Isandor. "What am I going to do?"

Myra touched her shoulder. "Bordertown should still be safe."

Loriane bit on her lip to stifle tears. "That's where he's taking us, isn't it?" She nodded at the invisible driver.

"It's our home," Myra said.

The bear veered to the right, where the horizon merged with the sky.

Eagles whirled overhead, as powerless as she.

Getting to Bordertown would take at least three days. They had no food and no shelter. Their clothing was not good enough for such a voyage. Tandor and Myra needed care. She was exhausted and her belly felt hard as a rock. Every bump in the ice hurt.

But the bear knew the way. It ran and ran and ran.

Continue the saga with book 2 of the Icefire Trilogy, Dust & Rain, in which we follow Loriane, Tandor and other refugees into Chevakia.

ABOUT THE AUTHOR

Patty Jansen lives in Sydney, Australia, where she spends most of her time writing Science Fiction and Fantasy. Her story *This Peaceful State of War* placed first in the second quarter of the Writers of the Future contest and was published in their 27th anthology. She has also sold fiction to genre magazines such as Analog Science Fiction and Fact, Redstone SF and Aurealis.
Her novels (available at ebook venues) include *Shifting Reality* (hard SF), *The Far Horizon* (middle grade SF), *Charlotte's Army* (military SF) and *Fire & Ice, Dust & Rain* and *Blood & Tears* (Icefire Trilogy) (dark fantasy). Her novel *Ambassador* was published by Ticonderoga Publications in 2013.

Patty is on Twitter (@pattyjansen), Facebook, LinkedIn, goodreads, LibraryThing, google+ and blogs at: http://pattyjansen.com.

MORE BY THIS AUTHOR

In the Earth-Gamra space opera universe

RETURN OF THE AGHYRIANS
Watcher's Web
Trader's Honour
Soldier's Duty
Heir's Revenge

The Far Horizon (For younger readers)

AMBASSADOR:
Seeing Red
Raising Hell

The Shattered World Within (novella)

FOR QUEEN AND COUNTRY
Whispering Willows
Innocence Lost
Willow Witch
The Idiot King

In the ISF-Allion universe

Charlotte's Army (novella)
The rebelliousness of Trassi Udang (short story)
His Name in Lights (novella)
Shifting Reality (novel)

Epic, Post-apocalyptic Fantasy

ICEFIRE TRILOGY
Fire & Ice
Dust & Rain
Blood & Tears
The Icefire Trilogy Omnibus

Short story collection
Out Of Here

Shorter works
Looking For Daddy (absurd horror novella)
This Peaceful State of War (Writers of the Future winning novella)

Visit the author's website at http://pattyjansen.com and register for a newsletter to keep up-to-date with new releases.

Printed in Great Britain
by Amazon.co.uk, Ltd.,
Marston Gate.